*Ace Books by Ilona Andrews*

*The Kate Daniels Novels*

MAGIC BITES
MAGIC BURNS
MAGIC STRIKES
MAGIC BLEEDS

*The Edge Novels*

ON THE EDGE
BAYOU MOON

# BAYOU
# MOON

ILONA ANDREWS

ACE BOOKS, NEW YORK

**THE BERKLEY PUBLISHING GROUP**
**Published by the Penguin Group**
**Penguin Group (USA) Inc.**
**375 Hudson Street, New York, New York 10014, USA**
Penguin Group (Canada), 90 Eglinton Avenue East, Suite 700, Toronto, Ontario M4P 2Y3, Canada
(a division of Pearson Penguin Canada Inc.)
Penguin Books Ltd., 80 Strand, London WC2R 0RL, England
Penguin Group Ireland, 25 St. Stephen's Green, Dublin 2, Ireland (a division of Penguin Books Ltd.)
Penguin Group (Australia), 250 Camberwell Road, Camberwell, Victoria 3124, Australia
(a division of Pearson Australia Group Pty. Ltd.)
Penguin Books India Pvt. Ltd., 11 Community Centre, Panchsheel Park, New Delhi—110 017, India
Penguin Group (NZ), 67 Apollo Drive, Rosedale, North Shore 0632, New Zealand
(a division of Pearson New Zealand Ltd.)
Penguin Books (South Africa) (Pty.) Ltd., 24 Sturdee Avenue, Rosebank, Johannesburg 2196,
South Africa

Penguin Books Ltd., Registered Offices: 80 Strand, London WC2R 0RL, England

This is a work of fiction. Names, characters, places, and incidents either are the product of the authors' imaginations or are used fictitiously, and any resemblance to actual persons, living or dead, business establishments, events, or locales is entirely coincidental. The publisher does not have any control over and does not assume any responsibility for authors' or third-party websites or their content.

BAYOU MOON

An Ace Book / published by arrangement with the authors

PRINTING HISTORY
Ace mass-market edition / October 2010

ISBN: 978-0-441-01945-8

ACE
Ace Books are published by The Berkley Publishing Group,
a division of Penguin Group (USA) Inc.,
375 Hudson Street, New York, New York 10014.
ACE and the "A" design are trademarks of Penguin Group (USA) Inc.

PRINTED IN THE UNITED STATES OF AMERICA

10   9   8   7   6   5   4   3   2   1

# Acknowledgments

A book is always a team effort. This one was no exception. We're deeply grateful to Nancy Yost, our agent, for putting up with numerous e-mails and phone calls, and being the lone voice of sanity in our big, fiery sea of crazy. We're also grateful to Anne Sowards for her constant support and encouragement. Without the two of you, our books would never see the light of day.

We would like to thank the following people: Michelle Kasper, production editor, and Andromeda Macri, assistant production editor, for taking the manuscript and turning it into a book, and for always finding an extra day or two to give us a little bit more time; Joan Matthews, copy editor—we're sorry about the confusion with the names and the general state of the manuscript, and we sincerely hope we didn't give you an aneurysm; Victoria Vebell, artist, for the stunning cover art—we wish we had a print of it to hang on the wall; Annette Fiore DeFex, cover designer, for taking a beautiful piece of art and turning it into an equally beautiful cover; Kristin del Rosario, interior designer, for creating a beautiful layout and making the book truly a pleasure to read; Kat Sherbo, editorial assistant—thank you for dealing with us, next time we'll send liquor along with chocolate just to dull the pain; and Rosanne Romanello, publicist, who tirelessly works to promote all of our books. We're very fortunate to work with all of you.

Many readers and friends helped us along the way. Here they are in no particular order: Reece Notley, Chrissy Peterson, Hasna Saadani, Ericka Brooks, Beatrix Kaser, and Ying Chumnongsaksarp. We also would like to extend our deepest gratitude to Jeaniene Frost, Meljean Brook, Shiloh Walker, and Jill Myles. We're eagerly awaiting bills for all of the over-the-phone therapy you have provided.

# BAYOU MOON

# ONE

WILLIAM sipped some beer from the bottle of Modelo Especial and gave the Green Arrow his hard stare. The Green Arrow, being a chunk of painted plastic, didn't rise to the challenge. The action figure remained impassive, exactly where he'd put it, leaning against the porch post of William's house. Technically it was a trailer rather than a house, William reflected, but it was a roof over his head and he wasn't one to complain.

From that vantage point, the Green Arrow had an excellent view of William's action figure army laid out on the porch, and if the superhero were inclined to offer any opinions, he would've been in a great position to do so. William shrugged. Part of him realized that talking to an action figure was bordering on insane, but he had nobody else to converse with at the moment and he needed to talk this out. The whole situation was crazy.

"The boys sent a letter," William said.

The Green Arrow said nothing.

William looked past him to where the Wood rustled just beyond his lawn. Two miles down the road, the Wood would become simply woods, regular Georgia pine and oak. But here, in the Edge, the trees grew vast, fed by magic, and the forest was old. The day had rolled into a lazy, long summer evening, and small, nameless critters, found only in the Edge, chased each other through the limbs of the ancient trees before the darkness coaxed predators from their lairs.

The Edge was an odd place, stuck between two worlds.

On one side lay the Broken, with no magic but plenty of technology to compensate. And rules. And laws. And paperwork. The damn place ran on paperwork. The Broken was where he made his money nowadays, working construction.

On the other side lay the Weird, a mirror to the Broken, where magic ruled and old blueblood families held power. He was born in that world. In the Weird, he'd been an outcast, a soldier, a convict, and even a noble for a few brief weeks. But the Weird kept kicking him in the teeth the entire time, until he finally turned his back on it and left.

The Edge belonged to neither world. A perfect place for the man who fit in nowhere. That was how he first met the boys, George and Jack. They lived in the Edge, with their sister, Rose. Rose was sweet and pretty and he'd liked her. He'd liked what they had, she and the kids, a warm little family. When William watched them together, a part of him hurt deep inside. He now realized why: he'd known even then that a family like that was forever out of his reach.

Still, he'd tried with Rose. Might have had a chance, too, but then Declan showed up. Declan, a blueblood and a soldier, with his flawless manners and handsome face. "We used to be friends," William told the Green Arrow. "I did beat the shit out of him before he left."

The joke was on him, because Declan left with Rose and took the boys with him. William let them go. Jack required lots of time and care, and Declan would raise him well. And Rose needed someone like Declan. Someone who had his shit together. She had enough trouble with the boys as it was. She sure as hell didn't need another charity project, and he didn't want to be one.

It had been almost two years since they'd left. For two years William had lived in the Edge, where the trickle of magic kept the wild within him alive. He worked his job in the Broken, watched TV on weekends, drank lots of beer, collected action figures, and generally pretended that the previous twenty-six years of his life had not occurred. The Edgers, the few families who lived between the worlds like he did, kept to themselves and left him alone.

Most people from either the Broken or the Weird had no idea the other world existed, but occasionally traders passed through the Edge, traveling between worlds. Three months ago, Nick, one of the traveling traders, mentioned he was heading into the Weird, to the Southern Provinces. William put together a small box of toys on a whim and paid the man to deliver it. He didn't expect an answer. He didn't expect anything at all. The boys had Declan. They would have no interest in him.

Nick came by last night. The boys had written back.

William picked up the letter and looked at it. It was short. George's writing was perfect, with letters neatly placed. Jack's looked like a chicken had written it in the dirt. They said thank you for the action figures. George liked the Weird. He was given plenty of corpses to practice necromancy on, and he was taking rapier lessons. Jack complained that there were too many rules and that they weren't letting him hunt enough.

"That's a mistake," William told the Green Arrow. "They need to let him vent. Half of their problems would be solved if they let him have a violent outlet. The kid is a changeling and a predator. He turns into a lynx, not a fluffy bunny." He raised the letter. "Apparently he decided to prove to them that he was good enough. Jack killed himself a deer and left the bloody thing on the dining room table, because he's a cat and he thinks they're lousy hunters. According to him, it didn't go over well. He's trying to feed them, and they don't get it."

What Jack needed was some direction to channel all that energy. But William wasn't about to travel to the Weird and show up on Declan's doorstep. *Hi, remember me? We were best friends once, and then I was condemned*

*to death and your uncle adopted me, so I would kill you?
You stole Rose from me?* Yeah, right. All he could do was
write back and send more action figures.

William pulled the box to him. He'd put in Deathstroke
for George—the figure looked a bit like a pirate and
George liked pirates, because his grandfather had been
one. Next, William had stuck King Grayskull in for Declan.
Not that Declan played with action figures—he'd had his
childhood, while William spent his in Hawk's Academy,
which was little more than a prison. Still, William liked to
thumb his nose at him, and King Grayskull with his long
blond hair looked a lot like Declan.

"So the real question here is, do we send the purple
Wildcat to Jack or the black one?"

The Green Arrow expressed no opinion.

A musky scent drifted down to William. He turned
around. Two small glowing eyes stared at him from under the bush on the edge of his lawn.

"You again."

The raccoon bared his small sharp teeth.

"I've warned you, stay out of my trash or I will eat you."

The little beast opened his mouth and hissed like a
pissed-off cat.

"That does it."

William shrugged off his T-shirt. His jeans and un-
derwear followed. "We're going to settle this."

The raccoon hissed again, puffing out his fur, trying
to look bigger. His eyes glowed like two small coals.

William reached deep inside himself and let the wild
off the chain. Pain rocked him, jerking him to and fro,
the way a dog shook a rat. His bones softened and bent,
his ligaments snapped, his flesh flowed like molten wax.
Dense black fur sheathed him. The agony ended and
William rolled to his feet.

The raccoon froze.

For a second, William saw his reflection in the little
beast's eyes—a hulking dark shape on all fours. The
interloper took a step back, whirled about, and fled.

William howled, singing a long, sad song about the hunt and the thrill of the chase, and a promise of hot blood pulsed between his teeth. The small critters hid high up in the branches, recognizing a predator in their midst.

The last echoes of the song scurried into the Wood. William bit the air with sharp white fangs and gave chase.


WILLIAM trotted through the Wood. The raccoon had turned out to be female and in possession of six kits. How the hell he'd missed the female scent, he would never know. Getting rusty in the Edge. His senses weren't quite as sharp here.

He had to let them be. You didn't hunt a female with a litter—that was how species went extinct. He caught a nice juicy rabbit instead. William licked his lips. Mmm, good. He would just have to figure out a way to weigh down the lid on the trashcan. Maybe one of his dumb-bells would do the job, or some heavy rocks . . .

He caught a glimpse of his house through the trees. A scent floated to him: spicy, reminiscent of cinnamon mixed with a dash of cumin and ginger.

His hackles rose. William went to ground.

This scent didn't belong in this world outside of a bakery. It was the scent of a human from beyond the Edge's boundary, with shreds of the Weird's magic still clinging to them.

Trouble.

He lay in the gloom between the roots and listened. Insects chirping. Squirrels in the tree to the left settling down for the night. A woodpecker hammering in the distance to get the last grub of the day.

Nothing but ordinary Wood noises.

From his hiding spot, he could see the entire porch. Nothing stirred.

The rays of the setting sun slid across the boards. A tiny star winked at him.

Careful. Careful.

William edged forward, a dark soft-pawed ghost in the evening twilight. One yard. Two. Three.

The star winked again. A rectangular wooden box sat on the porch steps, secured with a simple metal latch. The latch shone with reflected sunlight. Someone had left him a present.

William circled the house twice, straining to sample the scents, listening to small noises. He found the trail leading from the house. Whoever delivered the box had come and gone.

He approached the building and looked at the box. Eighteen inches long, a foot wide, three inches tall. Simple unmarked wood. Looked like pine. Smelled like it, too. No sounds came from inside.

His figures were untouched. His letter, pinned down by the heavy Hulk, lay where he'd left it. The scent of the intruder didn't reach it.

William pulled the door open with his paw and slipped inside. He would need fingers for this.

The pain screamed through him, shooting through the marrow in his bones. He growled low, shook, convulsing, and shed his fur. Twenty seconds of agony and William crouched on human legs in the living room. Ten more seconds and he stepped out on the porch, fully dressed and armed with a long knife. Just because the box seemed benign didn't mean it wouldn't blow up when he opened it. He'd seen bombs that were the size of a coaster. They made no noise, gave off no scent, and took your leg off if you stepped on them.

He used the knife to pry the latch open and flip the lid off the box. A stack of paper. Hmm.

William plucked the first sheet off the top of the stack, flipped it over, and froze.

A small mangled body lay in the green grass. The boy was barely ten years old, his skin stark white against the smudges of crimson that spread from a gaping wound in his stomach. Someone had disemboweled him with a single vicious thrust, and the kid had bled out. So much blood. It was everywhere, on his skinny stomach, on his hands, on the dandelions around him . . . Bright, shockingly red, so vivid, it didn't seem real. The boy's narrow face stared at the sky with milky dead eyes, his mouth opened in a horrified O, short reddish hair sticking up . . .

*It's Jack.* The thought punched William in the stomach. His heart hammered. He peered closely at the face. No, not Jack. A cat like Jack—slit pupils—but Jack had brown hair. The boy was the right age, the right build, but he *was not* Jack.

William exhaled slowly, trying to get a handle on his rage. He knew this. He'd seen this boy before, but not in the picture. He'd seen the body in the flesh, smelled the blood and the raw, unforgettable stench of the gut wound. His memory conjured it for him now, and he almost choked on the phantom bitterness coating his tongue.

The next picture showed a little girl. Her hair was a mess of blood and brains—her skull had been crushed.

He pulled more pictures from the box, each corresponding to a body in his memory. Eight murdered children lay on his porch. Eight murdered changeling children.

The Weird had little use for changelings like him. The Dukedom of Louisiana killed his kind outright, the moment they were born. In Adrianglia, any mother who'd given birth to a changeling child could surrender her baby to the government, no questions asked. A simple signature on a piece of paper and the woman went on her way, while the child was taken to Hawk's Academy. Hawk's was a prison. A prison with sterile rooms and merciless guards, where toys and play were forbidden; a place designed to hammer every drop of free will out of its students. Only outdoors did the changeling children truly live. These eight must've been giddy to be let out into the sunshine and grass.

It was supposed to be a simple tracking exercise. The

instructors had led the children to the border between
Adrianglia and the Dukedom of Louisiana, its chief rival. The border was always hot, with Louisianans and
Adrianglians crossing back and forth. The instructors
allowed the kids to track a group of border jumpers from
Louisiana. When William was a child, he had gone on
the same mission a dozen times.

William stared at the pictures. The Louisianans had
turned out to be no ordinary border jumpers. They were
agents of Louisiana's Hand. Spies twisted by magic and
powerful enough to take out a squad of trained Legionnaires.

They let the children catch them.

When the kids and the instructors failed to report in, a
squad of Legionnaires was dispatched to find them. He
was the tracker for that squad. He was the one who found
them dead in the meadow.

It was a massacre, brutal and cold. The kids didn't go
quick. They'd hurt before they died.

The last piece of paper waited in the box. William
picked it up. He knew from the first sentence what it
would say. The words were burned into his memory.

He read it all the same.

*Dumb animals offer little sport. Louisiana kills
changelings at birth—it's far more efficient than
wasting time and resources to try to turn them into
people. I recommend you look into this practice,
because next time I'll expect proper compensation
for getting rid of your little freaks.*

*Sincerely yours,*
*Spider*

Mindless hot fury flooded William, sweeping away
all reason and restraint. He raised his head to the sky and
snarled, giving voice to his rage before it tore him apart.
For years he'd tracked Spider as much as the Legion

would permit him. He'd found him twice. The first time he'd ripped apart Spider's stomach, and Spider broke his legs. The second time, William had shattered the Louisianan's ribs, while Spider nearly drowned him. Both times the Hand's spy slipped through his fingers.

Nobody cared for the changelings. They grew up exiled from society, raised to obey and kill on command for the good of Adrianglia. They were fodder, but to him they were children, just like he had once been a child. Just like Jack.

He had to find Spider. He had to kill him. Child murder had to be punished.

A man stepped out of the Wood. William leapt off the porch. In a breath he pinned the intruder to the trunk of the nearest tree and snarled, his teeth clicking a hair from the man's carotid.

The man made no move to resist. "Do you want to kill me or Spider?"

"Who are you?"

"The name is Erwin." The man nodded at his raised hands. A large ring clamped his middle finger—a plain silver band with a small polished mirror in it. The Mirror—Adrianglian Secret Service—flashed in William's head. The Hand's biggest enemy.

"The Mirror would like a word, Lord Sandine," the man said softly. "Would you be kind enough to favor us with an audience?"

# TWO

CERISE leaned over the tea-colored waters of Horse-shoe Pond. Around her, massive cypresses stood like ancient soldiers at attention, the knobby knees of their roots straddling the water. The Mire was never silent, but nothing out of the ordinary interrupted the familiar chorus of small noises: a toad belching somewhere to the left, the faint scuttling of Edge squirrels in the canopy above her, the persistent warbling of the bluebill . . .

She rolled up her jeans and crouched, calling in a practiced singsong, "Where is Nellie? Where is that good girl? Nellie is the best rolpie ever. Here, Nellie, Nellie, Nellie."

The surface of the pond lay completely placid. Not a splash.

Cerise sighed. A long wet smudge flanked by swipes from clawed paws marked the mud five feet from her. Nellie's trail. When she was fifteen, tracking rolpies through the swamp was an adventure. She was twenty-four now and trudging through the Mire in the middle of the night stumbling into water and sinking up to her ankles in sludge was a lot less fun. She could think of much better ways to spend her time. Like sleeping in her nice warm bed, for example.

"Here, Nellie! Here, girl. Who is a good girl? Nellie is. Oh, Nellie is so pretty. Oh, Nellie is so fat. She is the fattest, cutest, stupidest rolpie ever. Yes, she is."

No response.

Cerise looked up. Far above, a small chunk of blue sky

winked at her through the braid of cypress branches and Mire vines. "Why do you do this to me?"

The sky refused to answer. It usually didn't, but she kept talking to it anyway.

A chirp echoed overhead, and a white glob of bird poop plummeted from the branches. Cerise dodged and growled at the sky. "Not cool. Not cool at all."

It was time for emergency measures. Cerise leaned her sword against a cypress knee, anchoring the scabbard in the muck, shifted her weight, pulled the backpack off her shoulders, and dug in the bag. She fished out the tangle of a leather face collar. It was designed to hug the rolpie's muzzle and the extra strap locking behind her head guaranteed the beast wouldn't get out. Cerise arranged it on the mud for easy access and extracted a can opener and a small can.

She held the can out and knocked on it with the can opener. The sound of metal on metal rolled above the pond. Nothing.

"Oh, what do I have? I have *tuna*!"

A small ripple wrinkled the surface about thirty feet out. Gotcha.

"Mmmm, yummy, yummy tuna. I'll eat it all by myself." She locked the can opener on the can and squeezed, breaking the seal.

A brindled head popped out of the water. The rolpie sampled the air with a black nose framed with long dark whiskers. Large black eyes fixed on the can with maniacal glee.

Cerise squeezed the top of the can, letting some of the fish juice drip into the pond.

The rolpie sped through the water and launched herself out onto the shore. From the bottom up to the neck, she resembled a lean seal armed with a long tail and four wide half legs framed with flat flippers. At the shoulders, the seal body stretched into a graceful long neck, tipped with an otter head.

Cerise shook the can. "Head."

Nellie licked her black lips and tried her best to look adorable.

"Head, Nellie."

The rolpie lowered her head. Cerise slipped the collar on the wet muzzle and tightened it. "You'll pay for this, you know."

Nellie nudged her shoulder with her black wet nose. Cerise plucked a chunk of tuna from the can and tossed it at the rolpie. Razor-sharp teeth rent the air, snapping the treat. Cerise swiped her sword off the ground and tugged on the leash. The rolpie lumbered next to her, wiggling and pushing herself across the swamp mud.

"What the hell was that? Breaking out in the middle of the night and taking off for a stroll? Did you get tired of pulling the boats and decided to take your chances with Mire gators?"

The rolpie squirmed along, watching the can of tuna like it was some holy relic.

"They can bite bone sharks in half. They'll look at you and see a plump little snack. Brunch, that's what you'd be."

Rolpie licked her lips.

"Do you think tuna grows in the mud?" Cerise plucked another chunk and tossed it to Nellie. "In case you didn't know, there is no tuna in the Edge. We have to get our tuna from the Broken. The Broken has no magic. But you know what the Broken does have? Cops. Lots and lots of cops. And alarm systems. Do you have any idea how hard it is to steal tuna from the Broken, Nellie?"

Nellie emitted a small squeal of despair.

"I don't feel sorry for you." Tuna was a pricey commodity. It took four days to get to the Broken, and crossing the boundary between the Edge and the magicless world hurt like hell. Of the whole family, she and Kaldar were about the only ones who managed to do it. The rest of the Mars had too much magic to cross through the boundary. Trying to pass into the Broken would kill them.

Cerise slogged through the mud. Growing up, she was always told that her magic was a gift, a wonderful, rare, special thing, something to be proud of. The magic might have been a gift, but in moments of despair, as she sat poring over the ruins of the family's finances, she saw it for what it really was—a chain. A big heavy shackle that kept the family locked in the Mire. Were it not for all that magic, they could've escaped into the Broken long ago. As it was, the only way out of the swamp lay through the border with the Dukedom of Louisiana into the Weird, where magic flowed full force.

Louisianans used the Mire to dump their exiles. Criminals and troublesome bluebloods, anyone too inconvenient to keep but too risky to kill, were sent to the Mire. And once you crossed that boundary between the Weird and the Mire, the Louisiana Guard made sure you never made it back.

The vegetation parted, revealing the dark water of Priest's Tongue Stream. A green Mire viper lay in the mud. It hissed as they approached. Cerise hooked the snake with her sword and tossed it aside.

"Come on." She threw another bite of tuna to the rolpie and led her into the tea-colored water. Cerise wrapped the leash loop tighter around her wrist and slid her arms around Nellie's narrow neck. "You get the rest when we get home."

Cerise clicked her tongue and the rolpie took off down the stream.

TWENTY minutes later, Cerise shut the gate on the rolpie enclosure. Someone, probably the younger boys, had made a reasonable attempt to repair the chain-link fence, but it wouldn't hold if Nellie decided to ram it. In the twisted creeks and rivers of the swamp, rolpies were vital. In some places, the water was completely stagnant and the swamp vegetation blocked the wind.

The rolpies pulled the light swamp boats all over the Mire and helped save gasoline.

As long as a human was present, Nellie was an excellent rolpie: obedient, sweet, powerful. The moment you took the person out of the equation, the silly beast freaked out and tried to take off.

Maybe she had separation anxiety, Cerise reflected, starting up the hill toward the Rathole. Segregating Nellie into a smaller enclosure would just lead to disaster. Knowing her, she would bray night and day, because she was alone. And reinforcing the big fence would be too costly and take too much labor.

Cerise chugged up the hill to the Mar family house. Water dripped from her clothes and squished between her toes inside her boots. She wanted a hot shower and a nice meal, preferably with some meat in it. Things being what they were, she'd settle for fish and yesterday's bread. She'd have to oil her sword, too, but that was part of living in the swamp. Water and steel didn't mix very well.

The Rathole, a sprawling two-story monster of a house, sat on top of a low hill. Fifty yards of cleared ground separated the house from the nearest vegetation. The kill zone. Fifty yards was a lot of ground to cover when you had rifles and crossbones trained on you.

The ground floor had no entrance or windows. The only way in lay up the stairway to the second-floor verandah. As she approached the stairs, a small shape slipped from behind the verandah's colonnades and sat on the stairs. Sophie. Lark, Cerise corrected herself. Her sister wanted to be called Lark now.

Lark gave her a weary look from under dark tousled hair. Her skinny legs stuck out of her capris like matchsticks. Mud smudged her calves. Fresh scratches marked her arms over the old bruises. She hid her hands, but Cerise was willing to bet that her nails were dirty or bitten off, probably both. Lark used to be a bit of a neat freak, as much as an eleven-year-old girl brought up in the swamp could be. All gone now.

Worry pinched at Cerise. She kept her face calm. Show nothing. Don't make her self-conscious.

She came up the stairs, sat next to Lark, and pulled off her left boot, emptying the water out.

"Adrian and Derril are riding the Doom Buggy through the Snake Tracks," Lark murmured.

The dune buggy was a hell mobile made of pure fun. In fact, Cerise had snuck away with it before and had so much fun, she flipped it over. But touching the dune buggy without adult supervision was strictly forbidden. Stealing it and wasting expensive gasoline was punishable by three weeks of extra chores.

Of course, both fifteen-year-old Adrian and his fourteen-year-old sidekick, Derril, knew this and could handle the consequences. The most pressing issue was that Lark just tattled. Lark never tattled.

Cerise forced herself to calmly pull the other boot off. The very basis of her sister's personality was changing, and she could only watch, helpless.

"The boys didn't take you with them?"

The answer was so quiet, she barely heard it. "No."

Six months ago, they would have. Both of them knew it. The urge to reach out and hug Lark's bony shoulders gripped Cerise, but she kept still. She'd tried that before. Her sister would stiffen, slide away, and take off into the woods.

At least Lark was talking to her. That was a rare thing. Normally, Mom was the only person who could get through to her, and even she had a hard time drawing Lark out lately. The kid was slipping away into her own world, and nobody knew how to pull her out.

"Did you tell Mom?" Cerise asked.

"Mom isn't here."

Odd. "Dad?"

"They left. Together."

"Did they say when they would be back?"

"No."

Cerise tensed. In the Mire, the resources were few and the people were many. The families fought tooth and nail over the smallest things. Almost every clan was in a feud, and theirs was no exception.

The feud between the Mars and the Sheeriles had started eighty years ago and was still going strong. Sometimes it burned bright and sometimes, like right now, it smoldered, but it could burst into open warfare at any moment. The last time the feud had flared, Cerise lost two uncles, an aunt, and a cousin. The standing rule was: you go out, you let someone know where you're going and when you're planning on coming back. Even their father, who was the head of the family, never strayed from this rule.

Anxiety rolled over her. "When and why did they leave?"

"At sunrise, and they left because Cobbler got his butt bit."

Cobbler, an old wino, bummed about the swamp doing odd jobs for moonshine. Cerise never cared for the man. He was mean to the kids when he thought their parents weren't looking, and he'd stab anyone in the back just out of spite. "Go on . . ."

"He came over and told Dad wild dogs got into Grandpa's house. They chased him and one bit him on the butt. His pants had holes."

Sene Manor had been boarded up for years, ever since their grandparents had died there of red fever twelve years ago. Cerise remembered it as a sunny house, painted bright yellow, a spot of color in the swamp. It was an abandoned wreck now. Nobody went near it. Cobbler had no business going there either. Probably was looking for something to steal.

"What happened next?"

Lark shrugged. "Cobbler kept talking until Dad gave him some wine and then he went away. And then Dad said he had to go and take care of Grandpa's house, because it was still our land. Mom said she would go with him. They rode out."

Getting to Sene Manor by truck was impossible. They would've ridden out on horseback.

"And you haven't seen them since?"

"No."

Sene Manor was half an hour away by horse. They should've been back by now.

"Do you think Mom and Dad are dead?" Lark asked in a flat voice.

Oh, Gods. "No. Dad's death with a sword, and Mom can shoot a Mire gator in the eye from a hundred feet. Something must've held them up."

A muted roar rolled through the trees—the dune buggy's engine getting a workout. Dimwits. Didn't even have the patience to turn the engine off and roll the buggy back up to the house. Cerise rose.

"Let me deal with this, and if Mom and Dad aren't back by the end of the hour, I'll go and check it out."

An old dune buggy burst out from between the pines, splashing through the mud on its way to the house. Cerise raised her hand. Two mud-splattered faces stared at her from the front seat with abject horror.

Cerise drew in a deep breath and barked. "Cramp!"

Magic pulsed from her hand. The curse clutched at the two boys, twisting the muscles in their arms. Adrian doubled over, the wheel spun left, the dune buggy careened, and the whole thing toppled onto its side in a huge splash, sliding through the sludge. The hell mobile turned, vomiting the two daredevils into the mud, spun one more time, and stopped.

Cerise turned to Lark. "Feel free to go over there and kick them while they're down. When you're done, tell them to clean everything up and head straight to the stables. Aunt Karen will be overjoyed to have two slaves for the next three weeks."

Cerise took her boots and headed into the house. The vague feeling of unease matured into full-blown dread in her chest. She had to figure out what had held up her parents, and the sooner the better. For a moment she almost veered toward the stables, but riding out by herself would be just asking for trouble. She needed backup, someone steady in a fight. Better to spend an extra ten minutes gathering help now than regret it later.

This wasn't going to end well, she just knew it.

# THREE

WILLIAM leaned against the wall of his house. The two people in the yard watched him. If they found his toy army odd, they kept it to themselves.

The wild inside him snarled and growled, scraping at his insides with sharp claws. He held it in check. The images of dead children tore open an old scab, but anger would do him no good now. He'd run across the Mirror's agents during his time in the Red Legion. Rules didn't apply to them, and he'd learned quickly that turning his back on them wasn't a good idea. You screwed with those guys at your own peril, knowing that your next breath might come with a knife in it.

William didn't know what these two would do or why they came to bother him, and so he watched them the way a wolf watched an approaching bear: no hint of movement, no sign of weakness, no snarling. He wasn't afraid, but he had no reason to provoke them. If a reason did present itself, he wouldn't hesitate to rip out their throats.

The two people from the Mirror made no move either. Erwin stood on the left. Of the two, he seemed like the bigger threat. Most people would forget Erwin a minute after they'd met him. Of average height, average build, he had an unremarkable face and short hair, either dark blond or light brown. His voice was mild, his manner unassuming, and his scent was so saturated with magic that the whole place stank like a pastry shop the day before Thanksgiving. The way he held himself, loose, deceptively carefree, didn't bode well either.

The woman next to Erwin was a good deal older. Short, thin, ramrod straight, with skin the color of coffee, she wore a blue gown like it was armor. The gown's skirt split down the sides, showing gray pants and supple boots, letting the woman move fast if she needed to.

Her braided hair sat in a complex mess on her head. Her face drew the eye. She had dark eyes, black, sharp, and merciless. The eyes watched him with eerie intensity. Like being tracked by a bird of prey, cold and ready to kill. The woman's scent filtered down to William, a layered amalgam of perfume: blackberry, vetiver, orange, rosemary, roses. An in-your-face fragrance. She was in charge and wanted people to know it.

Erwin was a heavy hitter, and the way he hovered near the woman gave him away. The man acted as a bodyguard. Since he had no visible weapons, he had to be a flasher. Anyone with magic could learn to channel their power into a flash, a concentrated stream that looked like a ribbon of lightning—and if it was bright enough, it seared like one, too.

William shifted, a light transfer of weight from one foot to the next, and hid a smile when Erwin tensed in response. As a changeling, William had no flash, but he'd spent enough years in a unit full of superb flashers. If Erwin flashed pale blue or white, he was likely a blueblood or extremely talented, like Rose. If he managed a green or a yellow, he wasn't very high up the food chain.

The hotter Erwin's flash, the higher up the ladder of command the woman was. No sense wasting a good flasher to guard a mid-level paper pusher.

"Can you flash?" William asked.

Erwin offered him a mild smile.

"He wants to know who he is dealing with," the woman said. "You have my permission to demonstrate."

Erwin inclined his head to her and looked at William. "Name the target."

"Wasp nest, twenty feet to the left, on the oak. Second branch up."

It would have to be a hell of shot to hit that damn thing. Declan probably could, but he'd blow half the tree away with it.

Erwin turned. "Ah."

A white glow drenched his eyes. Tiny tendrils of white lightning sparked off his right hand and flared, combining into a current. A beam of pure white shot from him, severing the wasp nest in half, as if with a knife.

Erwin wasn't just a flasher. He was a sniper. Figured.

"You've heard of Virai," the woman said.

Most Red Legionnaires knew of Virai. The Red Legion did black ops, so when the Mirror needed muscle and raw numbers, they tapped the Red Legion first. Virai was the head of the Mirror, the power behind the agency. His name was whispered.

"Sure."

The woman raised her chin. "I am Virai."

William blinked. "*The* Virai?"

"Yes. You may call me Nancy, if you would like."

Nancy. Right. "Why did you bring me pictures of dead children?"

"Because you have spent the last two years living here, safe and cozy. You needed a reminder of who you are."

Arrogant crone. William bared his teeth in a slow wolf smile. "Your pet sniper won't stop me. I've taken his kind before." In his mind William leapt over his action figures, hit Erwin, breaking his neck on the way down, rolled . . .

"Perhaps," Nancy said. "But can you take two at once?"

Her eyes blazed with white. Magic unfurled from her in a glowing shroud, held for a long breath, and vanished.

The imaginary attack died as imaginary William got sliced in two by Nancy's flash. They had him. One superior flasher he could handle. Between the two of them, they would mince him into pieces before he got his fingers around anyone's throat.

William crossed his arms. "What is it you want?"

The woman raised her head. "I want you to go deeper into the Edge and find Spider. I want you to take away the object he's looking for and bring it to me. If you kill him, I would consider it a bonus."

Well, he did ask. "Why me?"

"Because he knows my agents. He knows the way they think, and he kills them. You've tangled with him twice and survived. So far, it's a record." She locked her teeth, making the muscles on her jaw stand out. "Spider is the worst kind of enemy. He's a true believer, convinced that he's serving a higher cause. He won't stop until he's dead."

"And you're here because you don't want to waste your people hunting him," William said. As a changeling, he was expendable. Nothing new there.

Nancy's voice cracked like a whip. "I'm here, because of all of the operatives available to me, you are the best man for the job and I can't suffer another failure. I can't compel you to help me. I have no authority over you. I can only ask."

If that was the way she asked, he hated to hear what her order sounded like.

She did *ask* all the same. That was new. He'd been given orders all his life. Declan was the only one who bothered to ask him anything. The dumb blueblood insisted on treating him as if he were a real person. Still, William reflected, he had a comfortable life. Asking alone wouldn't pry him free from it—but they also brought Spider to the table. The knowledge that the child murderer was within his reach would eat at him now, burrowing like a tick under his skin, until it would drive him crazy. He had to kill the man. It was the last bit of unfinished business he had. He'd murder Spider, taste his blood, and come back here without a weight on his soul.

Go deeper into the Edge, huh? The Edge wrapped the junction of two worlds all the way from one ocean to another, widening and narrowing whenever it felt like it. Sometimes it was three miles deep, sometimes fifty. "Where in the Edge is Spider?"

"In the swamps," Erwin said. "West of here, the Edge narrows down almost to nothing and then abruptly widens to encompass an enormous swamp the locals call the Mire. We estimate it to be at least six hundred square leagues, perhaps bigger."

Nine hundred square miles. "A hell of a swamp."

"The Mire is sandwiched between the Weird and the Dukedom of Louisiana and the Broken and the state of Louisiana," Erwin continued. "Most of it is mud and water, impassable and unmapped. The Dukedom has been dumping exiles into it for years. They're too full of magic to escape into the Broken, so they simply stay there, stranded between the worlds."

William raised his eyebrows. "A swamp full of criminals." He would be right at home.

"Precisely." Nancy nodded. "Spider is an urban agent. Nothing short of a dire need would drag him to the Mire, where he's out of his element. There are a dozen places where things are heating up, but instead his crew is scouring the swamps. They're looking for something. I want to know what it is and I want to own it."

She didn't ask much, did she? Just the moon and the stars.

"The Louisianans moved a detachment of Air Force wyverns to the border with the Mire," Erwin said.

William grimaced. "They expect to airlift Spider as soon as he gets out of the swamp."

Erwin nodded.

Whatever Spider was looking for had to be valuable if they were willing to park a wyvern for him.

A predatory light sparked in Nancy's eyes. "The Dukedom of Louisiana wants a war, but they're unwilling to

risk it unless they're certain of their victory. Spider has
been trying to deliver the means to win this war for the
last ten years. This time he must've found something
remarkable. If the war starts and the Dukedom wins,
every changeling within our borders will be murdered."

"Don't," William warned. "The pictures were unexpected, but I'm not an idiot. I know what you're trying
to do." Changelings had a harder time controlling their
emotions. That was one of Hawk's favorite tactics: rile
up the changelings, get them angry with the scent of
blood or a punch in the face, and send them into the fight
to rend everything they came across. He was an old wolf
and this wasn't his first hunt. "Cheap tricks don't work
on me."

Nancy smiled and he fought an urge to step back.

"I was right. You will do nicely. We will give you all of
the support at our disposal. Weapons, technology, maps,
intelligence on Spider's crew."

William showed her his teeth. "I don't like you and I
don't like this mission."

"You're not required to like me or the mission," Nancy
told him. "You're required to complete your task. That's
all."

"Suppose I do this for you. What do I get?"

Nancy arched her eyebrows. "First, you'll get venge-
ance. Second, I will owe you a favor. There are people
who would cut off their right arm for that alone. But
more importantly, you will know with absolute certainty
that Spider will never kill another changeling child.
Think on it, William Wolf. But be fast about it. Time is
short."


A cold drizzle sifted onto the swamp, blurring the trees and
obscuring the narrow road. The sounds of three horses
clopping merrily along blended with the noise of the birds
and chirping of insects.

Given a choice, Cerise would've galloped. Instead she kept the pace slow. The last thing they needed was to blunder at full gallop into an ambush.

"It's Sheeriles," Erian said from the right. Slim, blond, he rode like he was born in the saddle. The feud between their family and the Sheeriles had taken his mother when he was eleven, and Cerise's parents had raised him. He was more like a brother than a cousin.

"They have no reason to restart the feud," Mikita boomed. Nature had forgotten to install a volume control when he was born, and he came with two sound settings: thunder and louder thunder.

Unlike Erian, Mikita rode as if he was afraid the horse would somehow escape from underneath his huge blocky body. Six-feet-five, two hundred and sixty pounds, none of it fat, he was almost too big to be a Mar. Hard to grow that large on a ration of fish and swamp berries, but Mikita had somehow managed.

"The Sheeriles don't need a reason," Erian said.

"They do and you know it. If they can't show cause, the Mire militia will come down on them like a ton of bricks," Mikita said.

Mikita was right, Cerise thought, as they rounded the bend in the twisted road. The Dukedom of Louisiana was very generous in supplementing the Mire's population with exiles. None of them was law-abiding or peaceful. The Edger families stuck together, turning into clans full of half-starved locals with itchy trigger fingers. Feuds bloomed in the Mire like swamp flowers, and some of the old-timers threw around heavy magic. In their family alone, they counted four cursers and seven flashers, and then there were people like Catherine and Kaldar, whose magic was so specific they had no name for it. If the feuds had been left unchecked, pretty soon there wouldn't have been anybody left in the Mire to feud with.

That was why the Edgers finally banded together and instituted their own court and their own militia. Now to rekindle a feud, one had to show cause. The Sheeriles knew this. The problem was she didn't think they cared.

"They have all that money, and they managed to keep it through the years," Mikita said.

Erian frowned. "What does money have to do with anything?"

"People who keep their money that long aren't stupid. They won't take risks unless they think things will play out in their favor. Sniping Uncle Gustave and Aunt Gen without cause is a hell of a risk. They know our whole family will be howling for blood."

Cerise hid a sigh. Unlike the Sheeriles, the Mars were swamp-poor: they had land and numbers, but no money. That was how they'd earned their nickname: Rats. Numerous, poor, and vicious. The vicious part she didn't mind, the poor part she could do nothing about, and the numerous part . . . Well, it was true. In a fight, the Sheeriles would lose hired guns, while she would lose relatives.

The thought made Cerise wince. Her father's absence turned her into the head of the family. She was the oldest of his children, and she was the only fully trained warrior they had. If something did happen to her parents, she would be the one sending her family to die. Cerise caught her breath and let it out slowly, trying to release anxiety with it. This morning had gone from bad to worse in a hurry.

The path turned, and the decrepit husk of the Sene Manor came into view. Cerise's heart skipped a beat. A lanky man stood on the porch, leaning against the porch post, his straw blond hair falling over his shoulders. He glanced up, his eyes light on a tan face, and a slow, lazy smile stretched his lips.

Lagar Sheerile. The oldest of the Sheerile brothers. They and their mother ran the Sheerile clan now, since their dad fell off a tree three years ago. Sheerile Senior had busted his head so hard, he couldn't even feed himself anymore, let alone think. Served him right, too.

Behind her Erian swore softly.

Beside Lagar, Peva, his brother, rocked in a half-rotten wooden chair, whittling something from a block of wood. Above the two of them, the windows of the abandoned mansion stood wide open despite the rain. Men waited at the windows. She counted two crossbows, three rifles, and a shotgun. The Sheeriles had expected them and brought hired muscle. Paid top coin, too—the shooters with the Broken's rifles were expensive as hell.

All together, the Sheerile brothers, the dilapidated house, and the rifles in the windows made a perfect snapshot of the Mire. Like some sort of twisted postcard. She just wished she could shove it into the faces of the bluebloods from Louisiana. *You want to know what life is like in the Edge? Here you go. Think on that before you decide to pile more problems on us.*

Peva slid from his chair, a tall gangly form on legs that looked too long. His crossbow lay next to him on a rail. He was so proud of the damn thing, he'd named it. Wasp. Like it was Excalibur or something. Peva reached for it but changed his mind. Decided not to bother, did he? Apparently, they weren't enough of a threat.

Cerise stared at Lagar. *Where are my parents, you smug sonovabitch?*

The door banged, and the third Sheerile brother sauntered into view, carrying Lagar's sword. Arig, at eighteen, was the youngest and the dumbest. In a dark room in a crowd full of strangers, Cerise could've picked all three of them out in seconds. She had grown up knowing that one day she would have to kill the Sheerile brothers, and they knew they had to kill her before she did them in. She'd come to terms with it a long time ago.

Arig held the sword out to Lagar, but the blond Sheerile ignored it. They didn't mean to fight her today. Not yet.

Cerise brought her horse to a halt by the porch.

Lagar gave her a short nod. "Lovely morning to you."

"Same to you, Lagar." She smiled, making an effort to look sweet and cheerful. "You boys lost?"

"Not that I know of." Lagar gave her the same friendly smile.

"If you're not lost, then what are you doing on my land?"

Lagar peeled himself from the post with affected leisure. "My land, love."

"Since when?"

"Since your father sold it to me this morning."

Like hell he did. She pursed her lips. "You don't say."

"Arig," Lagar called. "Bring the deed to our pretty guest."

The youngest Sheerile brother trotted over to her horse and offered her a piece of paper rolled into a tube. She took the tube from him.

Arig leered. "Where's your cute little sister, Cerise? Maybe Lark would like some of what I've got. I can show her a better time than she's had."

A shocked silence fell.

Some things were just not done.

A lethal fire slipped into Lagar's eyes. Peva stepped off the porch, walked over to Arig, and grabbed him by the ear. Arig howled.

"Excuse us a minute." Peva spun Arig around and kicked him in the ass.

"What did I do?"

Peva kicked him again. Arig scrambled through the mud, up the rickety porch, and into the house. Something thumped inside, and Arig's voice screamed, "Not in the gut!"

Cerise glanced at Lagar. "Letting him go around without a muzzle again?"

Lagar grimaced. "Look at the damn deed."

Cerise unrolled the paper. The signature was perfect: her father's sharp narrow scrawl. Lagar must've paid a fortune for it. "This deed's false."

Lagar smiled. "So you say."

She handed it back to him. "Where are my parents, Lagar?"

He spread his lean arms. "I don't know. I haven't seen them since this morning. They sold us the manor and left in perfect health."

"Then you don't mind if we check the house."

He bared his teeth at her. "As a matter of fact, I do. Mind."

The crossbows and rifles clicked as one, as safety latches dropped.

Cerise fought for control. It flashed in her head: jump off the mare, use her as a shield against the first volley, charge the porch, split Arig's stomach with a swipe of the blade, thrust into Peva . . . But by then both Mikita and Erian would be dead. Six crossbows against three riders—it was no contest.

Lagar was looking at her with an odd wistful expression. She had seen it once before, two years ago, when he got drunk out of his mind at the Summer Festival. He'd crossed the field and asked her to dance, and she spun one time around the bonfire with him, shocking the entire Mire into silence: two heirs of feuding families playing with death while their elders watched.

She had an absurd suspicion that he was thinking of pulling her off her horse. He was more than welcome to try.

"Lagar," she whispered. "Don't screw with me. Where are my parents?"

Lagar stepped closer, dropping his voice. "Forget Gustave. Forget Genevieve. Your parents are gone, Cerise. There's nothing you can do."

The cold knot in her stomach broke and turned into rage. "Do you have them, Lagar?"

He shook his head.

Her horse sensed her anxiety and danced under her. "Who has them?" No matter how far away the Sheeriles had hidden them, she would find them.

A thin smile curved Lagar's lips. He raised his hand, studying it as if it were an object of great interest, watching the fingers bend and straighten, and looked back at her.

The Hand. Louisiana spies.

Ice slid down Cerise's spine. The Hand was deadly. Everybody heard stories about them. Some of them were so twisted by magic, they weren't even human anymore. What would Louisiana spies want with her parents?

Lagar raised his voice. "I'll send a copy of the deed to your house."

She smiled at him, wishing she could let her sword slide across his neck. "You do that."

Lagar bowed with a flourish.

"This is it," she said. "No turning back."

He nodded. "I know. Our great-grandparents started this feud, and you and I will finish it. I can't wait."

Cerise turned her horse and urged it on. Behind her, Mikita and Erian rode through the rain.

Her parents were alive. She would get them back. She would find them. If she had to paint their trail with Sheerile blood, all the better.

CERISE burst into the yard at a canter, her mare's hooves splashing mud. She'd asked Erian to ride ahead to get everyone together. He must've done a hell of a job, because Aunt Murid stood on the verandah with a crossbow. Up to the left, Lark sat in the pine branches, and to the right, Adrian had climbed up into a cypress. Both had rifles and neither missed often.

Derril ran up to take the reins from her, his eyes wide. "Is Richard here?"

Her cousin nodded. "In the library."

"What about your uncle Kaldar?"

Derril nodded again.

"Good."

During the ride, her fury had crystallized into a plan. It was a ridiculous plan, but it was a plan. Now she had to convince the family to follow it. By the last count, the Mar clan consisted of fifty-seven people, including the kids. Some of the adults had seen her in diapers. They listened to her father. Making them listen to her was an entirely different matter.

Cerise locked her jaw. If she had any hope of seeing her parents again, she had to catch the reins her father had dropped and grip them tightly now, before the family had a chance to think things over and argue with her. She had to hold them together. Her parents' lives depended on it.

Cerise walked up the stairs. Mikita followed at her heels.

She paused by Aunt Murid, who was standing at the door. Six inches taller, dark-haired, dark-eyed, Murid rationed words like they were precious water in the middle of a desert, but her crossbow never failed to make a point.

Cerise looked at her. *Are you with me?*

Murid nodded slightly.

Cerise hid a breath of relief, swung the door open, and stepped inside.

"No hesitation," her aunt murmured behind her. "Walk like you mean it."

The library lay at the end of the hallway. The largest room in the house, with the exception of the kitchen, it often served as the gathering place for the family. By now, the news of her parents having gone missing would have spread throughout the Rathole. The library would be full. Her aunts, uncles, cousins. All listening to her as she came down the hall.

Cerise took a deep breath and strode down the hallway, not caring about tracking mud.

She walked into the library, cataloging the familiar faces. Aunt Emma, Aunt Petunia—Aunt Pete for short— Uncle Rufus, in the chairs; Erian to the left, his slender blond body draped over a chair; Kaldar, his dark hair in wild disarray, leaning against the wall; half a dozen others; and finally Richard, the oldest of her cousins, tall, dark, with the poise of a blueblood, waiting by the table.

They all looked at her.

Cerise kept her voice flat. "The Sheerile brothers have taken Grandfather's house."

The room went quiet like the inside of a grave.

"Lagar Sheerile showed me a deed of sale to Sene Manor signed by my father."

"It's a forgery," Aunt Pete said. "Gustave would never sell Sene."

Cerise held up her hand. "My father and mother are missing. Lagar said they were taken by the Hand."

Richard's face paled.

"The Louisiana spies?" Kaldar, slim, his hair dark like Richard's, peeled himself from the wall. Where Richard radiated icy dignity, his brother lived to have fun. He had wild eyes the color of honey, a silver hoop in one ear, and a mouth that either said something funny or was about to break into a grin, sometimes just as he sank his blade into someone's gut. Richard thought like a general, while Kaldar thought like a criminal, and she desperately needed both of them on her side.

Kaldar leaned forward, a hard, vicious light sparking in his eyes. "What the hell does the Hand want with us?"

"Lagar didn't say. As of now, the feud is officially on. I need riders sent to Uncle Peter, Emily, and Antoine. We're pulling everyone into the Rathole. Someone needs to warn Urow, too."

"I'll take care of it," Uncle Rufus said.

"Thank you." Cerise wished she knew exactly what to say, but whatever words she had would have to do. *Here we go.* "We must take back Grandfather's house. First, my parents disappeared there. If any clues exist, they would be at Sene. Second, I don't have to tell you that the Mire runs on reputation. We're only as strong as others think we are. If we allow the Sheeriles to bite off a chunk of our land, we might as well pack it in."

No arguments. So far so good.

"Kaldar, how much time do we have to dispute the deed?"

Her cousin shrugged. "We have to file the petition with the Mirc court by tomorrow evening. The court date could be anywhere from ten days to two weeks from then."

"Can you stall?"

"I can get us a day, maybe two."

Richard's narrow lips bent into a frown. "If we go through legal channels, we'll lose. To dispute the Sheeriles' deed, we have to have the original document granting the Sene Manor to Grandfather. We need his exile order. We don't have it."

Cerise nodded. That document and many others had perished four years ago in a flood that had nearly demolished the storage buildings. She'd thought about that on her ride over as well.

"Can we get a replacement?" one of the younger boys asked.

"No." Kaldar shook his head. "When Louisianans sentence someone to exile, three copies of the orders are cut. One goes straight to Royal Archives, the second is carried by the marshals who transport the exile and is surrendered to the Border Guard when they reach the Edge, and the third is given to the exile. The Border Guard isn't going to fall over themselves to find that order for us. We'll never get close enough to ask. They'll shoot us and string our corpses on the trees along the border."

"Every exile carries the order?" Cerise asked.

"Every adult," Kaldar said. "What are you getting at?"

"There were two adult exiles, Grandfather and Grandmother," Richard said. "Grandmother's order wasn't among the papers ruined in the flood. I know, I sorted through them. Where is it?"

"Hugh," Aunt Murid said.

Cerise nodded. "Exactly. Before Uncle Hugh went into the Broken, he took certified copies of all archival documents with him for safekeeping, including the original copy of Grandmother's order. I remember this because Mother cried when she gave it to him."

Richard narrowed his eyes. He was the most cautious of all of them, the most reasonable, and the one who always kept his calm. You might just as well try to rattle a granite rock. The family respected him. If she convinced him to buy her plan, the rest would follow.

"Hugh is in the Broken," Richard said. "You can't go after him, Cerise. Not now."

"I'll do it," Kaldar said. "I'm the one who makes runs there anyway."

"No." She loaded enough steel into her voice to make the lot of them blink.

Erian looked ready to say something but clamped his mouth shut.

"The Hand took . . ." Cerise wanted to say *my parents* but checked herself. She had to remove the personal part out of the equation, or they would just decide she was hysterical. "Gustave and Genevieve for a reason. They must want something from them or from us. They will be watching us. That's why we must pull everyone into the main house now, before they pick us off one by one.

"It takes three days to get to the Broken, and that's with shortcuts and a good rolpie to pull the boat. The person who leaves runs the risk of walking right into the Hand's spies." Cerise looked at Kaldar. "You're a thief, not a fighter. Erian is too hotheaded, Aunt Murid doesn't know the way, Mikita has no survival skills, and you, Richard, can't pass through the boundary into the Broken. You have too much magic. The crossing will kill you."

She surveyed them. "That leaves me. I went with Kaldar the last few times, I know the way, and of all of us, I have the best chance of surviving a fight with the Hand."

Richard was on the fence; she could see the hesitation in his eyes. "We just lost Gustave. If we lose you, we'll lose our strongest flash-trained fighter."

"Then I'll just have to survive," she said. "We have no choice, Richard. Tomorrow, as soon as Kaldar files the dispute and we have a court date, I have to leave. If you or anyone else can find a different way around it, I'll be happy to hear it."

For a long moment silence held, and then everyone spoke at once. Richard said nothing. Cerise looked into his somber eyes and knew she had won.

# FOUR

THE Great Bayou Swap Meet met at a giant plastic cow wearing a straw hat. At some point the cow must've been black and white, William reflected, but years of rain and wind had bleached it to a uniform pale gray. He surveyed the gathering of stalls and makeshift booths, selling everything from cloth dolls and old baseball cards sealed in plastic, to dinner sets and tactical knifes. To the right, some guy screamed himself hoarse, trying to find a buyer for his Corvette. To the left, a skinny woman in a booth decorated with a velvet painting of Elvis muttered nonstop to a pair of macaws in a cage. The birds, wet from the damp air, huddled together and probably plotted to kill her if the cage was ever opened.

This was the Mirror's brilliant strategy. William shook his head to himself. Getting into the Mire from the Weird was near impossible: the boundary was thick with traps and heavily patrolled by the Louisiana Guard. Instead, the Mirror had arranged for him to sneak in through the back door, through the Broken. His instructions were simple: travel to the small town of Verite, located in the lovely state of Louisiana. Attend the Great Bayou Swap Meet. Wait by the cow at precisely seven o'clock. A guide would come and take him into the Edge. Great plan. What could go wrong?

If there was one thing he'd learned in his years of military service, it was that everything that could go wrong, would. Especially considering that the guide was a freelancer.

A homeless woman wandered over and took up a post by the cow's hind legs. A layer of grime obscured her features. She wore a dirt-smudged tattered field jacket that once must've belonged to some soldier in the Broken. A black ski cap hid her hair. Filthy jeans stuck out from under the jacket, tucked into what looked like a surprisingly solid pair of boots. Her scent washed over him. She smelled sour, like she'd rolled in a batch of old spaghetti. For all he knew, she was going into the Edge as well, and he'd have to smell that rotten tomato sauce for the whole trip. Last Sunday he'd watched a documentary about the Great Depression on the History Channel, and she would give any of those hobos a run for their money.

This was just getting better and better. He had nobody but himself to blame, William thought. He could be back in his trailer right now, drinking good coffee. But *nooo*, he had to be a hero.

The Mirror had given him a four-day crash course on the Mire, Spider's crew, and the operation of about a thousand gadgets they had stuffed into his rucksack. His memory was near perfect. All changeling children going through Hawk's were trained in memorization. They were meant to become soldiers, who were expected to remember mission maps and objectives. His memory was exceptional even among changelings.

William had practiced in the Broken out of habit, memorizing random things he read and watched, everything from gun catalogs to cartoons. He could recite the first hundred or so pages of an average paperback after having read it once. But the amount of information the Mirror had crammed into him strained even his brain, and now it hummed as if some phantom bees had made a hive in his skull. Eventually his mind would come to terms with the information, and he'd either learn it permanently or allow himself to forget it, but for now it was giving him a hell of a headache.

A man walked out of the crowd, heading for the cow. About forty, with gray hair cut in what would've been a mullet if he wasn't balding, the man walked with a slight limp, dragging his left leg. He wore black jeans, a black T-shirt, a gray flannel shirt, and a Remington rifle. Looked like a 7400 from where William was standing, but he'd have to see it closer to be sure.

The man stopped a couple of feet away and looked him over. William raised his chin and gave him a flat stare. The newcomer struck him as an enterprising sort of man. The kind that would slit your throat for a box of tissues in your bag while you slept.

The man turned to the woman, gave her a long once-over, and spat into the grass. "Here for the Edge?"

"Yes," William said.

The woman nodded.

Yep, he would be spending the next few days in the company of that enchanting stench. Could be worse. At least she didn't reek like vomit.

"Name's Vern. Follow me."

Vern limped his way from the swap meet into the brush. The hobo followed. William shouldered his rucksack and went after them.

They hiked through the brush for about twenty minutes when he sensed the boundary. The hair on the back of his neck stood up.

Vern turned around. "Here's the deal. We cross into the Edge here. You die in the crossing, that's your problem. Don't count on any CPR and shit. If you make it through, we've got a two-day trip up through the swamps. Both of you paid half. The second half is due when we land in Sicktree. If you give me any trouble, I'll shoot your ass and won't worry twice about it. You change your mind and want off the boat, you get off in the swamp. I ain't turning back, and I ain't issuing no refunds. We clear?"

"Clear enough," William said.

The woman nodded.

Vern grimaced at her. "You mute or something? Never mind, none of my business."

He turned and stepped into the boundary. *Here we go.* William tensed against the incoming pain and followed.

Thirty seconds of agony later, the three of them were bent double on the other side, trying to catch their breath.

William straightened first, then Vern. The woman stayed bent, sucking in the air in small pained gulps. Vern headed down through the brush to where sounds of running water announced a stream.

The hobo woman didn't move. Too much magic in her blood.

"You got it?" William asked.

She jerked upright with a groan, pushed past him, and followed Vern.

*You're welcome.* Next time he'd mind his own damn business.

He pushed through the brush and almost ran straight into the water. A narrow stream lay before him, its placid water the color of dark tea but still translucent. Giant cypresses with thick, bloated stems flanked the stream. They stood densely, as if on guard, their knobby roots anchoring them to the mud. At the nearest tree, Vern waited in a large boat, a wide, shallow vessel with peeling paint and dented sides. A wooden cabin took up most of it, more a shelter from the sun than a cabin really: the front and back walls were missing. Two ropes hung from the nose of the boat, dipping into the water.

"No motor?" William asked, stepping aboard.

Vern gave him a look reserved for the mentally challenged. "Not from the Edge, are you? One, a motor makes noise, so the whole swamp will know where you are, and two, you've got a motor boat, that's some valuable shit. The Edgers will shoot you for it."

Vern picked up the ropes. Two twin heads poked from the water on long sinuous necks, like two Loch Ness monsters that somehow grew otter heads.

"Rolpie power," Vern said. "Keep your damn hands inside the vehicle and stay away from the sides. The Mire's full of gators, most bigger than this boat. They see your shadow on the water, they'll lunge into the boat to get you. And I ain't jumping in to rescue your ass."

He slapped the reins, smacking his lips. The rolpies dove, and the boat took off, gliding across the dark water into the swamp.

WILLIAM leaned against the cabin wall and watched the swamp slide by. If someone had asked him yesterday morning what hell looked like, he would've said he didn't know. He'd spent twenty-four hours in the swamp, and now he had an answer. Hell looked like the Mire.

The boat crawled down the river, framed by dense clumps of vegetation and reeds. In the distance, cypresses rose, their bloated trunks grotesquely fat, like old men with beer guts squatting in the mud. Sunrise was due in half an hour, and the sky and the water glowed the pale gray of a worn-out dime.

William inhaled deeply, sampling the scents on his tongue. The feeble stirring of the air that passed for wind in this place smelled of algae, fish, and mud. His senses regained their sharpness in the Edge, and the stench rising from the mess of muck, rot, and water combined with the heat made him want to bite someone just to let out some frustration.

The constant movement of the boat grated on his nerves. Wolves were meant to walk on firm ground, not on this shell of fiberglass, or whatever the hell it was, that insisted on swaying and rocking every time one of the rolpies gulped some air. Unfortunately firm ground was in short supply: the shore was a soup of mud and water. When they had stopped for the night and he'd stepped onto what seemed like solid ground, his boots had sunk in up to the ankle.

He'd spent the night in the boat. Next to the spaghetti queen.

William glanced at the hobo girl. She sat across from him, huddled in a clump. Her stench had gotten worse overnight, probably from the dampness. Another night like the last one, and he might snap and dunk her into that river just to clear the air.

She saw him looking. Dark eyes regarded him with slight scorn.

William leaned forward and pointed at the river. "I don't know why you rolled in spaghetti sauce," he said in a confidential voice. "I don't really care. But that water over there won't hurt you. Try washing it off."

She stuck her tongue out.

"Maybe after you're clean," he said.

Her eyes widened. She stared at him for a long moment. A little crazy spark lit up in her dark irises. She raised her finger, licked it, and rubbed some dirt off her forehead.

Now what?

The girl showed him her stained finger and reached toward him slowly, aiming for his face.

"No," William said. "Bad hobo."

The finger kept coming closer.

"You touch me, I'll break it off."

Something splashed ahead. Both of them looked at the river.

A wave wrinkled the surface a few hundred yards out. The girl squinted at it.

Here it was again, a shallow ripple. It bopped up and down. Something sped to the boat.

"Sharks!" The girl lunged at Vern.

He gaped at her.

"Sharks, you moron!" She pointed at the water.

Ripples sliced through the surface. A huge fin emerged. A second followed.

Vern grabbed for his bag and jerked out a grenade. William grabbed the girl and threw her to the bottom of the boat, shielding her.

The grenade plunked into the water. Thunder slapped William's ears, the blast wave rolling against his skin. The boat careened.

He whipped about, just in time to see Vern dive into the river, aiming for the shore.

The sharks streaked toward the boat, no worse for wear. The leading fish darted up to the surface, flashing the ridge of thick bony plates armoring its back. The damn thing was bigger than the boat.

The rolpies sensed the sharks and flailed, whipping the river into froth. The twin guidelines that secured the animals to the boat went taut, jerking at the metal cleats bolted to the nose. The boat danced up and down.

The girl dropped to the ropes. A small knife flashed.

William jerked his heavy tactical blade from its sheath. "Stop."

She pulled back, and he chopped through the line in a single cut.

The rolpie leaped out of the water and dove deep. *Go*, William urged. *Go*.

He chopped the second line. The severed rope flew, and the second rolpie surfaced in a foamy fountain. Huge jaws pierced the foam. Triangular shark teeth flashed and tore into the rolpie's side. The creature screamed. The girl screamed, too, pounding her fist on the rail. William ground his teeth.

The shark ripped a bloody slab of flesh from the rolpie's flank.

William yanked a crossbow stock out of his rucksack and pulled the activation. The stock sprouted arms with a faint click. It was the latest in small arms models, only a foot long, and he was under strict orders not to use it unless absolutely necessary. William jerked back his sleeve, revealing a leather quiver strapped to his forearm, plucked a bolt, loaded in a single smooth move, sighted the fish, and fired.

A white star streaked through the air. The bolt sprouted from the shark's gills. The bolt head winked with green and exploded in a pulse of magic. The fish launched straight up, out of the river, its black mouth gaping, blood streaming from a hole in the side of its head, and crashed onto its back. The second shark hit the first, spinning it. Blood roiled through the river. The rolpie streaked away, fleeing for its life.

The injured shark thrashed and dived down. The second fish gave chase.

The boat crawled downstream.

William took a deep breath. The rush of the fight still sang through his veins, setting him on fire. He felt alive, more alive than he'd been in the last two years.

The old woman was right. He had forgotten who he was. He was a wolf and a killer.

"Thank you," the hobo girl said.

"We're fucked!" Vern announced from the shore.


THE boat drifted downstream at the speed of an invalid snail. Vern had no trouble keeping up even with his bum leg.

"They're bone sharks. The old kind. They swim up from the Weird sometimes and get trapped in the swamp. Of course they die from fresh water in a week or two, fuckers, but meanwhile they do their damage. It's over."

The boat's bottom slid against soft mud and stopped. About forty feet separated them from the nearest shore and Vern.

"What do you mean, it's over?" William said. "It's over when you get me to Sicktree."

Vern stared at him. "Are you daft? We have no rolpies, which means we've got no power and we can't maneuver for shit. Getting to Sicktree on foot would take days."

On the edge of William's peripheral vision, the hobo girl slid into the water. She did it silently, without a splash, and dove under. Even his ears picked up only the slightest hint of sound. The spaghetti queen had hidden talents. Where the hell was she going?

"Look around you, man!" Vern waved his arms. "That ain't a park out there. That swamp is gonna kill you. The Broken is only a day away by boat and about three by foot."

Everything that could go wrong . . . "I don't think so." William let some snarl into his voice. "I hired you to get me to Sicktree. That's where we're going."

Vern jerked his rifle up. "Get off my boat, you Weird fop."

William raised his crossbow. "Don't be stupid."

Vern sneered. "You ain't gonna hit me with that toy . . ."

A dark figure stepped out of the reeds behind Vern. A slender foot-long blade slid against his Adam's apple, reflecting light. William blinked. Smooth.

The hobo girl leaned to Vern's ear and whispered something.

Vern's fingers opened. The rifle fell into the mud with a wet splat.

The girl pulled the blade aside. William bared his teeth. She was trouble. Good for her, bad for him.

Vern limped away at top speed, yelling over his shoulder. "I won't forget this! I won't. You'll see."

The hobo girl hooked the rifle with her foot and kicked it into her hands. The rifle barrel glared at William. "You're in my boat."

*You've got to be kidding me.* "You can have this boat. You can have the whole damn swamp for all I care. After I get to Sicktree."

"That's a very nice crossbow," the girl said. "And you're very good with it. But I can shoot you twice in the time it takes you to load it."

William bared his teeth. "Want to test that theory?"

She smirked. "Are you sure you want to risk being shot? This bullet would make a very messy hole in your chest."

William pulled another bolt from the quiver.

The girl aimed to the left of him and squeezed the trigger. A feeble click echoed through the swamp. She popped the rifle open and swore.

"I emptied it last night while the two of you slept." William sighted her. "Vern didn't strike me as trustworthy. Looks like I keep the boat."

She lowered the rifle. "May I ask where you're going to pilot your new boat?"

"To Sicktree."

"And in what direction do you think Sicktree is?"

William stopped. The stream had turned at least half a dozen times. He knew the swamp settlement sat somewhere upstream, but where exactly he had no idea. The Mirror had no maps of this part of the Edge, but the parts that they did map looked like a labyrinth of tiny streams, ponds, and mud banks.

"I take it, you know the way to Sicktree."

She smiled. "I do. You should hire me to be your guide. Or you can spend the next couple of weeks blundering around the Mire."

She had him. William pretended to consider it. "Hire you? I think the privilege of riding in my new boat should be enough."

"Deal." She started toward the water.

"There are some conditions attached to my offer."

The girl rolled her eyes.

"One, if you're thinking of slitting my throat, don't. I'm faster and stronger than you, and I sleep light."

She shrugged. "Fine."

"Two, you bathe the first chance you get."

"Anything else?"

William thought about it. "No, that covers it."

The girl waded through the water, pulled herself into the boat, and dug in the bow compartment.

William watched her.

She pulled a large canvas bundle and dragged it to the side.

"What is that?"

"An inflatable boat. All runners carry them just in case." She patted the larger boat. "This bad boy is meant to be drawn by rolpies. It's heavy. The inflatable is light and we can carry it if we have to."

She pulled the cords, securing the canvas, dug in it, and swore. "Cheapskate. No inflatable—he's got his sleeping bag stuffed in there." She rose, stared at the cabin for a long moment, and tugged at the canvas covering its roof. "Are you going to help, Lord Weird? You can, of course, sit on your behind while I sweat, but it will take twice as long."

He grasped his end of the canvas and jerked. The camo fabric fell away, revealing a shallow, square-nose boat strapped to the cabin.

"A punt." The hobo girl sighed. "We'll have to pole it like a bateau."

William had no idea what a bateau or a punt was, but he didn't care. It was a boat and it could float, which meant it could get him to Sicktree to the Mirror's agent who waited for him there. He cut at the line securing the small vessel to the roof.

"Call me William."

"Cerise," the hobo girl said. "I've got a rule, too."

He glanced at her.

"No questions," she said.

Now that was interesting. William nodded. "I can work with that."

# FIVE

THE punt boat glided over the deceptively calm stream. Small speckled frogs perched on the wide queenscrown leaves. Somewhere to the left among the growth, a reed-walker traveled on long legs, emitting a staccato of clicks from his throat to ward off rival birds.

Cerise leaned into the pole, discreetly clamping her jacket tighter to herself. The stiff plastic packet hidden in the lining dug into her ribs. Still there. Tracking down Uncle Hugh took longer than planned—he'd moved and she had wasted two days trying to find his new house. Only four days separated her from the court date. She had to hurry. If she didn't show up with the documents on time, the family would be ruined. She had to move fast, and fast wasn't easy with a punt boat and some Weird knuckleheaded drylander who thought he owned it.

Lord William sat at the stern. Muscular, fit, wrapped in black leather, and more handsome than a man had a right to be. The first time she saw him, she almost did a double take. He had the whole tall, dark, and lethal thing going. Except at the moment he wore the expression of a man who'd just got a mouth full of soggy spinach. Maybe he was upset that his pretty leather pants got wet.

Lord William was bad news. That he was a blueblood from the Weird was plain as day: expensive clothes, well-groomed hair, and excellent weapons. She'd felt a spark of magic when that little crossbow went off. And he fired it fast, didn't even pause to take aim, and still hit that cursed fish in the gills. The man had training, the kind of training bluebloods from the Weird got when they wanted to play soldier. Excellent balance—he walked on the boat as if it were solid ground. Light on his feet. Very fast. Probably very strong, if the muscle on his arms was any indication. Bad news.

Why couldn't she have gotten another Edger or some dimwit from the Broken for a passenger? No, she got Lord Leather Pants here. In the Weird, nobles specialized. Some went into academics like her grandfather. Some devoted themselves to civil service. And some became killers. For all she knew, he was one of those multi-talented bluebloods, who cut down trees with their magic and sprouted weapons all over the place at the slightest hint of danger.

Cerise stole another look. The blueblood was surveying the Mire, and she let herself linger. He had the prettiest hair she had ever seen on a man: dark brown, almost black, and soft like sable, it fell down to his shoulders. She wondered what he'd do if she threw some mud in it. Probably kill her. Or at least try. Not that she had any intention of letting him win that fight. Talented or no, he wouldn't stop her sword or her magic.

She scrutinized his face. Strong chin. Narrow face without a trace of softness in it, square jaw, smart hazel eyes under black eyebrows. Interesting eyes, almost amber-yellow. That's what you looked at in an opponent—the eyes. The eyes told you what sort of person you faced. When she looked into William's eyes, she saw a predator. There he sat, all calm, but something behind those eyes promised violence. She sensed it the way one killer sensed another.

Bad news.

He caught her looking and scowled. "Give me that damn thing."

Cerise leaned into the pole. "Don't worry, you will get

your chance when we hit a stronger current. For now, sit pretty and enjoy the scenery. Look, there is a cute Mire gator to keep you entertained."

He glanced to the side, where two large yellow eyes looked back at him from a floating clump of waterweeds.

*Let's see what you're made off, Lord Bill . . .* "It's just a baby. Eighteen feet tops. He won't bother us. They grow much bigger."

No reaction. *Come on, tiny boat, big gator, that ought to worry anybody.*

"In a few years, he might get to be around twenty-five feet. Some old fellows grow to thirty. We call them *ervaurg*. Means 'big eater.'"

Lord Bill appeared unconcerned. *Hmm.*

Cerise pushed him a bit more. "The thing about ervaurgs is that they aren't like normal animals. When you feed a dog, he'll sit and wait for you to give him his food. When you feed a Mire cat, he'll grab the treat and rip it out of your hands. Feeding a Mire gator is like feeding a pair of giant, razor-sharp scissors. One moment you're holding a chunk of cow carcass on a hook above the water and then huge jaws come out and"—she snapped her fingers—"the meat is gone. No tug, no extra weight, nothing. Just jaws and an empty hook."

"Doesn't make much sense to feed them, then," William said.

"We do it for leather. A thirty-foot ervaurg packs a lot of leather, but his hide is too hard to make into anything. You might armor a boat with it, but other than that, it's not good for much. But when they're young, their leather is supple, so leather merchants breed them on gator farms like cows and kill them off with poisoned meat when they get too big. Mire gator leather is one of our few exports."

"It must've killed you not to talk for a whole day," he said.

*Handsome, scary, and an ass. As expected from a*

spoiled rich blueblood from the Weird. She imagined
thumping him on the head with her pole and gave him a
bright smile.

His eyes narrowed. "I get it. You kept your mouth
shut to hide the teeth."

And smart. Homeless people didn't have good teeth.
Kaldar had stressed that one to her before she left.

Cerise would've preferred a dumb Lord Bill over the
smart one—the smart one was more trouble—but in the
end, it didn't matter. She gave her word and she'd keep
it. They'd get to Sicktree, and then she'd drop him faster
than he could blink. She would just have to watch him
carefully and keep her sword close.

The swamp rolled by, savage and beautiful at the same
time. It'd been a few months since Cerise had come this
way, but she remembered it well enough. She was Kaldar's favorite partner in crime for his excursions to the
Broken. He'd wanted to come to look for Uncle Hugh so
badly even she couldn't convince him to stay behind. It
took Richard. He'd frowned and Kaldar gave in.

Cerise glanced at the sky. *Please keep the lot of them
safe in the Rathole. Please.* Someone had to meet her in
Sicktree to take her back to the house, and she'd agreed
to let Urow do it, because he was the best rolpie driver
the family had and because he nagged and piled on the
family guilt until she couldn't stand it anymore. Urow
was difficult. He was big and strong, and he thought that
made him a good fighter. He also had a chip on his
shoulder about being included in the family business.
She should've said no, but she knew it would crush him
and so she didn't. Now that decision was costing her a
bundle in frayed nerves.

But then Urow would come with a boat and a good,
fast rolpie, and she was late enough as it was. She would
need his boat and his crazy driving to get her to the Rathole on time.

Cerise brushed the jacket, feeling the stiff packet of
papers again. Still there. *Hold on, Mom, Dad. I'm coming.*

* * *

THE woman lay on the floor, curled into a fetal ball. Spider sighed. Her skin had acquired an unhealthy greenish tint. The matter wasn't helped by a patina of bruises covering her legs and arms. He always believed in the doctrine of maximum pain with minimal damage during torture—he wanted to break her spirit, not her body—and their sessions left only the lightest of injuries. Unfortunately Genevieve insisted on attacking the guards and trying to kill herself in her spare time. Subduing her without causing injuries proved difficult.

Her attempts grew more and more reckless. This last one was brilliantly executed and almost took her from him. He couldn't afford to lose Genevieve. Not yet.

Spider waited by the grimy wall. The place smelled of mildew. Gods, how he despised the swamp.

Genevieve stirred with a soft moan. Her eyelids trembled and she whispered, *"Non."*

Gaulish. Finally. She had reverted to her native language. It meant he had cracked her armor. Too little, too late. The Hand informed him that the Mirror was aware of his activities in the Mire and had sent an agent. They were unable to ascertain the agent's identity, but Spider expected the Adrianglians would send their best. The Mirror did produce worthy opponents once in a while, and he couldn't afford to jeopardize the integrity of the project. Some tough decisions would have to be made.

"Yes," he told her in Gaulish.

Genevieve pulled herself upright. A blue and black ring clutched at her throat.

"The bruise on your neck looks atrocious," he continued in the same language. "I have to admit, using magic to strangle yourself with your collar was an elegant move. Tell me, did you learn metal alteration before your parents were exiled to the Edge or after?"

She stared at him with intense, focused hatred.

"It saddens me that you hate me," he said. "I'm being sincere. You're a scion of one of the oldest blueblood

families, as am I. We should be having a civilized conversation, spiced with good red wine and an occasional witty
remark. Instead we find ourselves here." He spread his
arms. "In the drain for all of the world's muck, with you
reduced to a battered animal and me your batterer."

She didn't answer. He was wrong. She wouldn't break
anytime soon. A pity.

"It takes approximately five minutes to choke an adult
to death," Spider told her. "That's why people in my profession prefer to break the target's neck. We're frequently
short on time. It took my people thirty seconds to remove
the collar. At no point were you in danger of suffocating.
But in a way you did succeed. You see, now I'm short on
time. I can no longer gently choke you and wait for you to
comply. I have to break you now."

No reaction. As if she were a mannequin.

He leaned to her. "For Gods' sake, Genevieve, this is
your last chance. The war between Adrianglia and Louisiana is inevitable. It will be fought in my lifetime, if not in
yours. The diary holds the key to winning it. Thousands
of lives will be spared on both sides, if this war is resolved
quickly in a decisive show of force. That's why that translation is vital to me. I will have it."

She spat at him. He leaned just enough to avoid it and
shook his head. "I need an answer. Will you translate the
diary? Think before you answer, because you will sign
your death warrant with the wrong word. Think of your
husband. Your daughters."

Her cracked lips moved. "Go to hell."

Spider sighed. Why did people insist on frustrating
him?

"John?"

The door opened and John stepped into the cell. Tall,
gaunt, and stooped, his clothes perpetually rumpled, the
man had a wary manner about him, resembling a neurotic
buzzard. Spider had worked with several mages skilled in
human alteration, and John was neither the most difficult

nor the easiest to work with. He was, however, the best at what he did.

John dipped his head. "Yes, my lord?"

"We'll have to fuse her."

Shock slapped Genevieve's face. "You're a monster!"

Spider gripped her neck, swiping her off the floor, to bring her to his own eye level. "The world is full of monsters. I chose to become one, so the rest of my countrymen can sleep peacefully in their beds, knowing that their families are shielded by the likes of me. You've tied my hands, Madame. Take responsibility for your decisions."

He dropped her.

"Go ahead and fuse me," she hissed. "I will kill the lot of you. You will get nothing. My family will bury you in the swamp without that diary."

Tiresome. Spider glanced at John. "How much time?"

John surveyed the woman on the floor. "She's nearing fifty. Ideally a month, but I can do it in two weeks."

"Make it ten days."

"She won't be stable."

Spider looked at John for a long moment to make sure he had the man's attention. "She is my key, John. If you break her, I will be quite put out."

The alteration specialist swallowed.

Spider paused before the door. "Tell me when she is in the first stage. Her daughter left the family compound and traveled to the Broken. I want to know why."


AHEAD a bright green spot of fresh vegetation marked the mouth of Sandal Creek. Cerise turned the boat, steering it into the weeds. The bow mashed the green reeds. She laid into the pole, putting all of her weight into it. The boat tore through the green and landed in clear water.

A narrow channel stretched before them, flanked by

purple willows. Tiny magenta and blue leaves littered the calm water.

Lord Bill's eyebrows crept together, but if he had questions, he kept them to himself.

"That river back there gets a bit senile in another half a mile," she told him. "It forgets that it's flowing through the swamp and gets a good current going. Instead of paddling against the current, we're skipping the whole mess and saving ourselves a couple of hours. We should be back to the main river in about seven miles."

She tossed the pole at him. He snapped it out of the air. Good reflexes.

"Your turn. Don't use your arms, let your weight do the work. I'll see about lunch."

Lord Bill stood up, keeping his balance like he was born on water, and stabbed the pole into the water. The boat predictably slid from under him. It took him a couple of tries but he hit his stride.

Cerise sat down, dug in her bag, and pulled out a short fishing pole and the bait box she'd liberated from Vern's boat. She hooked a fat white grub and let the line fall into water.


"NOTHING yet?" William glanced at Cerise.

The hobo girl shook her head. The fishing line trailed forgotten behind the boat. She sat alert, her gaze scanning the banks, her body calm but ready. Like a veteran soldier expecting an attack.

"Something's wrong," she murmured. "The stream should be teeming with fish. It's too well blocked for sharks and too small for ervaurgs."

"Or you might suck at fishing." He surveyed the swamp. Torn clouds dappled the sky. The willows lined the shore, like slender women washing their locks in the water. No small noises, except for the distant shrieks of some insane bird.

William inhaled deeply. No odd scents, beyond the

usual smorgasbord of algae, fish, and vegetation. And Cerise. She was right. It was too quiet.

The hobo queen rolled into a crouch and reached into her jacket. *Here comes the blade.* He'd been waiting for her to pull it out again. A foot long, narrow, single edged, simple hilt. In good shape. She wasn't homeless—the sword gave her away before the teeth did—but the way she held it struck him as odd. Her grip was loose. Almost delicate, with the hilt caught in her long slender fingers. Clutching your weapon made you clumsy, but a firm grip was best. If you held you sword like it was a painting brush, sooner or later someone would knock it out of your hand.

Ahead an old willow leaned over the bank, its long branches cascading down to the river. A dark shadow shifted in the water under the willow leaves.

"Don't move," Cerise whispered.

He froze, pole in his hand. The boat glided slowly, using up the last of its speed.

Ripples pulsed under the willow, wrinkled the river, and vanished.

Cerise crouched at the bow, watching the water like a hawk.

A huge blunt head sliced through the river an inch from the surface, followed by a sinuous serpentine body. William held his breath. It kept coming and coming, impossibly long, moving in total silence, so enormous it seemed unreal. A low fin sliced through the water, sun glinted on the brown hide speckled with yellow flecks, and the creature vanished.

At least fifteen feet. Maybe more.

"A mud eel," Cerise whispered.

William nodded toward the pole. She shook her head.

The boat drifted downstream, heading for the right bank. The bottom scraped mud. They stopped. He raised the pole to push off.

The eel smashed into the side of the boat with a thud. The craft went flying. William leaped onto the bank. His feet touched the mud, it gave, suddenly liquid, and he sank to his hips.

The eel's blunt head reared from the water and hissed, its black maw flashing a forest of sharp needle teeth. The creature lunged onto dry land, clawing at the mud with short stubby paws. The damn thing had legs. Fucked-up place, fucked-up fish.

William spun the pole and rammed it into the night-marish mouth. Jaws locked on the wood, ripping it out of his hands. Round fish eyes fixed on him, expressionless and stupid.

He pulled a knife from his jacket.

The eel reared back. A bright red mark glowed on its forehead, a crimson skull with two gaping black circles for eyes.

William snarled.

The fish lunged.

Steel flashed, biting deep into the eel's left orbit, and withdrew. The milky gel of the fish eye slid free, its golden iris glistening like a small coin on wet cotton.

The eel jerked. Its huge body whipped around. The fish plunged into the river and sped away.

The hobo girl sighed and wiped the blade on her sleeve. "A single sinkhole on this bank for fifty feet in any direction and you managed to jump right into it. That takes real talent. Are you trying to make my job harder, Lord Bill?"

*Lord Bill?*

"The name's William. You stole my kill." He put his hands against the mud, trying to lift himself free, but it just crumbled under him. She could slit his throat from ear to ear, and there wasn't much he could do about it.

"Sure I did. You were just about to rip that big bad fish to tiny pieces." Cerise grabbed a willow with her left hand and leaned toward him. He gripped her fingers. She grunted and pulled him free.

Strong for a woman. And quick, too. That was one of the fastest strikes he'd ever seen.

Cerise was looking at him. "You look adorable."

Black slimy mud stained his pants, filling the air with the scent of old rot. Great. And he didn't even get to kill the fish.

"It's peat," she said. "It will wash right off. The eel won't be back for a few minutes, so if you want to clean up, now is your chance."

William pulled off his boots, emptying half a gallon of sludge onto the bank, and waded into the stream. The oily peat rolled off him in a slick wave, leaving no stains.

That was a hell of a sword thrust, fast, precise. Professional. The Mirror had no female agents in the Mire. Maybe she was Hand, one of Spider's crew. William ran through Spider's known flunkies in his mind, mentally comparing her to the women. No match. Either the Mirror had no information about her or they had neglected to share it.

William had a distinct urge to turn around, grab her, dunk her under the water, and wash all that dirt off her face, so he could see what she looked like.

He was a blueblood. He had to keep his cover.

William climbed out. The hobo queen greeted him with a huge smile. "So how are you enjoying your tour of the swamp so far?"

Smart-ass. He pulled on his boots. "Branded fish with legs weren't in the guidebook. I want a refund."

She blinked. "What do you mean, branded?"

"It had a skull etched between the eyes."

"Did it glow red?"

"Yes."

Her face dropped. She tilted her head to the sky. "That was rotten of you. I didn't deserve that. I have more than enough to deal with, so how about you stop throwing rocks at my windows? If you don't like the way I'm handling things, come down and try fixing this mess yourself."

"Who are you taking to?"

"My grandparents."

"In the sky?"

She faced him, her dark eyes full of indignation. "They're dead. Where else would they be?"

William shrugged. Maybe it was one of the odd human things changelings didn't understand. Or maybe she was just crazy. All Edgers were mad. He'd known that from the start. He was letting a crazy woman lead him deeper into the swamp. How could this not turn out well?

Gods, he missed his trailer. And his coffee. And dry socks.

Cerise strode to the overturned boat.

"What does the skull mean?"

"Never mind."

He picked up the pole and stepped in front of her. "What does the skull mean?"

She flipped the boat over. "It's Sect."

He followed her. "And that means what?"

"The eel belongs to the Gospo Adir Sect. They're necromancers. They alter eels and other things with magic and use them as watch dogs. The eels are vindictive as hell by nature, but this one is enhanced, which means it's smart and it's trained to hunt down trespassers. The damn thing will follow us around until we have to kill it, and if we do kill it, the Sect will want me to pay restitution for it."

Cerise pushed the boat from the shore and threw their bags into it.

"So let me get it straight—the fish attacks us, but you have to compensate this Sect for it?"

Cerise heaved a sigh. "Look before you jump, Lord Bill. It's a good rule. Learn it."

*Blueblood. Act like a blueblood. Bluebloods don't growl at the hired help.* "Wil-li-am. Do you want me to say it slower, so you can remember it?"

She clenched her teeth. "I hate dealing with the Sect. They aren't reasonable. We'll end up killing the stupid creature, and then Emel will eat a hole in my head over it."

"Who's Emel?"

"My cousin. The Red Necromancer. That's why I will have to pay restitution. The eel knows me by scent. It wouldn't have attacked me if I were on my own, so if you weren't with me, I wouldn't be in this mess."

He would strangle her before this trip was over. "Should I just let the fish eat me next time?"

"It would certainly make things easier."

William scraped the last of his patience together and tried to pretend to be Declan. "I'll pay you for the fish."

"Yes, yes, and that flock of pigs crossing the sky looks particularly lovely this time of day."

He lost it and snarled. "I said I'll pay for the damn fish if we have to kill it!"

She waved her hands in the air. "Do me a huge favor, Lord William. Keep your thoughts to yourself for the next few miles. If you keep talking, I'll have to hit you with this pole, and nobody wants that."


THE stream turned, spilling back into the river. Cerise leaned onto the pole, and the boat slipped into the wider water.

At this rate they'd reach Broken Neck by nightfall. She had no desire to chance crossing the labyrinth of peat islands and sunken cypresses in the middle of the night, not with the damn eel following them. They'd have to find a secure spot to camp. Maybe they would avoid Broken Neck altogether. Take one of the offshoot streams. It would be safer but slower. And her time was in short supply. More so because of the idiot blueblood.

*You stole my kill.* Ha.

Cerise glanced at him. Lord *William* had taken his crossbow out. His amber eyes scanned the water. There was something deeply predatory in the way he sat, silent and alert. Like a cat waiting to sink his claws into living flesh.

Cerise thought of the eel and William, stuck in the mud, only a knife in his hand. Most people would've panicked. He just waited for the fish to charge him. His eyes were predatory back then, too. Calculating, hot amber eyes, full of outrage, as if he was insulted the eel had attacked him.

She'd seen her share of exiles from the Weird. Once in a while, Louisiana would send a blueblood into the Edge. Some of them were powerful, some were desperate, but none were like William. She wanted to pry him open and figure out what he was made of. Why was he here in the Mire? What did he want?

He was only a blueblood, Cerise reminded herself. She would dump him in Sicktree. She had bigger things to worry about. She just liked looking at him, because he happened to have a handsome face and because with the two of them alone in the entire swamp, there wasn't anything else to look at.

"Looking for the eel?" Cerise asked.

He glanced at her and Cerise almost dropped the pole. His eyes luminesced like the irises of a wild cat hidden in darkness.

*Holy crap.*

Cerise blinked. William's eyes were back to their normal hazel. She could've sworn she'd seen them glow.

What the hell did she get herself into?

"I'm going to kill that damn fish," William growled.

*Oh, for Gods' sake.* "Crazy necromancers, anal cousin, financial liability, did any of that penetrate?"

"That fish is everything that's wrong with this place."

"And what, pray tell, is wrong with the Mire?" Cerise could write a book about what was wrong with the Mire, but she'd earned that right by being born and bred here.

He grimaced. "It's sweltering and damp. It smells of rotting vegetation, and fish, and stagnant water. It shifts constantly. Nothing is what it seems: the solid ground is mud and the fish have legs. It's not a proper place."

Cerise smirked. "It's old. The Mire was ancient before

our ancestors were born. It's a piece of another time, when plants ruled and animals were savage. Respect it, Lord William, or it will kill you."

His upper lip rose, revealing his teeth. She'd seen this precise look on her dogs just before they snarled. "It's welcome to try."

Ready to take the swamp on, was he? Cerise laughed. He glared. She was dying to know what his prissy behind was doing in the Edge, but she'd made the rule about personal questions and she had to stick to it.

"So what's a proper place?"

"A forest," William said, his expression distant. "Where the ground is dry soil and stone. Where tall trees grow and centuries of autumn carpet their roots. Where the wind smells of game and wildflowers."

"Why, that was lovely, Lord Bill. Do you ever write poetry? Something for your blueblood lady?"

"No."

"She doesn't like poetry?"

"Leave it."

*Hehe.* "Oh, so you don't have a lady. How interes—"

Magic prickled her skin. Her hands went ice-cold. A shiver gripped her. Her teeth chattered, her knees shook, and the tiny hairs on the back of her neck stood on their ends. Fear washed over her followed by a quick squirm of nausea.

Something bad waited for them around the river bend.


A familiar revulsion clamped William's throat and squeezed. His stomach lurched. Invisible magic sparked off his skin.

The Hand. Strong magic, coming fast. Ahead the river bent to the left. Someone from Spider's crew had to be just around the turn. Could be one man or could be fifteen. No way to tell.

Cerise froze at the stern. Her body trembled.

"Hide," he said. "Now."

She maneuvered the boat into the clump of reeds, sank the pole into the river's bottom, and crouched, keeping them put. He pulled a white coin from his pocket, locked his arms around her, and squeezed the metal. *Here's hoping the Mirror's gadgets work.*

The coin grew hot in his fingers. A faint sheen of magic flowed from his hand, dripping onto Cerise's arm, over her jacket and jeans, over his arms, swallowing the whole boat.

Cerise tensed. Her hands gripped the pole, until her knuckles went completely white. The pupils in her irises grew into dark pools.

A reaction to the Hand's magic. At least the hobo queen wasn't working for Spider.

Cerise shivered. The first exposure was always the hardest. He had built up tolerance, chasing Spider, but she had none. If he didn't contain her fast, she'd lose it and break the spell.

William pulled her tighter against him, clamping the pole in case she let go, and whispered into her ear. "Don't move."

A large boat rounded the river's bend.

Cerise shuddered. He clenched her to him, willing the spell to hold.

The magic sheen around them swirled with a dozen hues and snapped, matching the green of reeds and gray of the water with a mirror's precision.

The boat sliced its way against the current, drawn by a single rolpie. Men waited aboard, holding rifles. Not the Hand's regulars—the gear was too varied. Probably the local talent. He counted the rifles. Seven. Too many to kill easily. Someone in that crowd had to be from Spider's crew . . .

A man stood up at the stern. A long gray cloak hung off his shoulders.

The man raised his hand, and the boat drew to a stop. The rolpie's head poked through the water. The man at the

stern pulled off his cloak. He wore baggy pants and no
shirt. Too skinny, like someone had wrapped a skeleton in
tight muscle and poured a skin of red wax over it.

William ran through Spider's crew in his head. A couple of male operatives were skeletally thin, but only one
had brick red skin. Ruh. Spider's tracker. According to
the Mirror's intel, he and Spider were joined at the hip.
So the sonovabitch was in the swamp after all.

The skin between William's knuckles itched, wanting
to release the claws. One bite on that toothpick neck and
Spider would be out a tracker. Seven rifles and fifty yards
of water meant he wouldn't get a chance. Fine, he would
get his shot later. Ruh probably tasted vile anyway.

William breathed in deep and even. Hard to kill seven
men and the tracker. In cramped quarters on solid ground,
maybe. Especially if it was dark. He'd go through them
with knife or teeth, and they'd never know what hit them.
But out here, if the spell collapsed, they were sitting
ducks.

If Ruh saw them, he'd flip the boat in the air, use it as
a shield, and make a run for it. The girl would slow him
down, but if they got to the cypresses in one piece, he
could pick Ruh's crew off one by one.

Getting to the cypresses would be a bitch.

An older, stocky Edger pulled a line from a wheel
bolted to the boat's bow and caught the rolpie's long
fragile neck in a slip knot. Keeping one hand on the line,
he turned the wheel, winding it down. The rolpie jerked,
startled, and fought back like a fish on a wire, but the
line gripped its neck and dragged it against the side of
the boat. With no room to dive and its head trapped above
the water, the beast went limp.

Ruh anchored himself on the bow, his bare feet gripping the deck with toes like bird talons. He leaned forward
over the water, his body bent to a degree that would've
pitched a normal human into the river, and stretched his
right arm to the water's surface.

A bulge of flesh grew on Ruh's shoulder. It squeezed and relaxed slowly, growing thicker with each contraction. What the hell . . .

Ruh moaned. A huge drop of yellow ichor swelled over the tracker's right deltoid and burst, releasing a tentacle.

Acid burned William's mouth. Right, if he ever fought Ruh, stabbing him in the back from above, right between the shoulder blades, would be good.

The tentacle shivered above the tracker's shoulder, like a worm the color of raw muscle, and clung to Ruh's red skin. Lubricated by the ichor, the tentacle slid, winding its way down the arm. Another followed it, twisting about the first, then another.

Cerise gagged. He clamped her tighter. If she vomited, the body fluid would break the spell.

The tentacles plunged into the water. The rolpie moaned and screamed, trying to get away.

A sickening magic swept over them like an avalanche. If it was wind, it would've rocked the boat.

Cerise shuddered in his grip.

*Don't panic. Just don't panic.* "I've got you," he whispered into her ear.

Thin tendrils of magic stretched from the boat. Colorless, shimmering like hot air rising from the ground, they snaked their way along the surface of the river, through the reeds, toward them.

If the spell broke, they were fucked.

The magic hovered, waiting, probing. The colorless tendrils lapped at the edges of the mirror spell.

*Hold. Hold, damn you, hold.*

The coin burned William's hand. A spasm rocked Cerise. "Almost over," he whispered. "Almost done."

On the boat, Ruh peered straight at them.

William held his breath.

The magic tendrils swelled and split, flowing around the boat. They tasted the shore, slithered over the mud, and retreated.

Ruh turned to the Edgers. William strained. His ears
picked up the faint sound of Ruh's voice.

"Girl didn't . . . this way. Moving on . . ."

They were looking for a girl. The girl? This girl?

The tracker pulled his tentacles out of the river. William caught a flash of a complex web, covered with long
red eyelash-thin hairs dripping with water, and then the
net folded in on itself. The cilia slid into the tentacles;
the tentacles rolled into the shoulder like elastic rubber
cords, and the skin sealed over it. Ruh massaged the viscous ichor into his arm, rubbing it into the skin like a lo-
tion, and reached for his cloak.

The older Edger released the rope, and the rolpie shot
down the river, fleeing for its life and dragging the boat
with it.

William waited. A minute passed. Another. Long
enough. He let go of the coin. It lay useless and cold on
his palm, all of its charge spent. He had to give it to the
Mirror. They made neat toys.

Cerise slumped forward, curling into a ball. The parts
of her that weren't covered with dirt had turned so pale,
they looked green. The aftereffect of exposure to the
Hand's magic should be hitting her full force now.

If Spider wanted her, then William had to keep her
for himself. Sooner or later Spider would come looking
for her, and then they would finish the dance they'd
started four years ago.

Cerise coughed.

The wild in him bared its teeth. She was weak and
scared. Almost pitiful. Easy prey for anybody. He had to
guard her or she'd get herself killed.

"They're looking for you." He kept his voice brisk.

She clutched at her stomach. Her words came out
strained. "No personal questions."

"That's the Hand. Louisiana spies. Why do they want
you?"

She shook her head.

Fine. The aftereffects of the Hand's magic became

worse with time. He simply had to wait her out, the way a wolf pack waited out a bleeding deer. Sooner or later the deer would run himself into the ground and then it was dinnertime.

William took the pole from her and sank it into the water, propelling the boat upstream.

# SIX

CERISE shivered. Icy needles pricked her spine and stabbed into the muscles of her back. Her neck grew stiff. Her mouth had gone dry and bitter.

Something on many furry legs crawled up her arm. She brushed at it but her fingers closed over nothing. Her skin was clean. She rubbed her arm just to be sure, felt the touch of the little legs on her elbow, rubbed there, and then dozens of invisible bugs scattered up her shoulders and back. Stiff insect bristles and tiny chitinous claws scratched her, skittering down her neck. She jerked, raking at herself.

William leaned over to her and slapped her hand.

"Keep your hands off me."

"I will, if you keep them off yourself."

"What's it to you?" she clenched her jacket to herself, feeling the papers in the smooth plastic. Still there.

"That red freak you saw is a tracker. He needs very little, some spit, a few drops of blood in the river, and he'll know where you are. We're paddling upstream. If you claw yourself bloody, the current will drag it down, and at his next stop he'll find out what you taste like. Then they'll turn the boat around and come back this way with their seven rifles."

"How do you know?"

He touched his hand to her forehead, and she pulled back—his skin was burning hot. He showed her his palm, damp with her sweat.

"Right now you think there are ghost bugs crawling on

your skin. Your heart is hammering. Your tongue's dried up, and your mouth tastes like cotton; your hands and feet are freezing, but your body is hot. I know this because I've experienced it." He kept pushing the boat.

*Don't scratch.* She hugged herself to keep warm. Her teeth chattered. *Don't scratch.* "How did you m-m-manage?"

William grimaced. "I was a soldier in Adrianglia. We've run into the Hand's freaks before." He leaned into the pole. "The Adrianglian Mirror and the Louisianan Hand have been fighting a cold war for years. Adrianglia and Louisiana are too well matched. If a real war broke out, it would drag on for years, so instead they keep throwing spies at each other, looking for a back door to a victory. Adrianglian spies use magic, in their gadgets and their weapons. Louisianan spies *are* magic. They're so altered some of them aren't human anymore."

She knew all that already. "W-w-why does it make you sick?"

"Eventually the Hand's freaks get so fucked-up they start emanating their twisted magic. That magic is poison to us. It's like finding a rotten corpse—the stench makes you vomit, so you have no doubt that it's bad to eat. Same thing here. The more screwed up they are, the worse their magic is. They know it, too. They use it to weaken their prey. Eventually your body will adjust, but until then you'll be vulnerable."

"When d-d-does it wear off?"

"Depends."

What sort of answer was that? "How long d-d-did yours last?"

There was a tiny pause before he answered. "Eighteen hours."

"How d-d-did you k-k-keep from scratching?"

"I didn't. They chained me in a cell by the neck and let me go at it."

"That's h-h-horrible." What kind of army was he in exactly that they would let him claw himself bloody? "Couldn't they sedate you or s-s-s-something?"

His voice was matter of fact. "They didn't bother with it."

"That's not right." Her teeth danced, and Cerise bit down, sending her knees into an uncontrollable shiver. "It's going to g-g-get worse, isn't it?"

He leaned to her and peered into her eyes. "Do you see small red dots floating?"

"No."

He grimaced. "Then it's going to get worse."

Awesome. "W-w-w . . . w-w-w . . . w-w-w . . ."

"Take your time," he told her.

"W-w-w-weird assholes."

He barked a short laugh.

The bugs continued their mad jig. If only she could get warm . . .

"Is there another way to Sicktree?"

Her mind took a few long moments to digest his question. At last Cerise understood. "The tracker will d-d-double back eventually. We m-m-must leave the river."

He nodded. "That's right."

The bugs on her arms began gnawing at her skin, burrowing into it, trying to chew their way through muscles to her veins and the blood within. She clenched her fists to keep from scratching.

Her nose was running. She had an absurd feeling that if only she could get ahold of something sharp like a knife blade and scrape it against her skin, the bugs would disappear.

William turned the boat with a sharp stab of the pole. The punt rammed the shore. "Don't even think about it."

Cerise realized she was holding her short sword in her hand. She sniffled.

William held out his hand.

"It's m-m-mine," she said.

"You don't need it right this second."

Cerise took a deep breath, pronouncing each word with crisp exactness. "If you try to take my sword, I will kill you with it."

His eyes studied her. "Fine," he said. "I won't fight you for your knife if you tell me how we can get to Sicktree."

Cerise forced her mind to work. It started slowly, like a rusty water mill. "Small stream. Three miles up the river on the right side, between two pines, one of them lightning-scorched. It will take us to Mozer Lake, but we'll have to drag the boat for the last two miles."

Once she started scratching, she wouldn't stop. *There are no bugs, there are no bugs* . . .

"Hobo queen!"

"What?"

"Mozer Lake."

Mozer Lake. What about the damn Mozer Lake? She pictured the waterways. Sicktree. They were going to Sicktree, to that piss-and-shit sewer hole of a town. There was something vital about Sicktree.

Urow.

Urow was in Sicktree. She had to get to her cousin, so he could bring her home, fast, so she would make the court date, so they could take back the house, and kill the Sheeriles and the Hand, and get her parents back. *Save parents. Get to Sicktree. Right.*

"Mozer Lake opens into Tinybear Creek," she said. "Tinybear will become Bigbear. We can abandon the boat before the Bigbear joins the main river and cross the swamp on foot to Sicktree."

Cerise ran through the course in her mind. "Three miles, stream on the right, Mozer Lake, Tinybear, Bigbear, Miller's Path." She paused, not sure if she'd said it correctly. "Three miles, stream on the right, Mozer Lake, Tinybear, Bigbear, Miller's Path."

"Thank you, Dora. Put the sword back into Backpack and we'll go." He nodded at the river.

"Who is Dora?"

"You are. Dora the Explorer. *Vamanos.* Put the sword away or I will take it from you."

Arrogant prick. "Touch me and d-d-die," she told him.

He chuckled. It was a raspy deep sound. Wolves laughed like that.

Cerise sheathed the sword and hugged the scabbard. The bugs dug harder, tiny steel mandibles chewing on her ligaments, turning the muscle under her skin into bloody soft mush . . . Cerise locked her jaws, remembering the grotesque web of tentacles slick with crimson hair as it left the muddy water. *Damn freak. The next time we meet, I'll make your arms even. I'll keep mincing you into pieces until you tell me where my parents are.*

"It's g-g-going to rain," she said, pointing at the thick gray clouds.

William glanced at the clouds. "Rain's good for us. Covers our trail." He paused and leaned over to her. "It's all in your head. Don't let it push you around. I'll keep you safe until you're back on your feet."

Keep her safe, ha. She would keep herself safe. Huddled on the bench, Cerise pulled her jacket tighter around herself and tried not to scratch.


CERISE'S shortcut stream turned out to be mud slicked over with a foot and a half of water. Too shallow for the boat carrying the full load. William shifted his grip and waded on, dragging the boat and their bags in it. Cerise walked in front of him, sword out.

She hadn't taken it to her skin. She hadn't scratched either, but the Hand's magic took its toll: she stooped, as if carrying a heavy load, and hadn't said a word to him in the last hour. He wasn't sure if he was relieved or if he missed her needling.

The swamp had grown dark. Shadows disappeared. Storm clouds churned overhead, gray, thick, and heavy. A gust of wind ripped through the reeds and bushes, rustling the undergrowth. Rain was imminent.

Cerise kept trudging ahead. She was beginning to

drag her feet. The more sensitive you were to magic, the harder the Hand hit. Ruh was altered enough to make even William gag, and he'd been exposed to the Hand's magic before.

Ultimately it came down to willpower. She had guts and endurance—William gave her that—but the worst was yet to come. When the aftereffects really hit, and eventually they would, she could go into convulsions. If she died, his shot at Spider could die with her. He had to keep her alive and safe.

Lightning flashed. Thunder rolled, shaking the leaves. The air smelled of scorched sky. Heavy, cold drops drummed on the cypresses, at first a few, then more and more, until finally the clouds burst and a torrent showered the swamp, so dense even he could barely see beyond a few feet.

William raised his face to the dark sky and swore.

Cerise turned to him. The rain had soaked her, turning her clothes into a single dark mass and mixing with the mud on her face. She looked like she had sprouted from the Mire itself, like some shrub from a mud bank. Bloodshot eyes stared at him. She was running on fumes.

Cerise opened her mouth. The words came out slowly. "Don't worry, you won't melt. Not sweet enough."

"You see those dots I mentioned, you tell me."

"Will do."

They kept going. The boat scraped the ground and became wedged.

"We'll have to c-c-carry it," Cerise said, swiping her bag.

William shouldered his rucksack. She lifted the nose of the boat.

"I've got it," he told her.

"It's heavy."

"I'll manage." He flipped the boat over and hoisted it on his shoulders. He could carry her and the boat for several miles, but she didn't need to know that. His field of vision shrank to the small space directly beneath his feet, the rest taken up by dark boat and Cerise's jacket and legs. They moved on.

Water and mud soaked William to the bone. It was under his leathers and in his boots. His socks formed soggy clumps that bunched against his feet. He would give a year of his life to shed the wet clothes and run on all fours. But the girl and his load kept him in human skin.

He missed his trailer. His small, shabby trailer, which was dry and had a flat-screen TV and beer in the fridge. And dry socks. That was one of the things he loved most about the Broken. He could buy all the socks he ever wanted.

Cerise stopped and he nearly rammed her with the damn boat. "What is it?"

"We missed the turnoff!" she yelled over the storm. "The stream must've changed course because of the rain. We're too far to the left. We need to go that way, to the lake!"

She waved her hand to the right, at the gloom between the trees.

Everything that could go wrong did. Never failed.

William turned and followed her through the brush. A familiar ghostly pressure brushed his skin. They were near the boundary. For a furious second he thought she'd led him back to it in a circle.

She stopped again. He jerked back. Impossible woman.

Cerise pointed. "Look!"

He shifted the boat to see. In front of them the wide expanse of the lake stretched like a pane of muddy glass. On their left a dock protruded into the water and at the base of the dock sat a house.

Dark windows. No trace of smoke or human scents in the air. Nobody home.

The road by it looked too smooth—paved. William focused and made out the outlines of a satellite dish on the roof. A Broken house. He was right—they were near the boundary.

Cerise leaned closer. "Sometimes the Mire makes pockets that lead to the Broken. They're usually tiny and disappear after a while."

He bent to her. "We hit that pocket, the Broken will strip you of your magic. A cure for all your ills."

A tiny light flared in her eyes.

Lightning struck, the world's heart skipping a beat.

A dark object broke the surface of the lake, rising out of the water.

William hurled the boat aside and shoved Cerise back, behind him.

The dark thing stood upright. William stared, his eyes amplifying the low light.

Seven feet tall, the creature rose on thick columnar legs. Two eight-inch-long bone claws thrust from its wrists, protruding past its fingers. Its head looked human enough, but the rough bumps distorted the outline of its body, as if it had been carved out of rough stone by someone in a hurry.

Lightning flashed again and he saw it, clear as day in the split second of light. Mad bloodshot eyes stared at him from a human face ending in an oversized jaw. Its skin, the color of watery yellow mud, wrinkled on the creature's neck and limbs, as if it were too big for its body. Thick bony plates slabbed its back, stomach, and thighs.

Thibauld, his memory told him. One of Spider's crew. Severely altered, ambusher class. Shit.

Thibauld peered at them, looking from William's face to the girl and back. He blocked the way to the boundary. To get to the house, they would have to get past him. According to the Mirror's intel, Thibauld had a superior sense of smell. A bad opponent on land, he was hell in the water. Spider must've parked him in the lake on the off chance Cerise would come this way. He probably had most major waterways blocked.

William focused, judging the distance to the agent. His crossbow was in the pack on his back. A second to drop the pack, two to pull the crossbow, another second to load . . . too long. He'd have to rely on his knife.

The Hand's agent raised his arms. The long scimitar claws pointed at Cerise. His mouth gaped open, revealing rows of short triangular teeth. They would shred flesh like a cheese grater, and the jaws looked strong enough to bite through bone. Great.

A dull, deep voice issued from Thibauld's mouth, pronouncing each word with agonizing slowness. "It . . . is . . . mine."

"No," William told him.

The claws pointed at him. "You . . . die," the agent promised.

"Not today."

Cerise lunged. William sensed her move and thrust his arm out, knocking her down, before she got a taste of the claws. "Stay behind me!"

Cerise crashed into the mud and stayed there.

The muscle on Thibauld's frame expanded, snapping the loose skin tight. William eased the backpack off his shoulders.

An odd, warbling sound rolled in Thibauld's grotesque throat. The Hand's agent charged.

William dodged left. Claws fanned his face. He thrust under the tree-trunk arm and sliced at the exposed strip of skin over the ribs. The knife cut hard muscle. He sliced again, feeling the knife slide harmlessly across the bone plate. Damn armor-plated turkey. What wasn't covered by plates was shielded by thick muscle. His knife wasn't doing enough damage.

Thibauld spun, arms wide, aiming to backhand him. William jerked back. Thibauld missed but kept spinning like a windmill, claws rending. William ducked the first blow, dodged the second, and then Thibauld's arm smashed into his shoulder.

The blow took him off his feet. William flew, curling into a ball, hit the mud with his back, and rolled to his feet. His left arm had gone numb. Strong bastard. William couldn't afford to take another hit.

Ten feet away Thibauld blinked his bloodshot eyes, swiveling his head from side to side. Looking for Cerise. *No, you don't.*

"Over here, dimwit! Pay attention!"

The agent stared at him.

"Well, what are you waiting for? Do you need a special invitation?"

Thibauld stomped forward. *That's right, come to me, come closer, away from the girl.*

Thibauld was only six feet away. William lunged forward, obviously aiming for the agent's chest. Thibauld moved to counter, claws raised for the kill. *Fell for it.* William reversed his stroke. His blade carved at the inside of the agent's arm, slicing deep into the flesh just below the biceps. He ducked under the claws and pulled back.

Nothing. A cut like that should've disabled the arm, but Thibauld seemed no worse for wear.

No blood, no sound of pain, no wince. Nothing.

Thibauld raised his arms, shifting his stance. The agent couldn't catch him with his claws, so he decided to grapple. William bared his teeth. If he was by himself, he'd cut and run. The more Thibauld ran around, the faster he'd bleed out. But the moment he ran, Thibauld would lumber over to Cerise, who was still sprawled in the mud. In retrospect, he may have pushed her a bit too hard. Or the Hand's magic had battered her more than she showed.

A narrow line of red swelled across Thibauld's arm. Woo-hoo, he'd managed a scratch. Great. Now about a hundred of those and he would be set.

Thibauld stretched his neck and looked at his arm. "Is . . . that . . . all?"

"Don't worry, that's just a little foreplay." William waddled from foot to foot. "That's what you look like when you move."

Thibauld bellowed and charged.

William dashed, cutting, slicing, stabbing, turning his knife into a lethal metal blur. Thibauld struck back, huge arms swinging faster and faster. Claws raked William's side, ripping through the leather. Pain scorched him. He ignored it and kept slashing, carving at exposed flesh with precise savagery. Left, right, left, left, down, cut, cut, *cut* . . . Blood slicked Thibauld's massive frame.

Not enough. William drove the knife in to the hilt under the armored scales, aiming for the heart. The agent roared and swung. William jerked back, pulling the blade free. Not far enough. The fist caught him, spinning him around. The world turned fuzzy for a fraction of a second. William leaped straight up, knife in hand, aiming to slice Thibauld's neck, and . . . landed in the mud as the agent staggered back, a puzzled expression on his face.

Thibauld's huge legs trembled. He sucked in a hoarse breath.

The top half of him slid to the side and toppled in the mud, revealing Cerise holding a bare sword. The stump of the agent's torso remained upright for a long second and then fell, spilling blood onto the wet mud.

What the hell?

Cerise passed her sword to her left hand and walked over to him, sidestepping the corpse.

If he hadn't known better, he would've sworn she had cut Thibauld in half. Shell and all. How did she manage that? Swords couldn't do that.

Her eyes were huge and dark on her mud-splattered face. He peered into their depths and missed her fist until it was too late. A sharp punch hammered his gut. He didn't even have time to flex. Pain exploded in his solar plexus.

"Don't ever do that again," Cerise ground out.

He caught her hand. "I was protecting you, you dumbass."

"I don't need protecting!"

Behind her a bat crawled down the trunk of a cypress.

William grabbed Cerise, pulling her out of the way, and hurled his knife. The blade spun and sliced into the small body, pinning it to the tree. Cerise jerked away from him.

"Are you crazy?"

"It's a deader," he told her.

Purplish, translucent tentacles of magic stretched from the bat, clutching at the knife, trying to pull it out.

"What the hell is that?"

"A scout. Bats hide during rain." A "deader" meant a scout master who reported straight to Spider. He was pretty sure the bat hadn't seen them, but he couldn't be certain.

Cerise stumbled. Her legs folded; she swayed and half fell, half sat into the mud.

He crouched by her. "What is it?"

"Dots . . ." she whispered.

William scooped her from the mud and dashed through the rain to the boundary, swiping their bags on the way.


THE pressure of the boundary caught William in its jaws, grinding his bones. He tore through the pain, carrying Cerise. The changelings didn't have magic. They *were* magic, and while crossing hurt, it wasn't anything he couldn't handle.

He paused on the other side, catching his breath. Cerise lay in a small clump in his arms.

Oh, hell. He might have taken the boundary too fast for her to cope.

William lifted her higher so he could peer at her. "Talk to me."

Her bloodless face was like a white stain in the rain. He shook her a little and saw the long dark eyelashes tremble.

"It's gone," she whispered. She had pretty eyes, he realized, big and dark brown, and at that moment luminescent with relief. "The bugs are gone. The dots, too."

"Good." He strode to the house.

"Put me down."

That was a hell of a sword strike. A good punch, too. He was dying to see what she looked like under all that grime and mud. "If I put you down, you'll fall, and I don't want to pick you up again after your roll in the muck. I'm muddy enough as is."

"You're a thug and an ass," she told him, baring small, even teeth.

If she had energy to snap, she was coming out of it. Good. "You say the sweetest things. And that spaghetti perfume you're wearing is to die for. No hobo could resist."

She snarled. Heh.

"You sound like a pissed-off rabbit." He held her tighter in case she decided to punch him again, and he jogged to the house, up the porch steps, and to the door. The door looked good and solid.

"Wait."

The alarm in her voice stopped him cold. "What?"

Cerise raised her muddy hand to a small mark burned into the doorframe, holding on to him with the other hand for support. A letter *A* with the horizontal bar leaning at an angle.

Her bottomless eyes got bigger. "We need to leave," Cerise whispered.

"What does the letter mean?"

"Alphas."

He waited for more explanation.

"They're not from the Edge or from the Weird. They're their own thing in the Broken, and they're dangerous as hell. We see them sometimes, but they leave us alone if we leave them alone. This house belongs to them. If we break in and they find us here, we'll be dead."

William shrugged. "It will be fine. The house has been empty for months."

"How do you know?"

There were too many things to explain: the layer of grime settled on the edge of the door, the absence of human odors, the scents of small animals, some weeks, some days old, crossing over what they now considered their territory . . . "I just know. Whoever these alphas are, they're not around. We need a dry place to stay."

Cerise's face clenched in alarm. "Listen to me. We have to go. It's a bad—"

William kicked the door. It burst open. "Too late."

She froze in his arms.

The house looked dark and empty. No alarm broke the silence. Nobody emerged to fight them.

"Damn it, William."

He liked the way she said his name. "Don't worry, Your Hobo Highness. I'll keep you safe."

She cursed at him.

William stepped across the threshold and carefully set her down. She swayed and caught herself on the wall.

"Where are you going?"

"To check the house. Where else?" She pushed away from the wall and headed deeper down the hallway.

William inhaled. The scent signatures were old and his ears caught no noises. She was wasting her time.

Someone with military experience had drilled the basics of conduct in enemy territory into her. After everything they'd been through, a civilian woman should've landed on the first available soft surface. This one went to clear the house. She'd probably run out of steam and collapse in a minute.

The Edgers were an undisciplined, uneducated lot. They half-assed shit and got along on dumb luck and a prayer. Cerise didn't. He didn't know of any Edgers who could cut a body in half that way either. A very concentrated flash could have done that, but he didn't see the telltale glowing ribbon. Besides, most Edgers couldn't flash white, and to deliver that sort of damage, nothing less than a white flash would do.

He'd have to be careful not to underestimate the hobo queen, or it would cost him.

His ears caught a mechanical purr. The lightbulbs blinked and ignited with yellow light. She must've found a generator. He circled the living room, lowering the blinds.

Cerise appeared from the depths of the house. "Empty."

He gave her an elaborate bow. "I told you."

"I found the generator. There is a bathroom, too. The water is lukewarm but clean."

A vision of a shower and fluffy towels presented itself to William. He nodded. "Go. The sooner you bathe, the better it is for both of us."

The look she gave him was sharp enough to kill. She spun on her foot, picked up her bag, and headed to the bathroom. Smart. He wanted to see what was in the bag.

William searched the house, going from room to room. The place looked like someone's vacation getaway: relatively new and full of silly crap like model boats and seashells. Lots of knickknacks, no signs of the wear and tear that cropped up in a place where someone actually lived. The pantry was well stocked with cans. Food was good.

William returned to the living room, dimmed the main lights, turned on a couple of smaller lamps, just enough soft light to see, and waited.

His clothes sagged on him, clammy against his skin. His wet socks chafed his feet. William pulled off his boots and the soggy mass of ruined socks, and curled his toes. The hardwood floor felt nice and cool under his feet.

A model of a sailing ship sat on a shelf. He took it down and played with the tiny lines. The ship needed some small sailors. There were a couple of old small GI Joes from his collection at home that could've fit . . . No, they would be too big.

How long does it take to clean up anyway?

A door swung open behind him. "Done," Cerise announced.

He turned around and froze.

She'd lost the cap, the jacket, and the grimy jeans, and found a pair of shorts and an oversized T-shirt that hugged her breasts. Her hair, very long and dark, spilled down to her waist in a combed wave. William took in her tan face, full mouth, narrow nose, large almond eyes framed in sable eyelashes . . . The eyes laughed at him and he forgot where he was or why.

Her scent drifted down to him, her real scent mixing with the fragrance of soap. She smelled clean and soft . . . like a woman.

The wild in him lost its head, clawing at his insides.

*Want. Want the woman.*

"Lord Bill?" she asked.

His thoughts tumbled in a feverish cascade. *Want . . . So beautiful . . . Standing so close and so beautiful. Want the woman.*

"Earth to William?"

She was looking at him with those beautiful dark eyes. All he had to do was reach for her and he could touch her.

*No. Wrong.*

She hadn't given him permission. If he touched, he would take her. Taking women without permission was wrong.

William pulled himself back, regaining control. The wild buckled and snarled and screamed, but he reeled it in, forcing it deeper and deeper. Remember the whip? Right, everybody remembered the whip. Everybody remembered being punished for kissing a girl without permission. The scars on his back itched, reminding him. Humans had rules. He had to follow the rules.

He was a changeling. And a changeling could never be sure if the woman wanted him unless he paid for her or she said so. This woman didn't want him. She wasn't taking her clothes off, she wasn't trying to close the distance between them, and his instincts told him he couldn't buy her.

She was off-limits.

"My turn for a shower," he said. His voice sounded

flat. William walked past her, giving her a wide berth, and forced himself to keep walking into the bathroom, where he closed the door and bolted it to lock himself in.


CERISE swallowed, listening to the sound of the water hitting the shower tiles. Her whole body hummed with tension, as if she'd just survived a fight for her life.

The look of total shock as he'd stared at her in stunned silence had been priceless. She'd almost laughed. And then William had turned feral. Something wild glared at her through his eyes, something crazy and violent and full of lust. For a second she thought she'd have to fight him off, and then it vanished, as if his internal shutters had slammed closed.

She'd knocked his socks off. She'd planned to—if he had called her a hobo queen one more time, she would've strangled him. But she didn't expect . . . that.

She'd figured he might stare, maybe flirt. But he'd gone from zero to sixty in two seconds flat, as people in the Broken said. She had never seen a man do that before.

She'd never met a man who'd looked at her like that before. Like she was irresistible.

Cerise dug through her backpack, fished out a sweatshirt, and pulled it on. He'd made himself back down. Point for him, but no need to tempt fate.

The rush of adrenaline inside her cooled down. Warmth washed over her, followed by soft fatigue. What do you know—Lord Bill almost lost his head over a Mire girl. She grinned. *Hobo queen, shmobo queen, took you by surprise.* "Lost his head" didn't even begin to cover it. He'd stared at her like he was some sort of maniac.

It shouldn't have mattered. For all she knew, William looked at every woman that way. Well, maybe not quite that way, since he did manage to make it to adulthood somehow, without being murdered.

Still, it did matter. She sensed a sharp, dangerous edge to everything he did, and it pulled her in like a moth to a flame. She thought back to the fight. He'd pushed her out of the way. It wasn't a hard push, but she had been barely standing and she fell badly, flat on her back, the wind knocked out of her. For about half a minute, she lay there, woozy, trying to get up, and listening to William drawing the Hand's freak farther away.

He'd knocked her down with the best intentions, true, but she should've punched him harder for it. It's good that nobody had been there to witness it, or she would be the laughing stock of the entire Mire. Cerise grimaced. She'd really wanted to hammer one right to his jaw, but hitting someone in the jaw all but guaranteed a sore hand. That was one of the first lessons her grandmother had taught her: Take care of your hands. You need them to hold your blade.

When she had finally staggered upright, that brown monstrosity was almost fifty yards away. It was huge and armored and armed with claws. And William had gone after it with a knife. She would've said he was insane or stupid, except by the time she got there, the Hand's freak was bleeding like a stuck pig. She'd almost slipped on the trail of his blood. A few more minutes and William would've bled him dry.

The water in the shower stopped.

Cerise took off down the hallway before William stepped out and caught her staring at the door.

A pantry lay to the left. She sorted through the cans, looking for something with meat in it.

Cerise was pretty, she knew that. In the Mire, who she was and what she could do were always taken into account. She was Cerise Mar. She had the Rats at her back and her sword was famous. Her family wasn't exactly prime in-law material and some men had a problem with how well she handled her blade, but still there were enough guys out there who would work their asses off for a chance to be with her. If she wanted to, she could have her pick, and she did, for a while, until she got bogged down in fixing the family finances.

Knowing you were poor was one thing. But living with that knowledge, having it rubbed in your face again and again, being forced to hustle, scheme, and finagle so you could buy the kids new clothes for the winter or post bail for a relative, that was another thing. It drained her will to live.

And then there was Tobias. He turned out to be a piece of work.

Now if a man came on to her, the first thing that went through her mind was what did he really want? Was he after her or after the family's money, what little there was of it? Was he trustworthy? How badly could he screw up, and how much would it cost the family if they had to make the issue go away? That one drank too much, this one had a kid from the first marriage that he wanted to see well taken care of by someone else, the third one humped anything that moved . . . Too reckless, too stupid, too quick to anger . . . Soon she got a reputation for being choosy, and she didn't think she was. And even if she was, she couldn't afford not to be.

But William didn't know any of that. He didn't know the first thing about her and didn't give a damn about her family. She blindsided him and got an honest reaction.

Cerise recalled the look in his eyes and shivered.

The question was, what would she do when he came out of the shower? The thought stopped her in her tracks. He had to be in good shape. He was strong like an ox— dragging the punt through the swamp singlehanded was no picnic, and he'd picked her and the bags up and run, as if their combined weight were nothing. Her imagination tried to paint a picture of William coming out of the shower and toweling off, and she slammed the door on that thought real fast. It was fine if he was smitten. But she had other things to worry about.

A part of her really wanted to find out if his reaction was just a one-time thing or if she could get him to look at her that way again.

Cerise swiped two cans of beef stew off the shelf and

headed back to the kitchen. *Doesn't matter,* she told herself. *You're not fifteen. Put it out of your mind. You have parents to rescue.*

In a few minutes he'd step out of the shower, and she had to treat him like a potential enemy, no matter what he looked like. Safer that way.

Lord Bill was an enigma. He dressed like a blueblood, he talked like a blueblood, but he came to the Mire through the Broken. Nobles from the Weird usually couldn't enter the Broken. They were too full of magic, and they had to turn back or ended up dying. Either he was a dud magically or there was something very funky going on with his bloodline. Then there were the eyes full of fire. And now this.

He knew of the Hand. She had to make use of that. She could always kill him if he stepped out of line.

The stove had a fancy glass top. Cerise turned it on, waited until one of the burners glowed red, set a pot on it, and dumped the stew into it. Blueblood or not, she would figure Lord Bill out sooner or later. Or they would go their separate ways and the problem would solve itself.

The door opened.

It was curiosity, Cerise decided. Just normal healthy curiosity. She pretended to be occupied with the stew.

She could just look up at him and glance away . . . Oh, Gods.

Instantly she knew she'd made a mistake.

He wore jeans and a white T-shirt. His clothes molded to him. William wasn't built, he was carved, with hard strength and lethal speed in mind. No give, no weakness. He had the honed, lean body of a man who was used to fighting for his life and liked it that way. And he strode to her like a swordsman: sure, economical movements touched with a natural grace and strength.

Their stares met. She saw the shadow of the feral thing slide across William's eyes, and she stopped stirring the stew.

They stared at each other for a long tense moment.

Damn it. That was not supposed to happen.

She turned to grab two metal bowls, poured the stew into them, and set them on the table. He took his seat, she took hers, their stares crossed again, and Cerise wasn't sure which one of them was in more trouble.

William leaned forward, pulling his bowl closer as if she was about to take it from him. He needed a shave, but then he didn't look bad with the stubble. Quite the opposite, in fact. He kept his expression calm, but she knew with some sort of inborn female intuition that he was thinking about her and about doing things with her. She felt like a fifteen-year-old dancing with a boy for the first time, nervous, and shaky, and trying not to say or do the wrong thing but thrilled deep inside every moment.

Great. She couldn't decide which one of them was the bigger idiot.

"The food is crap. Sorry. But it's hot," she said, keeping her tone calm.

"I've had worse." His voice was flat, too.

"This stove is great."

William looked up from his bowl. "What do you cook on?"

"The main house has a huge woodstove and a small electric one. It's not nearly as nice." Cerise sighed, glancing at the glass-top stove with a small GE logo. "I want to steal this one."

"Good luck getting it past that damn eel." He dug into his stew.

"If we bring it along, you can always drop it on him."

He paused, as if he was actually considering dragging the stove through the swamp.

"I'm joking," she told him.

William shrugged and went back to his food.

A thin red stain spread through the side of his shirt.

"You're bleeding."

He raised his arm and looked at his side. "Must've reopened it. That asshole clawed me."

Those claws were half a foot long. "How deep?"

He shrugged again. More red seeped through.

"Stop shrugging." She jumped off her chair and walked over to him. "Lift your shirt."

He peeled the shirt up, exposing his side. Two deep gashes crossed his ribs. Nothing life threatening but nothing that would do him any good untreated either.

"Why didn't you bandage this?"

"No need. I heal fast."

Yeah. "Don't move." She grabbed her bag and pulled out a Ziploc bag with gauze and tape and a tube of Neosporin. "Did you at least wash it out?"

He nodded.

"Good. Because I'm not dragging you across the swamp if you pass out from an infection." She washed her hands with soap and squeezed Neosporin on the cuts. "This is medicine from the Broken. It kills infection in the wound."

"I know what it does," he said.

"And how would a blueblood know that?"

"No personal questions."

Ha. Walked into her own rule face-first. Cerise applied dressing and taped up the cuts. "Oh, look. You survived unscathed."

"Your Neosporin stinks."

"Get over it."

He pulled his shirt down, and she caught a glimpse of blue on his biceps. Cerise reached over and pulled his sleeve up. A large bruise covered most of his shoulder.

"You have ointment for that, too?" William asked.

"No, but now if I have to punch you, I know where it will hurt the most." She let go of the sleeve and went to put her supplies up. That was some biceps. His back was well muscled, and you could probably bounce a quarter off his abs. Either he still was a soldier or he did something nasty for a living. Men didn't stay in that kind of shape unless they had to.

She came back to the table.

"Thanks," he told her.

Now was her chance, Cerise decided. She had to get as much information out of him as she could. Who knew what would happen tomorrow. "I take it that turtle thing was one of the Hand's agents."

He nodded.

*Come on, Lord Bill, don't keep it all to yourself.* She tried again. "What about that bat? When we ran past it, it looked like it had been dead for a while. There was a hole in its side, and you could see its innards even before you put the knife into it. It stank like carrion, too."

He nodded again.

Maybe she was being too subtle. "Tell me about the Hand. Please."

"No questions. You made the rule, remember?" William hooked a piece of meat with the fork and chewed quickly. He ate fast—she had barely finished half, while he was almost done.

"I'm willing to trade."

William glanced at her from above the rim of his bowl. "An answer for an answer."

"Yes."

"And you'll answer me honestly?"

Cerise gave him her best sincere smile. She had two stories ready to go, depending on which way he was leaning. "Of course."

He barked a short laugh. "You're an Edger. You'd lie, rob me blind, and leave me naked in the swamp if you thought you'd get something from it."

Smart bastard. "I thought you said it was your first time in the Edge?"

"And now you're trying to sneak a question in. You think I was born yesterday."

If he was born yesterday, he sure matured fast. "I'll give you my word."

He choked on the stew, coughed, tossed his head back, and laughed.

For a blueblood, he was damn hilarious. Cerise rolled her eyes, trying her best not to laugh herself. "Oh, please."

William pointed up at the sky with his spoon. "Swear to them."

She raised her eyebrows. "How do you know my grandparents would be upset if I lied?"

"How do you know they wouldn't?"

Good point. She raised her eyes to the ceiling. "I promise to play fair."

William leaned back, watching her through half-closed eyes. "You want to know about the bat?"

"For starters."

"They're called deaders. I'm Adrianglian. I told you—we're all about gadgets and toys that amplify our magic. Some people have implants; some use military-grade magic amplifiers. Louisiana went the other way. They undergo permanent, irreparable body modification that makes them into freaks. Some of them sprout tentacles from their asses. Some spit poisoned barbs. From what I've heard, the kind of shit they do to their bodies is banned in other countries. The tracker you saw on the river—he wasn't born that way. The ambusher didn't grow all that armor by himself either. They cooked them up somewhere."

The armored freak was ugly, but the tracker deeply disturbed her. Something about watching those tentacles slither awoke a primal, deep-seated revulsion. She would never manage to scrub that image out of her mind, and she couldn't wait to pay him back. "I'll kill that tracker one day."

"Get in line."

The two of them grimaced at each other.

"The Hand uses a kind of necromancer, a scout master," William said. "You said your cousin was a necromancer. You know how the natural necromancers operate?"

They twisted the head off your favorite doll, stuffed a dead bird into it, and made it walk around. And then they were puzzled why you got upset. "More than I ever want to."

"Well, this one takes it to a whole new level. A scout

master sheds chunks of himself and stuffs them into corpses, turning them into deaders."

Ew. "You're pulling my leg, right?"

He shook his head. "These deaders become a part of him. He sees what they see. Then he finds himself a nice quiet spot, sends them out, and waits for the reports to roll in."

"That is incredibly disgusting."

"My turn." William leaned in, his hazel eyes fixing her with a direct stare. It was an odd gaze, magnetic and powerful, but betraying nothing. His voice was quiet, barely above a whisper, and Cerise leaned closer to hear it. She could've stared into those eyes for a thousand years and never noticed the time passing by.

"Why does the Hand want you?"

"That's a neat trick you do with your eyes, Lord William," she murmured. "Very scary."

"Answer the question."

"They have my parents."

"Why?"

She smiled at him. He actually thought he'd get an equal trade. "That's a second question. What are you doing in the Mire?"

"Looking for something that was stolen from my family. It's an heirloom, a ring. It was given to us by an Anglian king back on the Old Continent. The man who stole it ended up here, and I have to retrieve it."

If his family was truly that old, he should have been able to flash. He shot a crossbow, he was a master with a knife, and he could probably mow through opponents with his bare hands, but so far he hadn't flashed. Probably because he couldn't. He shouldn't have survived the trip to the Broken either. Cerise smiled to herself. She had guessed right. Someone in Lord William's long list of ancestors had dipped a toe in some muddy waters—the blood of either an Edger or a migrant from the Broken flowed through his veins.

"Why did the Hand kidnap your parents?" William asked.

"I don't know."

"You're lying."

She shook her head. "Our family is in a feud. Has been for the last eighty years. One generation slaughters each other, the feud dies down until the next crop of people grows up, and then we go at it again. A few days ago, my parents left to check an old house on the edge of our land. When they didn't come back, I went out to look for them. I found the family we're feuding with on the property. They told me the Hand took my parents. They neglected to mention why."

"You didn't do anything about them being on your land?"

She caught a hint of disapproval in his voice. Fury bubbled up in her. "That's an extra question, William. But fine. I'll answer it. I had three horsemen; they had six rifles. I did the math and the results weren't in my favor. But don't worry on my behalf. I'll see the light fade from their eyes before this is over."

She rose, washed her bowl, and went into the bedroom.

# SEVEN

WILLIAM finished the stew—it was food, and he had no idea when he'd get to eat again. He rinsed his bowl, padded to her bedroom on quiet wolf feet, and nudged the door open with his fingertips. The girl was already asleep. She slept sitting up against the wall, her legs crossed, her sword leaning on her shoulder. He had a feeling that if he came any closer, she would wake up with her blade in him, so he just stood in the doorway.

He studied the way the wave of her dark hair framed her face, spilling over her shoulders down almost to the floor. She was so pretty, it was like looking at a painting. Except this painting was alive and warm, and her scent made him want to whine like a puppy because he had to stay away.

She'd fixed the wound on his side. He'd sat very still and let her do it. He still remembered the feel of her fingers on his skin. If she'd known what he'd been thinking, she would have run away screaming. Then maybe not. Screaming didn't seem to be her thing.

Her story sounded genuine enough. The Edgers loved to feud over stupid crap, and once the feuds started, they never really died down. The smaller the stakes, the harder they fought.

Cerise hadn't given him a single name, except her own, and he had no guarantee that even that was genuine. She planned to dump him in Sicktree and vanish into the swamp. If they were on solid ground, he could track her, but in the swamp, where water broke up scent trails, he wasn't sure. She knew what she was doing.

If this was a normal conflict, things would be simple. She would be an enemy. But if she was telling the truth, she was a victim, a noncombatant. Noncombatants were off-limits. Until she made herself into an enemy by attacking him, he had no justification to treat her as such.

He wanted her to like him. Women rarely liked him, even in the Broken. They seemed to sense that something was wrong with him and gave him a wide berth.

What William needed was a way into her family, so he could figure out why Spider had decided to screw with them. Cerise was his way inside. He had to get her to like him or at least make her think he was useful enough to bring along. He had to think like a human and be sly.

Being sly wasn't among his virtues. Cats were sly. Foxes, too. He was a wolf. He took what he wanted, and if he couldn't have it, he'd bide his time until an opportunity to take it presented itself. She mentioned she expected to make Sicktree by the end of the next day. His window of opportunity was shrinking. He was running out of time.

William looked at her one last time and moved off into the living room. He pulled the cushions off the couch, made a makeshift pallet on the floor, and lay down, blocking the door. The Mirror had a man in Sicktree, Zeke Wallace. Officially he was a leather merchant and taxidermist. Unofficially he worked for Adrianglia and smuggled contraband in his spare time. According to Erwin, Zeke would provide him with up-to-date intelligence on Spider: where he and his crew had been seen, whom they contacted in the Mire, and so on. Zeke could help identify Cerise, but that was about it. The rest was on him.

*Think. You're a human, too. Think.*

He was still trying to come up with something, when sleep mugged him.

* * *

THE sound of faint steps tugged on William through his sleep. He opened his eyes in time to see Cerise's bare ankles as she slipped past him outside.

Running out on him. *I don't think so.*

William rolled into a crouch and followed her out. The dour lake stretched placidly under a morose gray sky. At the dock Cerise waded into the water up to her knees, still wearing her long T-shirt. He followed her, moving silently across the grass to the dock, padding across the boards until he could see her face. Her eyes were closed. She lifted her head to the dreary sky and stood, her arms out slightly, as if welcoming someone.

Her hair spilled over her shoulders in a glossy waterfall. Her face was sad.

William sat on the edge of the dock. What the hell was she doing now?

CERISE breathed in the morning air. She'd slept badly. Once she woke up because she dreamed that they had gotten to Sicktree and Urow was dead. The next time she'd dreamed the house was attacked. The dream had been so vivid, she actually got up and went as far as her doorway. From that point she could see the dining room and the living room, both dark, and William asleep in front of the door, barring the way for any intruders. In his dreams, the hard edge faded from the blueblood. He looked peaceful and calm. Watching him reassured her and she went back to sleep.

It was morning now, and she was awake, but the anxiety refused to go away. It saddled her and dug the spurs in. The responsibility for the whole family now lay with her, and it dragged her down like an anchor, so heavy, she wondered if she would sink if she dived into the lake.

Life was so much easier when she only had to obey Dad's orders. So much easier. She missed him and Mom so much, it hurt. If she didn't find them, the family would crumble. And Lark . . . She didn't even want to imagine what would happen to Lark.

*I will not sink. I will float.*

Cerise took a deep breath and let herself fall into the cold water softly. It picked her up and carried her along. She stretched, weightless, her long hair streaming around her in a soft veil. She had done this ever since she was a little girl. The water never failed to soothe her.

Failure happened. The trick was to accept the risk and try anyway.

The water lapped at her, washing away the jitters. Calm came.

She opened her eyes. The pregnant dark sky threatened rain. The dark boards of the dock slid past her. William's face swung into view, peering at her from the dock.

He stared at her with utter amazement, like a kid who had stumbled on to a bright odd-looking bug.

"Hi," she said.

"What are you doing?"

"Floating."

"Why?"

"It's relaxing. You should try it." Too late she realized that sounded like an invitation. Great. Just great. Would it have killed her to think before she opened her mouth? *Jump in with me, Lord Bill, I'm swimming here, half-naked . . .*

William shook his head. "No."

Wait a minute. What did he mean "no"? "Why not?"

"I don't like water."

"Why?"

William grimaced. "It's wet. And the pel . . . the hair stinks like fish for hours afterward."

Cerise blinked. Was he serious? "Swimming is fun."

"No, swimming gets you from point A to point B. What you're doing isn't swimming. You're not going anywhere."

Full of opinions, Lord Bill. "Swimming is good for

you, and you could always shampoo your precious hair afterward. Your hair looks good after you wash it."

He grimaced.

"I bet the women from the Weird tell you that you have great hair all the time, Lord Bill." She bet they told him he was handsome as sin, too.

His face turned grim. "Women from the Weird tell me nothing. They don't talk to me unless I pay them."

Well, that was neither here nor there. William peered at her. "If you're finished splashing in this muddy puddle, I'd like to get to Sicktree now."

Cerise raised her eyebrows. "Muddy puddle?"

"To you it might seem like a giant crystal-clear mountain lake, but trust me, it's a dirty little pond. I bet the bottom is squishy slime, too. I suppose trading the rotten spaghetti stench for the fish one is an improvement . . ."

He was going to take a dive into this lake. He just didn't know it. Cerise rose, finding footing in the soft mud. The water came up to just below her breasts and her wet shirt stuck to her body. William's gaze snagged on her chest. *Yep, keep looking, Lord Bill. Keeeeeep looking.*

Cerise raised her hand. William leaned forward, poised over the water. His strong dry fingers closed about hers. She smiled, gripped his hand, and bent her knees, hitting him with her full weight, trying to pitch him into the lake.

The muscles on William's arm bulged. He flexed and she felt herself lifted out of the water. He plucked her out and held her above the lake for a moment.

The tiny hairs on the back of her neck rose. Nobody was that strong.

A hint of a smile curved William's mouth. Carefully he set her on the pier and caught her by the shoulders. "You okay?"

He was standing too close.

Cerise tilted her face up. "Fine."

He had a peculiar look on his face, a slightly hungry,

possessive expression. His hands on her shoulders felt dry and warm.

If he took a small step forward, his chest would touch her breasts.

*Say something, you idiot. Snap him out of it.* "So do you often rescue hobo queens from filthy puddles, Lord Bill?"

"William," he told her quietly. It sounded like an intimate request.

"How's your side?"

He let go of her long enough to raise his shirt. The dressing was gone—he'd probably taken it off, the ass—but the cuts had scabbed over. That was some fast healing.

William dipped his head, looking at her. There was nothing threatening in his gaze, but she had a distinct sense of being stalked by a large, careful predator. They had to get out of the damn swamp and into town, where there would be other people and she could leave him . . .

"Maybe swimming would be good," he said.

*Oh no. No, no, no.*

Cerise looked past him, trying to think of something to say. Her gaze caught on chunks of battered wood bobbing in the lake just beyond the boundary. She squinted at them. Yep, sure enough. Cerise swore.

He turned. "What?"

"See those muddy broken boards in the lake?"

He looked to where she pointed. "Yes?"

"I think that's our boat."

CERISE stood at the boundary, staring into the Broken and listening to a torrent of cursing ripping from William's mouth. He had used a couple of words she'd never heard before, and she filed them away for later. She'd have to ask Kaldar what they meant.

The boat was no more. And the long smudge flanked

by clawed tracks left no doubt about who was responsible for demolishing it.

"I'll kill that damn fish with my bare hands!" He must have run out of swear words.

Cerise sighed. One chunk of the punt lay twenty feet to the left, the next was up on a bush, the third was in the lake . . . "Boy, he really must've flailed around to throw the pieces so far apart."

William took it as a sign to unleash another string of curses.

"It's a lake house," she said. "There is bound to be some kind of boat in there."

Twenty minutes later they climbed into a narrow canoe they'd found in the garage and paddled through the boundary. The crossing took her breath away. Tiny painful needles pierced her insides. Cerise slumped over. Everything had a price. This was how she paid for her magic. She was lucky. Most of her family couldn't even cross into the Broken.

"Are you all right?" William asked from the stern.

"Fine." She swallowed the pain. Lord Bill seemed no worse for wear. "We're aiming over there." She pointed at the opposite end of the lake where a narrow river spilled into the water.

They began to paddle. The canoe slipped along, light and easy.

In front of her William paddled, hard muscles working on his back. Why did she have to meet him now? Why not a month before? Then she could've actually flirted and had the luxury of doing something about it. She really wasn't handling this whole thing well. First, she practically invited him to frolic in the lake with her, then she let him ogle her, then . . .

The surface of the river dappled. Tiny silvery streaks burst from the waves in a reverse hail. Fish fry, scared out of their wits. Cerise grabbed her sword.

"Something's coming!"

William dropped the paddle into the boat and pulled his knife.

A long serpentine shadow slid under the water. Cerise caught a flash of stubby fat paws. Not again. Damn it all . . .

The eel shot under the boat. Cerise lunged, thrusting the blade into the water, and felt the sword's tip slide off the armored head. The creature dove, vanishing into gloomy depths, and she withdrew.

The lake lay placid.

A smooth wave rose and sped toward the boat. The fry leaped into the air in a futile attempt to escape. She gripped the canoe.

"He's going to ram. Get down!"

The blunt head smashed into the boat. The small vessel careened, propped on the eel's skull. A round fish eye stared at her.

William hacked at the head with his knife. The eel shot up, snapping at William's legs. The boat careened and he fell into the water.

*Oh no.* She let the eel eat the blueblood.

Cerise took a breath and dived in after him.

Cold water burned her skin. Cerise hung suspended in the dense gray-green depth, seeing nothing, hearing nothing.

An icy spark of Gospo Adir magic flared to the left. She swam like a rolpie, kicking her feet in unison.

An outline of a scaly body loomed before her.

She sank her blade into it, cleaving into the spinal column, before she realized that the eel lay motionless. Pale blood leaked and spread through the water in opaque clouds. Cerise tasted copper on her tongue.

She surfaced and saw William, one hand on the boat, looking for her. He reached her in two strokes.

"You aren't happy unless you're wet," he growled.

"There are times when wet is better than dry, but this isn't one of them," she snarled. "If you got down like I told you to, the fish wouldn't have knocked you out of the boat."

"It didn't knock me out. I jumped in."

Dear Gods. "You jumped into the water with a Gospo Adir eel in it?"

"I couldn't get a good cut from the boat."

Unbelievable. "Are you crazy?"

"Look who's talking, swamp mermaid."

"I jumped in to rescue you, you fool!"

He submerged and popped out of the water right next to her. There it was again, that wild thing he hid inside, looking at her through his eyes. If she just looked at it long enough, she would figure out what it was . . .

He grinned a crazy, happy grin. "You dived in to save me."

"Don't make too much of it." Cerise dived, picked up momentum, and climbed into the boat. Idiot blue-blood and his idiot eyes. What the hell was she doing? This was the last time she would let him throw her off-kilter.

William hooked the eel's carcass and swam, dragging it to the shore.

"What are you doing?"

"I'm going to cut off its head."

"Why?"

"I'll have it stuffed and mounted on my wall."

She stared at him in disbelief. Every handsome man had a flaw. It was just her luck that in William's case that flaw was lunacy. The man was nuts.

William's feet must've hit the ground because he stood up and began to wade. "That way," he said, "I'll be sure the damn thing is dead."


WILLIAM shifted his rucksack on his shoulder. The eel head he carried on a sharpened stick stank of rancid fish, and in retrospect he decided dragging it around probably wasn't the smartest idea. But that's what a blueblood would do, and he was too stubborn to toss it away now.

Cerise walked next to him. She hadn't said two words since they had gotten back into the canoe. Apparently he really pissed her off with that fish. His plan to get her to like him had gone up in smoke. She would leave him in Sicktree and disappear in the swamp. They were getting close to town, too—the muddy path had joined a narrow one-lane road.

He was out of ideas and out of time.

"We're almost there," Cerise said.

Think. "Got a favor to ask you. Before we split, will you help me find somebody to take the fish off my hands?"

She frowned. He concentrated, trying to read her expression. It would be a no, he could see it in her eyes.

He pulled a doubloon from his pocket, holding the small coin between his index and middle finger. "I'll pay for your time."

"There is a man. He sometimes stuffs fish." She held out her hand.

"Not until we get there."

"Fine." She turned away, but William caught a ghost of a smile on her lips.

He had done something right. He didn't know what it was, but he hoped he would keep doing it.

Ahead the road bent. The wind brought the smell of gun oil and a hint of human sweat. He stopped. "There are people ahead."

"How many?" Cerise asked.

"A few."

She pulled her sword out and kept walking.

"If they're waiting for you, we need to get off the road."

"They would just track us down," she said. "The road is better. Gives me space to work."

Crazy woman.

They turned. Six men waited across the lane. Five had blades, the sixth held a rifle. They wanted to take her alive, William decided. The more guns you had, the higher was the likelihood that someone would lose his shit and pull the trigger, so they gave the coolest head a gun as insurance and brought lots of manpower.

A bright smile painted Cerise's face. "Remember my family's feud? This is their hired muscle. Stay back."

"Very funny." He kept walking. He was feeling a bit frustrated, and he always made it a point to vent his frustration.

"It's not your fight."

"Six of them, one of you. I don't know what you think you'll do with your pretty little sword. I know they aren't playing."

"If you try knocking me out of the way again, I will cut your arm off. Stay back, William. You'll get hurt."

"Don't worry, I'll share this time."

"Don't do it."

Time to pick a fight. He jerked his fish head at the men barring the road and raised his voice. "Move."

"Lunatic," Cerise said under her breath.

The rifle's barrel sighted Cerise instead of him. Ah. So they knew about her sword tricks, too.

The Edgers looked him over. A tall balding guy with a machete smiled. "Where did you find the blueblood, Cerise?"

"In the swamp," she told him.

"That's nice. You shouldn't have gone off your land. Now you're all alone out here and your family can't help you."

Cerise's grin got wider. "You're looking at it the wrong way. I'm not all alone with you. You're alone with me. You should've brought more people. Six won't do it."

The Machete shrugged. "We got enough. Lagar says to bring you in one piece, so come along before anybody gets shot. You know Baxter. He doesn't miss much."

Baxter winked at them from behind the rifle.

"We're going to Sicktree," William said. "You're in the way."

The Edgers chuckled.

"This ain't the Weird. We don't care for bluebloods here," the man on the left called out.

"You'll get killed," Cerise murmured.

William thrust the stick into dirt. "I don't have time for this stupid shit. Move or I will move you."

Machete shrugged. "You heard the man. Baxter, move him."

The rifle barrel swung to William. He shied left. The bullet grazed his shoulder, burning across his flesh.

"That's it."

The rifle shot again, but he was already moving. He smashed the knuckles of his right hand into Machete's throat, hooking his foot with his right as the man fell, swiped the weapon from his fingers, rammed his elbow into the Edger to his left, and hurled the machete at Baxter. The knife hit the shooter between the eyes. The blow wasn't hard enough to kill, but the oversized blade cut at the man's scalp. Blood poured into Baxter's eyes. He screamed. As William broke the arm of the Edger to his right, he saw the rifleman take off into the brush.

William lost himself to the flurry of punches and kicks. Bones crunched, people howled, someone's blood wet his knuckles. It went fast and was over too quickly. He tossed the last man at Cerise, just for the fun of it. She reached out and very carefully popped the Edger on the head with the hilt of her sword. He went down.

William strode to her. *That's how it's done. Drink it in.*

She surveyed the carnage behind him. "Did you have fun?"

He showed her his teeth. "Yes. Now they won't take you anywhere."

Cerise stepped closer to him, so close he only needed to lean in and dip his head and he would kiss her. Since he saved her, maybe he could just grab her and—

"That was the stupidest thing you have done since I've met you," she ground out through her teeth.

Belay the grabbing.

"You're an outsider. Your kind exiled our kind into

this swamp. We hate bluebloods. Right now Baxter is out there telling wild stories about the blueblood who came to kill the Edgers. By nightfall, it will be you and some friends, who attacked defenseless locals. By morning, the whole town will be out looking for the mysterious army unit of bluebloods Louisiana sent in to exterminate us. They will hunt you down with torches, like a dog. Stay here, hero, while I fix this."

She strode over to Machete and crouched by him, the tip of her sword resting on the ground. "You're alive, Kent?"

Kent moaned something.

"Tell Lagar that he isn't the only one who can hire mercenaries. When we hire someone, we get the best. He would do well to remember that."

She rose from the crouch and nodded at William. He took his fish and followed her down the road.

Cerise's face was dark. "What were you thinking?"

"I was thinking that six against one wasn't a fair fight. I evened the odds a bit."

"You call that evening the odds? You demolished them."

Demolished. He liked that. "I left you one."

"I noticed."

"I promised to share," he told her. "Manners are very important in the Weird. Lying would be quite impolite."

Her mouth trembled and she hid a smile. It played on her lips for a second, lighting up her face, and vanished.

*Want.*

"I just told them that my family hired you," Cerise said. "Now instead of thinking you're some blueblood hell-bent on causing destruction, the locals will view you as a mercenary. That makes your presence a private matter between my family and the Sheeriles. Either way, you signed your death sentence—Lagar Sheerile will turn himself inside out to kill you now. Lagar isn't a pushover like those clowns. His brother Peva once shot the hearts off a card at a hundred feet with a crossbow."

"I'm very scared," William told her. "Are playing cards a real nuisance in your part of the Edge?"

She snickered.

"Shooting cards is dumb," he told her. "What is he, five? Or is he doing it to get women?"

Cerise waved her hands. "Never mind. You have two choices: you can either stay here and let them hunt you down while you look for your doohickey, or you can come with me to my house and wait until this blows over. We can probably smuggle you out once this mess dies down."

He wanted to jump up and down and pump his fist. "To your house? In the swamps?"

"Yes."

Play it cool, play it cool. "Hmm."

Cerise glared at him, her dark eyes bright. "What do you mean 'hmm'? You think I invite just anybody to our family home? If you'd rather be dead because you decided to play the hero and save me, you're welcome to it."

"What about your family? Won't they mind?"

"Until we get my parents back, I'm in charge of my family," she said.

The road broke through the trees, and they entered a small town. Wooden buildings, some on stilts, some on stone foundations, formed narrow streets. Somewhere to the left a dog bayed. The air smelled of food and people.

"Decide, Lord Bill. Yes or no?"

"Yes," he said.

"We might get killed along the way," she said.

"Nice of you to mention it."

"My pleasure." She pointed left. "Come on. Zeke's place is over there. We have to go that way anyway, and the more people see us together now, the better. It will reinforce the idea that you're working for me. And we can get rid of that awful thing."

He won. He won, he won, he won. He could see the method in Declan's madness now. Playing a hero had its advantages.

"I happen to think the fish head is an impressive specimen," William told her.

"It stinks."

"You wore a jacket full of rancid spaghetti for three days."

"It was a disguise! Nobody pays attention to homeless people in the Broken."

"Why were you in the Broken?" he asked.

"None of your business."

She stuck her chin in the air and strode down the street. He snuck a glance at her ass—it was a remarkable ass—and followed her.

# EIGHT

ZEKE Wallace's shop occupied a large wooden structure that in the Broken would've been a barn. In the Edge, it must've passed for a respectable storefront, William decided, since it had a giant gator head above the door and a sign that said ZEKE'S LEATHERS under it.

William swung the door open and remembered to hold it for Cerise. The inside of the store was cool and dim. A long counter sliced the floor in half, offering a variety of knives, gator leathers, belts, and assorted junk. A man sat behind the counter next to a large crossbow.

William glanced at him, evaluating. In his early forties, lean, probably still fast. Skin like a walnut—weather-tanned and lined. Hair, once black, now neither here nor there, worn on the longer side. Hooded dark eyes.

Their stares met. "What can I do you for?" the man asked.

"Looking for Zeke," William said.

"I'm Zeke. What are you and your lady looking for?"

Cerise turned to him. "Hi, Zeke."

Zeke flinched.

It lasted half a second, a mere flicker across the man's face, but William caught it: eyebrows raised, eyes wide, lips stretched back. That was the one human expression he was very familiar with—fear. Zeke Wallace was afraid of Cerise.

The man recovered fast, in the same breath. "Hello, Ms. Mar. And how are you this fine evening?"

"Good, thank you." She wandered down the counter looking at the knickknacks.

William raised the fish head. "I need this stuffed."

Zeke looked at the head. "That's a Gospo Adir eel."

Cerise grimaced. "Yes, and he's very proud of killing it."

"The Sect won't like it," Zeke said.

"Can you do it or not?" William let some growl into his voice.

Zeke frowned. "Fish mount is a tricky thing. You have to scrape the meat out from the cheeks and skull and then soak the thing in alcohol to get the rest of the meat to harden. I don't do them, but my nephew, Cole, has done some on occasion."

"If it's a question of money, I have it." William pulled one of the Mirror's coins from his pocket and tossed it to Zeke. It looked just like a normal coin, except for the engraving of the Adrianglian lion. The lion on the real coins had three claws, not four.

Zeke snapped the coin out of the air and looked at it. "Right. Well, you know what they say—money fixes everything. Like I mentioned, fish mounts are tricky, and there's a couple of ways to do them. I've got some samples in the back. If you pick out what you want, we can talk price."

He headed to a small door. William followed. They went into the back room and Zeke shut the door.

"I expected you yesterday," he whispered.

"We ran into some sharks," William said.

Zeke grimaced. "Figured it had to be something like that. That's Cerise Mar out there. I about broke my head trying to think up a way to get you close to the Mars, and you walk into my store side by side with her like you're bosom buddies."

William sat on the edge of a table. "What's the story with her family?"

"They're swampers—native Edgers. A big family, very old, land rich, money poor. They've got themselves a fam ily house out in the swamp. People call them Rats behind their back, because there's so damn many of them and they're poor and mean. The Mars aren't afraid of blood or lock-up, and they hold a grudge like it was their family treasure."

Zeke glanced at the main floor through a peephole in the door. "The Mars are feuding with their neighbors, the Sheeriles. The Sheerile family isn't that big—mother and three sons, but they've got money and use a lot of hired muscle. The old woman runs the whole thing, jerks her sons around like puppets on a string. Rumor has it, Gustave Mar and his wife, Gen, disappeared a few days ago and the Sheeriles were involved. That's a hard trick to pull off. Both the Mars and the Sheeriles are Legion families."

"What does that mean?"

"It means they have old magic," Zeke said. "The families take root from the ancient Legion marooned centuries ago in the swamps. The Sheeriles would've needed help to take Gustave alive. Lagar Sheerile is very good with his blade, but Gustave is one mean sonovabitch. His daughter is of the same stock—if you get in trouble with her, don't count on any mercy. A guy on the Sheeriles' payroll says the Hand was involved in the whole thing." Zeke frowned. "She's getting impatient."

Things were clearer but not by much. "Anything else?"

"That's all I've got. If I need to reach you, where will you be?"

"In her house."

Zeke's eyebrows crept up. "You got invited to the Rat-hole? You must be a miracle worker."

William hid a smile. Sure, he was.

Zeke pulled the door open. "Pleasure doing business with you."

"It's all yours," William growled.

Cerise looked up from the counter. "Are you done?"

"Yes." William nodded.

"Zeke, can we use your back door?"

"Sure thing," Zeke said.

A moment later they were outside, and William inhaled the scents of the swamp town swirling around him.

"Took you for everything you had?" Cerise's eyes laughed at him.

"I held my own."

"Sure you did." The back of the shop faced the Mire, and Cerise headed straight for it. "Our ride is this way."

"We have a ride?"

"My cousin," she said. "Come on, Lord Bill. We've kept him waiting long enough already."

**"GENEVIEVE . . ."**

The soft insistent voice reached through the fog clouding her mind and tugged on her, demanding attention.

"Genevieve . . ."

Slowly Gen opened her eyes to the blurry world wrapped in a shroud of light too bright for her dilated pupils. The pain came slowly, from some dark well within her. It built on itself, growing dense and heavy. Hot claws ripped into her insides, and the world reeled and shuddered. A face blocked her view. It seemed ridiculously large, bigger than her, bigger than the room, darker than light.

"Can you hear me, Gen?"

"Yes," she whispered through the tortured tempo of her breathing. She knew this voice. She knew it very well.

"Your daughter, Cerise, went to the Broken and came back. Why would she do that? Tell me." A hand stroked her hair, and the voice came again, gentle, friendly, caring. "I know you're tired. Tell me why Cerise went to the Broken, and I'll let you rest. Come on, darling."

Her dry cracked lips moved, shaping the words. "Go to hell, Spider."

The pain swelled larger and suddenly burst like a fiery explosion. Her ears filled with the ringing of countless bells. The fire slid down into her chest and lower to scald her legs. It scorched the skin, melted the muscle, and sank its teeth into the bone. Instinctively she tried to curl into a ball, like a newborn, but couldn't. The world spun in chaos, faster and faster with each rise of her chest, as if fueled by her breathing. Gen Mar retched and sank into oblivion.

CERISE strode down the twisted path, listening to the chorus of Edge cicadas seesawing in the underbrush. Night had claimed the Mire. It came on padded feet, soft and cautious, like a swamp cat, with its ears raised and its eyes opened wide. The reds and yellows of the sky burned down to deep indigo and purple. To the left the lazy, wide expanse of Deadman River stretched into the gloom. As the cooling air drained warmth from its calm current, the last of the nightweaver dragonflies streaked to the water, prickling the surface to snag water fleas in their chitinous claws.

She loved the night. The world seemed bigger somehow, the sky vast and endless, the soft darkness full of possibilities and excitement. Yeah. Right now excitement was the last thing they needed. Jogging down the path in hopes of watching Lord Bill trip on a stray root was as exciting as she wanted it to get. So far he hadn't stumbled once. It was like the man could see in the dark.

He went through Kent and his thugs like a sharp knife through a ripe pear. Didn't even break a sweat. She'd never seen anything like it. Kaldar once took her to an action movie in the Broken and she'd laughed the whole time at the ridiculous punches and kicks she could see a mile away, but she had to admit, the fights did look pretty. William's fight didn't look pretty. It was terrifying. He moved on liquid joints, so fast and sure, she just stood there and watched him until he was done.

She wished she could've watched again, in slow motion this time. He could've killed them all with his bare hands. He looked like he might have enjoyed it, too. And after all of that, he trotted over with a "Wasn't I cool?" look on his face and tried to make her laugh. *I left you one.* Heh. He wasn't even winded.

She glanced at the sky for a second. It spread above her, vast and cold. *Why now?* she asked in her head. *Why couldn't I have met him a month ago, when I could flirt, and laugh, and didn't have to worry about sending the family to the slaughter?*

She looked at him. Lord Bill trotted down the road, soundless, like a night shadow. She couldn't hear his steps, and she'd spent a lifetime listening for odd noises in the swamp.

*If he is that good with his hands, I wonder how he is with his blade.*

She could beat him. Of course, she could beat him. But it would be interesting to see what he could do up close.

She should've left him in Sicktree. That would've been the smart thing to do. But she never claimed to be smart. He knew the Hand and was willing to fight it, and that was good enough for now. She would sort out her own feelings later. When they were safely inside the Rathole, and she was clean and had a plate of food and a mug of hot tea.

It took all of her will not to laugh when he'd refused to give her money up front for guiding him to Zeke. It was such an Edger thing to do. He still hadn't paid her either. She killed a snicker. She bet Zeke took all of his money and Lord Bill was too proud to back out of the deal.

William stopped. One moment he strode next to her down the narrow path between the cypresses and the next he froze, caught in mid-step. His hand went to his blade.

"What is it?" she asked.

"I'm not sure." He stared at the old cypress up ahead.

Heh. He had found Urow. Cerise breathed a sigh of

relief. She'd figured Urow was all right when she saw Lagar's men on the road. If they'd known where he was, either the lot of them or her cousin would be dead by now.

"Come out," she called. "He sees you."

A huge gray shade peeled itself from the cypress. Urow stepped onto the path. He wore blue jeans, no shirt, and no shoes. As if on cue, the moon rolled out from behind a ragged cloud. Silvery light bathed Urow's gray skin. He stood five feet tall and seemed nearly that wide across his shoulders. Huge slabs of muscle lined his massive chest and biceps. His left arm was human. His right was at least six inches longer, with thicker longer digits. Black claws tipped his fingers and toes.

William stared. She didn't blame him. Urow would give anyone pause, especially in the dark. His looks won him no friends, but nobody was in a hurry to become his enemy either.

Cerise walked over to him and gave him a hug. "How are you?"

Urow hugged her back, patted her gently. "What took so long?" His voice sounded like it came through a gravel grinder.

"We had a date with the sharks."

Urow glanced at William. "Who's your friend?"

"His name is William. He's from the Weird. I found him in the swamp and he followed me home."

Urow's black eyes took William's measure. "Did you feed him?"

"Yes."

"There's your mistake. That will do it every time."

The blueblood hadn't moved.

"This my cousin Urow," she told him. "We keep trying to get him to work less on strong and more on tall, but he doesn't listen."

Urow tossed back the mane of coarse black hair and grinned, showing a mouthful of serrated teeth. William's face showed nothing. He simply waited, his attention focused on Urow.

Urow squared his shoulders, flexing. Just what she needed. Two knuckleheads in a tough man contest. She had to nip it in the bud. Urow outweighed William by at least two hundred pounds—her cousin weighed four hundred and then some, none of it fat, but Urow got along on brute strength and a loud roar, while William threw Lagar's crew around and made it seem effortless, like he was playing. Like he hurt people for fun.

"Stop trying to pick a fight with the blueblood." She patted Urow's arm. "He's my guest, and besides, he isn't the jumpy type."

She turned to where Urow's boat waited, tied to the cypress knees. He'd brought the smaller of his cargo boats, the smallest size that could be pulled by a rolpie without being tipped over. They'd go fast, and after the cramped canoe, extra room felt like a luxury.

"Is the blueblood coming with us?" Urow asked.

"He is."

"To the house?"

"Yes."

He chewed that over. "Are you sure?"

She let a note of steel slip into her voice. "Yes, I'm sure."

A rolpie popped out of the water. Cerise leaned over and patted the brindled head.

Urow frowned. "It might be a mistake. We don't know him."

Cerise turned and looked at him, copying her father's stare as best she could. It must've worked, because Urow clamped his mouth shut.

"If you have an issue with the way I make my decisions, you can take it up with my father, when he's back. Until then, I run the family and what I say goes. Now will the two of you get into the boat, please, before I take off and leave you standing on the shore?"

* * *

THE boat sped across the brown water, sending shallow
waves to lap at the nearest shore. William stood against
the rope rail, resting on it but not really leaning. At the
stern, Cerise sank to the bottom of the boat, leaned over,
and skimmed the water with her fingertips. Her face
seemed lighter, as if she had been carrying a heavy pack
and had finally dropped it. He decided not to tell her how
close he'd come to shooting her cousin in the throat.

Urow, whatever the hell he was, sat at the bow, guiding the Nessie wannabe with his reins and sulking. He
smelled odd. William wrinkled his nose. Not a changeling, definitely, but not all human either. Something
strange. If William had been wearing fur, the scent alone
would have made his hackles rise.

"Any news of my parents?" Cerise asked.

"Nope." Urow grimaced. "A woman was killed near
Dillardsville. She had claws between her knuckles. Bob
Vey said she shot a web at them. It hardened on their
skin and ate away half of his nose. He looks like a
Gospo Adir skull now."

"Serves him right," Cerise murmured. "Bob is a scum-
bag of the first order. Last year he beat Louise Dalton
bloody because she wouldn't spread her legs for him."

Urow nodded, shaking his black hair. "That's what I
said. I bet Louise is laughing now."

A long narrow island loomed ahead, on the left. In the
bright light of the moon, the cypresses and slash pines
crowding the shore stood out, etched against the river.

"What are you?" William asked.

Urow glanced at Cerise. "He doesn't mince words,
does he?"

She laughed. "What are you talking about? Subtle is his
middle name."

"I'm half-Mar, half-thoas," Urow said.

"What's a thoas?"

"The moon people," Cerise said.

"The swamp elders," Urow said. "The mud crawlers."

"They are an odd race." Cerise slumped against the short rope rail. "Some think they may have been human at some point, but they look different now. We don't know if they came from the Weird or from the Broken. They live deep in the swamp and don't like people much. Something about the full moon mesmerizes them. That's about the only way to see one—deep in the swamp, staring at the full moon with glowing eyes."

"My mother was raped by a thoas," Urow said. "Although the rest of the family seems to think otherwise."

Cerise cleared her throat. "We don't dispute the thoas part. We're just a bit unsure about the rape."

Urow leaned to him and wagged his eyebrows. William fought an urge to jump back.

"My mother was a woman of loose morals." Urow winked.

"You make her sound like a whore." Cerise grimaced. "Aunt Alina just liked to have fun. Besides, she was just about the only one of the family your wife could stand."

*Wife?*

"Don't say it," Cerise warned.

"You're married?" William asked.

She sighed. "Now you've done it. He'll never be quiet about it now. The whole trip will be, 'Oh, look at my pretty wife. Oh, look at my pretty babies.'"

Urow dipped his head and pulled a plastic wallet off his neck. "Just because you don't have a pretty wife . . ."

"I don't want one." She sighed. "Wives are too much trouble."

William barked a short laugh.

Urow passed the wallet to William. "The redhead is my wife. On the right that's my three boys and a baby."

"Three boys and a daughter," Cerise told him.

"Right now it's a baby. When it starts talking to me and comes when I call, then it's a daughter."

William opened the wallet, carefully holding it by the edges. A picture of a pretty redheaded woman looked at him from the left. Three adolescent boys crowded into the picture on the right. All had black hair and a grayish tint to their skin. The oldest looked like a younger copy of Urow, down to an oversized hand and claws. The smallest, the one holding a baby, could almost pass for a human.

William closed the wallet. Even this man got to have a family. But no matter how he tried, he just made a mess of things. He slapped a lid on the familiar frustration before it took over and made him do something he might regret.

They were looking at him. This was one of those human situations when he was expected to say something. "Your wife is very pretty."

He tensed, in case Urow lunged at him.

The gray man grinned and took the wallet from William's hand. "She is, isn't she? I have the prettiest wife in the whole of the Mire."

"Maybe you should stop rubbing it in," Cerise said softly.

She must've seen something in his face. William pushed his regrets deeper, away from the surface.

"Do you have any family, Lord Bill?" she asked softly.

"No." He didn't even know what his mother had looked like.

Urow's eyebrows crept up. "All right, all right." He slid the wallet around his neck.

A bolt thrust through Urow's shoulder. It was attached to a line.

William grabbed for Urow, but the line snapped taut and jerked the gray man off the boat.


UROW plunged into cold water. Webs snapped open between his toes, and he kicked, but the line dragged him to the surface. He skimmed the face of the river in a shower of spray. Water burned his stomach. He flipped on his side and back on his stomach again, digging deep into the waves, and thrust his hands into the current. His fingers found the line and gripped it. He searched for something to brace his legs against but met only water.

A dark form rushed at him through the waves and smashed into his gut. The last of the air burst from his mouth in a violent, silent scream. Pain bathed his left side. He clutched at the obstruction, gripping it with his limbs. Rotting bark, slick with algae, crumbled under his fingers. A log, Urow realized, and dug his claws into the soft water-soaked wood.

They shot him. The sonovabitches shot him with a harpoon and pulled him off his own boat. He'd rip out their guts and make them eat it.

The line pulled. The bolt tore at his flesh, hard, harder, ripping a growl from him. Urow clung to the tree and felt the heavy sodden mass move, compelled by the draw of the line. Pain burned him, reaching down across his chest to his ribs and his neck.

Something whistled through the air and punched the tree in twin thuds. The line snapped free, and the log rolled back under his weight. Urow submerged and surfaced. Two short black bolts punctured the wet bark of the log. Someone had shot the line, severing it.

Urow grabbed the bolt lodged in his shoulder and wrenched it free with a snarl. A piece of his bloody flesh still quivered on the barbs of the bolt's hooked head, and he rammed it into the sodden wood. Bleeding but free, he pulled himself onto the log and crouched on it.

A small river barge crowded with people headed for his boat, drawn by three rolpies. Cerise had her sword out, and the blueblood was reloading a crossbow. So that was where the bolts had come from. He'd have to thank the guy later. Right now he had work to do.

To the far left, a second boat struggled, its towing pulley spinning wildly, the way it did when the line had snapped. Four people manned it, as its driver tried to guide their rolpie into a tight turn.

*Hello, fellas. Shoot me, will you? Time to go over and say hello, in a friendly Mire way.*

An ugly snarl rippled from Urow's mouth, and he dived into the river, heading for the smaller cutter and its crew. They had no idea how fast the son of a thoas could swim.


WILLIAM reloaded. Thirty yards away a large boat sped toward them. He counted the shadowy figures on the deck. Ten. They weren't kidding.

Magic pricked his skin with a hot needle. "The Hand."

Cerise didn't answer. He glanced at her face and saw rage. She kicked aside a coil of docking line and stood in the center of the deck, leaning lightly forward, her sword pointing downward. A white glow rolled over her eyes.

So she could flash.

Twenty yards. Six men, three women. One undetermined in a long cloak.

They should've been shot at by now.

"No bows," William said. "They want you alive."

"Bad for them," Cerise whispered. "Good for me."

William raised his bow, sighted, and fired. A woman screamed and one of the figures stumbled back. The rest ducked, trying to take cover, all except the guy in the cloak, as expected. William reloaded and fired again at the man in the cloak. The bolt sprouted from his target's neck.

The man shuddered. The cloak fell from his shoulders, revealing a naked hairless body. The man gripped the shaft of the bolt and ripped it out of his throat. An odd clicking, like the sound of nut shells crunching under someone's foot, issued from his mouth.

One of the Hand's freaks. William bared his teeth. He'd met this kind before. He didn't even need the Mirror's intel to identify it. This type was called a hunter.

They specialized in tracking and apprehending. Spider really wanted Cerise.

The Hand's agent snapped the bolt in two, tossed it overboard, and licked his fingers.

"Stay back this time," Cerise said. "It's my fight."

"There are nine of them. Don't be stupid."

"Stay the fuck back, William."

"Fine." He took a step back and raised his crossbow. If that's the way she wanted it, he could always rescue her later. "Let's see what you got."

The larger boat slammed into them, sending a quake through the hull. Two men jumped onto the deck.

Cerise struck and paused, blood running down her blade.

The first two fighters died without a scream. One moment they stood on deck, and the next the top halves of their bodies slid down into the river.

William closed his mouth with a click.

The attackers drew back.

The edge of Cerise's sword shone once, as if a glowing silver hair were stretched along the blade. She leaped onto the larger boat.

They swarmed her. She whirled, cutting through them, slicing limbs in half, severing muscle and bone. Blood sprayed, she paused again, and the fighters around her fell without a single moan.

Four seconds and the deck was empty. Nothing moved.

She was the most beautiful thing he had ever seen.

He would have to fight her before this was over, just to find out if he could beat her.

A rapid staccato of clicks came from the back of the larger boat. The hunter was still alive.

"I see I missed a spot," Cerise said.

The hunter stared at her, his eyes solid black in the moonlight. His hand jerked up . . .

William jumped, shoving her out of the way.

Pale liquid sprayed the deck in the spot where she

had just stood and hissed, hardening into a corrosive paste.

The hunter creaked like he was crushing a load of beetles in his throat. "Give girl."

William snarled. "Come and take her."

The second stream of spray hit the spot where he'd just stood. Now both of the hunter's hands were empty. No more web.

The hunter charged him, clawed hands ripping the air in a wide swing. William dropped under the thick arms and swept at the agent's legs from a crouch. The hunter jumped, avoiding the kick, and struck, claws poised like daggers.

William dodged and laughed. The Louisianan thought that having claws made him a hotshot. *It's not the same, pal, unless you're born with them.*

The hunter whirled, slashing. William sidestepped and hammered a kick to the agent's kneecap. Cartilage crunched. The leg folded and the hunter dropped to his knees. William grabbed the man's bald head, locked the vertebra, and twisted. The neck snapped with a light popcorn pop.

Frothy yellow spit boiled from the hunter's mouth. His eyes rolled back. William let go and the agent toppled like a log, facedown.

It felt good. William chuckled and stepped over the body. "Weak knees and elbows. All that magic makes them easy to break."

He glanced at Cerise. She didn't look happy. She should've been happy. They won.

Her gaze slid over him. She was sizing him up.

William shrugged, popping his neck. *You want to dance, hobo queen, I'm ready. What do I get when I win?*

She thought about it. He saw it in her eyes. She wasn't sure if she could take him, but she was willing to try.

A scream ripped through the night. They both turned. Far to the left a smaller boat drifted off.

"Urow needs help," Cerise said.

"We should help, then."

She nodded.

He hid his disappointment and helped her fish the rol-pie reins out of the water

# NINE

CERISE brought Urow's boat alongside the Hand's second boat. A mangled corpse sprawled on the boat's deck, his chest a bloody mess of claw marks. A trail of slick bloody smudges led away from the cadaver to a small cabin.

*Oh no, Urow. No.*

Cerise jumped across the water, slid a little on the wet deck, and righted herself. William landed next to her, light on his feet like a cat. The salty metallic stench of fresh blood flooded her nostrils and coated the inside of her mouth, and for a few moments, she could smell and taste nothing else.

She rushed to the cabin. The door hung crooked on its hinges. Cerise peered inside. Empty except for a corpse slumped against the cabin door.

"Here," William called.

She circled the cabin. A woman's body lay crumpled on the deck by a pulley. Next to her Urow sagged, curled into a ball.

Stupid man. Stupid, stupid man. She ran to him, grasped the shoulders, and heaved, flipping him on his back. A thick purple swelling marked his shoulder.

Copper. Someone had poisoned Urow with copper. Heat washed over her. Only the family would know to do that: only Mars knew that Urow was meeting her. Someone had talked to the Hand. Cerise clenched her teeth. Why? Why would anyone do that?

She probed the swollen mass of tissue with her fingers. She couldn't even find the wound.

"That's not normal," William said.

"There must've been copper shavings in the head of the bolt. It's poison to thoas. He's dying."

"What can we do?"

Nothing. "We must get him to his wife."

She gripped his legs. William picked up Urow under his arms, grunted with effort, and lifted the body. They dragged him to the cutter.

"What the hell are you feeding him?" William growled.

"Bluebloods," she ground through her teeth.

They maneuvered around the cabin and carried him to the rail. A foot of water separated them from their boat.

"If we drop him into the river, he'll sink," she said. "He's too heavy."

"Let me have him." William knelt on one knee, and she wrestled Urow over his shoulders. William strained. Veins bulged under his skin. His face turned bright red. With a guttural snarl, William heaved and rose, Urow's massive form balanced absurdly on his back. He cleared the water in a single forceful step.

She exhaled and jumped onto their boat in time to catch Urow as William lowered him gently to the deck.


THE boat sliced through the dark water at a reckless speed. William held on to the rope rail. Cerise drove like mad, tearing up through the narrow streams away from the river, deeper into the swamp. The trees flew by. If they wrecked, he'd have to jump into the water. At least he'd get a soft landing.

The gray man shuddered, groaning quietly. Cerise had insisted on dragging the hunter corpse on board, and looking at the two bodies, William wasn't sure who looked more dead, the hunter or her cousin.

Urow's eyes snapped open. William knelt by him. The swelling had spread through the shoulder, up his chest. William touched the affected flesh. Hard as a rock. If the swelling reached Urow's neck, the man would suffocate. His own body would strangle him.

"Blueblood," the gray man said. "Thank you for shooting the line. One in a thousand shot."

"Not a big deal," William said.

Urow's lids slid closed. He trembled again and passed out.

Cerise took half a second to glance at him. Her eyes were full of ghosts.

William came to stand by her. Her scent washed over him and he savored it quietly.

The stream had narrowed, and she couldn't maintain the break-neck speed. Even if the narrow waterway allowed it, the rolpie couldn't take it. When she surfaced to gulp a breath, her sides heaved and foam dripped from her lips. Cerise saw it, too, and eased on the reins.

The gray man didn't have long. "Can we bleed the poison out?" William asked.

She shook her head. "I knew this was going to happen. Urow thinks that because he can lift a small boat by himself and he looks scary, it makes him a great fighter. He has no training. He doesn't battle, he brawls. Just waves his arms back and forth and hopes he'll hit somebody."

"When the shit hits the fan, brute strength doesn't cut it."

"You think I haven't told him that?"

"Then why did you have him pick you up?"

Cerise clenched her teeth. "Because I'm an idiot, that's why. He wanted to be useful. He sat there and bitched and moaned about how he never gets to do anything for the family and how if I just let him come and help this one time, he would feel that he belongs. Urow's invited to every family celebration. He's always welcome at the main house. He gets a portion of the family profits, just like everybody else. One of us goes to visit him at least once a month. How much more included can he be? I should've just said no, but he pushed all the right buttons and now he is dying and I don't have a scratch on me."

William looked at her face. Her lips pressed together in a rigid line. Her skin turned pale and her features looked sharper. She seemed smaller somehow, and she smelled like a cornered animal. He wanted to grab her and clench her to him, until she looked normal again.

William raked through his brain, wishing he knew the right things to say. "Let's say you're a soldier. They call a code-white mission and you volunteer. You assumed responsibility for your own safety and put yourself on the line. If you die, it's on your neck, not anybody else's. Nobody made you step forward and accept the mission. Your cousin volunteered. If he dies, it's not your weight to carry."

He checked her face, but she didn't seem any better.

"It's like a fight," William said. "You attack or you dodge. If you hesitate, you'll die. If you make a mistake and get cut, you ignore the pain until the enemy is dead. You made a decision and took a wound. Slap a bandage on it and move on. You can feel sorry and second-guess yourself later, after you've won and you've got leave, a bottle, and a woman."

Cerise stared at him for a second.

He probably shouldn't have said that last bit.

A powerful bellow rolled through the swamp. The hair on William's arms rose. Something ancient, huge, and brutal hid in the gloom, watching them with hungry eyes, and when it roared, it was as if the swamp itself gained voice to declare its might before swallowing them whole.

Another bellow joined the first, rolling from the left. William raised his crossbow.

"The old gators are singing," Cerise told him.

He peered at the darkness between the colossal cypresses guarding the stream, but saw nothing except twilight gloom.

"Thank you," she said softly. "For trying to make me feel better and for saving Urow. It wasn't your fight."

"Yes, it was," he told her.

Something shifted in the branches to the left. William raised his bow. Whatever the thing was, it was humanoid and fast.

The shape scuttled through the branches, wearing gloom like a mantle, and leaped to the next tree. Stocky body, black hair. A second thing dashed through the branches on the right. This one within crossbow range.

"Don't shoot," Cerise said. "It's Urow's children."

The one on the left sprinted and dived into the water off the branch. The gray body shot through water, and the boy launched himself onto the deck.

They swam like fish. William made a mental note never to fight one in the water.

The kid rose, dripping water. His face was young, sixteen or seventeen, but his body was thick and muscled like that of a bear. The boy glanced at the gray man's body and bared his teeth in a feral snarl.

"Copper poisoning," Cerise barked. "Tell your mother, Gaston."

The boy dived into the water.

The stream made a tight turn and opened into a pond, cradled by giant cypresses. A house perched on stilts, with a small dock. Built of logs and stone, with a roof sheathed in green moss, the house looked like it had grown from the swamp like a mushroom.

A woman ran onto the dock and clutched a rail. Bright red hair fell in a braid from her shoulders. Urow's wife.

Cerise snapped the reins, pulling a burst of speed from the exhausted rolpie. They docked with a bump.

The woman glared at them. William had a feeling that

if her eyes could shoot fire, both he and Cerise would've been burned to a crisp.

"Damn it, Cerise. What did you do to him?"

Cerise's face clenched into a rigid mask. She turned her back to the woman. "William, can you help me lift him?"

"Follow me," Urow's wife snapped and took off.

William grasped Urow under his arms and paused, unsure how to get four hundred pounds of deadweight onto the dock. Another of Urow's kids surfaced and pulled himself onto the boat. This one was older, layered with thick slabs of muscle like his father. He grasped his dad's legs and together they hauled him onto the pier and to the house.

"Hurry!" Urow's wife yelled. "On the floor here."

William followed the boy through the door. They maneuvered through the cramped inside into a dimly lit room and lowered Urow on the stack of quilts.

Urow's wife bent over her husband. The swelling was half an inch from her throat. "Mart! Herbs!"

The boy ran into the kitchen.

Urow's wife dropped on her knees, threw open a large box, and pulled out a scalpel sealed in plastic. "Cerise, tracheotomy tube, now."

Cerise tore at another plastic bag.

The red-haired woman crossed herself and sliced her husband's neck with the scalpel.

William escaped outside.


WILLIAM stood on the dock and watched hundreds of tiny worms crawl up the roots of the cypress. The worms glowed with gentle pastel colors: turquoise, lavender, pale lemon. The entire pond was bathed in the eerie glow. He once had a drink in a bar with LED glasses that lit up when you tapped the bottom. The effect was strikingly similar.

He'd waited on the dock for at least two hours. At

first he caught brisk orders filtering through the walls from the inside, then magic had brushed against him. Now all was quiet. He couldn't tell if the gray man had survived. William hoped he had. The gray man had children, and children had to have fathers.

He had no father. He'd never find him, even if he wanted to look for him, which he didn't. At Hawk's some changelings had talked about finding their parents. William saw no point in it. Why? When he was twelve, he'd broken into the archive at the academy and read the records. His father hadn't stuck around to see him born. His mother gave him up as soon as she was strong enough to walk after giving birth. That was the Adrianglian No Questions policy. If a woman had a changeling child, she could give her baby up, no questions asked. The state would assume responsibility for the kid. They would stick him into Hawk's and grow him into a monster.

He'd been whipped for breaking in. It was worth it. Before he'd wondered if he had a family. Afterward he knew. Nobody wanted him. Nobody was waiting for him. He was alone.

Steps approached. William straightened. The door swung open, and Urow's wife came out and leaned on the rail next to him.

Up close she wasn't as pretty as the picture made her out to be. Her skin stretched too tightly over her sharp features and bony face. She reminded him of a haggard fox, driven crazy by her pups.

Cerise was much prettier.

"I was short with you back there," she said. "I didn't mean to be."

"Will your husband make it?"

"The worst has passed. He is sleeping now. The swelling has dropped and we took the tube out."

"That's good," William said to say something.

Urow's wife swallowed. "Cerise said you saved my husband. Our family owes you a debt."

What was she going on about . . . The rope, William remembered. "I shot at the rope and happened to hit it. No debt."

The woman straightened. A spark of pride flared in her eyes. "Yes, we do. And we always pay our debts. You're called William?"

"Yes."

"My name is Clara. I'm going to return the favor, William. In the morning, we'll get our fastest rolpie and our best boat, and my sons will take you back to town."

"I can't do that."

She nodded. "Yes, Cerise said you're invited to the main house. Don't go."

Now that was interesting. "Why not?"

Clara sighed. "Cerise is a beautiful girl. Woman, I should say, she is twenty-four now. Striking. But you have to understand something about Cerise: she is a Mar. Mars are loyal to the family first."

"You're a Mar."

She nodded. "Yes. And I'm loyal to the family. They treat my husband as if he's one of them. It's not every clan that will take in a half-thoas bastard. They treat my children well, too."

Her gaze flicked to the base of the tree, where one of her sons climbed out of the water to sit on the roots. "My problems with the Mars are complicated. You don't need to know them. If you go to the Rathole, there will be no turning back, William. We have our own law here in the Mire. We do a lousy job of enforcing it, but we manage better than other places in the Edge, from what I've heard. You aren't one of us. Your clothes are good, and you hold yourself like you aren't from around here. The Mire law won't shield you. You go to the Rathole, and if you step an inch out of line, Cerise or one of her cousins will cut your throat with a pretty knife and bury you in the mud. They won't lose any sleep over it. You seem like a decent man. Walk away. It's about to get real bloody down there between the Mars and the Sheeriles, and it's not your fight."

She was wrong. It was his fight. Until William figured out how Cerise's parents were connected to the Hand, he had to stick to her like glue. He wouldn't leave her now anyway. Not after he'd seen the way she fought. But he wasn't about to explain that to anyone.

"Thanks for the warning," he told her.

She shook her head. "You're a fool. Cerise will never fall for an outsider."

"I don't expect her to fall," he said.

Clara slumped over the rail. "Well, I've tried."

"Why are you with Urow?" William asked.

She looked up and he saw warmth in her eyes. "You could get shot for a question like that."

With what? "I don't see any rifles."

"You're an odd man, William."

She didn't know the half of it.

"Why do you want to know?" Clara asked.

He saw no point in lying. "Because he has someone and I don't."

Another of Urow's kids dropped from the branches, swam across the pond, and sat next to his brother. That, plus the youngest one inside, made three. They'd all gathered around him to protect him. His own pack.

Clara sighed. "I've had men before him. Some were nice, some were bastards. But when I'm with him, he treats me like I'm his world. I know that no matter what happens, he will do all he can to keep me and the kids safe. His all might not be enough, but no matter how bad it gets, he will never run off and leave me to pick up the pieces. He will never hurt me."

There had to be more to it than that. "And is that enough?"

She smiled. "That's more than most people have. They're alone in the world, but I'm not. When I lay in his arms at night, there is no safer place. Besides, what would that big lug do without me? I let him go away for four days by himself, and he gets himself shot."

The smile drained from her face.

She'd thought of something bad. William focused on her face. "What is it?"

"If you're bound and determined to go down to the Rathole, you need to know this: thoas aren't common to the Mire. Someone told those men my husband was meeting Cerise down by Sicktree. Someone who knew what copper does to a thoas."

A traitor, William realized. She was trying to tell him there was a traitor in Cerise's family.

"She will go down there and start a witch hunt. Don't let yourself get caught up in it. Don't let yourself be used. Let my kids take you back to town. You have nothing to gain and everything to lose."

Cerise walked out on the dock.

Clara's face shut down. "Are you leaving?"

"Yes," Cerise said.

"Not while it's dark? It's pitch-black out there."

"It will be fine," Cerise said.

Urow's youngest son had followed her out. Gaston, William remembered.

"Lagar sent people out to watch the waterways." Gaston's voice was a deep guttural snarl. Trying to make himself seem older, like his father. If he were a cat, he would've arched his back and puffed out his fur. "Ry said he saw Peva out in the Mire."

"The court is tomorrow," Cerise said. "If I wait, I won't make it to the hearing. I'm late enough as is." Her gaze flickered to William. He looked into her dark eyes and lost his train of thought.

*Want.*

His ears heard her speak, but his brain took a couple of seconds to break the words down to meaning.

"If you would rather stay . . ."

"No." He walked down the dock and stepped into the boat. He had to figure out some way to keep her from catching him off-guard like this.

Cerise hesitated. "Clara, at first light, you should come, too."

"Don't be ridiculous." Clara crossed her arms.

"The Hand has a tracker," Cerise said. "He may follow us here."

"The Hand wants you, not us."

"It's not safe here."

Clara raised her chin. "You may be in charge of the family, and if Urow was awake, he might listen to you, but he isn't awake and I'm not about to take orders from the likes of you in my own house. Be on your way."

Cerise clenched her teeth and climbed into the boat. Anger rolled off her in waves. She touched the reins, and the rolpie took off, pulling them across the pond.

"Why doesn't she like you?" William asked.

Cerise sighed. "Because of my grandfather. He came from the Weird. He was a very smart man. He taught me and all of my cousins. We don't have normal school here in the Mire. Some people can't even read. But our family had Grandfather. We know some things that most Edgers don't, and that makes us different."

"Like what?"

Cerise switched to Gaulish. *"Like speaking other languages. Like knowing the basics behind the magic theories."*

*"Anyone can learn another language,"* William told her in Gaulish. *"It's not difficult."*

She peered at his face. *"You're full of surprises, Lord Bill. I thought you were Adrianglian."*

*"I am."*

*"Your Gaulish has no accent."*

He overlaid a thick coastal drawl over the Gaulish words. *"Is that better, mademoiselle?"*

She blinked those huge eyes, and he switched to a harsher Northern dialect. *"I can do a fur trapper, too."*

*"How do you do that?"*

*"I have a really good memory,"* he told her in refined upper-class Gaulish.

She matched his accent. *"I have no doubt of that."*

Her grandfather must've been a noble and from the East, too. She stretched her *a*'s. William filed it away for further consideration.

*"That's really impressive,"* she said.

Ha! He'd broken bones, killed an altered human, carried her rhino of a cousin, and she didn't blink an eye. But the moment he said two words in another language, she decided to be impressed.

Cerise dropped into Adrianglian again. "People like Clara don't like it. She thinks we 'put on airs,' as she says, as if what we can do somehow makes her less. She is right, you know. You're heading straight into the den of cutthroats. You should've taken her up on her offer and gone back to town."

She'd heard their conversation. William shook his head. He had a mission to complete, and if he walked away now, he would never see her again. "I said I would come with you. If I don't, who'll protect you?"

Her lips curved a little. "You saw me fight. Do you think I need protection, Lord Bill?"

"You're good. But the Hand is dangerous, and they have numbers on their side." He waited for her to bristle, but she didn't. "Besides, you're my ride to a safe, warm house, where it's dry and I might be given hot food. I have to take care of you, or I might never have a decent meal again."

Cerise tossed her head back and laughed softly. "I'll make an Edger of you yet, before this is over."

He liked the way she laughed, when her hair fell to the side and her eyes lit up. William looked away, before he did something stupid. "You have a plan about the sniper?"

She nodded at the corpse. "I think we should let the dead man do the work."

William glanced at the hunter and bared his teeth at the corpse.

# TEN

THE door opened silently under pressure from Spider's hand, admitting him into the hothouse. Fifty feet of glass sheltered a narrow strip of soil divided by a path in two. During the day sunlight flooded the hothouse, but now only the weak orange radiance of the magic lamps nourished the greenery. The previous owner of the mansion had used the hothouse to coax cucumbers out of the Mire's soil; he would've been shocked to discover the oddities that filled it now.

Spider surveyed the twin lines of plants and saw Posad's misshapen form, hunched over by the roots of a vernik midway down the path. A large bucket and a wheelbarrow sat next to him.

Spider strode toward the gardener, the gravel crunching under his feet. Posad dipped his small, almost feminine left hand into a bucket and administered a handful of black oily mud to the soil around the roots of a young tree. Translucent blue, it stood seven feet tall, spreading perfectly formed leafless branches.

The blue branches leaned toward Spider. Tentatively, like a shy child, one touched his shoulder. He offered his hand and the branches nuzzled his palm.

He plucked a bag of feed from the wheelbarrow and offered a handful of grainy gray powder to the tree. A small branch brushed it, scooping the powder up with tiny slits in its bark. Its fellows reached to his palm, and the entire tree bent closer to the food.

Posad continued working the mud into the soil with a three-pronged garden fork. "You spoil him," he said.

"I can't help it. He is so polite." Spider fed the last of the feed to the tree and shook his hands to the remaining branches. "Sorry, fellows. All gone."

The branches brushed his shoulders as if in gratitude, and the tree righted itself. Spider watched the grains of feed float down the trunk, opaque and glowing like snowflakes turned into tiny stars by light.

The tree was vital to fusion. Only with it could John combine Genevieve's body with the plant tissue. The process would destroy her will and ensure complete compliance. The fusion carried its own dangers, Spider reflected. Genevieve could lose all cognitive ability, which would make her useless to him. She could retain too much will, and then she would try to murder him. But he had little choice in the matter. The diary was simply too important.

Posad swung the rag over his shoulder and pushed the wheelbarrow forward. The growth on his back and right side had gotten larger in the last few days, the way it always did when the colony was about to split. Thick purple veins clasped the flesh of the hump under the pink, glistening skin. It drew the eye.

Like most of the Hand's altered humans, Posad had been conceived as a weapon. He was meant to be the Bee Master, commanding swarms of deadly insects. In combat conditions the idea proved grossly impractical, but Posad found his niche, taking care of the plants that provided them with chemicals for alteration.

"I can't find Lavern," Posad said, brushing the dirt from his pants with his shovel-large right hand.

Spider pondered that for a moment. Lavern was one of their strongest hunters but more unstable than most. He showed cannibalistic tendencies, which meant he was close to being replaced. He was deployed only under strict supervision, and as far as Spider knew, Lavern shouldn't have left the house.

"Do tell," Spider said.

Posad grimaced. "Karmash said to keep an eye out. Lavern was fine last night, but he isn't fine now."

His second in command had sent Lavern out. Spider felt a wave of fury begin to swell and counted to three in his head. "Are you sure?"

"The Goldmint isn't picking him up. Come, see for yourself."

They walked down the path. The wheelbarrow creaked with steady regularity, the sound of worn wheels mixing with the dry scratch of gravel.

The stench of old urine hit Spider's nostrils. The path turned, and they halted before an enormous blossom. Seven feet wide and pale yellow in color, it hugged the ground, rising to Spider's waist. Boils, as big as his fist and filled with murky liquid, covered the thick flaps of the meaty petals. A network of pale false stamens rose to the ceiling, anchoring itself to the wooden framework of the greenhouse roof.

Up close the reek of sewage squeezed moisture from Spider's eyes. He stared into the tangled web of the filaments, seeking the true stamens among the mess of the false. He counted thirty-one. The thirty-second stamen drooped to the side, its antler thick with white fuzz. The stamen had matured and produced pollen. The link between Lavern's magic and the flower no longer suppressed its development.

"Lavern is dead," Posad said. "I thought you should know."

Spider nodded. The gardener reached over and hacked the stamen off with a short thick knife. The second man they had lost in the Mire since Cerise had left the Rathole. First Thibauld, who failed to report in and whose stamen had been cut yesterday. Now Lavern, who should have been safe at base.

Spider left the hothouse, striding briskly to his study. A small rush basket perched at the bottom of the staircase. He looked at it for a second and climbed the stairs. Two more baskets sat on the landing. He passed them and reached the upstairs hallway. More items woven of rush littered the narrow corridor. Stacks of carriers, linen hampers, and bread bowls leaned against the walls; round waste bins set into each other formed rush colonnades; intricate hampers vied with flower panniers for space. Their dried plant odor mixed with the stench of algae that always permeated the house.

Spider growled under his breath, dodged a tower of round planters teetering precariously with his every step, and pushed into the small room that served as the reception area for his office. Veisan hunched in her chair, her fingers plaiting the rushes into a rug. A heap of rushes lay at her feet next to an equally large pile of baskets.

At his approach, Veisan surged to her feet, her strong hands tearing the braided rug. "M'lord!"

"Have Karmash see me," he ordered.

"Yes, m'lord."

A huge rush creation resembling a hollow duck sat between him and the door. Spider kicked it into the corner.

"And stop cluttering the place. We're not basketry merchants."

"Yes, m'lord."

He entered his study and walked past the rectangle of a massive antique table to the window. Pitch-black. It took a fraction of a breath for his enhanced eyes to adjust, and then the darkness blossomed, unfolding before him like a flower to reveal the strand of cypresses next to the flooded plain.

Karmash had disobeyed him. Yet again.

Spider's anger pushed his senses into overdrive, as the implanted glands squirted catalysts into his bloodstream. He unlatched the frame and swung the window open. A cascade of night scents and noises washed over him. His acute hearing caught Karmash's particular gait, and he faced the door. The steps drew closer, and Spider smelled the musky scent of the breaker's sweat.

"Enter," he barked. There was a momentary pause. The door swung open. Karmash stepped inside, his hulking form dwarfing the doorway, and shut the door behind him. His white hair dripped moisture. Spider's nostrils caught a hint of swamp water.

"Were you swimming?" Spider asked.

"Yes, m'lord."

"Was the water warm?"

"No, m'lord." The big man shifted from foot to foot.

"So it was more of a brisk, invigorating kind of experience?"

"Yes, m'lord."

"I see."

He turned to the table and stared at the array of papers. He could hear the elevated tempo of Karmash's heartbeat.

"My lord, I'm very sorry . . ."

Spider smashed his fist into the table. The thick top board broke with a wooden scream. The drawers burst open, releasing a flood of loose papers, small boxes, and metal ink jars. A pungent cloud of expensive incense billowed from the wreckage. Spider seized half of the ruined table, top-board, drawers and all, and hurled it across the room. It crashed against the wall and shattered in an explosion of splinters.

Spider turned on his heel, slowly, deliberately. All blood drained from Karmash's face, and his skin matched his hair in whiteness. Spider took two steps to the remaining table piece and studied it.

"I'm disappointed in you," he said.

Karmash opened his mouth to answer and closed it. Spider perched on the edge of the table wreck and looked at him. Karmash's skin smelled of fear. It shuddered in his eyes, broke through in the clenched fingers of his big hands, showed itself in the way he bent his knees lightly, ready to run. Spider studied that fear and drank it in. It tasted sweet like a well-aged wine.

"Let's go over this again," Spider said, pronouncing the words with a glass-sharp clarity in that patient, slow tone one used with a disobedient child or a woman one desired to infuriate. "Which part of my instructions wasn't clear to you?"

Karmash swallowed. "All parts were clear, m'lord."

"They mustn't have been, since your actions didn't match my words. A miscommunication has occurred. Let's pin it down. Reiterate what I ordered you to do."

Spider stared at Karmash, hard, unblinking. Their gazes locked, and Spider saw terror wash away any semblance of thought from Karmash's eyes. The big man snapped into panicked stiffness. Karmash opened his mouth. No sound came. Sweat broke at his hairline and slid across pallid skin to the shield of white bushy eyebrows.

"Go ahead," Spider said.

Karmash strained and forced a small word from his mouth. "You . . ."

"I can't hear you."

Karmash glanced away, muscles knotted along his jaw. He blinked rapidly, rigid as a board. Spider studied his neck, imagined himself reaching out, grasping the throat in the steel hold of his hand, crushing the windpipe until the cartilage popped with a light crunch under his fingers.

Karmash tried again. "You told me . . ."

"Yes?"

The voice caught in the big man's throat. He stared at the floor, his eyes wide and almost black from the dilated pupils.

Too easy. Cringe, Karmash. Cringe and submit.

Karmash swayed a little. His nostrils didn't flutter—he had forgotten to breathe. Another dozen heartbeats and he would faint. Spider toyed with the idea of bringing him to that point and decided against it with some regret. Too much trouble to wait for Karmash to come to.

"How long will you keep me waiting?" He let his tone and his stare ease just a fraction.

A fraction was enough. Karmash's knees trembled. His nostrils flared, drawing the air in a frenzied rhythm, and Karmash shuddered, every nerve and muscle shaking. For a moment he looked limp like a rag doll, ready to come apart.

Spider waited. The second stage of fear, the release. Petrify the body in a panicked freeze, and the mind locked as well, cycling on the same thought. Release the body, and logic came back with ready fluidity. It was an animal response, a defensive mechanism of Mother Nature, who realized that given a chance, her bastard children would think themselves into the ground, so she freed them of the handicapping burden of their minds in times of imminent danger. *At the core, we're but animals,* Spider thought. *Come on, Karmash. Obey and don't make me bare my teeth and roll you on your back again. I enjoy it entirely too much for my own good.*

"You told me to find the girl," Karmash's voice came in a shaky gush.

"And what did you do?"

"I sent Lavern to fetch her."

Spider put the fingers of his hands together, making a tent, and touched his index fingers to his lips, as if thinking. "So let me see if I got this right. I told you to find the girl, and you sent the dumbest, the most contumacious hunter we have. A hunter who has been twisted by his upgrades to the point of becoming fond of human flesh. Is that right?"

"Yes."

"Suppose he did somehow manage to disarm Cerise Mar, although how he would accomplish this escapes me. Suppose he did apprehend her. What made you think that he would deliver her safe and healthy instead of dropping her withered husk on my doorstep?"

"I thought . . ." Karmash hesitated.

"No, please continue. I'm extremely interested in your thought process."

"I thought Lavern would be sufficient, m'lord, since she was only a civilian. I told him it was his chance to rehabilitate himself. I was wrong."

Spider closed his eyes and let out a deep cleansing sigh. Only a civilian. Of course.

"M'lord . . ."

Spider raised his hand. "Shhh. Don't talk now."

Karmash's size had gotten away from him again. Occasionally the man's obsession with his own strength cut off the flow of air to his brain. His only saving grace was that at the moment Spider had nobody to replace him.

"Let me explain something to you," Spider said, slowly, with gravity, making sure every word was understood. "I hate the swamp. I hate the way it looks. I hate the way it smells. It repulses me. I'm forced into inactivity until John finishes fusing Genevieve, and I sit here, restless and bored, while my best slayer is compulsively braiding rush baskets on my doorstep, because unless she occupies herself with something intricate, she might snap and slaughter the lot of us."

Spider smiled, baring his teeth. "And you, whether by ignorance, ineptitude, or design, seem determined to keep me here longer than necessary through botching up tasks I give you. Don't give me an excuse to take an interest in you, Karmash. Don't make yourself the thing I choose to shrug off my boredom. You won't like it."

Karmash's eyes widened.

"That's not an order," Spider said. "Just a bit of friendly advice." He stood up and walked to the large bookcase set against the back wall. A mismatched assortment of books filled the shelves, some tall, some short. He ran his fingers along the tattered spines and pulled out a thick leather volume. Gilded golden letters curved across the front page: *The Empire: The Third Invasion.*

He handed it to Karmash. "I realize that you weren't present during the apprehension of the Mars. I wish to correct that oversight. Read this. It will give you a basic understanding of what Cerise Mar is and the casualties we can expect when dealing with her. And this is an order."

Karmash's long fingers closed about the book. Spider held on to his end, fixed Karmash with a stare, and let go.

"I wish you had seen it," he said. "Gustave Mar was truly a sight to behold."

"I'm sorry I missed it, m'lord."

They had missed the one opportunity to grab Cerise, and she was likely gone behind the shield of warding spells that guarded her family house. Still, a chance that she would leave the compound for some reason existed, and his people had to have something to do. Spider nodded toward the map on the wall, and Karmash obediently turned to it.

"There is a small road running southeast from the Mar compound."

"The White Blossom Trail, m'lord?"

"It's the only land route from the Rathole to the town. The rest, as you can see, is swamp. I want you to put Vur and Embelys right there. They do nothing but watch. If she leaves the compound, one must follow, the other must report in."

"Yes, m'lord."

"No mistakes this time."

"Yes, m'lord."

"You may go."

Karmash shifted from foot to foot. "Do you wish me to send a retrieval team to find Lavern's body?"

"No. I'll go myself. I think the fresh air would do me good."

Karmash fled.

Spider sighed. Perhaps the girl would make a mistake. He hoped so. He wanted to sit her down and try to figure out how her mind worked. She would make a fascinating conversationalist.

Spider walked over to the door and opened it. Veisan dropped the load of baskets she was carrying and stood at attention, her collection of rolled blue-gray locks spilling onto her shoulders like a nest of thin snakes.

"Have the wall repaired. I'll need a new table, too." A pang of regret stung him—it had been a very nice table.

"Yes, m'lord." Her lapis lazuli eyes watched him from a face the color of raw meat.

"And I'm sorry about the baskets. You can continue weaving. I was tired and under a lot of stress."

"Thank you, m'lord."

He nodded and walked past her.

She turned her head, following his movement. "Where are you going, m'lord?"

"Out. I'm going out. I'll be back soon." He kept walking. Perhaps he could kill something during his search for Lavern's corpse. He was so mercilessly bored.

# ELEVEN

**PEVA** Sheerile sat leaning on the trunk of a slash pine
and watched the dark water. Around him bronze-flicked
feathers of rust ferns rustled gently, swayed by the night
breeze. To the left a bush-brow owl hooted, trying to
scare shrews from their hiding places. An old ervaurg
lay in the water like a half-sunken log.

Peva had staked out the stream early in the evening.
The second fastest waterway to the Rathole from Sicktree, it would be the one he himself would've taken in
Cerise's place. The Rat bitch was pressed for time. She
had a court hearing in the morning, and since the Ridge-
back Stream was the fastest and thus too obvious, and
Priest's Tongue was too crooked and slow, she would
pass this way. The night swamp being too chancy to
travel by boat, she would try to creep in at first light,
quiet and humble, thinking she was slick, and she would
meet Wasp and her bolts. He patted the crossbow's walnut tiller. Wasp was thirsty, and Cerise had much blood
to offer.

It would be good to dump her body by the Rathole.
With his bolt still in it. He tried to picture Richard's face,
grief-shocked from its usual haughty calm into a slack
mask, and grinned. It was high time that bastard recalled
who he was—a mud rat, just like dozens of others all
swarming, snapping, breeding in the muck of the Mire
together. None better, none worse, all mongrel Edgers
together. Yes, high time.

In his mind Richard's face somehow morphed into La-

gar's. The joy fled. Damn. He wondered what he would
read in his brother's face when he showed him the body.
On second thought, it would be best if Lagar didn't see
her corpse at all. There was no need.

The thing between Lagar and Cerise puzzled him. It
wasn't like she would ever roll on her back for him.
Hell, it wasn't like Lagar even tried. Never bought her
presents or flowers or whatever it was women liked, but
Cerise would pass by and Lagar would look. And there
was that damn dance. Spinning by the fire, Lagar drunk,
his eyes crazy, Cerise grinning. Wasn't that something?
He pictured them side by side and had to admit to himself that if those two bred, they'd make a pretty litter.

In another life.

No, in another world. Even if they weren't feuding, it
would be a warm day in hell before their mother would
let someone like Cerise into the family. The old hag wasn't
keen on competition. If she had her way, none of them
would ever marry, unless it was to a slow deaf-mute.

It was for the best, Peva decided. Kill Cerise quick,
dump the body, and tell Lagar it's been done and done
clean with no pain.

A trace of movement flickered through the narrow break
in the trees, where the stream made a sharp bend. He concentrated. A shadow darker than the others was sliding
along the water. A boat, and before dawn, too. Damn. The
brazen bitch had chanced the night after all.

Instantly he was hot: his heart thudded, his mouth
went dry. The excitement surged in him. He leaned forward, alert eyes fixed on the dark silhouette at the bow.
His breathing slowed. Peva aimed. The figure on the
cutter sat slumped over. Tired from the sleepless night. It
was all too easy.

He held her in his sight for a brief delicious moment.
In that precious instant they were linked, he and his target,
by a bond as ancient as the hunt itself. He felt her life,
quivering like a fish on a line, and drank in the rush it

brought him. Only two things made man equal to Gods: creating life and destroying it.

Slowly, regretfully, Peva squeezed the trigger.

The bolt punched the silhouette in the chest, knocking it to the deck.

"Back to the mud, Cerise," Peva whispered.

Something whistled past him, smashing into the pine trunk with a loud thump. The night exploded with white light. Blinded, Peva dropped into a crouch, fired in the direction of the boat, and rolled into the ferns. A magic bolt. Damn.

A whine sliced through the air. He heard two solid thuds: bolt heads punching the ground where he had sat a moment ago. Circles of searing white light swam before his eyes. Peva reloaded on feel alone.

His heart fluttered as if a small bird were caught in the cage of ribs and now fought to escape in a frantic frenzy. He caught his breath and forced himself to slow down.

Hugging the ground, Peva reached with one hand toward the area he had guessed the bolts had hit. His hand found a shaft. He pulled it free, letting his fingers explore the length of the bolt. Short shaft. He'd almost been hit with a short bolt.

Cerise couldn't have him from ten yards with a short bolt. The bitch had help. She must've dropped a bowman off on shore, and Peva had given himself away with that shot.

Peva's fingers touched the bolt head. Smooth, balanced. Professional. Too good for a casual bowman. Peva dropped the bolt before he cut himself on the razor-sharp edges. Feathery ferns brushed his face. He still couldn't see. To move was to die. To stay was to die, too—eventually the bowman would figure out where he hid. He felt the bolt coming, felt it speeding along that same ancient connection he had savored earlier. Peva dashed to the side, fired two shots at a wide angle, and reloaded again.

The blinding fire in his eyes began to dim. He saw the ferns, dark strokes against the bright haze. A few more breaths and he would have his vision back. He had to buy some time. To the left, a dim outline of a large cypress loomed, its base bloated and thick enough to shelter him.

Peva Sheerile wouldn't die in the swamp today.


CERISE halted in the sea of rust ferns. Peva died on his knees, hugging the cypress. William had pinned him to the tree with two bolts, one through the neck and one through the chest. Death turned Peva's face into a bloodless mask. She looked into his eyes, hollow and sad in the moonlight, and felt guilty for no reason.

Cerise looked away. That was the dumbest thing. The man would've killed her without a moment's thought, but she'd known him for so long, it was almost like family dying. What would it be like when one of the family did die?

She swallowed. Now wasn't the time to lose it.

William walked out of the ferns, sliding bolts into a leather quiver. Cerise tensed. She'd watched the whole thing from the boat, hiding behind the body of the Hand's spy. She'd guessed that Peva would set up an ambush somewhere along this route. Lagar would give him plenty of people, but Peva, the arrogant snob that he was, would send them off to cover other routes, so he could get the kill all by himself. She and William did the simple math: one man was easier to take down than several. They'd set the corpse up as the rolpie driver, she stayed low, steering, while William had trailed the boat along the shore for the past mile. The moment Peva showed himself, William would take him down. Except it didn't quite go that way.

"You made him run," she said, keeping her voice neutral.

William gripped the bolt in Peva's back. The dark shaft was deep in there. Only the fletch and about an inch stuck out. It would take a lot of strength to pull it out. He strained and the body released the bolt with a wet sucking sound.

"Did you have fun playing with him?"

"I didn't do it for fun." William wiped the bolt on Peva's back and examined the sharp head. "I fired the flare bolt to blind him and then ran him around on an off chance he had some help hiding in the bushes. When he didn't flush out any friends, I killed him."

He reached for the second bolt. The shaft had gone clear through Peva's neck and into the tree, at least three inches. She probably could've stood on it and it wouldn't have budged. Mikita with all of his strength wouldn't be able to wrench it out.

William's fingers closed on the bolt. He put his foot against Peva's back and grunted, his face jerking with strain. The bolt popped out of the cypress. William sniffed it and grimaced. "The head's bent, but the shaft is still good."

William wasn't human. Couldn't be.

She'd suspected it before, the first time at the Alpha house, because he was dead certain it was empty. The fight with Kent made her wonder, but the battle with the hunter had settled it. The way William had moved sent ice down her spine—too fast, too expert—but the look on his face cinched it. They were facing a human altered beyond what she would have guessed possible, and William had looked ice-cold, as if emotion was beyond him. She would've settled for fear or anger, but what she saw was the ruthless calculation of a cunning predator. He surveyed his prey, decided that he would win the fight, and proceeded to do so. And now she had indisputable proof. His strength wasn't beyond human limits, but it was beyond his lean body.

Cerise took a step back.

William went very still.

She had to settle it now. "You lied to me."

His eyes were clear and cold. Calculating. "Fine, here

is the truth: I did enjoy it. He wanted to kill you and I killed him instead. I didn't tell you, because I don't want you to be scared of me."

"That's not what I meant."

"What did you mean?"

"Your story about the lost ring and searching for it is pure bullshit."

"Ah. That."

He jerked the crossbow up. A black bolt stared at her.

Cerise clenched her sword. Magic sparked deep in her, singing through her body, and leaked from her eyes and the fingers of her right hand onto the sword. A brilliant point of white ran along the blade and died.

William's eyes glowed like two amber coals. She met his gaze and flinched. No emotion reflected in the amber, only intelligence, cruel in a way the eyes of a hunting Mire cat were cruel. She saw no worry, no softness, no thoughts at all, only waiting. He seemed barely human now, not a man but some feral *thing*, knitted of darkness and biding his time for an opportunity to pounce.

William glanced at her sword. His upper lip rose, showing her his teeth. *My, my, Lord Bill, what* big *fangs you have.* That was all right. She wasn't Red Riding Hood, she wasn't scared, and her grandmother could curse his ass so hard, he wouldn't know which way was up for a week.

William nodded at her blade. "That's what I thought. You cut through bones like butter, because you stretch your flash onto your sword."

"And it's such a nice flash, too. All pretty and white." *And it will cut you to pieces.*

"Won't do much against a bolt in your chest."

"How do you know I can't shield myself with the flash?"

The thing that was William chuckled low. "You can't do it. It would be nice if you could, but we both know you can't."

*Bull's-eye, William.* Blade flashing took years of training and every ounce of her concentration. As long as she flashed, her blade would cut through anything, but she could only do it for a split second at a time. Flash defense was beyond her. He'd just pegged her for a one-trick pony, and he was right.

Still, there was no reason she couldn't bluff. "So eager to die?"

"If you can stop my bolt, show me."

*Oh, crap.* Cerise tensed, ready to dive into the stream behind her the moment he fired. "Any time."

William just stood there. The amber eyes tracked her every twitch, but he showed no sign of moving.

It dawned on her that if he were going to fire, he would've done so already. "You won't shoot me, will you?"

William growled. "If I do, you'll be dead."

And why would her being dead bother him? True, he thought she was pretty, but she wasn't naive enough to think that would stop him.

Cerise took an experimental step back.

The crossbow shifted a quarter of an inch. He was aiming for her legs. "Don't move."

"Let's part our ways here, William. You go one way and I go the other."

"No."

"Why not?"

He said nothing.

"What if I run?"

He leaned forward. "That would be a mistake, because I would chase you."

*Oh, dear Gods.*

His voice was wistful and tinted with an odd longing, as if he were already running through the dark woods in his mind. The tiny hairs on the back of Cerise's neck rose. Whatever she did, she couldn't run, because he would love to chase her and she wasn't quite sure what would happen at the end of that chase. By the way he looked, he wasn't quite sure either, but he was pretty sure he would enjoy it.

A small part of her wanted to find out what it would be like to be chased by William through the Mire woods. What it would be like to be caught. Because he wasn't looking at her as if he wanted to kill her. He was looking at her as if he had something completely different in mind. All she had to do was dash into the woods. The thought of it sent tiny shivers down her spine and she wasn't sure if it was alarm or excitement.

She was in over her head. Just a smidgeon.

Cerise raised her eyebrows. "I've lived my whole life in this swamp. What makes you think you could catch me?"

William grinned, baring white teeth, and chuckled in his wolfish way. The quiet raspy sound made her shiver. In that moment Cerise knew with absolute certainty that he would stalk her, chase her, and catch her. She wouldn't get away. Not without a fight neither of them wanted.

Cerise glared back at him, right into those fiery eyes. He leaned forward a little, the hungry thing inside him focused on her completely.

He wanted her. She could see it in his eyes, in the way he held himself, loose and ready. It would take the slightest trigger, a smile, a wink, a hint, and he would close the distance between them and kiss her.

Warmth washed through her, followed by the prickly needles of adrenaline. One step forward. That was all she had to do. A month ago she would've taken that step without a moment's pause.

A month ago she wasn't responsible for her family. Now was no time to be selfish.

If either of them forced a fight, she would kill him, and she would regret not knowing why. Dealing with William was like playing with fire: no right way to do it.

"What would happen if you caught me?" Besides her slicing him to ribbons. Or losing all her sense.

"Run and you'll find out."

William took a small step forward.

Cerise jerked back. If he touched her, she would have

to make a decision: to cut or to seduce, and she didn't
know which way she would go.

The fire in his eyes sparked and died a little. "Nothing . . . untoward."

Cerise swallowed. She was wound so tight, the muscles in her legs hurt. Untoward? What the hell did that
mean, untoward? "Can you just answer the damn question
straight?" Her voice vibrated a note too high. Damn it.

William sighed. The feral edge slipped away. His
shoulders dropped slightly. He put the crossbow down.
"I won't hurt you. Don't be afraid. If you have to go, go.
I'll be good and won't chase you down. Straight enough
for you?"

He meant it, Cerise could see it in his face. He thought
she was scared of him and he backed down.

Tension leaked out of her. Suddenly she was tired.
"And what will you do here, alone in the swamp?"

He shrugged. "Find a way out."

Yeah, right. He would wander for days in the Mire.
She had no doubt he would survive, but he wouldn't make
it out anytime soon.

"Here is what I know: you're fast, you know about the
Hand, and you're trained to kill with your bare hands. You
look like you've been doing it for a while and it doesn't
bother you. I think you like it. And your eyes, they . . ."
She raised her hand to her face.

"What?"

"They glow."

He blinked. "I'm wearing lenses to keep that from happening."

"Well, they aren't working."

"No?"

She shook her head. "You got screwed."

"No point in keeping them in, then." He sat on a log,
pulled his lower eyelid down, fished a lens out, and tossed
it into the mud. The second followed. He raised his head
with obvious relief, like a kid who was told he could get
out of his church clothes. His eyes were actually light hazel,

and when he blinked, the amber glow rolled over his irises like fire.

In her head, Cerise walked over to him, put her arms around his neck, and kissed him, looking right into those wild eyes. And in her head it would have to stay. For now.

"Better?" she asked.

"Much." He sat there, blinking, crushed that his scheme had fallen apart. He looked . . . sad. One moment he was some sort of hellspawn with glowing eyes, the next he was a sack of gloom, and all of it looked and felt completely genuine.

She should've walked away, except that he knew the Hand, knew it better than anyone she could think of, probably better than anyone in the Mire, and she needed his knowledge desperately. Yes, that was it.

*Stop,* she told herself.

The path to becoming a flash fighter was paved with years of training, but it started with one simple rule: never lie to yourself. It meant accepting your true motivations, owning your emotions and desires without pretending they were noble or evil. It was easy to understand but hard to follow. Just like now.

She had to admit and accept the reality: William with his amber eyes and his wolfish laugh, crazy, lethal William, made her head spin. He was like a dangerous puzzle box full of razor blades—press the wrong switch and the blades would slice your fingers to ribbons. And she was the fool who couldn't wait to press the switches and find out the right one.

Cerise exhaled. She wanted him, fine. No use denying it. But that alone wasn't enough to let him into the house. Now that she admitted it, she had no trouble putting it aside.

"A man like you wouldn't be out in the Mire looking for some trinket, William. You lied to me, and I almost took you to my house, where my family lives. I can't afford to be lied to."

"Fair enough," he said.

"Still, you could've killed me when I slept. You didn't. You helped me hide from the Hand, and you saved my cousin. Level with me, William. Why are you here? Are you working for somebody? Tell me."

*Tell me because I don't want to leave you in this swamp. Tell me so I know we have a chance.*

"If you can't, no hard feelings. We'll go our separate ways from here. I'll even draw you a map to get you back to town. If you can't tell me why you've attached yourself to me, just say nothing. But don't lie to me, or I swear, you'll come to deeply regret it. I may work together with you, but I won't let you use me or my family." Cerise raised her chin. "What will it be?"

HE had to lie.

Cerise was a granddaughter of Louisiana bluebloods. They killed his kind in Louisiana. To her, he was an abomination.

In his head, William had somehow managed to gloss over that fact. But now it stared back at him. He would have to be very careful, William decided. She was scared enough as is. He would have to hide who he was until she was used to him.

He didn't mean to scare her, but damn, she would be fun to chase. He would give her a head start. And when he caught her, he would make sure she wouldn't want to run away again.

But she didn't run. She just stood there, waiting for his answer.

The Mirror would have to be kept out of it as well. The Hand was one rock, the Mirror was the other, and her family was caught in the middle as they clashed. Cerise would think he would use her—and he would—and she knew that in the greater scheme of things, a few Edgers mattered very little.

He had to lie.

That's what spies did—they lied to get what they wanted.

He had to be slick about it, because if he failed, she would wander off into the Mire, leaving him holding the severed end of their conversation, and he wouldn't do a damn thing about it. It would be a low thing to hurt her. She was protecting her family. If he had one, he would do exactly what she was doing.

He had to convince her that he was working for himself, out on his own personal goal of revenge. And that he was human.

William looked at her. "The man who took your parents is called Spider. I'm here to kill him."

Cerise blinked. "Why?

She had to ask that. William looked away at the river, trying to keep the memories under control. "Four years ago he slaughtered some children. They were important to me."

"Were they your children?" she asked softly.

He exhaled slowly, as the wild in him howled. "No. I don't have any family."

"I'm sorry," she said.

William almost snarled. He didn't want her to feel sorry for him. He wanted her to see that he was strong and fast and he could take care of himself. "The first time I got to him, he broke my legs." William got up, shrugged off his jacket, and pulled up his T-shirt, showing her the long scar that snaked its way up his back. "This was the second time. He had something on his knife, some sort of poison."

She took a step closer. "And what did you do to him?"

William smiled, remembering. "I beat the shit out of him with a boat anchor. Would've done him in, but he knocked me into the water and then the damn boat blew up. I was bleeding a bit by that time from the cut and my throat had closed up from the poison, so there wasn't much I could do about it."

"So you're thinking the third time might be the charm?" she asked.

It better be. "I'll kill him this time," he promised. Thinking about ripping Spider apart laced his voice with a happy lupine growl.

She took another step forward. Getting closer and closer. Another step and he would be in her striking range. She was sneaking up on him.

"How did you know Spider is in the Mire?"

He had to give her more information or she wouldn't believe him. "The man in Sicktree. The taxidermist."

"Zeke?"

"He works for me."

Her eyes went wide as saucers. "How?"

"Zeke has contacts in the Weird." Technically that was true. "People know I'm looking for Spider and will pay for the information." Also true. "He let his people know that Spider is in the Edge, and they got in touch with me." True again. The trick to lying was to tell the truth.

"So when the two of you went to the back . . ."

"He was explaining to me all about you and the Sheer-iles."

"Sonovabitch. And I stood there like an idiot, waiting for the two of you and thinking, 'He sure is taking his time. Zeke must be milking him for every coin he has.' You made me feel . . ."

He took a wide step and stood next to her. "Yes?"

She looked up at him. *Want. Want the woman, want, want, want . . .*

"You made me feel stupid." Her voice went soft. "Are you even a blueblood?"

"Technically."

"What does that mean?"

William smiled. "It means they call me Lord Sandine, but aside from that, I've got nothing. No power, no land, no status. I've got some money saved from the service, and most of it is on me right now." Well, that was an outright lie. The Mirror had supplied him with money.

"So you *were* a soldier?"

She didn't catch him. William nodded. "I was."

Her posture was still wary, and her eyes tracked his movements. But she no longer looked like she was about to bolt into the wilderness. He was going in the right direction.

"What unit did you serve in?"

"The Red Legion."

"The red devils?"

He nodded again. "Look, I want to kill Spider. The only lead I've got right now is you. Spider wants you, which means you're my bait."

"Don't I feel special." She cocked her to the side. "How do I know you didn't make the lot of it up?"

He spread his arms. "You could ask Zeke, who'll tell you the same story. If you've got a way of learning things outside the Edge, you could ask about the Massacre of Eight in the Weird. But all of that takes time. You need me, Cerise. You don't know how to fight the Hand. I do. We're on the same side."

"Is there anything else you need to tell me?"

*Every time I look at you, I have to put a leash on myself.* "No."

"If you lied to me, I'll hurt you," she promised.

He showed her his teeth. "You'll try."

She sighed. "You worry me, Lord Bill. You're trouble."

He won again. William hid a laugh. "You should be worried, and I am." He folded the arms of the crossbow and headed toward the boat.

She put her hand on her hip. "Where are you going?"

"To the boat. You called me Lord Bill again. That means we're cool."

Cerise slapped her forehead with the heel of her hand and followed him.

"Fine. I'll take you with me. But only because I don't want to run into the fight blind."

They walked to the boat side by side. He breathed in her scent, watching the way her long hair shifted as she moved. She was graceful and she stepped so carefully, picking her way along the mud, almost as if she was dancing. It finally sank in—he'd spend the next few days under her roof. In her house, filled with her scent. He would see her every day.

She would see him every day. If he played his cards right, she might even do more than see. He had to stay cool and bide his time. He was a wolf. He had no problem with patience.

"I just want to know one thing," Cerise said.

"Yes?"

"When you kill Spider, are you going to chop off his head and have Zeke stuff it to make sure he's really dead?"

# TWELVE

THE porch boards creaked under Lagar's foot. The whole manor was rotten. The inside of the house smelled musty, the paneling damp and slimy, dappled with black mildew stains.

He'd wanted the manor so much, he got in bed with the Hand for it. Fucking freaks. He shrugged his shoulders, trying to shed the memory of their magic, hot and sharp, brushing against him like a bunch of heated needles. And all for what? For this piece-of-shit house.

The only reason he'd wanted the damn house was because it belonged to Gustave. Gustave had everything: he ran his family and they worshipped him, he was respected, people asked him for advice . . . And Cerise lived in his house.

Chad appeared from behind the house, hands clutching the rifle.

"What is it?"

"I can't find Brent."

Lagar followed the guard around the house to a garden overgrown with weeds and ickberry. A small puddle, burgundy-dark in the gray dawn light, slicked the mud on the edge of the bushes. Blood.

Chad shifted from foot to foot. "I came to relieve him . . ."

Lagar raised his hand, shutting him up. Long scratches marked the wet slime, wide apart, driven deep by a massive weight. Footprints approached the tracks. Brent must've seen the scratches and hesitated in this spot. The momentary pause cost him his life. Something leapt at him and carried him off.

Behind him Chad shifted from foot to foot. "I thought maybe a Mire cat . . ."

"Too big." Lagar peered past the sea of weeds to the crumbled stone wall that separated the once cultivated piece of land from the pines. Quiet.

"Where is the rifle?" he thought out loud.

"Uh . . ."

"The rifle, Chad. Brent had one. Why would an animal take it?"

It began to drizzle. The rain wet the gray-green ickberry leaves, the red milkwort, the tall spires of laurel that kept their purple flowers locked in green against the rain. Cold wetness crept from Lagar's scalp down his neck and across his brow. He didn't bother wiping it away.

"Pair the men," Lagar said. "From now on, nobody stands watch or goes anywhere alone. Send Chrisom to town and have them buy some crvaurg traps."

"The nest kind or the shredders?"

"The shredders." There was no need to be subtle. "Put a shooter up in the attic to cover the garden, make three teams of two, and comb it. Let's see if we can find that rifle. After you're done searching, trap the place."

Lagar waved him off, and Chad departed at a brisk run. Lagar crouched by the tracks and spread his hand, measuring the distance between the scratches. The front paws were almost ten inches across. Lagar moved into the thicket. There it was, the deep indentations, marking a place where an animal had crouched. He glanced back to the claw marks. Seven and a half yards.

He touched the edges of the paw prints and dipped his fingers into the imprint to measure its depth. Round, thick fingers. If this was a cat, then it was male, four yards long and weighing near seven hundred pounds. His mind struggled to picture an animal that large. Was it something from the Weird? Why did it come here?

Lagar walked out of the thickets and rubbed the claw marks with the sole of his boot until only slick mud remained. Panic was the last thing they needed.

He paused before reaching the porch, stopping where mud had been churned by many feet two weeks ago. The rain had obliterated the tracks. They had taken Gustave down here. He fought for his freedom, fought for his wife, but he lost.

Lagar tugged at a loose strand of hair, thinking of the way Gustave looked when the web spawned by the Hand's magic finally let them wrestle the sword from his fingers. It had been a sweet sight, Gustave helpless in his fury, but they paid for it with four of their men.

Four men who worked for him. He knew their families. He gave their wives money for their dead husbands. The way Emilia Cook looked at him when he gave her her cut made him want to drown himself. Like he was the scum of the earth.

A crazy thought danced in his mind. Walk away, abandon the manor, leave the Mire, and go someplace new, where nobody knew him. He was barely twenty-eight.

Lagar hunched his shoulders. A sardonic smile tugged at the corners of his mouth. He had paid too much for this false diamond. Like a runner who had given all of himself to the race, he had reached his finish line but found he couldn't stop.

The sound of a horse at full gallop startled him. He ran to the porch in time to see Arig shoot by him on a gray gelding.

"Lagar!"

Unable to stop the horse, his brother circled the house, slowing down, and leaped to the ground, red-faced and huffing.

"What?"

"Mom says you got to go out in the swamp. Something happened to Peva."

\* \* \*

WILLIAM sat at the bow, as far away from the corpse
of the hunter as the length of the boat would allow. Why
she insisted on dragging it with them was beyond him.
He'd asked her about it, and she'd smiled and told him it
was a present for her aunt.

Maybe her aunt was a cannibal.

The rolpie pulled with steady force. There was a serene, almost severe beauty to the fog-smothered swamp,
a kind of somber, primeval elegance. The haze obscured
the chaotic vegetation, filtering it to individual congrega-
tions of plants. Isolated groups of cypresses adorned
with maiden hair moss loomed out of the fog and sank
back into it as the boat passed them. The water resembled quicksilver, a glossy, highly reflective surface that
masked the pitch-black depth.

"Is it deep here?" William wondered.

"No. Looks that way because of the peat in the bottom."

Magic brushed against him, like a gentle feather.
"What's that?"

Cerise smiled. "A marker. We're on my family's land,
getting close to the house. We've got the house and some
outlying land warded. Good wards, old, rooted into the
soil. They don't go very far, though."

He squinted at the shore. A large gray rock sat at the
edge of the water, about two feet tall and a foot wide. An
identical pale stone sat halfway in the water. Ward stones.
He'd seen them before: magic connected them like mushrooms in a mushroom ring, creating a barrier. Even Rose
had used them to protect the house and the boys. Rose's
ward stones were tiny, but they grew with time. These
looked centuries old.

"What about the river?" he asked.

"The river, too. There are ward stones crossing the
bottom. You can't get to the Rathole unless we want you
there. But the wards don't go very far. Most of our land
isn't covered."

That explained why Spider didn't just raid the house. A safe base was good. "What about your grandparents' house?"

She shook her head. "No wards there. Grandfather refused to have the place warded."

The fog retreated. They turned into a smaller stream. Cold drizzle sifted from the sky. William ground his teeth. Did it ever stop raining in this fucked-up place?

Being back at his trailer would've been very nice right now. He'd make himself a cup of good strong coffee and watch some TV. He'd bought a new season of *CSI* that begged to be cracked open. He liked *CSI*. It was like magic. If he felt in need of some comedy, he could always find *COPS*. He'd started watching the show to find out how good the Broken police were in case he had to have a run-in with them, but the shirtless drunken idiots proved too hilarious and stole the show. The only thing he'd learned about the cops was that they had to run a lot.

He pictured himself on the couch, Cerise tucked next to him. Nice. *Never happen,* he reminded himself.

He just wanted to be dry. Just for a few minutes. And to wash his hair. The pelt had to be kept clean or it would itch and get bugs in it. He didn't spend money on expensive toys, like pricy cars or phones, but he did buy decent shampoo and he went to a salon to have his hair cut. Salons smelled good, and the pretty women who cut his hair flirted with him and leaned close.

The constant dampness drove him crazy. At this rate, he'd sprout waterweeds on his head before the week was out. The next time he had to have a haircut, they'd have to trim the mushrooms from his scalp.

The stream opened into a cove, framed by pines and stout picturesque trees with round yellow leaves. William leaned to get a better look. Pretty.

A small dock protruded into the water, a natural extension of the dirt path that led up a hill. To the left a heavy wooden gate barred what was probably another stream.

He smelled rolpies. His ear caught the distant grunting squeals beyond the gate. The Edgers must've kept them penned up like cows.

A man stepped out onto the dock and looked at them. Black hair, fit, tall, about thirty. If they were in the Weird, William would've sworn he was looking at a blueblood. The man held himself very straight, taking up more space than his lean body needed and radiating enough icy, stuck-up elegance to give Declan's relatives a run for their money. William growled in his mind and pulled Declan out of the recesses of his memory. If this guy was a blueblood, he'd have to concentrate not to give himself away.

"That's Richard. My cousin," Cerise said.

A small mud-slathered creature sat by Richard's feet. He was lecturing it. William couldn't quite catch the words but it looked like a serious chewing out. William focused on the little beast. A kid. Looked like a girl, sitting with her knees clasped to her chest, long hair a mess of mud and leaves.

Cerise drew a deep breath. He glanced at her. She was looking at the little girl. Her black eyebrows knitted together. Her mouth quivered once, wanting to droop at the corners. He glimpsed sadness in her eyes. Then she hid it and pulled the smile on like a mask.

Richard's words floated down to them. ". . . absolutely not appropriate, especially hitting him in the head with a rock . . ."

The little girl saw them. She shoved past Richard and dove into the water. Richard stopped in mid-word.

"Oh, Lark," Cerise whispered.

The little girl swam through the water, limbs flashing. Cerise slowed the rolpie. The kid dove and scrambled onto the boat, wet and dripping mud. She lunged at Cerise and clutched at her, burying her face in Cerise's stomach. Cerise put her arms around the child and looked like she was about to cry. Her smile broke. She bit her lip.

"Don't leave," the girl whispered, her arms locked around Cerise.

"I won't," Cerise said softly. "I'm home now. It will be okay. You're safe."

"Don't leave."

"I won't."

The kid looked like a stray cat, half-starved and skittish. She clasped on to Cerise, as if she were her mother, and she smelled of fear.

William reached over, took the reins from Cerise's hands, and slapped them on the water. The rolpie pulled, and he guided the boat to the dock. The boat bumped against the support beams, shuddering. Richard leaned over, and William handed him the mooring line.

"Hello," Cerise's cousin said.

"Hi."

"Lark, you have to let go now," Cerise murmured gently.

The kid didn't move.

"I can't carry you to the house. You're too big. And if I did, the other kids would make fun of you. You have to be strong now. You must let go and stand on your own feet. Here, hold my hand."

Lark pulled away. Cerise took her hand. "Shoulders back. Look at the house. You own this house and this land. Walk like you mean it."

Lark straightened her spine.

"That's it. Show no weakness." Cerise gripped her hand, and they stepped onto the dock in unison.

William picked up their bags and followed. Richard strode next to him on long legs. He walked with a light step and good balance. A sword fighter, William decided.

"My name is Richard Mar. A pleasure to make your acquaintance."

Like someone had plucked the man out of the Weird and dropped him into the Edge, with all his manners intact. Except bluebloods didn't wear black jeans.

William raised his chin a slight fraction, channeling Declan. "William Sandine."

"Lord Sandine?" Richard asked.

Go figure. He must be doing better than he thought with his disguise. "Occasionally. When it suits me."

"I hate to pry, but how did you and Cerise meet?"

"Something tells me you love to pry."

Richard permitted himself a small spare smile.

Cerise turned around. "We got stranded together coming in from the Broken. He's here to hunt the Hand."

Richard's expression remained polite but impassive. "Oh?"

"He saved Urow," she said.

No change. "What happened?"

"The Hand shot him with a copper harpoon."

A flicker of fury shot through Richard's eyes. William filed it away. The man had a temper.

"I see," Richard said. "So you're our guest and ally, then, Lord Sandine?"

"Just William will do, and yes."

"Welcome to the Rathole. A word of caution, William. If you betray us, we will murder you."

Ha! "I'll take it under advisement."

"A couple of days in our company and you may view it as the superior option." Richard regarded him with his dark eyes and turned to Cerise. "The papers?"

"I have them."

An adolescent boy came riding down the road, leading three horses.

Cerise wrinkled her nose. "What are the horses for? We're just going to the house to wash."

"You don't have the time," Richard said.

"I'm covered in mud and blood."

"It will have to wait, cousin. Dobe moved the court date."

Cerise blinked a couple of times. "How much time do we have?"

Richard glanced at his wrist. He wore a G-Shock, a durable plastic watch. William had bought one for himself in the Broken. The watch didn't look too good, but it was shockproof and waterproof and it was precise. For all of his blueblood airs, Richard was practical, and Mars made frequent trips to the Broken.

"Fifty-two minutes," Richard said.

Cerise raised her head to the sky and swore.

WILLIAM had seen some piece-of-shit towns in his lifetime, but Angel Roost took the cake. It consisted of a long muddy street, flanked by about a dozen houses and terminating in what Cerise kindly termed "a square," a clearing about the size of a hockey field. On one side of the clearing sat a two-story structure with the sign HOUSE OF WORSHIP. On the other side rose a long rectangular box of a building, put together with giant cypress logs and graced with an even bigger sign that read HOUSE OF COURT. Its barn-style doors stood wide open and a steady stream of people made their way inside.

"This is the town?" William murmured to Cerise.

"The county seat," she said.

He blinked.

"We decided we didn't want Sicktree telling us what to do, so we formed our own county. Our own judge, militia, and everything."

William pretended to look around.

"What are you looking for?" Cerise asked.

"The one horse that all of you share."

She snickered like a kid. William preened. She thought he was funny.

Richard was frowning.

"He's implying this is a one-horse town," Cerise told him.

Richard raised his eyes to the sky briefly.

"Are you appealing to your grandparents as well?" William asked.

Richard sighed. "To my dead father, actually. He sees it fit to put me through all sorts of foolishness lately."

They dismounted before the courthouse, tied their horses to the rail, and joined the crowd filtering into the building. Dozens of scents swirled in the wind, assaulting William's nose. His ears caught bits and pieces of broken conversations. People edged too close to him, trying to make it through the doors.

A nervous giddiness squirmed through him. Crowds were dangerous and exciting, and usually he made it a point to stay away from them.

*Keep a lid on it,* he told himself. He had to get through this court thing, and then he'd be home free.

"We're a bit provincial. Nothing ever happens here," Richard said. "A court hearing is a big event." He smiled.

Cerise smiled back.

"Did I miss a joke?" William asked.

"We're going into battle smiling," Richard said.

"To show that we aren't worried," Cerise added. "The Mire is watching and here reputation is everything."

William leaned to her. She smelled like mud, but he caught a mere whiff of her real scent underneath and it made him want her. "Are you worried?"

"If I didn't have to smile, I'd be pulling my hair out with both hands," she said softly.

"Don't. You have pretty hair, and it will take a long time to grow back."

Her eyes sparkled, and she bit her lip, obviously trying not to laugh.

Inside the air proved colder than on the street. A fresh pine scent floated on the draft. Several pine saplings grew from barrels set in the corners. Opaque lamps hung from the ceiling on long chains. As they made their way through the crowded aisle, the lights came on in yellow electric glory.

William looked at Cerise.

"We have a power plant," she said. "It runs on peat."

This had to be some sort of human joke he didn't get.

She looked at his face and grinned. "Seriously. Peat burns really well once you dry it. We heat the house with it."

That had to be the craziest thing he'd heard. At some point they must've looked around and said, *"Hey, what do we have a shitload of?"*

*"Mud! It's cold and wet. I know, let's burn it!"*

*"Well, it ain't good for nothing else."*

What the hell? He supposed if fish could have legs, then mud could burn. Spider or no Spider, if their cats started flying, he would be out of here like a rocket.

Cerise took a seat in the front row, behind a table. Richard stopped by the row directly behind her and offered him a seat with a short bow. "Please."

William sat. The other side of the courtroom had an identical table. The accused's side, he guessed. Past the two tables, a raised platform supported the judge's desk and chair. Two small lecterns, one for the plaintiff and the other for the defendant, faced the judge. The arrangement was familiar enough. He'd gotten intimately accustomed with the way courts were laid out at his court martial.

His memory served up another courtroom, a much larger sterile chamber he'd viewed through the bars of his cage. They had locked him up like an animal at the court martial. Even his advocate took care to stand outside of his reach. William recalled being pissed off about it at the time. Looking back, it might have been for the best. He'd been bitter and so full of pain, he didn't care whom he hurt.

He caught Cerise looking at him and pulled himself back to the present.

A gray-haired woman, wizened like a dry apricot, slipped into a chair to William's left and smiled at him. Her small black eyes sat like two pieces of shiny coal on her wrinkled face. Barely over four feet tall, she had to be pushing a hundred at least—some Edgers lived as long as people in the Weird.

Richard leaned forward an inch. "Grandmother Az, this is William. He's a friend of Cerise."

William bowed his head. Older people had to be treated with respect. "Honored, my lady."

Grandmother Az raised a tiny hand. Her fingers grazed his hair. A spark of magic shot through William. He recoiled.

"Such a polite puppy you are," Grandmother Az murmured softly and petted his arm. "You can sit by me anytime."

She'd made him. Alarm shot through William. He opened his mouth.

Cerise turned in her chair. "Hi, Grandma."

"There you are, sweetie." Grandmother Az reached over and petted Cerise's hand. "Your friend is a very nice boy."

Cerise smiled. "I'm not sure about that . . ." She surveyed the building. "Half the county showed up to see us lose."

"I was just telling William that our court hearings are our entertainment," Richard said.

"It's not that bad." Grandmother Az snorted. "You should see the funerals. All those old geezers, glad they aren't dead themselves, gloating over the poor deceased. When I die, I want you to burn me."

Cerise rolled her eyes. "Here we go."

"Why burn?" William asked.

"So they can make a big bonfire and get drunk," the old woman said. "Hard to sit there moping with a big fire going."

A tall blonde entered the room, wearing a yellow sash that marked her as an advocate. Two men followed her, carrying papers. She was lean and long-legged, with a graceful neck and nice ankles, and William took a minute to watch her come down the aisle. She looked highstrung and difficult. Still, good legs.

Mmm, smelled of mimosa, too. Expensive scent. Cerise smelled better, when clean.

"It appears the Sheeriles obtained a Weird lawyer," Richard said. "Bringing out the big guns."

"Where the heck is our lawyer?" Cerise grimaced.

"I told him the time," Richard said. "Twice."

A small door on the side swung open. A huge bald man shouldered his way into the courtroom, planted himself to the right of the judge's desk, and crossed his arms, making his carved biceps bulge. His face broadcast "Don't screw with me" loud and clear. All that was missing was a big tattoo across his chest that said BACK OFF.

A bodyguard. William took his measure. Big. Probably very strong but not young, approaching middle age. With that kind of man, you'd have to keep your distance. He'd break bones with one lucky punch. William scrutinized the legs. If he had to get past him, he'd go for the knees. All of that muscle made for a lot of weight to drag around. His knees were probably shot, and he wouldn't react fast enough to block.

"That's Clyde, our bailiff." Grandmother Az wiggled her fingers at the giant.

Clyde winked at her without breaking his scowl and looked straight ahead.

A large beast trotted through the side door. At least thirty-five inches at the shoulder, shaggy with greenish fur sprayed with brown rosettes, it resembled a lynx. The beast sauntered over and lay at Clyde's feet, surveying the crowd with yellow eyes.

Great. A green cat. Why the hell not? This place came in two colors: green and brown, and the beast had both.

"That's Clyde's pet bobcat, Chuckles," Grandmother Az said helpfully. "Clyde, Chuckles, and Judge Dobe. Three peas in a pod."

A man dropped into the chair next to Cerise and grinned, black eyes slightly wild. Lean, quick, with the sure movements of a born thief, he wore a mud-splattered shirt over mud-smeared jeans. His brown hair fell on his shoulders, and a two-day stubble stained his chin. A silver hoop earring shone in his left ear. He looked like he'd spent the night in lockup after a drunken binge and was up to no good. "Did I miss anything?"

"Kaldar," Cerise reached over and poked him with her fingers. "You're late."

"Couldn't you have cleaned up for the court?" Richard growled.

"What wrong with the way I look?"

Grandmother Az slapped him on the back of his shaggy head.

"Ow! Hello, Meemaw."

"Did you bring the map?" Richard asked.

Kaldar's face turned panicky. He patted himself down, reached under Cerise's hair, and pulled a folded paper free. "I knew I put it somewhere."

Richard looked like a man who'd bitten into a lemon. "This isn't a circus."

"Look around you," Kaldar said.

"A circus has more elephants," William told him. He'd gone to the P.T. Barnum show once in the Broken, and his scent had scared an elephant half to death. For all their size, they were hysterical creatures.

Kaldar squinted at him. "Who are you?"

"His name is William. He's my guest and the reason Urow is still breathing," Cerise said.

Kaldar glanced at her, then back at William. He had sharp eyes, almost black, and William felt like the man had just sighted him through the scope of a rifle. Clown act or no, Kaldar would try to slit his throat if he stepped an inch out of line.

"Try" was the key word.

A hint of a knowing smile passed across Kaldar's lips, as if he had figured out some secret, and then his face split in a happy grin. "Welcome to the family."

"Are you her brother?" William asked.

"Cousin." Kaldar nodded at Richard. "I'm his brother."

Richard looked at the ceiling. "Don't remind me."

"You and I are going to be friends," Kaldar told him. William caught a hint of threat in his voice, but Kaldar's face remained blissfully happy.

Clyde stepped forward, leveled a hard stare at the audience, and bellowed. "All rise!"

# THIRTEEN

THE audience stood up in a shuffle. Somewhere in the back a thud announced a fallen chair and a woman cursed.

A middle-aged man scurried into the room. The billowing blue robe hung off his shoulders like a sheet drying on a clothesline. The face above the robe was brown, weather-edged, and sun-dried like a raisin. Two enormously wide eyebrows severed his face, like two fat, hairy caterpillars. His jaw moved as he walked to the seat, as if he were an old, decrepit bull chewing cud.

"The Angel County of the Edge District Court is now in session," Clyde boomed. "Judge Dobe presiding. Be seated."

Everybody sat.

Clyde stepped toward the judge. "Case number 1252, Mars versus Sheeriles."

Judge Dobe reached under his desk, took out a small metal bucket, and hacked into it. "All right," he said, sliding the bucket back in its place.

William wondered if Kaldar was right and this was a circus.

"Advocates, rise," Clyde barked.

The blond woman stood up and so did Kaldar.

The judge's massive eyebrows crept up. "Kaldar. Are you the one speaking for the plaintiff today?"

"Yes, Your Honor."

"Well, shit," Dobe said. "I guess you're familiar with the law. You hit it over the head, set its house on fire, and got its sister pregnant."

A huge grin sparked on Kaldar's face. "Thank you, Your Honor."

The blonde cleared her throat. "With all due respect, Judge, this man isn't qualified to serve as an advocate. He's a convicted felon."

Dobe's gaze settled on the blond woman. "I don't know you. Clyde, do you know her?"

"No, Judge."

"There you have it. We don't know you."

"I'm here to represent the Sheerile family." The blond advocate stepped forward, holding out a parchment. "I'm a practicing Jurist in New Avignon. Here are my credentials."

"New Avignon is in the Weird," Dobe said.

The blonde smiled. "I've made an extensive study of Edge law for this case, Judge."

"What's wrong with local talent that Lagar Sheerile has to go into the Weird to find himself an advocate?" Dobe squinted at the row of empty chairs. "Where is Lagar? And the rest of his kin?"

"He waived his right to appear," the blonde said. "The Code of the county gives him that right in Statute 7, Section 3."

"I know the Code," Dobe told her. His eyes gained a dangerous glint. "I wrote half of it. So Lagar thinks he's too good for my courtroom. Fine, fine. Kaldar, this Jurist over there says you aren't qualified, because you're a convicted felon. You got anything to say to that?"

"I'm a convicted felon in the Weird and in the Broken," Kaldar said. "In the Edge I was only fined. Besides, the same statute also states that any Edger can serve as his own advocate. Since the matter concerns the communal property owned by the Mar family and I'm a member of that family, I contend that I'm representing myself and, therefore, may act as my own advocate."

"Good enough." Dobe waved his hand. "Proceed."

Kaldar cleared his throat. "The Mar family owns a

two-acre parcel named Sene, consisting of land and the Sene Manor house."

Kaldar passed the maps to Clyde, who passed them to Dobe. Dobe squinted at them for a while and waved his hand again. "Proceed."

"On the seventh of May, Cerise Mar, Erian Mar, and Mikita Mar traveled to the aforementioned manor house and found Lagar Sheerile, Peva Sheerile, Arig Sheerile, and several men in their employ on the premises. Cerise Mar voiced a polite and a nonviolent request that they get the hell off our land, which was refused."

Dobe peered at Cerise. "And you let it go why?"

Cerise rose. "We're a peaceful family, and we let the court handle our disputes."

The spectators guffawed. Dobe cracked a smile. "Come again?"

"They had rifles and we had riders," Cerise said.

Dobe's silver-dusted eyebrows performed some sort of wiggling maneuver. "Noted. And why do you look like something an ervaurg stored for a lean day?"

"Tough day in the swamp, Your Honor."

"Noted. Sit your behind down."

Cerise sat.

Dobe glanced at Kaldar. "So what do you want from the court today?"

"We want the Sheeriles off our property."

"Fine." He looked at the blonde. "Your turn. Just to be fair, I'll bring you up to speed. I run a clean hearing, no long speeches. Don't quote me precedent, argue from the law. I don't give a pig's ear for precedent—they let any idiot be a judge nowadays."

The blonde muttered, "No kidding," under her breath.

Chuckles raised his head and hissed. His yellow eyes locked on the blonde. William smiled to himself. He'd seen that intense look before. He wore it from time to time. If he could crack the big cat's skull and search it, he would come up with one clear thought: *How fast can you run?*

"You said something?" Dobe asked.

"No, Your Honor."

"Good, then. Proceed."

The blonde's lips stretched in a flat smile. "The property in question was legally sold to the Sheerile family by Gustave Mar. Here is the Deed of Sale and the Deed of Ownership to the Sene Manor and the land attached to that dwelling."

She held up two papers. Clyde ambled over, took them to Dobe. Dobe squinted at them and waved the papers at Kaldar. "Looks good to me. And I don't suppose Gustave is around to dispute it since his daughter is sitting at the table."

"We haven't seen him since that morning," Kaldar said. "But we'll find him."

"That's fine and dandy, but meanwhile we have these deeds here. You got anything to say about this?"

Kaldar looked down.

The room fell silent.

So that's it? William wondered. This was how it ended. She'd risked the Hand and raced through the swamp for this?

"Well?" Dobe asked.

Kaldar's dark head drooped. He rummaged through the tangle of his hair.

"Answer the court," Clyde boomed.

Kaldar raised his head. "Your Honor, Gustave couldn't have sold Sene."

"And why is that?" Dobe asked.

"Because this parcel was purchased by the Dukedom of Louisiana from Angel Roost County twenty-seven years ago under the Exile Relocation Act. It was subsequently awarded to an exile, one Vernard Dubois, who then became related to the Mar family through the marriage of his daughter, Genevieve Dubois, to Gustave Mar. As such, Sene Manor and its land constitutes a nontransferable Senatorial grant. It can't be sold, in whole or in part, only inherited by the exile's offspring. Since both Vernard and his wife had passed away, and their offspring, Genevieve, is missing, the parcel rightfully belongs to her daughter Cerise Mar. Even if Gustave did sign those deeds, his signature has no power. He doesn't own the parcel. Cerise does and she isn't selling."

Someone gasped.

Kaldar raised his arms, holding folded documents in a fan. "Copy of original Deed of Sale to Louisiana, signed and stamped. Copy of Senatorial Grant, with Genevieve listed as an heir. Copy of Gustave's and Genevieve's marriage certificate. Copy of Vernard Dubois's and Vienna Dubois's death certificates. Copy of Cerise Mar's birth certificate."

He bowed with a flourish and dumped the papers into Clyde's hands.

Dobe scanned the papers and cackled. It was a gleeful snide kind of cackle, and as he laughed, his eyebrows bounced up and down. "Blondie, you've been buggered."

The blonde advocate's face twitched. "I want to examine the papers."

"Examine all you want. I'm ready to rule. I love them when they're that simple, don't you, Clyde?"

"Yes, Your Honor."

Cerise rose.

"The Sheerile family has one day to vacate the Sene parcel. If by the morning of the second day, they fail to do so, the Mar family can use whatever they've got to get their property back. If the Mars fail to handle the Sheeriles on their own, they may appeal to the Mire Militia for assistance. That's it."

Dobe picked up his robe and scurried off.

They had won the right to attack the Sheeriles, William realized. Now there would be a bloodbath.

"Show-off." Cerise slumped onto her chair. He read exhaustion in the curve of her spine.

"Oh, everyone enjoyed it. Let me have my fun." Kaldar patted her shoulder. "You don't look so good."

"Just really tired," she said. "It's been a while since I slept. Or ate."

"We should go home," Richard said.

"Yes." Cerise rose and immediately dropped back into her chair. "Emel."

A man in a long crimson robe was making his way to them from the back of the room. He was dark-haired and very lean, and looked a bit like Richard, if you took Richard's face and stretched it a couple of inches. William riffed through his memory. Emel, her cousin, the necromancer who supposedly would eat a hole in her head over the fish on legs.

"Is there a particular reason you don't want to meet our dear cousin?" Kaldar gathered the documents. "He's a bit grim and smells like dead people, but he is family . . ."

"William killed his eel." Cerise ducked lower, crouching by the seat.

The four Mars stared at him. William shrugged. "It tried to eat me."

"Emel will want money," Cerise murmured. "I can't handle that right this second."

Kaldar jerked his head toward the door. "Go. We'll stall him."

Cerise slunk from her seat, melting into the crowd. William tensed, but there was no way to follow unless he threw her cousins aside.

Kaldar turned and stepped forward with a big smile. "Emel!"

Emel looked a bit perplexed. "Cousin."

They embraced.

Kaldar winked at William over Emel's shoulder. Grandmother Az watched them with an affable smile.

"Congratulations on the battle fought and won." Emel's voice was surprisingly pleasant.

"Thank you," Kaldar said.

Emel braided the fingers of his hands, in the manner of a pious priest. "Lagar won't leave peacefully. Kaitlin won't let him. Let me know if you need assistance. Officially I can't do anything—the Sect doesn't wish to be involved—but I can still pull some strings. And, *hrhm*, I myself am not without some modest skill."

Kaldar nodded. "Thank you, Emel."

Emel's face took on a mournful cast. "Speaking of needs. I've come to see Cerise. There is a certain delicate matter that I would like to discuss with her."

Yeah, a delicate matter of the fish with legs who attacked random peaceful travelers in the swamp. William opened his mouth. Grandmother Az put her hand on his elbow and shook her head. He clamped his mouth shut.

Kaldar nodded gravely. "I'm sorry, she left. But I'll do my best to give her a message."

"I need to speak to her concerning a certain animal belonging to the Sect . . . Normally I wouldn't bring this up, but the Sect believes some restitution is in order."

"Lost your pet, did you?" Grandmother Az snapped out of her reverie.

Emel paled. "Why, Meemaw Azan, I didn't see you there . . ."

"Serves you right." Grandmother's eyes blazed with fierce fire. The flow of the crowd around them slowed, as the audience sensed a new attraction. "When she was a little girl, you stole her dolls, stuffed dead things into them, and made them dance! What kind of a person expects a little girl to be happy with a stinky dolly that's full of maggots? What were you thinking?"

Emel winced.

"I say it's right that she killed your eel. What kind of a pet is that for a respected man anyway? Couldn't get a dog or a cat. No, this knucklehead gets himself a bald fish with legs!"

Light giggling pulsed through the crowd.

"Meemaw Azan—" Emel started but she cut him off.

"I don't care if you're a necromancer! Coming over here, all important, doesn't say hello to his granny. Too good for your family, are you, Emel? I know I brought my grandchildren up better than that. I think I'll have me a talk with your mother!"

A spark of fear flared in Emel's somber eyes. "I should go," he said softly.

"It's for the best," Kaldar murmured. "I'll give Cerise your message."

Emel bowed to his grandmother and took off toward the door amid the cackling audience.

Grandmother Az put her tiny fists on her hips. "And don't you walk away from me, Emel Mar! I am not finished with you! Emel!"

The necromancer grabbed his robe, broke into a run, and escaped through the door. Grandmother Az waved her arm around and poked William in the shoulder. "Can you believe that child? Well, doesn't that just sink my boat! And he was such a sweet baby, too."

LAGAR pulled the boat to the shore, threw the reins on a cypress knee, and stepped on the wet grass. A lake of ferns rustled before him.

"Peva?"

No answer came. He took a step into the ferns and saw a trail of broken stems leading away from a pine. A small bag of tracker's mix lay on the roots, the nuts and raisins scattered on the ground. Above it, a circular black mark, the kind a flare arrow made, glared at him from the pine's trunk.

Peva had no flare bolts. The hair on the back of Lagar's neck stood on its end.

He unsheathed his sword in a single fluid motion and searched the ground.

Twin puncture marks, two wounds in the dirt, marked the spot by the pine root. Someone had shot at his brother and lived to retrieve the missiles. Unless Peva took them for his own.

Lagar jogged to the edge of the fern field. Several stems lay broken on the ground. His gaze snagged on a bolt pro-

truding from a cypress trunk. A green glyph marked the
shaft. One of Peva's. Too low for a target. Besides when
Peva aimed, he always hit. He'd shot to distract someone's
attention from himself. Lagar crouched, pointing the tip of
his sword in the direction of the bolt, and turned the other
way.

A large cypress blocked his view twenty feet away.
He ran to the cypress, circled the bloated stem . . .

Peva lay on his back on the ground. The blue tint of the
bloodless skin, the rigid features, the brown stain of blood
on the chest, it all rushed at Lagar at the same time and
punched him deep into the gut, where the nerves met. He
dropped to his knees.

Rain came, drizzling the swamp with cold water. It
plastered Peva's hair to his head, filling the dead eyes with
false tears. A phantom hand squeezed Lagar's throat until
it hurt.

Lagar pulled his brother close and held him.

# FOURTEEN

CERISE rode quietly, letting the horse pick the pace. The swamp rolled by on both sides of the road: pale husks of the dead trees rising from the bog water that was black like liquid tar.

They won the first round. Peva was dead. The court had ruled in favor of the family. They had the right to retrieve Grandfather's house. Now they just had to do it.

She should've been happy. Instead, she felt empty and worn-out to the core, as if her body had become a threadbare rag hanging off her bones. She was so weary. She wanted off her horse. She wanted to curl up somewhere dark and quiet. And most of all, she wanted her mother.

Cerise sighed. It was a ridiculous urge. She was twenty-four years old. Not a child by any means. If things had gone differently, she would've been married and had children of her own by now. But no matter how she tried to rationalize herself away from it, she wanted her mother with the desperation of a child left alone in the dark. The need was so basic and strong, she almost cried.

She couldn't remember the last time she had cried. It had to be years.

The logical part of her knew that winning the hearing was only the first step on a long road. For the past ten days she'd had a clear purpose: find Uncle Hugh, get the documents, and return in time for the hearing. She lived and breathed it, and now it was done. She had accomplished her goal, and inside, in the same place she wanted her mother, she felt deeply cheated because her parents failed to magically appear.

Hoofbeats came from behind her. Cerise turned in her saddle.

Two riders came down the path at a brisk canter. William and Kaldar. William carried Peva's crossbow. Some women waited for a knight in shining armor. She, apparently, had ended up with a knight in black jeans and leather, who wanted to chase her down and have his evil way with her.

When she was a teenager, she used to imagine meeting a stranger. He would be from the Weird or the Broken, not from the Mire. He would be lethal and tough, so tough, he wouldn't be afraid of her. He would be funny. And he would be handsome. She'd gotten so good at imagining this mysterious man, she could almost picture his face.

William would kick his ass.

Maybe that was why she couldn't get him out of her head, Cerise reflected. Wishful thinking, hoping for things that would never be.

The two men reached her and halted their horses.

"See?" Kaldar grimaced. "She's in one piece."

William ignored him. "You rode out alone. Don't make a habit of it."

He was worried about her safety. Charming Lord Bill. And phrased it so delicately, too. Why, he was the very picture of gallantry. "Worried about your bait?"

"You're no good to anyone dead."

Kaldar had a peculiar look on his face.

"What is it?" she asked.

"Nothing. I think I'll ride ahead a bit." He rode on.

Cerise sighed. "Did you get under his skin?"

William shrugged. "He makes bad jokes. I told him they weren't funny. Riding out alone was sloppy. If you keep making small mistakes, they will become habits and then you'll die."

Just what she needed. "Thank you for the lecture, Lord

Bill. How I survived without your help to the ripe age of twenty-four, I will never know."

"You're welcome."

*When sarcasm flies over a blueblood's head, does it make a sound? No, I guess not.*

"Don't tell me what to do." She nudged her horse and the mare followed Kaldar. William rode next to her. He was looking intently at her face. Cerise looked back.

The problem with Lord Bill was that not only was he hotter than July in hell, but he existed blissfully unaware of his hotness, which, of course, made him even more attractive. Looking at him for too long was bad for her. He was a challenge, and she had so many other things to worry about: her parents, the feud, the rest of the family . . .

"Are you upset?" he asked.

"Yes."

"With me?"

"No."

The rigid line of his jaw eased a little. "Then with what?"

Cerise glanced at the sky, gathering her thoughts. "I realized that I'm a child."

William looked point-blank at her chest. "No."

Laughter bubbled up and she couldn't hold it in. "Up here, Lord Bill." She pointed to her face. "It's not polite to stare at a woman's breasts, unless of course, she is naked in bed with you. Then you can look all you want."

Amber flashed in William's eyes, betraying intense, unfiltered lust. And then it was gone.

*Oh, Lord Bill, you devious thing you.* Everything he thought registered on his face. His wife would have no guesswork. If he was sad, she'd know. If he wanted sex, she'd know. If he wanted another woman, she'd know, too. He wasn't capable of lying, even if he wanted to.

"Why do you think you're a child?" he asked.

"Because I want my mother," Cerise told him. She was probably foolish for letting him see that deep inside herself, but then she couldn't exactly share any of it with the family. "I never knew until now that I was spoiled. My parents shielded me from the really important decisions. They made things easy. As long as I did as instructed, and even if I didn't always, things would be okay, because they would always be there to fix it or at least to tell me how to fix it. I complained and thought I had it rough. Now they're gone. All of the decisions are mine now, and all of the responsibility is mine, too. Tomorrow I'll be sending my family into slaughter to take back my grandfather's house. Some of them won't come back. And all I want is for my parents to tell me I'm doing the right thing, except they can't. It's up to me to know what the right thing is. I feel like I'm taking a test and somebody just stole my cheat sheet. I have to pack a few years of growing up between tonight and tomorrow morning, and I better do it fast."

There. More than he'd bargained for, she had no doubt.

"It's like being a sergeant," William said. "At first you're an enlisted man, a rank-and-file Legionnaire. As long as you're where you're told to be when you're told to be there, you can do no wrong. And then you make a sergeant. Now you have to figure out where everyone has to be and when. Everybody is waiting for you to screw up: the people above you, the people below you, and the people who knew you before and think they should be where you are. Nobody holds your hand."

"I suppose it is like being a sergeant." she murmured.

"The rule is: often wrong but never in doubt. That's what makes you different. You show doubt, and nobody will follow you."

"But what if you *are* in doubt?"

"Don't let it show or you're fucked."

She sighed. "I'll keep it in mind. You liked the military, Lord Bill. You keep mentioning it."

"It was easy," he told her.

"Why did you leave?"

"They sentenced me to death."

What? "I'm sorry?"

William looked ahead. "I was court-martialed."

What did he do? "Why?"

"A terrorist group had taken over a dam in the Weird. They took hostages and threatened to flood the town if their demands weren't met."

"What did they want?"

William grimaced. "Many things. In the end, they just wanted money. The rest of it was trying to dress themselves up as something other than robbers."

"What happened?"

"The dam was very old, honeycombed with passageways. I was picked for the mission, because I don't get lost easily and because they counted on me to do what I was told. The mission came with a strict set of orders: take out the terrorists, keep the dam from being destroyed. Keeping the dam intact had the highest priority."

It sank in. "Higher than keeping the hostages alive?"

He nodded and fell silent.

"William?" she prompted softly.

"There was a boy," he said quietly.

Oh no. "You let them blow up the dam to save a child."

He nodded.

"And they sentenced you to death for it? What sort of people were these Weird bastards? Didn't your family protest? Your mother should've been screaming at every politician she could find!"

He stared straight ahead, his expression bored and haughty, looking every inch a blueblood. "I don't have a mother. Never knew her."

All the fight went out of Cerise. "I'm so sorry. I guess Weird or Edge, women still die in childbirth."

His chin rose another fraction of an inch. "She didn't die. She gave me up."

Cerise blinked. "She what?"

"She didn't want me, so she surrendered me to the government."

Cerise stared at him. "What do you mean, surrendered? But you were her son."

"She was young and poor, and she didn't want to raise

me." His voice was light, as if he were telling her their afternoon stroll was canceled due to the rain.

"What about your father?"

He shook his head.

"You grew up in an orphanage?"

"Something like that."

It wasn't a nice orphanage. She could tell it wasn't because he had this perfectly calm expression on his face. She'd seen that same expression on his face when Urow boasted about his family. Now she got it. That's why he compared everything to the army. He grew up in an orphanage from hell and joined the military right after, and then even they kicked him out. The army was all he knew and it had been taken away from him.

Her aunt Murid had managed to sneak out through the Broken and from there back into the Weird. She'd joined the Louisiana military and served for twelve years before someone figured out she was related to an exile. She had to run home. It nearly killed her, and at the end of every March, on the anniversary of her escape, they had to hide the wine, because she drank herself sick.

William didn't drink. William hunted Spider instead. He'd probably done things to his body so he could keep up with the Hand. He had failed at the only profession he'd ever had, and he made sure he wouldn't fail at this one.

"I'm not one to judge," Cerise said. "I don't know what your mother's circumstances were. But no matter how poor or how badly off I was, they would have pried my son from my cold dead fingers. How quickly did she . . . ?"

"The day after I was born."

"So she didn't even try?"

"No."

There were times when it was best for the child to grow up with someone other than his parents, but William's mother didn't exactly give him to a loving family. She gave him to some sort of hellhole. "I'm so sorry."

Cerise shook her head. "You know what, screw her. You can make yourself a new family."

William spared her a glance, and she found herself on the receiving end of a thousand-yard stare. "Families aren't for people like me."

"What are you talking about? William, you're kind and strong and handsome. There are tons of women who'd climb over razor wire for a chance to make you happy. They'd be insane not to."

And she had pretty much just admitted to being one of those women. Cerise sighed. She was too tired to think straight.

William shrugged. "Sure, there are women who'd do anything for a steady paycheck or to get out of their crappy life or to piss off their parents. If you're desperate enough, even sleeping with someone like me sounds good. But those women aren't looking for a family. It's much easier to just pay the woman for her time. That way you can do what you need to do and be on your way. That's the way I prefer it."

*Wait just a minute here.* So, the way he looked at it, she was either trying to get out of her crappy life or desperate, and it would be much easier for everyone involved if he could just pay her for her time.

Maybe he didn't get it. Or maybe he was trying to tell her that she was good enough to screw but not good enough for anything else. *Stupid, Cerise. So, so stupid.*

Maybe she should stop playing footsies with a blueblood she met a week ago in the damn swamp.

"Well, if you're hoping for a roll in the hay with me, you're out of luck, William," she said, keeping her voice light. "I'm not for sale."

She urged her horse on, before he could answer.


**WILLIAM** killed a growl. He couldn't explain Hawk's to her, and he didn't even want to try. He was a blueblood in her eyes. He didn't want to kill that, not just yet. She'd figure him out eventually and realize that he was a changeling, poor and happy being a nobody. He knew exactly how it would go. In the Weird, women would occasionally come up to him, smiling and inviting, and then, when he explained what he was, the smiles would slide off their faces. Some would walk away without another word. A few nice ones would make some excuses, trying to soothe his feelings, which he hated even more, and then leave. A couple had been indignant as if he'd tricked them, as if every changeling had to wear a sign announcing what he was. Or a chain. That would've suited them even better.

He didn't want to imagine what it would be like when Cerise found out. It would happen soon enough. For now, he needed to stay a blueblood. He had a job to do.

They rode to the top of a hill. A huge house sat in a clearing, two stories high and big enough to shelter a battalion. The ground floor was built with red brick and caged by sturdy pillars that supported the second-story wraparound balcony. The pillars passed through the balcony's floor, transforming into light wooden collonettes, carved and painted white. A single wide staircase led up to the balcony and the only door he could see.

It was built like a fortress. Maybe the Mars planned to hold off a siege.

Smaller buildings flanked the house, rising on the sides and slightly behind, like a flock of geese led by the largest bird. To the left, a small water tower jutted against the sky. Why would they need a water tower in the swamp? If you dug a six-inch hole, it filled with water in seconds.

"The Rathole, Lord Bill," Cerise said. Her voice was cheerful, but her eyes had narrowed. He read anger in the tense lines of her mouth. When he told her about himself, the compassion in her eyes was like that ointment she slathered on his wounds—soothing and warm. She dulled the sharp memories, and he was grateful to her for it. But now she was mad at him.

"What did I say?"

She arched her eyebrows. "I don't know what you mean."

"Don't do this. What did I say to piss you off?" He had to fix it. It gnawed at him now and wouldn't let go.

Cerise shook her head. "I don't want to talk about it right now."

He clenched his teeth to keep from pulling her off the horse and shaking her until it spilled out of her. "Tell me what I did."

She turned in her saddle and looked at him over her shoulder, hair spilling down, eyes on fire.

"What?" he growled.

"Think about it. You'll figure it out."

William ran through the conversation in his head, recalling her reactions. He couldn't for the life of him find anything offensive in what he said. Military, orphanage . . . She seemed upset by what he told of his life, but it wasn't directed at him. It was directed at people who made his life hell. Blah, blah, blah . . . *"It's much easier to just pay the woman for her time. That way you can do what you need to do and be on your way. That's the way I prefer it."* *"Well, if you're hoping for a roll in the hay with me, you're out of luck, William. I'm not for sale."*

She was pissed off, because she thought he'd lumped her in with whores. Why the hell would she think that? He never called her a whore . . .

*"William, you're kind and strong and handsome. There are tons of women who'd climb over razor wire for a chance to make you happy. They'd be insane not to."*

Understanding dawned in his head. She *liked* him.

She liked him. She thought of herself as one of those women, and she was pissed off because he told her that he preferred to pay for his sex and leave. She didn't want him to leave. She wanted him to stay. With her.

William searched his memory, trying to find some indication of flirting. He'd watched countless women flirt with Declan, everyone from random passersby at the market to blueblood ladies at the formal balls.

*"I bet the women from the Weird tell you that you have great hair all the time, Lord Bill."*

*"I jumped in to rescue you, you fool!"*

*"You demolished them."*

*"What would happen if you caught me?"*

She liked him. The beautiful girl with eyes like black fire wanted him. William almost laughed, except she would have killed him on the spot. *You tripped, hobo queen.* She should have never let him know, but now he'd figured it out and it was too late. He'd have to stalk her, he decided. Carefully and patiently. He would bring her flowers, swords, and whatever else she liked, until he was sure when he pounced, she wouldn't want to run away.

He looked at her, showing her the edge of his teeth.

"Look, I didn't mean to imply that you were a slut," he told her. "I know nothing about you. And just if there is any question, I never hurt a woman, never forced anyone to do things with me. It was always a clear-cut deal, half the money up front, half when we were done. You and I agreed to work together. Whatever I did or didn't do in the past doesn't matter. My private life doesn't matter. It only matters what I do from this point on."

She shrugged.

"Are you done being mad?"

"Yes."

"Good." *Insane woman.*

They rode into the yard. He hopped off the horse and caught a thick scent of wet fur and the sharp piss signature marking the territory. Dogs. Shit.

A loud hoarse baying erupted from a dozen furry throats. William tensed. Some dogs didn't mind his scent, but most reacted as they should when a wolf walked into their territory. They fought him for dominance and lost.

*Hi, Cerise, sorry your dogs attacked me and I slaugh*

*tered the lot of them, but good news, now you have lots
of nice pelts . . .*

A dog pack burst from around the corner. Big dogs,
too, a hundred pounds at least, some black, some tan, all
with the square heads of a mastiff breed and docked tails.
Damn it all to hell.

The dogs charged him, running at full speed.

The knife jumped into his hand, almost on its own.

The first dog, an enormous pale male, lunged at him
and went down on his front paws, ass in the air, tail wiggling.

What the hell?

The mob swirled around him, paws scraping dirt, noses
poking him, tongues licking, drool flying in long sticky
gobs. A smaller dog squealed—someone stepped on her
paw.

"All right, down! Calm the hell down!" Cerise barked.
"What has gotten into you?"

He reached over and petted the alpha's giant head.
Sad brown eyes looked at him with canine adoration.
Dogs were simple creatures, and this one seemed to love
his scent.

"That's Cough," Cerise told him. "He's the idiot in
charge."

The dog sniffed his hand and licked it, depositing
muddy slobber on his skin. Ugh.

"Cough, you dufus. Sorry, usually they're more reserved. They must like you."

"They do," a calm female voice said from above.

A woman stood on the balcony, next to Kaldar. Tall and
lean, she looked like Cerise if Cerise were twenty years
older and had spent those decades in the Red Legion doing
shit that kept her awake with nightmares. Where Cerise was
muscle, this one was made mostly of sinew and bone. Her
gaze fastened on him, focusing, measuring the distance, as
if she were a raptor sizing up her prey. A sniper.

If the eyes didn't give her away, her rifle would have.
He'd seen it only once in an obscure catalog. A Reming-

ton 700 SS 5-R. A sniper rifle. Remington produced only about five hundred of those a year. The Edge was the last place William expected to see one.

"My aunt Murid," Cerise told him.

"The man with Peva's crossbow," Murid said, nodding at Peva's weapon. "The enemy of our enemy is our friend. Welcome."

"What she said." Kaldar swung the door open. A whiff of cooked beef floated through, reducing William's world to a simple thought.

*Food.*

Cerise was already moving. William heaved the crossbow up, pushed his way through the sea of dogs, and headed up the stairs. He made it through the door in time to see her turn into a side room on the left.

"You and I are going straight." Kaldar popped up at his side with the buttery grace of a magician. "Keep the pace now, that's it. I think I'll take you to the library. My sister is in there, and she'll keep an eye on you while I go scrounge us some food. The kitchen is a madhouse this time of day, and if you go down there, there will be no end of questions. Who are you? Are you a blueblood? Are you rich? Are you, by the way?"

"No," William said.

"Married?"

"No."

Kaldar moved his head from side to side. "Well, one out of two isn't bad. Rich and unmarried would be perfect, married and poor would be two strikes out, nothing good there. Poor and unmarried, I can work with that. Library it is. Besides, you'll get to meet my sister."

William tried to imagine a female version of Kaldar and got a mud-splattered woman with Kaldar's face and blue stubble on her cheeks. Clearly he needed food and some shut-eye.

"This way. And we turn here through that door, and here we are." Kaldar held the door open for him. "This way, Lord . . . What is your name, I don't think I ever got it."

He could not strangle Kaldar because he was Cerise's cousin and she was fond of him. But he really wanted to. "William."

"William it is. Please. Into the library."

William stepped through the door. A large room stretched before him, the walls covered with floor-to-ceiling shelves and crammed with books. Soft chairs stood in the corners, a large table waited to the left, and at the opposite wall by a window, a woman sat in a chair working yarn into some sort of lacy thing with a metal hook.

She sat in a rectangle of afternoon light spilling through the window. Her hair was soft and almost gold, and the sunlight played on it, making it shine. She looked up with a small smile, the glowing hair around her head like a nimbus, and William decided she looked like an icon from one of the Broken's cathedrals.

"Catherine! I bring you Lord Blueblood William. Cerise found him in the swamp. He must be fed and I need to go get him some food, so can you please babysit him while I'm gone? I can't have him wandering through the house. We don't know what he's made of, and he might snap and devour the children."

Catherine smiled again. She had a soft gentle smile. "My brother has the tact of a rhino. Please come sit by me, Lord William."

Anything was better than Kaldar. William walked over and sat down in a chair next to her. "Just William."

"Nice to meet you." Her voice was calm and soothing. Her hands kept moving, weaving the yarn with the hook, completely independent of her. She wore rubber gloves, the kind he'd seen on *CSI*, except it looked like she wore two pairs, one on top of the other. Her lacy thing rested on a rubber apron, and her yarn came from a bucket filled with liquid.

Odd.

"How did the hearing go?" she asked.

"We won, sort of," Kaldar said. "We die at dawn."

"The court gave the Sheeriles twenty-four hours," William corrected.

"Yes, but 'we die at dawn the day after tomorrow' doesn't sound nearly as dramatic."

"Does it have to be dramatic all the time?" Catherine murmured.

"Of course. Everyone has a talent. Yours is crocheting and mine is making melodramatic statements."

Catherine shook her head and glanced at her work. The yarn thing was a complicated mess of waves, spiked wheels, and some odd mesh.

"What is that?" William asked.

"It's a shawl," Catherine said.

"Why is the yarn wet?"

"It's a special type of crochet." Catherine smiled. "For a very special person."

Kaldar snorted. "Kaitlin will love it, I'm sure."

He'd heard the name before . . . Kaitlin Sheerile. Lagar and Peva's mother.

Why the hell would they be crocheting a shawl for Kaitlin? Maybe there was a message on it.

William leaned forward and caught a trace of an odor, bitter and very weak. It nipped at his nostrils and his instincts screeched.

*Bad! Bad, bad, bad.*

Poison. He'd never smelled it before, but he knew with simple lupine certainty that it was poisonous and he had to stay away from it.

He made himself reach over for the shawl.

"No!" Kaldar clamped his hand on William's wrist.

"You mustn't touch," Catherine said. "It's very delicate and it will stain your fingers. That's why I'm wearing gloves. See?" She wiggled her fingers at him.

She lied. This pretty icon woman with a nice smile lied and didn't blink an eye.

He had to say something human here. "Sorry."

"That's all right." Kaldar's fingers slipped off his wrist. "She isn't offended, are you, Cath?"

"Not at all." Catherine offered him a nice warm smile. Her hands kept crocheting poisoned yarn.

Hell of a family.

"Right, well, I'm off to procure some vittles." Kaldar turned on his toes and sauntered off.

Catherine leaned to him. "Drove you crazy, yes?"

"He talks." *A lot. Too much. He jabbers like a teenage girl on a cell phone. He stands too close to me, and I might snap his neck if he keeps breathing on me.*

"That he does," Catherine agreed. "But he's not a bad sort. As brothers go, I could've done much worse. Are you and Cerise together? Like together-together?"

William froze. Human manners were clear as mud, but he was pretty sure that's something you weren't supposed to ask.

Catherine blinked her long eyelashes at him, the same serene smile on her face.

"No," he said.

A faint grimace touched Catherine's face. "That's a shame. Are there any plans for the two of you to be together?"

"No."

"I see. Don't tell her I asked. She doesn't like it when we pry."

"I won't."

"Thank you." Catherine exhaled.

This family was like a minefield. He needed to sit still and keep his mouth shut, before he got into any more trouble. And if someone offered him a handmade sweater, he'd snap their neck and take off for the woods.

Lark came into the library carrying a basket that smelled of freshly baked bread and rabbit meat with cooked mushrooms. William's mouth filled with drool. He was starving. Almost enough to not care if the food was poisoned.

The kid knelt by him. She was clean and her hair was brushed. She looked like a smaller version of Cerise. Lark pulled the cloth off the basket and pulled out a pocket of baked dough. "Pirogi," she said. "Are you the one who killed Peva?"

"Yes."

Lark reached over and touched the tiller of Peva's crossbow.

"Okay, then. You can eat our food." She tore the pocket in two, handed him half, and bit into the remaining piece. "Uncle Kaldar said to do that. So you would know it's not poisoned."

William bit into his half. It tasted like heaven. "Can you shoot a crossbow?"

Lark nodded.

He picked up Peva's crossbow and offered it to her. "Take it."

She hesitated.

"It's yours," he said. "I already have one and mine is better." The Mirror's crossbow was lighter and more accurate.

Lark looked at him, looked at the bow, grabbed it out of his hands like a feral puppy stealing a bone, and took off, bare feet flashing. She whipped about in the doorway. Black eyes glared at him. "Don't go in the woods. There is a monster there." She whirled and ran down the hallway.

He glanced at Catherine. Her hands had stopped moving. Her face was sad, as if at a funeral.

Something was wrong with Lark. He would figure it out, sooner or later.

Light footsteps floated from down the hall, and a man appeared in the doorway. About five-ten, slightly built, blond, but still tan like a Mar. He leaned against the doorframe and looked William over with blue eyes. "You're the blueblood."

William nodded.

"You know about the Sheeriles."

William nodded again.

"I'm Erian. When I was ten, Sheerile Senior shot my father in the head in the middle of the marketplace. My mother had died years before that. My father was all I had. I was standing right there, and my father's blood splashed all over me."

And?

"Cerise's parents, my aunt and uncle, took me in. They didn't have to, but they did. Cerise is like a sister to me. If you hurt her or any of us, I will kill you."

William bit into his pirogi, measuring the distance to the door. Mmm, about eighteen feet give or take. He'd cover that in one leap. Jump, punch Erian in the gut, ram his head into the door, and boom, he could finally get some peace and quiet. He nodded at the blond man. "Good speech."

Erian nodded back. "Glad you liked it."

# FIFTEEN

RUH leaned forward, casting his web into the stream. Spider watched the carmine cilia that sheathed the blood vessels of Ruh's net tremble in the dark water. A long moment passed, and then the net closed on itself, folding, retreating, and sliding back into the tracker's shoulder.

"They passed this way." Ruh's grating yet sibilant voice reminded Spider of gravel being swept across stone. "Lavern's blood is in the water. But they're gone. I can taste two traces of the hunter's body fluids, one more decomposed than the other. So they came this way and went back out."

Spider looked up to where a small house sat perched on stilts, stretching a weathered dock into a cypress-cradled pond. "They came here, lingered for some reason, and left, taking Lavern's body with them."

"I also found that odd trace, the same as in the river. It's blood, but it tastes of something other than man."

Spider propped his elbow on his knee and leaned, resting his chin against his fingers. The blood was interesting. "A wounded. They had a wounded with them, and they dropped him off here."

"Yes, m'lord."

"Why here? Why not take him to the Mar house, behind the wards?" Spider tapped his cheek with his finger. "How much time does Lavern's body have left?"

"Twenty-two minutes. Although I may be mistaken and it's twenty-three."

Spider smiled. "You're never mistaken, Ruh. Let's wait then and find out if we're right."

He touched the reins, and the rolpie obediently pulled the small boat under the cover of a gnarled tree bent over the water.


CERISE descended the small staircase hidden in the back of the kitchen. The wooden steps, worn out by four generations of feet, creaked and sagged under her weight. They would have to be repaired before too long. Of course, that would keep Aunt Petunia from the lab, and she wasn't suicidal enough to become the object of her aunt's wrath. And it would be wrath. No doubt about it—Aunt Pete did nothing halfway.

Fatigue filled Cerise, making her legs terribly heavy. She had to do this and then she could go upstairs, shower, and collapse into her bed for a couple of hours. She couldn't remember the last time she ate.

The staircase ended in a solid door, fitted so snugly that no light escaped along its edges. Cerise rapped her knuckles on the metal.

The door swung open, revealing the Bunker. Uncle Jean had built it for Aunt Pete following the instructions for a fallout shelter, and it looked like one, too—concrete walls and harsh lighting spilling from the cones of electric lamps in the ceiling. She never could figure out how he'd managed to keep the water out, but the Bunker never leaked. In the event something contaminated it, one pull of the chain hanging from the far wall and the water tower would empty into the bunker, flooding it with magic-treated water, neutralizing the problem. The neutralizing solution then drained into a cistern outside the house.

Mikita closed the door behind her. She walked along the wooden platform bordering the walls, jumped off to the bottom, and headed past the decontamination shower to the examination table and Aunt Pete bent over it with a scalpel.

Short and plump, Aunt Pete frowned at her, a look of intense concentration on her face. That look was a killer. Aunt Petunia made the best pies, and that's exactly how she looked when she mixed the crust. Every time Cerise saw that expression, it catapulted her back in time, and she was five years old again, hiding under the table with a stolen piece of piping hot berry pie and trying not to giggle, while Aunt Pete made a big show of looking for the thief and bumping into the table for added drama.

Unfortunately, this time Aunt Petunia wasn't working on a pie. The body of the hunter lay on the table, split open like a butterflied shrimp. The organs had been carefully removed, weighed, and placed into ceramic trays. Soft red mush filled the bottom of the trays. It shouldn't have been there.

"I like you, child. You bring such interesting things home," Aunt Petunia said through a cloth mask.

"Put your mask on," Mikita boomed.

Cerise took the mask from his hand and slipped it on.

"He's decomposing too fast," Aunt Petunia said. "In a few hours there will be nothing left. There." She nodded at the microscope on the side.

Cerise looked into the ocular. Long twisted ribbons glistening with faint blue flailed among the familiar globules of blood cells. "What is that?"

"Worms."

"I gathered that."

"Hold the sass, missy. I don't know what they are, but they must've hatched when the body began to cool and they're devouring our cadaver. That's high-grade magic right there. Someone probably was set for life after making these little monstrosities. There is more. Come look at this."

She clamped the hunter's upper lip with metal forceps

and curled it up, revealing fangs. "Look at those choppers. And these two have poison glands."

Aunt Petunia moved on to the arm. "And here we have claws between the knuckles. The claw goes back like so, the small sack behind it contracts, and we get a nice stream of sticky goo."

The small black claw slid back under the pressure of her forceps, and a drop of opaque goo swelled around it.

"It doesn't shoot out now, because our boy is dead and the sack is empty, but I'm guessing a jet of about four to five feet."

"More like nine," Cerise said.

Aunt Petunia's eyebrows rose. "Nine. Really?"

Cerise nodded.

"He's one sick puppy." Aunt Petunia leaned back. "Your grandfather would've loved this. He would be appalled, of course, but he would be able to appreciate the workmanship. When you change someone with magic this much, well, they aren't human anymore."

No, they weren't human. Cerise hugged herself. This thing, this was something monstrous and uncontrollable. People she could deal with. People had weaknesses—they didn't like being hurt, they cared for their family, they could be intimidated, outwitted, bribed . . . The way the hunter had looked at her had made her hair stand on end. As if she were an object, a thing, something you could break or eat, but not a person. How did you fight something like that? She couldn't think of anything that would stop it, short of completely destroying it.

They would need her flash or a really big gun. Or William. William seemed to work very well.

"So when do I get to examine the other one?" Aunt Petunia peered at her from above her glasses.

"What other one?"

"The gorgeous one you supposedly found in the swamp."

Cerise raised her arms in the air. "Does nothing stay put in this house?"

"Of course not." Aunt Petunia snorted. "I was told he's so handsome that Murid actually spoke to him."

"He isn't that handsome." Cerise hesitated. "Okay, yes, he is."

"Hrmph," Mikita said.

"You like him!" The older woman grinned.

"Maybe a little." Understatement of the year. "He's an ass."

"Hrmph!" Mikita said.

"I believe my son is trying to tell us that we're offending his delicate sensibilities with our girl talk." Aunt Petunia grimaced. "You look tired, dear. And you smell like humus."

*Thank you, Auntie.* "It's been a long week."

"Go. Bathe, eat, sleep, flirt with your blueblood. It's good for the soul."

Mikita lumbered off to unlock the door.

"He isn't so much on flirting," Cerise murmured. "Either he doesn't like me or he doesn't know how."

"Of course he likes you. You're lovely. He probably just doesn't get it. Some men have to be hit over the head with it." Her aunt rolled her eyes. "I thought I'd have to draw your uncle Jean a giant sign. That or kidnap him and have my evil way with him, until he got the message."

"Hrrrmph!!"

"Go," Aunt Petunia waved her on. "Go, go, go."

"All right, all right, I'm going." Cerise climbed up and stepped out.

Mikita carefully closed the door behind her and locked it.

*Flirt with your blueblood, yes, yes.* Cerise started up the stairs. How do you flirt with a man who doesn't know the meaning of the word?

"THREE," Ruh whispered. "Two . . ."

"One," Spider said.

* * *

**AN** explosion shook the staircase.

Oh, Gods.

Cerise whirled, covering the ten steps in two jumps.

Heavy thuds hammered against the door. A hoarse scream ripped through the cacophony of shattering glass.

"Mikita!" She pounded the door. "Mikita, open the door!"

Something thumped inside. Boards splintered with a dry snap. Metal screeched against the stone.

"Aunt Petunia?"

A dull thud answered her and dissolved into the drum of drops on metal. The decontamination shower. Someone was alive in there.

"Mikita!"

Above her a door banged and people rushed down the staircase. Erian landed next to her, light on his feet. Above him William popped into her view and jumped, clearing the stairs in the single leap.

"The door won't open!" she told him.

He glanced at the door and ran back up the stairs, almost knocking Ignata, her cousin, out of the way. A moment later Ignata ran down, her worried face a pale oval in the tangle of curly reddish hair. "Mom? What's going on?"

"Something exploded in the lab. Your brother and your mother are both in there, and I can't get through. The decontamination shower is on."

"Mikita! Mom! Mother!" Ignata waited for a breath. "We must open the door."

"We can't," Erian said quietly. "They've triggered the shower."

"They're hurt," Ignata said.

William had taken off. She had no time to wonder where he was going.

"Erian is right." It hurt her to say it, but it had to be said. "If we open it, we risk spreading whatever it is they're trying to contain all over the house."

"You two are out of your minds."

"There are children upstairs," Cerise said.

Ignata starcd at her. "They could die in there!"

"If they do, you can blame me for it later." Cerise clenched her teeth.

Richard appeared in the doorway above. "What's going on?"

Erian held up his hand. "Noise. Water running."

Ignata leaned against the wall and hugged herself, her hands white-knuckled on her forearms.

A faint scratch cut through the sounds of water. Cerise put her ear to the door. "Mikita?"

"Here." His voice came in a hoarse whisper.

She closed her eyes for a second, overwhelmed by relief. Alive. He was alive.

"Aunt Pete?"

"Hurt."

*Oh no.*

"Can you open the door?"

"Stuck . . . tight."

"Hang on, Mikita," she breathed. "Hang on. We'll get you out."

*Think, think, think.* The magic-treated neutralizing solution would kill any contamination. She had no doubt about it—her grandfather had taught Aunt Petunia to make it, and his magic never failed. "Erian, do we have any neutralizing solution left?"

"How much do you need?"

"As much as you can carry."

He ran up the stairs, taking them two at the time.

Cerise glanced at Ignata. "I need you to move, so I can have room."

Ignata climbed up the steps.

She had to cut the lock out. "Richard, I need a knife."

He passed her his knife. She concentrated on the blade. The door was three inches thick. It would take more than onc strike.

Cerise flashed, slashing at the door handle with the blade. A three-inch-long gouge scoured the metal.

*Slash.* She broke through the metal.

*Slash.*

*Slash.*

Sweat broke out on her forehead. Not fast enough.

*Slash.*

*Slash.*

Finished. A ragged crescent cut cleaved the lock from the rest of the door. Cerise rammed the door and bounced off. Stuck tight.

William landed on the stairs next to her, a roll of pale bubble gum lined with paper in his fingers. He tore a chunk of bubble gum, pressed it against the upper hinge, tore another strip, stuck it on the lower one, peeled the paper away in one single-layered movement, grabbed her hand, and ran up the stairs, pulling her into the crowded kitchen, away from the door.

"Explosives!" Richard barked.

The family pressed against the wall.

A second passed.

Another.

The explosion popped, small, almost like a firecracker going off.

William dropped her on her feet and dashed back down the stairs. Richard followed. Cerise chased them.

"Mikita, get away from the door," Richard called out.

Erian reappeared, carrying a bucket of the neutralizing solution. Cerise grabbed one side of the bucket, he grabbed the other.

Richard and William rammed the door with their shoulders in unison.

The door creaked, careened, like a tooth about to fall out, and crashed down. Cerise and Erian heaved and dumped a glittering liquid cascade into the opening. The water fell, leaving Mikita, drenched and pale, holding his mother in his arms as if she were a child. He took a step and crumpled. They lunged forward and caught his big body before he hit the floor.

# SIXTEEN

SPIDER raised his eyebrows. No explosion.

"You were right," he said. "They're gone and they've taken Lavern's body with them."

Gone to the Rathole. Gone behind the wards where they couldn't be touched. He braided his fingers, thinking. *Cerise, Cerise, Cerise.* Such workmanship with the sword. A single strike per body, flash stretched over the blade—an almost forgotten skill. But who was with her? Who was the second person in the boat?

"What now?" Ruh's yellow eyes regarded him.

"We could return to the base." Spider smiled. "But then there is that trace of odd blood in the water. There were three people in that boat. One of them was Cerise, we know that. One of them was her cousin, the thoas. The question is, who was the third person? The thoas had bled and was poisoned. From what we know, it was likely copper poisoning, which would rob him of consciousness. Cerise wouldn't be able to move him by herself. She had help from her passenger, who was likely a man and a strong one. I want to know who he is. Aren't you curious, Ruh? I'm curious. It's such a nice little cottage. Looks very hospitable. I think that I shall call on them."


CLARA tugged at the woolen blanket, freeing Urow's feet. He couldn't sleep with his feet covered and usually wriggled until his clawed toes emerged from under the blanket. Her gesture served no purpose now. Urow had sunk so deep into his herb-induced sleep that a roar of an ervaurg in his ear wouldn't wake him. Let alone the feel of wool on his feet.

She brushed his hair from his forehead, feeling the cool skin of his face. The fever had ebbed, and his breathing slowed to an even rhythm, still a touch too shallow, but steadily improving. Her fingers traced the deep lines at the corners of his eyes. The laugh lines. He called them Clara's wrinkles. He claimed she was responsible for most of them. Before meeting her, he hadn't laughed enough to make them.

She felt tears swelling up and held them back. She had almost lost him. Just like that, he would've been gone, ripped away from her.

For a space of a breath she closed her eyes and dared to imagine what it would be like if he were no longer there. His smile, his strength, his voice, all gone. Her throat hurt. She tried to swallow and couldn't, struggling with a hard lump until it finally burst from her mouth in a small sob. Nothing would ever be the same. *Gods, how do people survive that?*

She opened her eyes. He was still breathing.

*My Urow.*

She blinked the tears from her eyes and looked away to keep from crying, looked to the walls of the room, which bore bundles of dried herbs and small wooden shelves. An assortment of knickknacks filled the shelves: a ceramic cow, painted deep red; a tiny teapot with bright red stars of bog flowers painted on the pale green; a small doll in a cheery yellow and blue dress. She had always wanted a girl, ever since she gave birth to Ry nineteen years ago, and so she had bought the doll, determined that one day she would give it to her daughter. Her gaze traveled to the crib. She finally had her wish. Took three boys, but she had her little girlie. Everything seemed to be going so well . . .

Why? Why did the feud have to flare now? Was it because they were happy?

Urow's fingers moved under the blanket, and she bent forward, afraid she woke him up. His lips moved a little, but his eyes remained closed, his breathing even. Still asleep.

She could sit like this till he awoke, watching his chest rise and fall. For a moment it was almost too tempting, but then she had three boys to feed and the dinner wouldn't make itself. Clara let her fingers graze his cheek one last time and rose.

On her way to the kitchen, she paused by the shelf and picked up the doll. The painted blue eyes looked at her. A single line made a happy smile on the doll's face. Five months ago, when she gave birth, she had decided that she was going to wait until Sydney grew big enough to play with the doll before she would give it to her.

Life was too short and ended too suddenly. If you didn't take advantage of what you had today, tomorrow it might be ripped from you.

Clara tugged the doll skirt straighter and took a step to the crib. Sydney lay curled; her blanket kicked free, the dark fuzz of baby hair sticking straight up from her head. Clara tucked the doll in the fold of her daughter's little arm and put the blanket over them.

In the kitchen she fired up the stove and checked the fish stock she'd made in the morning. She'd clarified it a good two hours ago by stirring a beaten egg and crumpled eggshell into the pot and carefully simmering it at a near boil to separate the grease.

It needed more pepper. She checked the glass jar, but there was none left. She could send Gaston out for some water-bright. It wasn't as good as real pepper but would do in a pinch.

But then, one of the boys had to stand guard. With Mart and Ry gone, only Gaston remained to keep watch. Those were Urow's rules, and she would follow them to the letter. Especially now. The soup would survive without the pepper. Besides, when the two oldest returned from herding the rolpies into the shelter, she could ask one of them to fetch some.

*You'd think we are at war.* She dropped the sieve into the sink, irritated, stirred up the fire to warm up the stock, and reached into the cold box for the widemouth fish caught by the boys the night before.

The odd thing was, she liked Gustave Mar. She never cared for Genevieve that much—too smart and too . . . not prissy exactly, but too . . . too something. Like she was just born better than they were, with better manners and a prettier face, and she wasn't unapologetic about it either, as if that was a natural thing to be. Genevieve made her feel like a stupid mud rat. Clara had never cared for the woman, and her daughters weren't much better either.

Clara hacked the fish's head off with a cleaver and filleted it with deft precise strokes. But Gustave was always pleasant, she had to admit that. Still, he was gone now, and nothing would bring him back. And even if it did, how many lives would it take to rescue him? Nobody was worth that much blood. No matter what that daughter of his thought.

The stock was close to a boil. She bent and scraped the fish bones off the cutting board into the garbage vat and saw feet in black boots in her kitchen.

Clara straightened very slowly, her gaze rising from the boots and black trousers to the jacket, to the wide shoulders, and then to the face above the dark collar. It belonged to a blond man of indeterminable age, somewhere between late twenties and early forties. The face was pleasant enough. She glanced into his eyes and froze. They were empty and stone-hard. Trouble eyes. Fear shot through her.

How did he get by Gaston? She'd heard no noise, no commotion.

"Limes," the man said, offering her a handful of the bumpy citrus fruit. "You'll need some for the fish soup, so I took the liberty of picking some up on my way through your storeroom. I understand the trick is to cut them paper-thin so they'll float on top of the soup when you pour it into the bowls."

Those eyes, they made her want to raise her hands in the air and back away slowly, until it was safe to run for her life. But there was nowhere to run. This was her house. In the next room Urow and the baby lay helpless. Clara kept her eyes firmly on the man's face. *Stay asleep, Sydney. Stay asleep, because if he gets you, I'll do whatever he says.*

"Well, are you going to take the limes or aren't you?"

She opened her mouth, knowing that saying anything was a mistake and unable to help herself. The words came out hoarse. "Get out of my house."

He sighed, put the limes on the counter, and leaned against the cabinet, like a black crow come to caw on her grave. "Two people came here less than eight hours ago. They brought a thoas with them and left him in your house. That thoas, who is he to you? Your husband, perhaps?"

"Get out," she repeated, moving back. The cleaver in her hand was useless. He'd take it away from her and chop her to pieces with it.

"I see. A husband, then. He was hurt. My sympathies. I hope he recovers." The man nodded gravely. "But he doesn't interest me as much as the two who brought him. One of them was Cerise Mar. I'd like to learn about her companion. I want to know everything about this other person. Looks. Age. Accent. Anything that you might find helpful to contribute."

He smiled at her, a bright dazzling smile. "If you tell me what I want to know, I'll depart and let you get back to your cooking. That stock smells divine, by the way. So what do you say?"

He fixed Clara with his stare, and she hesitated, suddenly panicky, like a bird caught in a glass cage. The menace radiating from him was so strong that deep inside she cringed and tried to shield the gaping hole that sucked at the bottom of her belly.

"It's an honest offer." He leaned forward. "Tell me what I want to know and I'll vanish." He weaved his long fingers through the air. "Like a ghost. An unpleasant but harmless memory that will fade with time."

His stare offered reassurance like a crutch, and Clara realized that he wasn't bluffing. He wouldn't harm her if she told him what he wanted to know. She felt the need to please him. It would be so easy . . .

But he had hurt Urow. The thought sliced through her hesitation. He or someone who worked for him almost took her husband away from her. He would take her children if she let him.

"I'm afraid that I'm rather pressed for time," he said.

Clara took a deep breath and threw the cleaver at him. As he caught the wide spinning blade by the handle, she swiped at the stock pot off the stove and hurled it at him.

The boiling stock splashed over the man in a wide shower. She dashed away through the doorway, leading him away from the baby, away from Urow.

An animal snarl of pure rage whipped her into a frenzy. She scrambled through the familiar cluttered rooms, through the den to Ry's room, to the window. Her fingers grasped the windowsill and she pulled herself up.

A steel hand clasped Clara's leg and jerked her down with impossible force. She screamed as the back of her head hit the floor. He jerked her ankle up, nearly lifting her body with one hand. His eyes burned her with deranged fury. Somewhere deep inside a small part of her refused to accept what was happening, stubbornly chanting, *It's not real, it's not real, it's not real . . .*

The heel of his left hand hit her knee. Her ears caught the sharp snap of the broken bone. In the first second she felt nothing. And then the pain ripped from her knee through her femur into her hip, as if someone poured molten lead into her leg bone. Clara screamed, clawing at the air.

"Hurts, doesn't it," he snarled.

She barely heard him, trying to roll, trying to draw her

ruined leg to her. *Oh, Gods, it hurts so much, it hurts, oh, Gods. Help me!*

He wrenched her ankle higher. She saw the cleaver in his hand and shook, her eyes opened wide and frozen with shock. *No. No, you can't do this to me. No.*

The cleaver fell in a shining metal arc. Ice bit her, and then he was holding the bloody stump of her leg, her foot still in the brown shoe. He tossed it aside as if it was a log. It hit the wall and bounced, leaving a bloody smudge.

Blood fountained from the stump in a crimson spray. She couldn't speak, she couldn't breathe. All sound fled the world and time slowed to a terrible crawl. She saw the man's lips move, and then he twisted, shockingly fast to her underwater-sluggish eyes. He leaped up over her, and through the window. Glass fragments showered her like a glittering rain, falling, falling . . .

Urow's face swung into view, his fangs bared, eyes burning with mad rage. She saw him drop the enormous crossbow. He had been meaning to mount the thing up on the roof for ages. It was too heavy for him to wield. How silly.

His eyes met hers. His lips moved, but she couldn't hear him. He looked so scared, like a lost child. *Don't be frightened, darling. Don't be.*

She could feel the darkness encroaching, ready to pounce on her. She tried to reach out to him, to touch his face, but her arm wouldn't obey.

*I think I'm dying.*

*I love you.*

# SEVENTEEN

CERISE slumped in a chair, painfully aware of William waiting next to her like a dark shadow. He didn't seem to want anything, he just . . . stood guard over her. It was absurd—she was in the family house—but for some odd reason it made her feel better.

Across from her, Richard leaned against the wall, watching William with sharp eyes. The rest of the family mulled about. People came and went. Cerise didn't pay much attention to them.

"How strong are you, William?" Richard asked.

"As strong as I need to be," William answered.

Richard's face showed very little, but she had been reading his expressions since they were kids and she found concern in the minute bend of his mouth. Something about William deeply troubled her cousin.

The door swung open, and Ignata stepped out, wiping her hands with a towel. Cerise rose from her chair.

"Mikita has two broken ribs," Ignata announced.

"What about Aunt Pete?" Erian asked.

Ignata squared her shoulders, and Cerise knew it was bad. "Mom lost her left eye."

The words punched her. Cerise rocked back. She should've dumped the damn body into the river. First Urow, now Mikita and Aunt Pete. Urow and Mikita would recover, but eyes didn't grow back. She'd managed to disfigure her aunt for life.

Ignata pulled at the towel, twisting it. "We aren't out of the woods yet. The cadaver was full of tiny worms.

When the body exploded, both of them were showered with bone shards and decomposing tissue. The worms are circulating through their bloodstream. So far all of them seem to be dead, but I don't know if that will persist."

"Transparent worms?" William had a look of intense concentration on his face, as if trying to remember something.

"Yes," Ignata said.

"The parasites will activate only when the temperature of the body drops below 88.7 degrees Fahrenheit. Do you know how to purge malaria?"

Ignata nodded. "And we have Chloroquine."

"What's that?"

"It's a type of medicine people in the Broken use to stop malaria."

"Give it to them," William said.

Ignata pursed her lips. Her gaze found Cerise.

"Do it," Cerise said.

Ignata turned and went back into the room.

Cerise glanced at William. "Did you know the body would explode?"

"No."

"But you knew about the worms?"

William nodded. "Sometimes the Hand does it to keep the altered bodies from being examined by their enemies."

"Why didn't you warn me?"

"My memory doesn't work that way. If you'd asked me specifically about worms or if the Hand ever infected their operatives with parasites, I could answer."

That wasn't the way normal memories worked. William had done something to himself, Cerise was certain of it now. He was enhanced somehow, just like the Hand's freaks. Either he was one of them or he'd made himself like them in the name of revenge.

Cerise wished she could open his head and search it. Since that wasn't possible, she would have to settle for going with her instincts, and they told her he wanted re-

venge, yearned for it, the way a man dying of thirst
yearned for a drink. When he spoke about Spider, his
whole demeanor changed. He tensed, his eyes focused
with predatory alertness, his body ready as if it were a
coiled spring. She wanted to find her parents with the
same desperation.

And now it had cost her aunt an eye. How the hell was
she supposed to live with herself after that? How many
more injuries would it take?

Often wrong, but never in doubt. Right. "Richard?"

"Yes?"

"The Hand has a tracker. They may track the body
down the river. Let's put some sharpshooters on our side
of the wards. If they show, maybe we could even out the
score."

"Very well." Richard turned, stabbed William with a
long look, and left the room, Erian in tow.

"You're still winning," William said.

"Urow is hanging by a thread, my aunt is blind in one
eye, and my other cousin has two broken ribs."

"Yes, but they're still breathing."

Good point. So why didn't it make her feel any better?

Ignata reemerged, carrying a box. She set it on the table. "Wallowing in self-hatred or self-pity?"

"Right now it's hatred for the Hand," Cerise told her.
"When I switch to self-pity, I will definitely let you know.
I should've dumped the body overboard."

"Oh, please." Ignata rolled her eyes. "Mom had the
time of her life playing with it. I've told her again and
again: wear the damn goggles. Kaldar stole those special
for her. I told her, Mikita told her: wear eye protection,
Mom. But no, the lot of us are apparently stupid. We
don't know anything, and she can see just fine, and when
she wears her goggles, the lenses fog up . . ."

Ignata pulled the towel off her shoulder and threw it
across the room.

"It helps to throw something heavy," William said.

Ignata waved him off. "You, hush. Look, Ceri, we all make mistakes, and we pay for them, especially if they're made out of arrogance."

Ignata plucked a vial from the box, and the scent of dirty socks and rotten citrus spread through the room. Valerian extract.

"So as much as you'd like to own this particular mistake, it belongs to my mom. She owns it all by her own lonesome self and she knows it. If she had worn the goggles, she'd have gotten away with a couple of broken ribs like my brother."

Ignata counted off ten drops into a glass and poured some water into it from a bottle. "Drink. You need sleep."

Cerise took the glass.

"I wouldn't," William murmured.

Ignata fixed him with her glare. "You—be quiet. You—bottoms up. Now."

It was only valerian, and arguing with Ignata was like trying to reason with a pit bull. Cerise gulped the water in one big swallow. Fire and night rolled down her throat.

"What did you put in this?"

"Water, valerian, and a very strong hypnotic. You have about five minutes to get to your room and shower, or you'll pass out where you stand."

"Ignata!"

"Ignata-Ignata-Ignata!" Ignata waved her arms. "When was the last time you ate or slept? What, nothing to say? You have tonight to sleep, tomorrow to rest, and the day after tomorrow you're going to take our posse to the Sheeriles, and after that, I won't have time for you. I'll be busy patching up everybody else. So you just go on! Shoo! And take your blueblood with you." She pointed a long finger at William. "You, walk with her and make sure she doesn't pass out someplace on the stairs."

Cerise sighed and headed up the stairs. William followed her.

"She's mad," he said.

"No, she is trying to keep it together and not cry. Her mother and brother could've died. There isn't much she can do, so she's bossing me around."

He frowned. "You mean, in revenge?"

"A little, yes. My father used to tell me, 'When you're in charge, everything is your fault.' She blames me a little." Her feet grew heavier with each step, as if someone slowly poured lead into her bones. "She'd never admit it even to herself, but she blames me."

"So that's what it's like to have a large family," he said.

Now her head grew too heavy. Her eyelids tried to close on their own. She stopped by the door to her room. "Something like that. You haven't seen the worst of it. Did they give you a room?"

William bared his teeth. "Yes. Kaldar showed it to me." He said Kaldar's name like he wanted to strangle him.

"I'm not mad at you about the worms," she told him, trying to force her thoughts into a coherent pattern. She yawned. "I'm sorry, I'm very sleepy."

"That's okay," he said. He was standing a little too close.

"What kind of blueblood says *okay*, Lord Bill? You need to work on your cover some more." She yawned. "You would make a horrible spy. Promise me that while I'm asleep, you won't injure any of my cousins, not even Kaldar."

William looked at her.

"I'm exhausted and miserable. Promise me. No snapping people's heads off their necks, no broken bones, nothing to make me regret taking you to my family."

"You got it," he said.

"Thank you."

"You're welcome."

"The little girl says there is a monster in the woods," he said.

Something lurched in her chest. "It's her."

William was looking at her.

"It's Lark," she said, her chest hurting. "She thinks she's the monster."

William's arms closed about her. She should've said
something. She should have pushed him away. But she
felt so tired and so down, and his arms were strong and
comforting. He held her to him, and the dull ache gnawing at her receded. It felt so nice, that she just leaned
against him. He dipped his head. She watched him do it
but didn't realize why he was doing it until his lips
grazed her mouth.

"Sleep well," he said. "I'll watch your family for you."
He let her go.

Cerise closed the door and stared at it for a long moment, unsure if they had really touched or if she had
imagined it. She got nowhere and sat on her bed to pull
off her boots. She got the left one off, and then the bed
turned upside down and fell on the back of her head.


**WILLIAM** awoke to the darkened bedroom. The air was
cool and a narrow sliver of moonlight sliced through the
draperies to fall at the floor. For a moment he lay still,
looking at the ceiling, his arms behind his head.

He'd kissed Cerise and she let him. His memory had
preserved the moment with near perfect recall. He remembered everything: the tilt of her face, the angle of
her hair, the puzzlement in her dark eyes, the feeling of
holding her against him, the delicate trace of her scent
on his lips. He would kiss her again, even if her entire
family lined up to shoot him while he did it.

William rolled off the bed, moving on quiet feet, and
tried the door handle. Still locked. They had shut him in
like he was a child.

He smiled, pulled open his backpack, and fished out
the night suit. He stripped and pulled on the pants and
the shirt. The fabric, stained with dark and light gray,
clung to him like a second skin. The first time he'd seen
the thing, complete with a hood and a face mask covering everything except his eyes, he'd told Nancy that as
far as he knew, he wasn't a ninja. She'd told him to wear

it and like it. He still wasn't sure if she had even known what a ninja was.

William had to admit, the suit had a certain logic to it. True night was never just black; it was a shifting ethereal mix of shadow and darkness, of dappled gray and deep indigo. A man wearing solid black stood out as a uniform spot of darkness.

He drew the line at the hood and the mask, though. A man had to have standards, and he had no desire to cover his ears or to breathe through a cloth. Besides, it made him look like a total idiot.

Since Cerise went to bed, he'd been passed from one relative to another, with Kaldar checking on him every half an hour or so until he was ready to wring the man's neck. Kaldar had the slick easy charm of a talented swindler. He said whatever popped into his mouth, laughed easily, and talked too much. During the evening William had watched him steal a hook from Catherine's basket, a knife from Erian, some sort of metal tool from Ignata, and a handful of bullets from one of Cerise's cousins. Kaldar did it casually, with smooth grace, handled the item for a couple of moments, and slipped it back where it came from. William had a distinct suspicion that if Kaldar was caught, he'd just laugh it off, and his demented family would let him get away with it. They knew Kaldar was a villain. They didn't care.

William found a small box with camo paint, and darkened his face, splaying the gray, dark green, and brown on in irregular blotches. That done, he slid his knives into his belt and swiped up the Mirror's crossbow. He loaded it with two poisoned bolts from the quiver, careful not to touch the complicated mechanical bolt heads. The toxin was potent enough to take down a horse in mid-canter. The bolts' heads were too large and oddly shaped, and his accuracy would suffer, but it didn't matter. The crossbow was a weapon of last resort, to be used at close range, when death had to be guaranteed.

Someone in Cerise's family didn't play by the rules.

Someone had told the Hand about Urow. He was sure that many locals were aware that the Mars had a thoas relative, but only a family member would know that this thoas went to pick up Cerise in Sicktree.

If there was a traitor in the family, he would have a direct line to Spider or someone on Spider's crew. And given that Cerise had just arrived home with some strange blueblood in tow, the traitor should be dying to tell Spider about it.

The traitor would wait until most of the house had gone to bed for the night, and the Mars seemed to suffer from a critical inability to be quiet. The giant house buzzed like a beehive for most of the evening. It was close to midnight now, and Cerise's noisy family had finally settled down.

William strapped the sleeper to his wrist. It was a complicated gadget, all clockwork gears and magic, embedded into a leather wrist guard. Four narrow metal barrels sat in a row on top of the sleeper. William pulled three thin wire loops from the underside of the wrist guard and threaded them on his index, middle, and ring fingers. He spread his fingers. The barrels rotated around his wrist like chambers on a revolver. If he flexed his wrist, driving the heel of his hand forward, the lowest barrel would fire, spitting a small canister armed with a needle. The canister held enough narcotic to put a large man into a deep sleep within three seconds.

It was an elegant weapon. He would miss the Mirror's toys when this was over.

The traitor would head for the Mire. He was sure of it. First, he had already learned that nothing that happened within earshot of the Mar house stayed private. Second, Lark mentioned a monster in the woods. Cerise said Lark thought of herself as a monster, but he wasn't sure she was right. The kid might've been confused. She might've seen something in the fog and the trees she couldn't explain to her sister. Some of the Hand's agents had enough enhancements to give a grown man nightmares, let alone a child. If Lark had found an odd, scary creature in the woods, he wanted to meet it.

He had a very simple plan: keep watch, identify the traitor as he or she left for the woods, then follow their trail to the wonderful presents that waited on the other end. He might get a drop on the Hand's agent and follow him to whatever deep dark hole Spider claimed as his lair in the swamp.

Perhaps he might even let the Hand's agent see him, William decided. Then they would have to have a conversation. Maybe some bones would even get broken. He chuckled soundlessly.

The window slid open without a sound. He eased through it onto the long balcony and crouched down, moving away into the deeper shadow by the rail.

The moon dipped in and out of ragged clouds. In the distance an old gator voiced a lazy roar. The wind smelled of water and the mimosa-tinted perfume of night needle flowers.

It had been a while since he'd hunted, and the night was calling.

Below, past the rail, the yard lay empty. William sat still, quiet and patient.

Minutes stretched like honey.

A faint shiver troubled the cypress branches to the left. A boy with a rifle. No older than twelve.

Another stir, to the right. A young woman in the pine. Judging by the distance between the trees, a third lookout probably waited on the opposite side of the house. They faced out, watching the Mire. None saw him.

A door closed shut with a quiet thump up ahead.

He slipped along the balcony, staying in the shadows, and sank down by the rail again. The spot gave him a view of a narrow slice of the front balcony and most of the staircase.

Measured footsteps, followed by a barely audible second set. He'd learned that second sound very well by now. Kaldar. Ugh.

The wind fetched their scents for him. Yeah, Kaldar and Richard. Those two were on the top of his traitor suspect list. Kaldar had the air of a man who always needed money but never had enough. The Hand paid well. When they didn't murder their hirelings, that was.

Richard was a different story. William had picked Catherine's brains while sitting in the library and listened to the family's chatter for the entire evening until he'd pieced together the family tree. Grandmother Az had seven children. Of the seven, Alain Mar had been the oldest. Alain had three children, Richard, Kaldar, and Erian. When the Sheeriles had shot Alain in the market place, Richard was seventeen, Kaldar was fourteen, and Erian was ten. The family reins passed to Gustave, Cerise's father. Cerise's parents had taken Erian, because his brothers had been too young to take care of him.

Richard smelled like a natural alpha. Rational, calm, respected, from what little William had seen. People looked up to him, Cerise included. But Richard wasn't in charge. Cerise was. Why?

He liked Richard for the traitor. The bulk of Cerise's relatives consisted of her cousins, their children, and relatives by marriage, but only the core of the family knew about Urow meeting Cerise. He'd managed to narrow it down to eight people: Cerise, Richard, Kaldar, Erian, Murid, Petunia, and Ignata.

Catherine mentioned that Richard's wife had left him about a year ago. Spouses didn't seem to last among Mars.

If he had a wife and she left him, he would feel powerless, William decided. He would try to find the biggest, baddest asshole and take him down. It wouldn't matter if he won or lost the fight. Either way, he'd replace the emotional hurt with real physical pain, something he could deal with, something that did eventually get better. They were similar, Richard and he. They both kept things contained inside. He'd sat next to Richard during the evening for a few minutes. They didn't say a word to each other, sharing a calm silence. Richard had shown emotion only once. They'd both watched Kaldar slip the knife back into the sheath on Erian's belt, and Richard had permitted himself a long-suffering sigh.

Maybe Richard wanted to prove to everyone that he wasn't as powerless as his wife had made him feel.

"The man carries military-grade explosives in his pack," Richard said quietly. "They came from the Weird. The magic aftershock was so strong, my teeth hurt."

"Cerise said he used to be a soldier." Kaldar's tone was light. "William's obviously on a hunting expedition. As long as he hunts the other side, we win."

They were talking about him. Ha!

The two men stayed silent for a long moment.

"I didn't hit that door," Richard said.

"Hm?"

"The door to the Bunker. It was all him. He knocked it out, before I hit it. I barely grazed it."

"So you're sore, because you missed out on a bruise on your shoulder?" Kaldar asked.

"After we got Mikita out, I looked at the Bunker. One of those big storage shelves had fallen against the door. The weight of the door plus the shelf . . ."

"Richard, I told you today that you're like a mother hen." Kaldar took a few steps down the stairs, coming into his view. William stayed still.

"You have to loosen up, brother. You're so tense, you'll get the lot of us killed."

"The man is dangerous."

Kaldar raised his arms. "Of course he's dangerous. You've got to have balls to come out after the Hand. They hunt; they don't get hunted. Besides, you know she wouldn't have brought him here if they didn't reach some sort of agreement. She trusts him and I trust her."

"She's young. Don't tell me you can't see what's going on. I saw the way she looked at him when he dragged her up the stairs. Her parents are gone. She isn't thinking clearly."

Kaldar turned on his foot on the stair. William had to give it to the man—Kaldar had balance.

"Richard, how old do you think she is?"

"She's . . ." Richard didn't finish.

"Yeah," Kaldar said. "She is twenty-four. And you're thirty-three. In your head you must still be a teenager, while she and Erian are toddlers. They grew up. We all grew up. I come here more often that you do. Gustave runs the family, but Ceri runs the house."

"What do you mean?"

Kaldar heaved a sigh. "I mean that our dear uncle Gustave drove the Mar family ship right into the ground. He has no head for business. You could give him a free crate of guns from the Broken, and he'd manage to sell it at a loss. Genevieve's too busy, she's dealing with Lark and trying to keep the rest of the kids fed and watered, but when it comes down to it, she just doesn't want to deal with money. Can't say I blame her. I wouldn't want to do it. So three years ago they dumped the accounts onto Ceri. She balances the books, she pays out our allotments, and she picks up our expenses. Why do you think she's been going with me to the Broken? She knows how bad it is, and she's pinching every penny, looking for some sort of angle to get us more money. We're clawing out of the hole Gustave put us in, but it's slow going. And there are too damn many of us, and everyone keeps having emergencies that bleed the money."

"I had no idea." Richard's voice was clipped.

William grimaced. He had no idea either. Money wasn't something he had in abundance, but he knew it had to be rationed. Back in the Legion, his food and gear were free, so what money he had, he spent on leave, on booze, books, and women. The first few months in the Broken turned his world upside down. He'd almost gotten himself evicted before he learned to pay bills first and spend on other things later. He'd seen enough of the Mars—their clothes were patched, their equipment was old, with the exception of a rare piece here and there, but everyone looked well fed. To keep the horde of Mars in line, Cerise would have to squeeze every cent.

Kaldar kept going. "They make a pretense of Gustave still approving everything, but trust me on this, it's all her. If you go into her room, wake her up, and ask her how much money we have, I bet you she'll tell you the balance down to a penny. If any of us are thinking clearly, she is it."

Richard's voice gained an icy haughtiness. "I'll speak to Gustave, once we find him."

"And say what? That it doesn't sit well with you that our funny baby cousin is scrounging for change to keep us in this oh-so-rich style we've become accustomed to?"

Richard didn't answer.

Kaldar's face jerked. "When I found out, I asked Gustave about it, and he looked at me like I'd sprouted a water lily on my head. She was twenty-one then, and when Gustave was twenty-four, he'd taken over the family."

"It's not right," Richard said.

Kaldar shrugged. "She works hard, Richard, and the Hand just pulled the rug out from under her feet. If this blueblood makes her happy, I'm all for it. She hasn't gone out with a man in three years, since that asshole Tobias. Now, that isn't right. Sure, the timing stinks. Trust me, if the blueblood bastard fucks up, I'll be the first in line to slit his throat. But until then, he's her guest, and you and I will be making him feel welcome."

"And if she falls for him and he leaves her? Last time I looked, Weird nobles weren't in the market for exile brides."

"Then at least she would've lived a bit," Kaldar said. "She's allowed her mistakes. You and I both made plenty. We're the big fucking rock around her neck. She can't leave until the family is on its feet again, and by then she will be your age. Let her have some fun. She could die tomorrow. We could all die tomorrow."

Kaldar walked off down the stairs and turned left, an-gling toward a smaller building. A few moments later Richard's retreating steps told William he had gone inside.

So they knew Cerise liked him, and Kaldar, at least, was all for it. William made a mental note to find out about Tobias.

William gave Richard a few seconds to make his way from the door, crossed the front porch, and dropped into the grass, pressing against the wall, hidden from the sentries.

He heard a tiny noise and turned toward the thicket of ickberry bushes flanking the cypresses. A long shoot covered with thorns shivered, then another.

William leaned forward. Heat surged through his muscles, making him fast and focused.

The shrubs shook, as if taunting him, and a big square head thrust through the leaves. Two brown eyes fixed on William from across the clearing.

Idiot dog.

Cough pushed through the brush and trotted toward him, not so much walking but falling from paw to paw. If the lookouts decided to follow Cough's course, they'd run right into him.

William bared his teeth. *Go away.*

Cough kept coming, a lopsided canine grin on his furry face and not a thought in his head. If the dog could hum, he'd be singing "La-la-la!" in tune with his footsteps.

Cough sauntered over to him.

William pressed against the wall. No bullets. So far, so good.

Cough clenched, and vomited something chunky onto the grass.

Terrific.

The big dog sat on his haunches and looked at William with a perplexed expression on his face.

"Well, eat it back up," William hissed. "Don't waste it."

Cough gave a tiny whine.

"I'm not eating your puke."

Cough panted at him.

"No."

A lean shape leaped off the porch and ran past them into the woods. William caught a glimpse of dark hair and small brown boots. Lark. Why would a child be sneaking out into the woods in the middle of the night? Was she meeting "the monster" there?

Cough got up and trotted after her.

Good idea. William peeled himself from the wall and sprinted across the clearing. As he passed the tree with the sentry, he looked up and saw the kid asleep between the branches, the rifle leaning on his lap.

Finally something was going his way.

# EIGHTEEN

WILLIAM glided through the grove. The cypresses gave way to the Edge pines. Huge pine trunks surrounded him, black and soaring, like a sea of masts that belonged to ships sunken deep under the carpet of blue leaf moss.

Dense thickets crowded the pines, punctuated by the patches of rust ferns. Stunted swamp willows with startling pale bark protruded through the brush like white wax candles. This wasn't his Wood. This was an old treacherous place, a garish decay and new life mixed into one, and William felt uneasy.

The dog by his side didn't much care for the wood either. The sleepy-eyed, good-natured idiot had raised his ears, and his brown eyes scanned the woods with open suspicion.

A breeze touched them. They both sniffed in unison and turned left, following Lark's trail.

Where was that kid going? William leapt over a fallen branch. He hoped with all of him that Lark wasn't meeting some "nice" monster in the woods and telling him all of the secrets of her family.

A large white oak loomed in the woods, a lone giant tinseled with maiden hair moss. The air currents slapped William with a dozen odors of carrion, some old, some new. What the hell?

With all this carrion, he could smell nothing else.

Cough barreled on ahead. Dogs. Stupid creatures.

William jogged closer.

A dozen small furry bodies hung from the oak's branches.

Two squirrels, a rabbit, an odd thing that looked like a cross between a raccoon and an ermine—something the Edge had cooked up, no doubt—fish . . .

A skinny shape scrambled through the branches above him. Lark's small face poked through the leaves.

"You shouldn't be here. This is the tree where the small monster lives," she said. "This is the small monster's food, and that's the small monster's house."

He looked up to where she pointed. A haphazard shelter sat in the branches of the oak, just some old boards clumsily nailed and tied to make a little platform with an overhang. A small yellow something sat on the edge of the platform. William squinted. A stuffed teddy bear next to Peva's crossbow.

Cerise was right. Lark thought she was a monster. A small one. Who the hell was the big monster?

The teddy bear looked at him with small black eyes. Looking at it made him feel uneasy, as if he was sick or in serious danger and he wasn't sure when the next blow would be coming. He wanted to take Lark and her teddy bear away from the tree, just carry her off to the house, where there was warmth and light. His instincts told him she'd bolt if he tried.

Human children didn't do this and she wasn't a changeling. If she was one, he would've recognized her by now and Cerise wouldn't be surprised by his eyes.

William tapped the tree. "Can I come up?"

Lark bit her lips thinking. "I can trust you?"

He let the moonlight catch his eyes, setting them aglow. "Yes. I'm a monster, too."

Lark's eyes went wide. She stared at him in silent shock for a long breath and nodded. "Okay."

William took a couple of steps back and launched himself up the trunk, scrambling up like a lizard. It took him less than two seconds to crouch on the branch across from Lark.

"Wow," she said. "Where did you learn to climb that fast?"

"It's something I do," he said.

Cough whined below.

Lark scuttled down the branches, pulled out a small knife and cut the rope holding a water rat. The rat's body fell with a wet plop. Cough sniffed it and sat on his haunches, panting, long sticky drool stretching from his mouth.

"He never eats them." Lark frowned.

That's because they're rotten. "Do you come here a lot?"

She nodded. "If we don't find my mom, I might move here. I like it. Nobody bothers me here. Except for the big monster, but I usually run away when I hear him."

"The big monster?"

She nodded. "It moans and snarls when the moon is up."

The Hand's agents were freaks, but he doubted they would howl at the moon. "Is it something that's always lived here?"

"I don't know. I only started this tree four weeks ago."

"What does it look like?"

She shrugged. "I don't know. It gives me the creeps, and I usually run straight to the house." Her face shut down.

"Do people bother you at the house?"

Lark looked away.

"Monsters belong in the woods," she said. "They don't belong at the house. Were kids mean to you when you were a small monster?"

William considered the question, trying to sort through the mess that was his childhood to find something a human girl would consider mean. "I grew up in a house with a bunch of kids who were monsters like me. We fought. A lot." And when they really went at it, only one changeling got up in the end.

Lark scooted closer to him. "The adults didn't stop you? We aren't allowed to fight."

"They did. They were strict. We got whipped a lot, and

if you really screwed up, they would put you on a chain in a room by yourself. Nobody would talk to you for days."

Lark blinked. "How did you get food?"

"They would slide it through a slot in the door."

"And bathroom?"

"There was a hole in the floor."

She pursed her lips. "No showers?"

"No."

"That's nasty. How long did you stay in there?"

He leaned back, lowering one leg down. "The longest was three weeks. I think. Time is odd when you're in that room."

"Why did they put you in there?"

"I broke into the archives. I wanted to find out who my parents were."

"Did you?"

He shook his head. "No."

"So you didn't ever have a dad? Or a mom?"

William shook his head. This conversation had gotten deeper than planned.

"How can you not have a mom? What if you got sick? Who would bring you medicine?"

Nobody. "What about your mom? Is she nice?"

A small hint of a smile crossed Lark's lips and twisted into a pained frown. He guessed she was trying not to cry.

"My mom's very nice. She makes me brush my hair. And she holds me. Her hair smells like apples. She makes really good food. Sometimes, I come and sit by her in the kitchen when she cooks, and she sneaks me hot cocoa. It's hard to get, because Uncle Kaldar has to bring it from the Broken, and we only get it when something big happens. Like birthdays and Christmas, but I get it a lot . . ." Lark clamped her mouth shut and looked at him. "Do you know when your birthday is?"

He nodded. "Yes."

"Did you ever get any presents?"

William sucked the air in through his nose. She asked

bad questions. "I'm a monster, remember? The birth of little monsters isn't something people celebrate."

Lark looked away again.

Great. Now he made the kid feel bad. *Nice going, asshole.*

William reached over and touched one of the ropes holding a squirrel carcass. "Did you catch all these?"

"Yes. I'm good at it."

Both rats bore bolt marks. She probably did shoot those. But the rabbit carcass was at least eight days old, and there weren't maggots on it. William picked up the rope, pulled the rabbit up, and looked at it. His nose told him not to eat—there was some sickness in it.

Water rats were ugly, but the rabbit was cute. She wouldn't shoot one. She probably just found the corpse somewhere. A changeling child wouldn't have any problem killing a rabbit. It was good meat, slightly sweet.

William let go of the rope. "You're planning to eat those?"

She stuck her chin in the air. He'd touched a nerve. "Yep!"

"All right. First of all, squirrels aren't good to eat. The only thing you can make with them is stew, and even then, they're bony and they stink. Rats, same. Don't eat rats. They carry a sickness that will give you fever, cramps, and chills, and your skin and eyes will turn yellow. All these over there are too rotten to eat. That one over there has been picked on by birds, and that one's got maggots. Your fish over there is hanging too close to the trunk and there are spots on it—that's because the ants from that hill over there have been going up the tree and eating your kill."

Lark's eyes turned as big as saucers.

William pulled the rope, lifting the ermine thing. "Not sure what this is . . ."

"It's a Mire weasel. He killed those squirrels over there and ate their babies."

That explained things. The weasel raided a nest and

was punished. "I wouldn't eat him either," William said. "Unless I was really hungry. But since he's fresh, he'll do."

He cut the corpse from the rope and laid it on the tree. "The reason you hang things is to drain the blood, cool them down, and keep creatures like that dimwit under us from eating your food. If you take a creature's life to keep you going, you have to treat it with respect and not waste it." He split the carcass. "The first thing you do is pull the insides out. That's called dressing. Pay attention to the stomach and the guts, you don't want to cut them. This right here is the liver. This dark blob is full of bile. You cut that open and the whole thing is shot. It's too bitter to eat."

He dumped the innards on the ground and shook the weasel to fling off any of the old blood.

"Now you skin it. Like this. If you leave a bit of fat on it, the meat won't dry out. Also, you have to keep flies off of it. Steal a can of black pepper and sprinkle that on the meat. Flies don't care for it." He finished skinning and held up the bare carcass. "Now, you can cook it, or you can store it. If you want to store it, you can—freeze it—but I don't see how you could here, so your choices are curing it or smoking the meat . . ."

The tiny hairs on the back of his neck rose. He felt the weight of a gaze on his back sharp as a dagger.

William turned slowly.

Two eyes glared at him from the darkness between the branches of a pine.

"What the hell is that?" he whispered.

Lark's voice trembled. "The big monster."

The eyes took his measure. William looked deep into them and found an almost human awareness, a cruel and malevolent intelligence that shot a wave of icy alarm down his spine. He tensed like a coiled spring.

The diamond pupils shrank into slits, looking past William, at the girl in the branches behind him.

William pulled the crossbow from his back and locked the weapon's arms.

The eyes shifted, tracking Lark. Whatever it was in the pine was about to pounce.

"Run."

"What?" Lark whispered.

"Run. Now."

William raised the crossbow. *Hello, asshole.*

The eyes fixed on him.

*That's right. Forget the kid. Pay attention to me.* William gently squeezed the trigger. A poisoned bolt whistled through the air and bit below the eyes.

A snarl of pure pain ripped through the night.

Behind him Lark scrambled down the tree.

The creature didn't go down. He hit it with a poisoned bolt, and it didn't go down.

The eyes swung up, the bolt moving with them. He caught a glimpse of a nightmarish face, pale, hairless, with elongated jaws flashing a forest of teeth.

The beast bunched its powerful back legs and launched its enormous bulk into the space between them. William fired a second time and leaped to intercept it.


The huge body hit William in midair. Like being hit by a truck. William slammed against the oak, the creature on top of him. The air burst from his lungs in a single sharp grunt. Pain blossomed between his ribs. Huge jaws gaped an inch from his face, releasing a cloud of fetid breath. Sonovabitch. William snarled and sliced across the beast's throat. Blood poured.

A thick muscled paw smashed his head. The world teetered. Colored circles burst before his eyes.

He sliced again, pinned down by the creature's weight. Two bolts, two cuts across the neck. It should've been dead.

The next hit knocked him into a woozy, furious haze.

Half-blind, William thrust the knife into the beast's flesh and locked his hand on it.

A thick leg swiped him, clenching him in a steel-hard clamp. William shook his head, gripping the knife. The woods slid by him in a flurry of green stains—they were moving. The beast clutched at the trunk of the oak like a lizard and climbed up to the crown, dragging him with it.

William twisted, spreading the fingers of his left hand, jammed the sleeper against a vein bulging underneath the creature's pale skin, and squeezed. The needle punched into the blood vessels, squirting the contents of the capsule into the bloodstream. Enough narcotic to drop a grown man where he stood.

The creature snarled and shook him like a dog shakes a rat. William snarled back, punching the needles into the beast's neck in rapid succession: one, two, three. The sleeper clicked, out of ammo.

The beast hissed and dropped him. William plummeted in a shower of broken branches. His fingers caught a tree limb. He grabbed it, nearly dislocating his shoulders, swung himself up and over like a gymnast, and dropped down to the forest floor.

His vision cleared. He jerked his head up. Above him, the beast descended the tree, moving down the trunk upside down, headfirst.

Bolts, poison, knife, enough narcotic to drop a twelve-hundred-pound bull in mid-charge, and it still moved. William backed away.

The brute leaped to the ground. The moon tore through the clouds, flooding the beast in silvery light. Long and corded with hard muscle, it stood on four massive legs, equipped with five thick, clawed fingers. Coarse brown fur grew in patches on its powerful forequarters and along the sides, thickening to cover the pelvis but failing to completely hide the wrinkled flesh-colored skin. Flat cartilaginous ridges guarded the curve of its spine, flaring into bony plates to sheath the top of its narrow skull. The long serpentine tail lashed and flexed, coiling. Two deep bloody gashes split his neck.

In his entire life, William had never seen anything like it.

The creature dug the ground with a clawed paw, more simian than canine. The malevolent eyes glared at William. The flesh around the wounds on its neck shivered. The edges pulled together, the red muscle knitted, the skin stretched, and suddenly the cuts were gone. Nothing save the lines of two thin scars remained.

Fuck.

The beast's mouth opened wide, wider, like the unhinging jaws of a snake. Crooked fangs gleamed, wet with foamy drool.

"Nice." William raised his knife and motioned with the fingers of his left hand. "Come closer. I'll carve you up the old-fashioned way."

A pale furry body shot from the bushes, baying like some hell dog. Cough danced around the beast, snapping and barking and foaming at the mouth. The beast shook its ugly head.

William gathered himself for a charge.

The beast recoiled, as if shocked by a live wire. A moment later William heard it, too, a low female voice singing, rising and falling, murmuring Gaulish words.

The beast shuddered. Its maw gaped open. It howled, a low lingering wail full of regret and pain, whirled, and took off into the night.

"Come back here!" William snarled.

The voice came closer. The tiny glow of a lantern swayed between dark pines.

William dived into the thicket, leaving Cough alone in the mangled weeds.

The bushes parted, and Grandmother Az emerged. She raised her lantern, the shaky light carving the age lines deeper into her face. Lark peered from behind her, dark eyes huge in her pale face.

The dog trotted over and pushed against the old woman's legs, nearly knocking her off her feet.

"There you are, Cough." Grandmother Az reached over to pet Cough's foam-drenched head. "It's all right."

"Is it gone?" Lark asked.

"Yes, he's gone now, child. He won't come back tonight. You have to stay out of the forest for a while. I wish you would've told me he had come around. Come. Let's go home."

Grandmother Az took Lark's hand with a soothing smile and walked back into the woods. The dog followed them, growling quietly and talking shit under his breath.

William sat up. His chest hurt, and his shoulder felt like it was a single continuous bruise. The thing had regenerated before his eyes. Not even the Hand's freaks healed that fast. What in the bloody hell was that?

Slowly the reality of the situation sank in. He got his ass kicked, learned nothing, and got saved by a dumb dog and an old lady.

If he lived long enough to make a report to Nancy back in Adrianglia, he would have to gloss over this part.

# NINETEEN

THE morning came way too fast, William decided as he finished shaving. He'd slipped back into the house and caught a few hours in bed, but most of him still felt like he had been run through one of the Broken's dryers with some rocks added for the extra tumble.

At least his room had a bathroom attached to it, so he could clean up in relative privacy. His shoulder had gone from blue to sickly yellow-green. The yellow would be gone by the evening—changelings did heal fast. But then, healing fast often just invited more punishment, he reflected.

Something had happened early in the morning. He remembered waking up to some sort of commotion, but his door had stayed locked, so he went back to sleep.

William dressed and tried the door handle again. Open. Good. It had taken all of his will not to bust it last night. Being locked up had never been his favorite.

He slipped into the hallway. The house was quiet and sunlit; the air smelled of cooked bacon. He decided he liked the Rathole. With its clean wooden floors and tall windows, it was an open, uncluttered place, welcoming, comfortable, but not overwhelming. He caught a faint hint of Cerise's scent and followed it down the stairs and into a huge kitchen. A massive table, old and scarred, dominated the room. Behind it an enormous wood-burning oven sat next to an old electric one. Erian sat at the table doing his best to empty his very full plate. Kaldar leaned against the wall. No Cerise. Great.

"Here you are." Kaldar saluted him with a wave of his hand. "You missed breakfast, friend."

"I thought you were supposed to watch me," William said. "What the hell?"

Kaldar grimaced. "Things happened. Anyway, I figured you'd find your way here sooner or later. Besides, we all watch you. Can't have a stranger in the house unsupervised. No offense."

"None taken. Urow's wife explained to me where I stand."

Kaldar's eyes narrowed. He glanced away.

Something had happened to Clara or Urow. Something that made Kaldar wince.

"That's Clara for you," Kaldar said. "Anyway, you've met my younger brother before, yes, no?"

"Yes. Erian."

Erian waved at him with his fork. He ate slowly, cutting his food into small pieces. His face was smart but slightly melancholy—the man worried a lot.

"Usually we have to introduce everyone three or four times before guests start remembering names." Kaldar picked up a metal platter covered by a hood and took the lid off. William took in a pile of fried sausage, chunks of battered fried fish, scrambled eggs, and two stacks of golden pancakes glowing with butter, and tried not to drool.

"Leftovers," Kaldar said. "Sorry about the fish. We don't get much meat here. The plates are in the cabinet behind you."

William retrieved two plates and traded one of them with Kaldar for a fork and a knife. They sat down on opposite sides of Erian. William attacked the pancakes. They were sweet and fluffy and perfect.

Kaldar passed him a small jar of green jam. "Try this."

William slathered a small bit on his pancake and put it in his mouth. The jam was sweet and slightly sour, but mild. It tasted like strawberry and kiwi and some odd fruit he once tried . . . persimmon, that was it.

"Good, yes?" Kaldar winked at him. "Cerise makes it. She's a great cook."

Erian stopped chewing. "Did you just try to broker Cerise to him?"

Kaldar waved at him. "Shut up, I'm working here."

"No," Erian said. "For one, we barely know the man."

William loaded his plate with sausage. Rabbit. Mmm. If Kaldar thought Cerise would let him sell her, he was deeply mistaken. That much he knew.

"And I'm practically her brother, and I'm sitting right here," Erian said.

Kaldar regarded him. "And that concerns me how?"

"You don't try to sell a man's sister right in front of him, Kaldar."

"Why not?"

"That's just not right." Erian looked at William. "Tell him."

"You've got to be careful about that," William said. He'd learned very early on that there is a fine line between joking among men and pissing a soldier off by saying something bad about his sister. He never could tell the difference, so he stayed away from the subject altogether. "People take offense. You might get your throat slit."

"Well, I don't see a problem with it," Kaldar said.

"That's because you're a scoundrel," Erian said dryly.

Kaldar put his hand to his chest. "Oh, Erian. From you, that hurts."

Erian shook his head. "I don't know about a slit throat, but Ceri will cut your balls off if you keep meddling."

Now that was something William could believe. "Where is she?"

Both men took a bit too long to chew their food before Erian answered. "She's in the small yard. Cutting things."

"So," Kaldar leaned back. "You're a blueblood, and you said you aren't rich."

"He isn't?" Erian glanced at him.

"No," William said.

"So how do you earn your cash?" Kaldar asked.

*I lay floors in the Broken.* "I hunt."

"Men or beasts?" Kaldar asked.

"Men."

Erian nodded. "Any money in that?"

William washed his pancake down with a gulp of water. "Some. If you're good."

Erian's eyes fixed him. "Are you?"

*Keep pushing and you'll find out.* William stretched his lips, showing his teeth to Erian. "How badly do you want to know?"

"Oh, now that's not nice . . ." Kaldar clicked his tongue.

Footsteps approached the stairs. William turned to the door. "Company."

"I don't hear anything," Kaldar said.

"Perhaps if you shut up?" Erian wondered.

The stairs creaked. The door swung open and a massive form dwarfed the doorway. Urow pushed his way into the room. Haggard, his gray skin pale, he staggered to the table, his right arm in a sling. Kaldar got up and pulled a chair from the table. Urow sat.

All the strength seemed to have gone out of him, as if he'd grown too heavy for his muscle.

"Blueblood," he said, offering William his left hand across the table.

They clamped hands. Urow's handshake was still hard, but William sensed weakness in his grip.

"You all right?" he asked.

"Been better." Urow's eyes were bloodshot and dull.

"How's your wife?"

"Hurt."

He thought as much. Clara was hurt and Urow's world had been split open. He could've taken on a lot of punishment, but failing to protect his wife broke him. "Sorry to hear that."

"I have a favor to ask," Urow spoke slowly, as if straining to push the words out. "You already helped me once, so I'd owe you two."

"You owe me nothing. What's the favor?"

"I'm leaving my youngest son here. He needs to stay busy, so if you need something done, tell him to do it for you. The harder the job, the better."

Strange. "Fine," William said. "I'll do that."

Urow reached into his pocket, pulled something out, and pushed it across the table. It was a round thing, about two inches wide, made with braided twine and human hair. A black claw stained with dried blood protruded from the circle. It smelled of human blood and looked like one of Urow's claws, except he had all of his.

"Keep this for me, so my son minds your orders."

Behind Urow, wide-eyed Kaldar furiously shook his head. Erian's face was carefully neutral, while his hand was making "don't take it" motions beside the table, out of Urow's view.

"What is it?" William asked.

"It's a thing. A sign." A faint tremble laced Urow's hoarse voice, and William realized that this was the closest the man could come to begging. The urge to get up and walk away gripped him.

"I've got nobody else to take it," Urow said. "Family won't work, and the rest of the Mire, well, there isn't anyone I'd trust with my boy. They would use him badly." Pain filled his eyes. His voice fell to a rough, broken whisper. "Do this for me, William. I don't want to kill my son."

William sat utterly still. Pieces clicked in his head. He'd read about this custom before, in a book about the tribes on the Southern Continent of the Weird. When a child committed an offense punishable by death, his family could surrender him to another guardian and keep him alive. The child would serve the guardian until maturity.

Urow's youngest boy had done something punishable

by death and Urow could no longer keep him. The only way the kid would survive would be if he belonged to someone else.

William sat very still. When he was born and his mother didn't want him, she could've thrown him in the gutter and walked away. In Louisiana, he would've been strangled at birth. He survived because he was born in Adrianglia and because his mother cared enough to surrender him to the government instead of tossing him into a ditch like garbage. For better or worse, they took him, they fed him, they gave him shelter, and while his life had never been easy, he never regretted being born.

It didn't matter that the kid wasn't exactly a changeling and this was not Adrianglia, and he didn't know Urow or what to do with his son.

It was his turn. Only a fool didn't pay fate back, and he wasn't that fool.

William took the amulet.

Urow exhaled slowly through his nose. Kaldar pretended to hit his face against the cabinet. Erian leaned forward, rested his elbows on the table, and put his head on his fists, hiding his face.

"If you ever need anything . . ." Urow pushed to his feet.

William nodded. The rest went without saying.

Urow turned and walked out of the room.

"You shouldn't have taken that." Erian raised his head. "It's done now."

Kaldar sighed. "You're a good man, William. Stupid but good."

William had just about enough. "You talk too much."

"I've been telling him that for years," Erian said.

A door swung open the second time and one of Urow's kids came in. Gaston, William remembered. The kid was about sixteen or so, judging by the face, still leaner than Urow but already a couple of inches taller and on the way to his father's massive build. Same temper, too, judging by the shallow scars on his muscular forearms. Fighting with his brothers probably. William scrutinized his face: hard jaw, flat cheekbones, deep-set eyes, startling pale gray under black bushy eyebrows. The kid could pass for human, if the light was bad enough. Bruises marked his jaw and neck. Somebody had pummeled him.

William pointed to the chair across the table. "Sit."

The kid sat, his shoulders hunched, as if expecting to block a punch. His left hand was missing a claw. The wound had barely had time to scab over.

"Hungry?"

The kid eyed the food and shook his head.

William got another plate, loaded it, and passed it to him. "Don't lie to me, I'll know."

The kid dug into the food. William let him eat for a couple of minutes. Slowly the kid's posture relaxed.

"How old are you?"

"Fifteen."

Three years older than George, Rose's brother.

"What's your name?"

"Gaston."

William touched the amulet. "What did you do?"

Gaston froze with his fork halfway to his mouth.

William said nothing.

The kid swallowed. "You left. Dad was sleeping. Ry and Mart went to herd rolpies into the shelter, because Mom was worried that if the Sheeriles showed up, they'd kill the rolpies first. I was supposed to watch the house. We have a hand crank siren up in the tree. If anything went wrong, I was supposed to crank the siren so Mart and Ry would run home. Mom was cooking carp." Gaston stared at his plate. "Dad hates carp. Says it tastes like waterweeds. I had lines set up in a creek. I went to check my lines."

Gaston looked at his plate. "I abandoned my family."

"Who came to the house while you were gone?" William asked.

Gaston slid into a toneless monotone. "A man. He attacked Mom. He . . . cut off her leg. Ignata says that there is nothing she can do. My mom will be a cripple now. Because of me."

The kid was dumping buckets of self-loathing on himself. The fault wasn't his. Clara should have left when Cerise told her about Ruh. Gaston wasn't pushed out of his family because he'd left his post. He was a child and likely not properly trained. Gaston was pushed out because Urow loved Clara, and now every time he looked at his youngest son, he would be reminded of her injury. Urow had injected himself into the situation, his wife failed to evacuate, and now they loaded all of their guilt and their mistakes onto their child and removed him from the family. A clean sweep.

The wild scraped at his insides. That was fine. The kid was his now.

"What did the man look like?"

"I only saw him for a second, when he jumped out of the window. Tall. Blond hair."

"What else?"

"He offered Clara limes for her soup," Kaldar said quietly.

Spider. William hid a growl. Only Spider could walk into a house of a woman to interrogate her and start the conversation by offering her fruit.

William leaned forward. "The man dove into the water and didn't come up for air."

Gaston blinked. "Yes. Dad and the guys didn't believe me, but he didn't come up."

"He has gills that feed air into his lungs. What did he want from your mother?"

"He was asking about you and Cerise."

William expected as much. Clara didn't tell Spider what he wanted to know, but there had to be more to it than that. Something made him forget why he'd come there and lose himself to blinding rage. "What did she do to him?"

Gaston stared at him.

"He lost it. Otherwise, he wouldn't have attacked her. He's very good at inflicting pain to get people to talk. Hacking off someone's leg just makes them bleed to death. The target goes into shock and becomes useless for interrogation. They're too focused on their own pain and injury to respond."

Everyone winced. Apparently, he'd said the wrong thing, but William really didn't care. He had to get to the bottom of this. "What did your mother do to him?"

"She threw boiling soup at his face."

That explained everything. William leaned back. "Yeah, that would do it."

"And then Dad grabbed his crossbow, and the guy jumped out of the window," Gaston said.

"I've seen it. It's a big crossbow," Kaldar said. "I'd jump, too."

It wasn't the crossbow. It was Urow with his gray skin and serrated teeth popping up behind Spider right after he'd been scalded.

"This guy." Erian took his plate to the sink. "He has a thing about soup?"

"He has a thing about being scalded. When he was a child, his grandfather dumped boiling water on him."

"Why?" Gaston asked.

"He thought his grandson was a changeling. He was trying to get the demon beast to come out."

"Lovely family," Kaldar murmured. "I take it, that's the fellow you're hunting."

"Yes."

"You have a history?" Erian asked.

William nodded.

The boy gripped the table. The wood creaked under the pressure of his fingers. His voice came out as a ragged snarl. "When I see him, I'll kill him."

Spider would break him in half and toss him aside like a dead rat. "When you see him, you'll get me. That's an order."

Gaston opened his mouth. William looked at him the way he looked at wild wolves when he wanted them to move out of his way. The kid clamped his mouth shut. "Yes, sir."

"You fucked up," William told him. "You never leave a post you're assigned to. If you do, people get hurt."

Gaston nodded. "I understand."

"However, your mother set herself in harm's way. She was told the house wasn't safe and she had to leave, and she refused."

Gaston clenched his teeth.

"I know it's not what you want to hear. But your mother got into a pissing contest with your aunt and made a bad decision. You are a kid. You aren't responsible for her decisions. So stop wallowing in self-hatred. You're no good to me that way."

William rose. He wanted to see Cerise. He hadn't seen her since last night, and he wanted to smell her scent and see her face and know that she was all right. "Where is the small yard?"

"I'll take you." Kaldar started toward the door. Gaston jumped to his feet, dropped his plate into the sink, and followed them.

CERISE finished the combination and lowered her swords. The sun was out, and the small yard looked so nice this morning. Sheltered by the walls of the building trailing the main house, it was completely secure, a small haven in the swamp. The sunlight danced on the short grass, turning it a cheery green, and at the western wall, flowers bloomed in the small garden. Grandma Az sat on the short brick wall bordering the flower beds. Their stares connected and the old woman waved. Surrounded by white and blue blossoms, Grandma looked ancient and serene this morning, like one of the harvest goddesses the old ones worshipped.

Cerise launched into another combination, twisting, slicing at invisible opponents with her swords. The exertion felt so good . . . When she'd come out here two hours ago, twisted up inside from seeing Clara on crutches, she thought the weight that rode in her chest would never disappear. It wasn't gone now, but it was so much lighter.

She'd warned Clara. She told her to come to the Rathole. In the end it was Clara's decision, and there wasn't a thing Cerise could've done to change it. But it was she who'd started this chain of events. If she had never put Urow in danger in the first place, Clara wouldn't be missing a leg.

Gods, she was so pissed off. She wanted to run upstairs to Clara's room and slap the woman across the face. She'd endangered the kids, endangered Urow, got her leg cut off, and all for what? For a little bit of pride.

Cerise unclenched her teeth. More exercise was in order.

The door swung open. William stepped into the sunlight.

*Don't look straight at him, don't do it, don't do it . . . Too late.* Fine, she would just have to pretend that she didn't do it.

Cerise slashed the air, glancing in his direction out of the corner of her eye. He stood completely still, watching her. Kaldar was saying something, but William didn't seem to be listening.

The look on his face was all the confirmation she could've wanted. He did kiss her yesterday. She didn't dream it up.

*Keep watching, Lord Bill.* Cerise spun into the Thunderstorm, her swords a whirlwind of precise strikes, spinning faster and faster, as she gathered her magic. Left, right, left, down, churning the air like the fury of the wind churned the storm clouds. She paused for a fraction of a second, poised on her toes in the middle of her lethal storm, and let her flash leak into her eyes. The magic sparked like lightning and shot to her swords. She broke into her dance again, the flash riding on the edge of her blades; she was lost to its rhythm, so deep in it she drowned in the flow of magic. When she glanced up, he stood two feet away, watching her, utterly focused on her every move.

She arched her back, twisted in the last smooth cut, and straightened.

"Lord Bill." *I hope you enjoyed the show. I need to lie down now.* "Didn't see you there."

He stared at her with such open, raw longing it sent tiny needles of adrenaline through her. She wanted him to cross the distance to her and kiss her.

William pulled back. She saw it in his eyes. It cost him, but he pulled back, almost as if he put himself on some invisible chain. She felt so disappointed it actually hurt.

"Very pretty," William said. "Small problem."

"What's that?" She turned away to put down her swords.

"The air doesn't fight back."

She pivoted back, narrowing her eyes. "And you do."

He nodded.

*Oh, you sad thing, you.* She stepped aside and bowed, inviting him to the weapon rack with a wave of her hand. "Take your pick."

William surveyed the weapons on the rack. "Too big. Do you have a knife?"

"You can't fence with me using a knife, Lord Bill. I would slice you to ribbons."

He growled a little and picked up a short sword.

Behind him Kaldar nudged Urow's youngest son. "Bet you he lasts at least thirty seconds."

"Umm . . ." Gaston looked at him. "No, he won't."

"Bet me something."

"I don't have anything."

Kaldar grimaced. "Pick up that rock."

Gaston swiped the rock off the ground.

"Now you have a rock. I bet this five bucks against your rock."

Gaston grinned. "Deal."

Kaldar's face took on a look of intense concentration. Cerise glanced at him. Yep, he was trying to work his magic. When a bet was involved, occasionally luck was on Kaldar's side against all odds. It didn't work every time, but it worked often enough, and right now her cousin seemed to be straining every ounce of his will to help William spar with her. She had no idea why. The inside of Kaldar's head was a mysterious place better left alone by all sane people.

Cerise raised her swords. "Any time, Lord Bill."

William struck. She swiped his blade aside with her longer sword, turned, reversing her short blade, and rammed the pommel into his face, tripping him. He fell down.

That felt almost too good. Guilt nipped at her.

Kaldar and Gaston made some sucking noises.

"Are you okay, blueblood?" Kaldar called out.

William twisted his legs and rolled back up, shifting his stance, the short blade raised above his shoulder, his knees lightly bent. Amber rolled over his eyes and vanished. He was smiling. Interesting. She'd never seen that stance before. No matter.

Cerise charged. He thrust into her attack, sliding his blade against hers. She moved to parry, and he smashed his left fist into her ribs. The blow took the air out of her lungs. She slashed at his ribs, opening a light cut across his black shirt. *You want to play? Fine.*

William muscled her back. She was no pushover, but he was freakishly strong and he wasn't kidding. They danced across the yard, cutting and punching and grunting. He punched her shoulder—her arm nearly went numb—and knocked the shorter sword from her hand.

Sonovabitch! She elbowed him in the gut, which must've been made of armor, because he didn't even wince. The next time she smashed her fist above his liver. He laughed, dropped his blade, and grabbed her right wrist. Cerise hammered a kick to his knee. William dropped down, and she kicked him in the jaw, knocking him into the grass.

"Weak knees and elbows, Lord Bi—"

He grabbed her ankle and twisted her off her feet. She hit the ground hard. Her head rang, and when she blinked the ringing off, her arm was caught between his legs. An arm bar. Nice.

"Done?" William looked into her eyes and put on a bit more pressure.

She groaned.

"How about now?"

Pain shot through her shoulder. "Done."

He kept the arm in the lock. "So help me out here, does this mean I win?"

"Could you gloat a little more?"

He grinned, nodding. "I could."

"Okay. You win."

He dropped his voice. "What's my prize for winning?"

She blinked. "What do you want?"

The feral thing in his eyes winked at her.

"No!" she told him. "Whatever it is you're thinking of, I'm not doing it in front of my whole family. And threatening to dislocate my shoulder isn't the best way to ask for it."

"Get off the ground, children," Grandma Az called.

He let her go. Cerise twisted and kicked him in the head, not very hard. The blow took him just below the ear. He shook his head, looking a bit dazed. Cerise rolled to her feet.

"What the hell was that for?" he growled.

"For being a jackass."

She picked up her swords and went to sit by Grandma Az. It was highly unlikely he'd follow her there.

Their audience had grown. Aunt Pete and Ignata sat next to Grandma. Aunt Pete was sporting a black eye patch that made Cerise's heart lurch. Aunt Murid leaned against the tree behind them.

Cerise sat on the grass between Aunt Pete's and Grandma's legs and gave William the evil eye. He grimaced, got up, and headed to the large, round sink at the other end of the yard to wash up.

"Pummeled you pretty good," Aunt Pete said.

"I could've cut his head off."

"But you didn't," Ignata said.

"No."

Ignata gave a little innocent smile. "I wonder why that is."

William pulled his shirt off. Shallow cuts crisscrossed the muscle on his back and sides. She'd nicked him more than she'd thought.

"Oh my," Aunt Pete murmured. "What are they feeding them in the Weird?"

A hand touched Cerise's hair. Grandma Az. Cerise leaned her head over, brushing against familiar fingers.

"So how is your romance going?" Grandma Az asked.

"It's not going."

"What are you talking about?" Ignata squinted at her. "He was giving you a look."

"That was not a look," Auth Pete said. "That was *the* look."

"Looking is as far as it gets," Cerise murmured. William was rinsing blood off his side, presenting her with a view of carved chest and lean stomach, and she had trouble concentrating on the conversation. You'd think a man washing off his blood would be the least attractive thing ever. Yeah.

It wasn't his body, she reflected. It was in his eyes. In the way he looked at her.

"Have you tried dropping hints?" Ignata asked.

"I dropped boulders of hints," Cerise said. "He pulls himself back every time. It's not working."

"I don't see how it couldn't." Ignata bit her lips. "He's obviously all about getting with you."

"Maybe he doesn't get it," Aunt Pete said. "Some men—"

"Have to be hit over the head with it. Yes, Mother, we know." Ignata rolled her eyes.

"I don't want to just throw myself at him." Cerise grimaced.

"No, that would be bad." Aunt Pete frowned. "You said he was a soldier. You don't suppose . . . ?"

"Oh, Gods." Ignata blinked. "You think something could be wrong down there?"

All of them looked at William, who chose this precise moment to slide the wet shirt back on his back, which required him to flex, raising his arms.

"That would be a shame," Cerise murmured. Maybe he was impotent. That would explain the frustration she saw on his face.

"Such a waste," Aunt Pete said mournfully.

"There is nothing wrong with his body," Grandma Az said. "It's in his head."

William turned. He walked past them to where Kaldar and Gaston haggled over a rock, pausing for a moment to look at her. Something hungry and sick with longing glared at her through his eyes, and then he turned away.

Like being burned.

"Oh, boy," Ignata murmured.

"Now isn't a good time for this sort of thing anyway." Cerise sat up straighter.

"Are you crazy?" Aunt Pete stared at her. "Both of you could die tomorrow. Now is the perfect time for this. Live while you can, child."

A hand rested on Cerise's shoulder. She looked back. Aunt Murid nodded to her and walked away on her long legs, heading straight for William.

She said something, William nodded, and the two of them took off, Gaston at their heels. Kaldar stood there for a second, looking at a rock in his hands, shrugged, and followed them.

"What do you suppose all that was about?" Ignata asked.

"Who knows?" Aunt Pete shrugged.

# TWENTY

SPIDER opened his eyes. He lay submerged on the bottom of the pool, in the cool shadowy depths. Above him, a wet sky glistened where the water kissed the air. He felt neither hot nor cold. Nothing troubled the water. He was utterly alone, floating weightless, watching from the shadows as the sunrays filtered through the water, setting it aglow.

If he closed his eyes, he could pretend that he was diving in the translucent waters far to the south, where a chain of the New Egypt islands stretched from the eastern tip of the continent far into the ocean. Swimming there, gliding above the coral reefs, surrounded by life but blissfully free of humanity, brought him a sense of peace and the simple thrilling exhilaration of being alive.

Alas, he wasn't diving in the ocean now. Spider allowed himself one last moment of regret and surfaced with a single kick, emerging without a sound.

The air was unpleasantly cool. The skin flaps on his sides closed, hiding the pink feathery fans of his gills. Among his many alterations, this was the least useful but the most enjoyable.

Spider grasped the edge of the well and pulled himself up. Above him the sun shone bright. The sky was a clear crystalline blue, but despite the rare sunshine, the swamp still looked the same, a primeval mess of rot and mud. To the left, the manor where he'd made their base rose among the trees, struggling for stately elegance and failing.

Veisan's peacock blue eyes greeted him. The contrast between those turquoise irises and her red skin never failed to surprise him. She looked at him with earnest expectation. Like a puppy, Spider thought. A murderous, lethal, psychotic puppy.

"Hello, m'lord," Veisan whispered.

"Hello, Veisan."

"Your skin has healed remarkably well, m'lord."

Considering the amount of catalyst he'd dumped into the well water, the rapid progress was expected. "Veisan, why are you whispering?"

Her eyebrows crept up, making her look pitiful. "I'm not sure, m'lord," she said in a slightly louder voice. "It seemed appropriate."

She offered him a fuzzy towel. He gripped the stone rim of the pool, pulled himself out, and dried off. The liquid left light pink smudges on the yellow towel. It had been a few months since he'd sustained an injury severe enough to require underwater restoration. Spider touched his face, pleased with the smoothness of the skin on his cheek, where the burn blisters had been.

Veisan traded a meticulously folded stack of clothing for his towel. He began to dress. "Anything vital happen while I was under?"

"Judge Dobe ruled in the Mars' favor. The Sheeriles have been given one day to clear the Sene Manor. Their reprieve expires tomorrow morning. Advocate Malina Williams sent the Sheeriles a letter detailing her apologies. She intends to appeal."

Spider shrugged. "She'll get nowhere with it. They should've gone with one of the local hacks. The Edgers prize familiarity more than skill."

"We've received a message from Lagar Sheerile."

Spider grimaced. "He wants reinforcements before the Mars attack him tomorrow."

"Yes, m'lord."

"He's on his own. I don't need him anymore." Let the mud rats fight it out between themselves. It saved him the trouble of wiping them out to cover his trail, and this way none of his people risked injury. There was always a chance that Lagar would kill Cerise, but considering how well her mother was progressing, it was unlikely they would need her. Spider flung the water off his hair in a vigorous shake. He'd spare a few moments of regret for her death, the way one would mourn the destruction of a prized painting—the girl represented a forgotten martial art, and it was a shame to lose her. But in the grand scheme of things, she was of little use to him.

"Send a Scout Master out there. I want to know about the crossbowman."

"Yes, m'lord."

Veisan handed him a brush, and he dragged it through his wet hair.

"Lagar also reported an attack by a feline of unusual size."

He looked at her.

"There are two attacks to date. The first was a sentry on duty. The second was a man returning from the settlement with purchases. In both cases the animal took the weapons belonging to its victims. Lagar Sheerile estimates it to be about four yards long and seven hundred pounds heavy. The circumference of the paw prints—"

"Back up. The bit about the weapons."

"In both cases the animal took the weapons belonging to its victims." Veisan repeated the sentence exactly, reproducing the same intonation and pauses she had used the first time.

"Does Lagar have an opinion as to why it's attacking his men?"

"No, m'lord."

Odd. Spider dismissed the rest of it with a flick of his fingers. "Any news of Embelys and Vur?"

"They are still in hiding at the perimeter of Mar territory."

He didn't really expect them to capture Cerise. But

one could always hope . . . Spider ran his hand across his cheek. Stubble. He'd have to shave.

Veisan produced a shaving kit, the soap already whipped into thick foam. He took it.

"What else?"

"John reports that the subject has regained consciousness. He says that in two days she will either be ready for instruction or her brains will ooze out of her ears, m'lord."

"I take it he's still frustrated with the rushed schedule."

"I believe so."

Prima donna. "He'll get over it."

"And if he doesn't, m'lord?"

"Then you can have him. Assuming you can limit yourself to one death."

Veisan licked her lips nervously. "I'll try. It's been . . . a long time."

He put his hand on her shoulder, feeling steel cables of muscle tense under his fingers. "I understand, Gabrielle. I apologize for keeping you idle."

She sniffled and a slow purple blush spread through her red skin. Like all agents, she had taken a different name when joining the Hand. He only used her birth name on special occasions. Spider made it a point to know the birth names of all agents under his command. Funny how a single word could have a devastating effect.

"Thank you, m'lord."

Spider strode to the manor, Veisan following at his heels.

"My lord?"

"Yes?"

"What's in that diary?"

He grinned at her. "A weapon, Veisan. A means to win the war."

"But we're not at war."

He shook his head. "When we obtain the diary, we will be."

* * *

WILLIAM raised his head from the rifle he'd finished cleaning and handed it to Gaston. Murid, Cerise's aunt with the sniper eyes, had asked for his help. He'd spent the last three hours cleaning the rifles and checking the crossbows with her at the range behind the house.

Murid didn't say more than two words to him, which suited him just fine, but she watched him. She wasn't too subtle about it, and the constant scrutiny put him in a foul mood. At first William had guessed she was keeping him away from Cerise, but now he decided she had something else in mind.

Murid had empty eyes, the kind of eyes a man got after he'd been through some rough shit and redlined. Lost his brakes, lost himself. It made her unpredictable, and so William didn't try to guess what she would do. He simply waited for the moment she would do it and prepared to react.

Murid test-fired a crossbow. The bolt bit into the target. She was good. Not as good as he, but then he was a changeling and his coordination was better. If she'd turned and fired at him instead, he wouldn't have been surprised.

His ears caught the sound of light steps coming. He glanced back. Lark, running from the house, Wasp in her hand. She saw him looking and slowed down, a scowl on her face. Upset at being caught. She sauntered over and stood on his left next to Gaston.

William picked up the last crossbow from his stack, raised it, and fired without aiming, purely on muscle memory. The bolt sliced into his target next to the other ten or so he'd put into the bull's-eye in the past hour.

Lark snapped her crossbow, imitating him, and fired. The bolt went wide.

"It won't work," Gaston told her with an expression of complete gloom on his face. "I've been trying to shoot like he does for the last hour."

He'd been picking up the bolts out of the grass for the last hour, too, William reflected. The kid shot well enough.

Good hand-to-eye coordination, good perception. With proper training, he would be an excellent shot.

Lark jerked her crossbow up, fired another bolt, and missed. "How come you can do it?"

"Practice," William said. That and a changeling's reflexes. "I've been a soldier for a long time. I can't flash, so I had to use the crossbows a lot."

Lark hesitated. "I can flash."

"Show me."

She grasped a bolt in her fist. Pale lightning sparked from her eyes down to her hand, clutched the bolt, and vanished. Another white flasher. Figured. Flash usually ran in the family.

"Nice!" he told her.

Lark offered him a narrow smile. It was there and gone almost as fast as her flash, but he saw it.

William turned to Gaston. "You?"

"None of the thoas can flash." The boy shook his head, sending his black mane flying. The damn hair reached nearly to his waist. On the one hand, it was too long. If you grabbed the hair, you could control the kid's head in a fight. On the other hand, the hair hid his face. He looked human enough in passing, but he'd fail close scrutiny. His jaw was too heavy, his eyes were too deep set under the wide black eyebrows, and his irises luminesced with pale silver when they caught the light.

Still, the kid needed a shock to the system. Proof that he was done with his family. A rite of passage. William pulled a knife from the sheath. "Cut it."

Gaston's eyebrows crept up.

"Cut the hair."

Gaston glanced at him, glanced at the knife, and took the blade, his teeth clenched. He grasped a strand of hair in his hand and sawed at it with the blade. The black strands fell on the ground.

Lark crouched and picked them up. "It's not good to leave the hair out," she said quietly. "Someone could curse you with it. I'll burn it for you."

"Thanks." Gaston grabbed another handful of his hair and sliced it off.

Murid opened her mouth.

*Here it is.* William tensed.

"It's almost time for lunch."

He nodded.

"It would be good if we knew what they were cooking in the kitchen," she said. "If they're cooking fish, we need to head to the house. Fish doesn't take much time. If they're cooking a pig, we have another half an hour."

"I can go and ask," Gaston said.

William sampled the wind. "They're cooking chicken."

Murid turned her expressionless dark eyes on him. "Are you sure?"

"Chicken and rice," he said. "With cumin."

"That's good to know," Murid said. "We have time, then."

William had an odd feeling that something important had just happened, but what he had no idea. Behind him Gaston sliced another handful from his mane and deposited it into Lark's hands. William loaded the next crossbow and fired. He would figure it out sooner or later.


LAGAR closed his eyes. It did no good—Peva was still there, even in the darkness of his mind.

"Look at your brother," his mother's voice whispered like the rustling of snake scales across the floor. "It's because of you he's dead. You weren't smart enough to keep your brother safe."

Slowly he opened his eyes and saw Peva's body, blue and nude, on the washing table. A single lamp hung above it, its harsh glow concentrated by the fixture into a cone. The light clutched at the faces of two women, bleaching them into pasty masks. He watched them dip thick cloths into the buckets of scented water and rub the mud from Peva's limbs. The dirty water ran off Peva's skin into the groove on the table.

Peva was dead. He would never rise, never speak again. There was a horrible finality in death, an absolute and total ending. There was nothing to be done. No way to help it.

Lagar rolled his head back and took a deep breath. They spent their lives jerking and clawing their way to the top, and for what? To end up like this. On the table.

Tomorrow Cerise would come for him. Tomorrow evening either he or she would be on the table, just like this. This wasn't what he wanted. In his dreams, when he was alone with nobody to spy on him, this wasn't what he wished for.

"Why do you bother?" Lagar's voice caught, and he forced the words out, raspy and strained.

Kaitlin stared at him from the gloom, a squat ugly thing, wrapped in her shawl. His mother. Like an old poisonous toad, he thought.

"Why do you bother?" he repeated. "He's dead. The soul's gone. Peva's gone. Nothing left but this . . . shell. Dump it in the ditch. Give it to the dogs. He isn't going to care."

She said nothing, clamping her lips together. Disgust swelled in him. Lagar spun and left the room, slapping the door shut behind him.

CERISE padded out onto the verandah and closed the door behind her, shutting off the busy noises fluttering from the kitchen. Earlier, tired of making plans and choosing weapons, she'd come down there hoping to cook. Being in the kitchen, in the middle of bustle, standing over the fire, smelling spices, tasting food, and catching up on the Mire gossip usually comforted her. Today she cooked in a daze, listening to her aunts and cousins, while her mind cycled through tomorrow, wondering who else would die.

Then, before she knew it, dinner came. The entire family had gathered at the main house, those who lived in the outer buildings, those who lived farther in the swamp, everyone came for the dinner before the fight. Every seat was filled. The kids had to be sent off to a smaller kitchen to eat there, just to make room.

Then she sat at the head of the table, in her father's place. She listened to the chatter of familiar voices, looked at the familiar faces, watched small fights break out and dissolve into teasing, and knew with absolute certainty that tomorrow some of these chairs would be empty. Guessing and calculating which ones made her colder and colder, until she was shivering, as if a clump of ice had grown in the pit of her stomach. Finally Cerise could take it no more and snuck out.

She just needed some peace and a little quiet. She started along the balcony, heading to the door that led to her favorite hiding spot.

Steps followed her. Maybe it was William . . . She turned.

Aunt Murid chased her.

Figured. William snuck around like a fox. She'd seen very little of him. First, Murid took him off, then Richard and Cerise rode out and climbed a pine, to get a better look at Sene. At dinner William ended up in a corner, with Gaston next to him. She barely recognized the boy with his hair shorn off. What the hell was Urow thinking? Gaston was family. What was done was done, but it still felt rotten.

Cerise stopped. Aunt Murid stopped, too. Cerise read hesitation in the older woman's posture and tensed. What now?

"Your uncle Hugh is a good man," Aunt Murid said softly.

Well, that came out of nowhere. Murid didn't speak of her younger brother, especially since he'd left for the Broken about twelve years back. He'd visit at the house every few years for a week or two and then leave again. When Cerise had gone to get the documents from him, he looked pretty much the same as she remembered him: fit,

tall, muscular. His hair was an odd salt-and-pepper shade,
but aside from that, he was pretty much a male version of
Aunt Murid. But where Murid was harsh, Uncle Hugh
was mild and soft-spoken.

"I only saw him for about an hour," Cerise admitted.
"Just to get the papers for Grandpa's house. He looked
well."

"I'm sure he did. Come, I'll walk with you."

They strolled along the balcony.

"Hugh was difficult as a child," Murid said. "Some
things he just didn't understand. Our parents and me, we
tried our best to take care of him, but his mind just didn't
work the same way. You had to spell things out for him.
Obvious things. Hugh always liked dogs and other animals better than people. Said they were simpler."

Cerise nodded. Where was this going?

"He wasn't mean," Murid said. "He was kind. Just odd
in his way and very violent."

"Violent? Uncle Hugh?" Cerise tried to imagine the
quiet man flying off the handle and couldn't.

Aunt Murid nodded. "Sometimes he'd take offense to
things, and you wouldn't even know why. And once he
started fighting, he wouldn't stop. He would kill you,
unless someone pulled him off." She stopped and leaned
against the rail. "Hugh wasn't like other people. He was
born different and there was no help for it. It runs in our
branch of the family, on my father's side. I don't have it
and my dad didn't have it, but our grandfather did."

So Uncle Hugh was a crazy person and it was heredi-
tary. Cerise leaned on the rail next to Murid. He never
seemed crazy, but then she barely knew him. All she had
to go on were childhood memories.

Murid swallowed. "I want you to understand: If you
were Hugh's friend, he would take a bullet for you. And
when he loved, he loved absolutely, with all his heart."

The older woman looked at the night-soaked cypresses.
"When Hugh was nineteen, he met a girl. Georgina Wal-

lace. She was very pretty, and Hugh was very handsome. So she took him for a ride. They saw stars together for a few weeks. Then Georgina decided that she was all funned out and broke the news: she was engaged to Tom Rook over in Sicktree. Hugh was her last fling before the wedding."

"Ugh."

"Hugh didn't understand. He loved her so much, and he couldn't imagine that she didn't love him. I tried to calm him down and to explain that sometimes things didn't turn out. I tried to explain that Georgina lied, but he couldn't let it go. To him, she was everything. She accepted him, she made love to him. In his mind, that meant they belonged to each other forever. Hugh thought she was his mate. His soul mate."

Cold washed over Cerise. "What happened?"

"Hugh took off. The next morning they found Tom Rook and Georgina, and Tom's brother, Cline. Tom and Georgina were torn to pieces. Cline survived. He's crippled for life, but he survived. He said a huge gray dog broke into the house and ripped into them."

"Hugh set one of our mastiffs onto them?"

"No." Murid closed her eyes. "Not a mastiff. Cline never left the Mire. All he knew were dogs. But I saw the tracks the animal left. It was a wolf. A big gray wolf."

"There are no wolves in the Mire," Cerise said.

"There was one that night."

Cerise frowned. "What do you mean?"

Murid looked at the swamp. "That night Hugh left for the Broken. There are a lot of Louisianans from the Weird here, and in the Weird's Louisiana they kill people like Hugh. Do you understand, Ceri? They kill his kind. They strangle them at birth or drown them, like rabid mutts."

The realization hit Cerise like a rock between her eyes. Uncle Hugh was a changeling.

It couldn't be. Changelings were demonic things from scary slumber party stories. They were mad, murderous,

evil things. There was a reason why the Dukedom of Louisiana killed them—they were too dangerous. They turned
into wild animals, and they slaughtered and ate people.
Everything she'd heard about them made them out to be
monsters.

No matter how hard she tried, she couldn't picture
Uncle Hugh as a monster. Uncle Hugh was family. He
built the wooden tree house where she used to play. He
trained the dogs. He churned ice cream. He was calm
and strong, and his eyes were kind and she'd never
seen him angry.

"Has he killed anyone else since?"

Murid shook her head. "Not unless the family asked
him to."

"Does Father know?"

Murid nodded.

There had to be a reason for this story. Maybe her father
made him leave. Maybe Murid saw this as a chance to
bring her brother back.

"Changeling or not, he is my uncle. He's welcome in the
house anytime."

"He knows that. He's in the Broken by his choice."

Okay. "Then why did you tell me this?"

"Hugh is a very strong man." Murid looked into the
distance. "Very good with a crossbow and a rifle. His
reflexes are better honed, and he barely needs any time
to aim at the target. Death doesn't bother him at all. He
accepts it as a fact and moves on."

*William.*

Her heart hammered against her ribs. *No. Please, no.*
"Uncle Hugh is very fast, isn't he?"

Aunt Murid nodded.

"And his eyes glow in the dark?"

Murid nodded again. "He could always tell me what
was cooking when we were at the range, because he could
smell it from the kitchen."

The range was a good ways from the house. Far enough

that if you were at the house and you needed to get the attention of somebody down there, you had to yell at the top of your lungs. Cerise cleared her throat, trying to keep her voice even. "You took William down to the range with you today."

Murid looked away at the swamp. "Chicken with cumin and rice."

"I see." Things made so much sense now. Cerise bit her lip. William was a monster. The orphanage, the military, that wildness she sensed in him—everything made sense.

"You have to spell things out," Murid said. "No games, no hints. You have to be very, very clear with him, Cerise. Be very careful and think before you act. He's dangerous. Hugh didn't change shape often, but William does, because he knows how to hide it. He's been trained to fight and whoever trained him knew how to make the most of William's strengths. So far he's behaving himself, but if you're alone with him and you don't have a blade, you don't stand a chance. Don't send him the wrong messages and don't get yourself raped. William may not even know it's wrong to force a woman."

Her memory thrust the lake house before her. Oh, he knew. He knew very well.

"If you let him, he'll love you forever and he won't know how to let go. Make sure you truly want him before you take that plunge. And . . ." Murid hesitated. "Your children . . . If you were to have any."

Their children would be puppies. Or kittens. Or whatever William was.

*"Families aren't for people like me."*

Oh, dear Gods. She finally found the man she wanted, after all this waiting, and he turned out to be a changeling. Maybe she was cursed. "It can never be easy, can it?"

Aunt Murid leaned toward her. "I had my chance with a man. I didn't take it, because it was too hard and too complicated. Look at me now. How so very happy I am, old and alone. Fuck easy, Ceri. If you love him, fight for him. Nothing worth keeping is free in this world. If you don't love him, cut him loose. Just don't take too long to decide. Our future might be short."

She turned and walked away, into the gloom.

WILLIAM padded through the night, following Cerise's scent trail. He'd always paid close attention to female scents. Some were smothered with perfume, some were tinted with whatever the woman had eaten last. Some fragrances tantalized, others shouted, and a few cringed and proclaimed, "Easy prey."

Cerise smelled the way he imagined his woman would smell. Clean, with a slight trace of shampoo from her hair, a touch of sweat, and a hint of something he couldn't quite describe, something healthy, dangerous, and exciting that primed his nerves.

*Mmmm, Cerise.*

He chased her scent down the balcony, around the house, separating it from Murid's trail. The two women stopped here for a while, then Murid left, but Cerise remained, resting her hands on the rail and looking at something . . . He leaned over the rail. Down below him Mire pines stretched to scratch at the night sky. Pale blossoms of maiden-bells bloomed between the roots, delicate like cups made of frosted glass. Cerise stood here looking at the flowers. If she liked flowers, he would get them for her.

William leaped over the balcony's rail, landing in soft dirt. Five minutes later, he climbed back up, with a handful of flowers in his hand, and followed Cerise's scent. It led him to the back of the house. He turned the corner and ran into Kaldar, carrying a bottle of green wine and two glasses.

Gods damn it.

Kaldar looked at his flowers. "Nice touch. Here." He thrust the bottle and glasses at him. William took them on reflex. Kaldar pointed behind him. "Now you're all set. Small door, up the staircase."

He turned the corner and went off the way William had come.

*Crazy family.* William looked at the bottle. *Why the hell not?*

The door led him to a narrow staircase. He jogged up the steps into a large room. The floor was wood. Bare rafters crossed over his head—the room must've been sectioned off from the rest of the attic. To the left, the wall opened into a narrow balcony. Two soft chairs waited on the right. Cerise curled in the left one, by a floor lamp, reading a book.

*I found you.*

She saw him and blinked, startled.

He knocked on the stair rail with the bottle.

"Who is it?" she asked.

"It's me. Can I come in?"

"It depends. If I don't let you in, will you huff and puff and blow my house down?"

She had no idea. "I'm more of a kick the door open and cut everyone inside to ribbons kind of wolf."

"I better let you in, then," she said. "I don't want to be cut to ribbons. Is that wine for me?"

"Yes."

William crossed the floor and handed her the thick bottle. The light of the lamp caught the wine inside, and it sparkled with deep emerald green.

"Greenberry." Cerise checked the label. "My favorite year, too. How did you know?"

He decided not to lie. "Kaldar gave it to me."

She smiled and he had to hold himself back to keep from kissing her. "My cousin is trying so hard. It's not his fault—he's been trying to marry me off for years."

"Why?"

"It's his job. He arranges the marriages for the family: haggles over the dowry, makes preparations for the weddings, that sort of thing." Cerise looked at the flowers in his hand. "Are those from Kaldar, too?"

"No. I picked those."

Her eyes shone. "For me?"

"For you." He offered her the flowers.

Cerise reached for them. He caught her hand in his. His whole body snapped to attention, as if he'd awoken from a deep sleep because someone had fired a gun by his head. *Want.*

She took the flowers and smelled them. "Thank you."

"You're welcome."

He watched her pull the stems apart on her lap. She took three flowers, added a fourth, and wrapped its stem around the first three. "Will you pour us some wine?"

Yeah, because wine was exactly what he needed right now. William opened the bottle and poured the shimmering green into the two glasses. It smelled nice enough. He sipped it. Nice, a bit sweet but nice. Not as nice as she would taste, but he had to settle for the wine for now. "Good."

"It's homemade." Cerise kept weaving flowers together. "It's a family tradition. Every fall we go to Fisherman's Tree to pick the berries, and then we make wine."

She sipped her wine, he drank his, and for a while they sat quietly next to each other. He wanted to reach over and touch her. She made him feel like a child made to sit on his hands. William drank more wine, feeling the warmth spread through him. Maybe he should just grab her. If he did, she'd try to cut off his head right there. His beautiful, violent girl.

"Why are you smiling?" she asked.

"Because I thought of something funny."

Cerise wove the last flower into her tangle. It looked like a large circle now. She picked it up and put it on her head.

Oh, yeah. He would bring her more flowers and wine and anything else she wanted, until she liked him enough to stay with him.

"Is this your place?" William asked to say something.

"Yes. It's where I hide when I have a fight with some-one."

He didn't remember her fighting with anyone. She sat at the table for a while and then slipped out quietly.

"Who are you fighting with now?"

Cerise got up and walked over to the wall. He followed her. Pictures hung on the wall behind the glass. Cerise touched one of the frames. A man and a woman stood by the pond, both young, almost kids. The man was a Mar: lean, dark, tan. The woman was blond, soft, and slender. Fragile. If she was his, William thought, he'd be worried about breaking her every time they touched.

"My parents," Cerise murmured. "Gustave and Gene-vieve."

"Your mother looks like a blueblood."

She glanced at him. "What makes you say that?"

"Her hair is curled, and her eyebrows are plucked down to nothing."

Cerise laughed softly. "I pluck my eyebrows. Does that make me look like a blueblood?"

"Yours still look natural. Hers look odd." He grimaced. "She looks very well taken care of. Like she never saw the sun."

"It's their wedding. My dad was eighteen, my mother was sixteen. She'd only been in the Mire for a year. Here look at this one. You'll like this one better."

He looked at the next picture. In it a young woman about Cerise's age sat on top of a huge dead gator, lean-ing on its head with her elbow. Her grin cut through the mud caked on her face.

He nodded. "I do like this one better."

"She caused my grandmother no end of misery. Grand-ma Vienna and Grandpa Vernard. Grandpa used to joke that together they made a *W*. He really wanted to name my mother something that started with *W*, but Grandma wouldn't let him."

Cerise reached to a fist-sized glass box with a small

crystal at the bottom and pushed a button. A tiny spark
ignited within the crystal and a three-dimensional por-
trait of a couple sprang into life above the box. One
of the Weird's keepsakes, and not a cheap one either,
since it survived the trip to the Edge and lasted all these
years.

William scrutinized the couple. The woman resembled Genevieve in her wedding picture. Same brittle
quality, like she was made with fine crystal. A man sat in
the chair next to her, leaning back and looking awkward.
Long skinny legs, long skinny arms. Even sitting, he was
very tall.

They were bluebloods, no question, and ones with
long pedigrees. And money. The clothes looked expensive, and the emeralds on the woman's neck had to have
cost a small fortune.

"I told you before that my grandpa and I were very
close. He was brilliant. So, so smart. He always made
time for me. We used to garden together. And tomorrow we'll have to go and drive the Sheeriles out of his
house."

Cerise's shoulders went rigid. "My grandparents were
from an old Weird family. My grandfather did medical
research. He was famous actually. They had status and
money. My mother used to tell me about their castle. It
was somewhere north. They had dogwood trees and they
would bloom white in the spring. She said they would
host balls, and people would gather from all over and
dance . . . Have you ever been to a ball, William?"

He'd been to too many of them. Casshorn, Declan's
uncle, had adopted him to get him out of jail in hopes
that he and Declan would kill each other. The adoption
came with etiquette lessons. "I have."

Cerise glanced at him. "Is it fun?"

"I was bored. Too many people, too many colors. Everything is too bright and too vivid. Everyone is talking
but nobody is listening, because they're too concerned
with being seen. After a while it all just blends."

"I'd like to go to one," she said. "It might not be my thing even, but I'd like to go at least once to say I've done it. Sometimes I feel cheated. I know it's selfish, but sometimes I wonder what it would've been like if my grandfather didn't get himself exiled. Who knows, I might have been a lady."

He didn't have much use for ladies. A lady was someone else's wife or daughter or sister. They were not real, almost like trophies forever out of his reach. She was real. And strong.

She looked about to cry.

"Would you like to dance?"

Her eyes opened wide. "Are you serious?"

Once he learned something, he never forgot it. William took a step forward and executed a perfect deep bow, his left arm out. "Would you do me the honor of dancing with me, Lady Cerise?"

She cleared her throat and curtsied, holding imaginary skirts. "Certainly, Lord Bill. But we have no music."

"That's fine." He stepped to her, sliding one arm around her waist. She put her hand on his shoulder. Her body touched his, and he spun with her around the attic, light on his feet, leading her. It took her a moment and then she caught his rhythm and followed him. She was flexible and quick, and he kept picturing her naked.

"You dance really well, Lord Bill."

"Especially if I have a knife."

She laughed. They circled the attic once, twice, and he brought them to the center of the room, shifting from a quick dance to a smooth swaying.

"Why are we slowing down?" she asked.

"It's a slow song."

"Ah."

She leaned against him. They were almost hugging.

"What's bothering you?" he asked.

"I'm scared to death." Her voice was barely above a whisper. "And mad. I'm so mad at the Hand for putting me through this hell, I can't even breathe. I have to save my parents. I love them so much, William. I miss them so bad it hurts. I would have to rescue them, even if they were horrible people, because if I don't, our reputation will plummet. People will think we're weak, and they will peck us apart little by little. But to save my parents, I have to sacrifice some of my family. Tomorrow they will die, their seats at the table will be empty, and for what? So we can keep living in this mud and squabbling over it. Gods, there has to be something more to life than this . . ."

She closed her eyes.

He held her close. "You'll do fine. You're a natural."

"A natural what?" she asked.

"A killer. I've known people who were better swordsmen, but they didn't have that thing inside that let them kill. They hesitated, they thought about it, and I killed them. You have it. You're good and you're fast. I'll be there to keep you safe."

"I don't want to be a killer, William."

"You don't get to pick."

She pulled away from him. He didn't want to let her go, but he did.

Cerise hugged herself. "On the wall to your left."

He turned. Two photographs waited at eye level. The first showed three men standing close. The middle one was Peva Sheerile. He had one arm around an adolescent kid with the face of a spoiled child and the other around a tall blond man with mournful gray eyes.

"The Sheeriles. That's who we're killing tomorrow." Cerise sounded bitter.

He looked at the second photo and stopped. Cerise and Lagar danced silhouetted against a bonfire.

She was dancing with her enemy.

*Why?*

*Was he better than me? Did she like him?*

*Did she want to dance with him again?*

"Did you think of him while we were dancing?"

"What?"

He wanted to rip Lagar's head off his shoulders. Instead he turned and went down the stairs.


CERISE watched him leave. The door closed and she slumped into her chair. So there he was, Lord Wolf. He might have been a bear, for all she knew, but somehow wolf just suited him better. He was predatory, fast, and cunning. And made ninety-degree turns that made her head spin. One moment they were dancing, the next he took off snarling under his breath.

She looked at Lagar on the wall. William didn't understand the pictures. Lagar would, though. He would know exactly why she kept him on the wall. It was a snapshot of what might have been but could never be.

Cerise sighed and drank the wine from her glass. If things were different, if their families hadn't been in a feud, if Kaitlin, Lagar's mother, wasn't a raging ball of hate, if Lagar was his own man, he would've courted her. She was sure of it. She'd seen it in his eyes that night by the fire, that look of desperate, hopeless longing. If things were different, she might have accepted his courtship. He would've been a good match: handsome, smart, with the strong magic of an old Legion family, and enough money to make sure she would never need to hustle again. She didn't love him, but who knew, maybe if things were different, she might have given him a chance.

That snapshot on the wall showed Lagar's wistful thinking for all to see. Her grandparents' picture showed hers.

She'd wanted so much to have been born out of the Mire. The swamp had its savage beauty, but it was no place to live. No place to build a family and raise children. Half of the people her age couldn't read and didn't want to learn, which was the sadder still. But everyone

from the age of twelve and up could fire a crossbow and
wouldn't hesitate to shoot a person with it. There was
no hope in the Mire. No way to improve their lot. Even
Lagar, with all of his money, still dragged the same mud
on his boots.

She thought of her grandmother, standing delicately
behind her husband and sighed. She didn't want to be
Grandmother Vienna. She didn't want wealth. She could
live her whole life without wearing a single gold ring,
and it wouldn't make a bit of difference. She just wanted
to know that there was light at the end of the tunnel.
That they could send Lark to a school, a real school with
actual teachers, and to someone, a therapist, a doctor, who
could help her, because the family didn't know how. That
they could earn enough to clothe and feed everyone
without resorting to stealing. That they wouldn't have to
look over their shoulders, knowing any minute they might
have to fight with another family like two rats snapping
at each other in the muck. That they could live somewhere else, not in a place where her parents got kidnapped and nobody did anything about it.

Cerise shook her head. If they were slowly crawling
out of the mud, she could live with it. But they were
sinking deeper and deeper. Her children wouldn't know
her grandfather, and her grandchildren, if she were to
have any, wouldn't even know he existed. All his knowledge would be lost. Already she was forgetting things,
and the books didn't help, because half of the time she
was too tired to read them.

It was wrong. Cerise clenched her teeth. The whole
point of working so hard was so her children and their children would be better off than she was. But they wouldn't.
They would be worse. The more time passed, the more
exiles Louisiana stuffed into the swamp, the more vicious it
would become.

No matter how hard she tried, no matter how hard the
family worked, they made no progress. They just slid

backward into the swamp, and all she had as a consolation were useless dreams of "what if" filled with pathetic self-pity.

And then there was William. She should've known that nothing in life came without a catch. He was everything she could ever want in a man: smart, strong, funny, handsome, a hell of a fighter . . . and he turned into a monster. Gods damn it.

She picked up the book she had been reading before William came in. *The Nature of the Beast.* It was an old text from Louisiana. She knew it was biased, but it was her best resource at the moment. She'd taken it out of the library a few months ago to read to Lark, to try to convince her that there were real monsters out there and she wasn't one of them. It's not that she didn't trust Aunt Murid, but since Uncle High was involved, her aunt wasn't exactly objective.

She wouldn't have guessed that her uncle Hugh was a changeling. Would've sworn on her life he wasn't. So not all the stories were true. Yes, her uncle was a murderer, but it wasn't out of bounds for the Mire.

Maybe William was a wolf like Uncle Hugh. They were supposed to be noble creatures . . . She set the glass down. What was she thinking? He's a murdering beast but that's okay, because he is a noble murdering beast?

Poor William. She'd gotten a shock to the system, but it was nothing compared to what he got. Here he was, hunting his enemy. He met a girl in the swamp that made his head spin. And then he realized that the girl came with a clan of insane relatives, an eighty-year feud, and a horde of the Hand's agents. That was a hell of a price tag. Being related to Kaldar alone would make most men run for their life.

Cerise toyed with her glass. William was hers. The way he looked at her, the way he held her while they danced, told her that better than any words. When she'd seen him come up those stairs, her heart had sped up, and it wasn't because she was scared he'd rip her to pieces. She wanted him. But want alone wasn't enough, because he was trouble. Aunt Murid was right—when William loved, he would love absolutely, but when he became jealous or angry, he would be uncontrollable. Life with him would never be dull. It wouldn't be easy either.

She had to decide yes or no. To let him love her or to cut him loose.

All of this was useless speculation, she decided. In the morning they would attack the Sheeriles, and she had no guarantee she would make it out of that fight alive.


WILLIAM burst onto the balcony. She had a picture of another man on the wall.

He swung onto the rail and crouched there staring into the swamp. He needed a fight. A long exhausting brawl.

"What are you doing on the rail, child?"

He whipped around.

Grandmother Az stood next to him, smiling. "It's not good to stare too long at the Mire. It might look back." She reached over and patted his hand with her tiny wrinkled one. "Come on down off that rail. Come now."

Snapping at sweet old ladies was beyond him, no matter how mad he'd gotten. William jumped off the rail.

"That's it," she told him. "Come, help an old woman to a chair."

He followed her around the corner, to where the balcony widened and three wicker chairs sat facing the Mire. William held the chair out for her. Grandma Az sat. "Such a well-mannered child you are. Come sit with me."

William sat. Everything about the old woman was soothing, but he didn't trust her any more than he trusted the rest of them. She knew what he was, too, and kept it to herself. The question was, why?

Grandmother Az reached to a narrow wicker table on the side and picked up an old leather photo album. She flipped it open. "Look right here."

A tall man stood next to a young woman. The man was dark-haired and lean, the woman looked like Cerise, but her features were harsher.

"This is me and my husband. Henri was a good man. I loved him." Her eyes sparkled. "My father didn't like him. My father was a great swordsman. In the old way."

"Like Cerise?"

"Like Cerise. Do you know of the old way, William?"

"No." The more information he got, the better.

"I'll tell you. Once the New Continent of the Weird was filled with people. They built a great empire."

That he'd heard before. In the Broken, the Europeans settled the Americas, killing the native tribes. In the Weird, the history had been almost completely turned around. The *tlatoke* had built a great kingdom, fueled by the magic born in the forest and jungle, and they had raided the Eastern Continent for years until they built a world-destroying weapon, which predictably destroyed them. When the Easterners finally scraped enough courage together to cross the ocean and make landfall, they found an empty north continent and a huge wall that sealed off the southern landmass.

"They called their kingdom the Empire of the Sun Serpent," Grandmother Az continued. "They were great warriors, with a long tradition and great skill in magic. Their magic was their undoing. They brought about their own destruction and had to flee. Some of them fled here, into the Edge, and here they remained, secure in the swamps for centuries to come. That's where we take our root. We keep their arts of sword and magic alive."

"So that's what Cerise does?"

The old woman nodded with a serene smile. "The path of the lightning blade. Very old art. Very hard to learn." She picked up a small letter opener from a narrow side table and raised it straight up. A thin streak of brilliant white dashed down the blade.

Damn it all to hell.

Grandmother Az smiled. "Who did you think taught her?"

"Her father."

"Spoken like a man."

The old woman turned the blade sideways, and the flash danced across her fingers. "She was a good student for me. This art takes much practice and discipline. You have to be chosen from childhood, the way Cerise was. You have to give yourself to it and practice and practice and practice. Long hours every day. When you work that hard, you start thinking that you should be rewarded for your efforts, so when you decide you want something, you fight tooth and claw to get it."

She had some sort of purpose for this conversation, but for the life of him, William couldn't figure out what it was.

"My father was a great swordsman. I told you that. My husband . . ." Grandmother Az moved her wizened hand from side to side.

"Not so much?" William guessed.

"No." The old woman smiled. "He was from the Broken, from a place called France. Very handsome. Very valiant. But not that good with his sword. My father didn't want me to marry him, so he told Henri they had to fight."

"Did Henri win?"

She shook her head. "No. But when my father put his blade against Henri's heart, I put mine against my father's throat. I told him that I only lived once and I wanted to be happy. Do you understand what I am saying to you, child?"

"No."

"That's all right. You will. Think on it."

He had no idea what she was talking about. "Tell me about the monster."

Her face fell. "Stay away from him. He is a terrible thing. Terrible, terrible thing."

"Who is he? Why is he here?"

"He senses trouble. It will all be over soon. Things are coming to an end."

William hid a growl. She would tell him nothing.

"What happened to Lark?"

Grandmother Az shook her head, that same serene smile plastered on her face. William exhaled frustration.

"Tell me about Lagar Sheerile."

"He is handsome. Rich. Strong in the old way."

Great. "He can stretch his flash on his sword like Cerise?"

"Our feud is old, child. Do you think the Sheeriles would've lasted this long if they didn't hold on to the Old Way?" The old woman heaved a heavy sigh. "But there is trouble in Lagar's house. Good blood has gone to bad. The tradition will die soon."

"What do you mean?"

"Kaitlin." She spat the word like it was a poisonous fruit. "She came from a good family. We were friends once, back then, before she married the Sheerile. Her father was a hard man. Once her mother passed away, he never remarried. Kaitlin was his only child, his legacy. He had an iron grip on her, and nothing, not even his death, could break it."

She flicked her hand in disgust. "Kaitlin's done the same to her children. She drives them, steers them at every turn, like they are horses pulling her carriage." The old woman snorted. "Lagar . . . He had promise, that one, but she killed it, smothered his will with hers. Kaitlin doesn't understand—a swordsman must be free to carve his own path in the world, however long it takes him. Her husband understood."

Her voice turned bitter. "Such good blood. They've stood against us for four generations and survived. And she spoiled it all, the old half-wit. Not even her magic will save her now."

A vicious blaze flashed in the old woman's eyes. Her

fingers curled into claws. Her lips wrinkled, baring her teeth, and a specter of magic, dark and frightening, flared behind her. Alarm shot through William.

Grandmother Az stared through him, raised her chin high, her eyes afire. Her voice rolled, deep, frightening. "Gone will be Kaitlin, gone will be her children and her house. We'll purge the memory of the Sheeriles from the world. Ten years from now nobody will recall their name, but we will still be here, watching trees grow from the ground watered with the Sheerile blood we spilled."

William struggled to draw a breath. All around him the air hung thick with the odorous stillness peculiar to the swamp, fecund, violent, and primal. Rotting mud, the pungent scents of night flowers, the stench of wet dogs from the kennel . . .

A door bumped to the left, and a woman's laughter, incongruously normal, sounded through the house.

The savage fury died in Grandmother Az's eyes, and she patted his hand gently, her face wrinkled by a smile. "Well, look at me, rambling on and on, showing my age. Time to go to bed, I think."

She rose. "I have a favor to ask of you. I need to borrow Urow's youngest from you for tomorrow."

"You can have him, if you don't put him in harm's way."

Grandmother Az's face split in a smile. "Silly child. He's my own grandson. I wouldn't harm my family." She turned and went inside.

William slumped in the chair.

Insane woman.

Insane family.

And he was mad to think he could lure Cerise away from them. They would never let her go.

Lark climbed over the balcony rail and sat in one of the chairs. Her hair was filthy again.

"Are you going to chase me off to bed?" she asked.

He shook his head.

"I can't sleep." Lark gathered her knees to her. "I'm scared about tomorrow. Do you think Cerise will die?"

William crossed his arms. "Anything is possible, but no, I think she will live. I'll be there and I'll do my best to keep her safe."

They looked at each other.

"What do you know about Tobias?" he asked. Maybe she would answer his questions. Nobody else would.

"It was a long time ago," Lark said. "Like three years or more. I don't know very much. Him and Cerise were engaged. He was very nice. And pretty."

Figured. "Why did he leave?"

"I don't remember it very well." She frowned. "I think Mom was doing my hair. And Grandma was there. Then Cerise came. She was really upset about some sort of money missing. I think she thought Tobias took it. And then Mom told her to keep calm and not do something she would regret for the rest of her life and that sometimes you had to let things go and give the person another chance. And Grandma said that in the Legion times death was not an improper punishment for stealing from the family. Cerise got this really crazy look on her face. And then Mom said that the Legion times were long over. And Grandma said that that was exactly what was wrong with the Mire, and if it wasn't for the exiles, it would still be a proper place and that Cerise knew what had to be done. And then Cerise took off, and Mom sent me out because her and Grandma needed to have an adult conversation. I didn't see Tobias after that."

A hell of a story. "Do you think she killed him?" William asked.

Lark bit her lip. "I don't know. I don't think so. Cerise gets really calm before she kills somebody. Icy. I think she was too mad that time."

They sat together and looked at the moon for a while.

Lark turned to him. "I'm coming to fight tomorrow. For my mom."

William wanted to tell her that she was too small, but he'd seen his first fight by her age. "Watch yourself and don't do anything stupid."

"I won't," she told him.

# TWENTY-ONE

CERISE raised her head and squinted at the morning sky. It was a beautiful, intense shade of turquoise that promised a gorgeous day. Except today, the family rode out to kill and die, and she was at the head of the column.

Behind her two dozen Mars rode on horseback. She had already sent the kids out to scout the road ahead. She'd glanced over her shoulder. Everyone was here. Richard, Kaldar, Erian, Aunt Murid, Uncle Ben . . . Her gaze snagged on William riding at the edge of the column on the left, next to Adriana. He scowled at her. *Yes, yes, I see you scowling, Lord Bill the Jealous.*

If something happened to her today, Richard would assume command of the family and Aunt Pete would take care of Lark. Cerise's heart lurched. Lark wouldn't do well with Aunt Pete, but she didn't know where else to turn.

Grandma Az would help, but Grandmother and Gaston had their own fight to fight. The Sheerile family was a hydra: the two brothers would be at Sene, but the clan wouldn't die until Kaitlin, their mother, breathed her last. Grandmother had decided today was the day for it, and none of them were stupid enough to stand in her way.

They rounded the bend in the road. It would've been so much easier if Grandpa's house sat somewhere off a main road. They'd ram it with a truck, throw a stinker into it, and sit back and shoot whatever came out. But no, the manor perched deep in the swamp. No truck would make it through the narrow, half-flooded trails.

That meant they would have to lay siege to the house. Even with the Sheeriles alone, the odds wouldn't be good. But with the Sheeriles and the Hand together . . . Who knew what sort of insane monsters the Hand would stuff into it?

Whichever way you looked at it, they'd have to get the stinker into the house somehow. They had to get the Sheeriles out of the house with the least damage, or they risked destroying whatever clues the manor held.

It had been sixteen days since her parents were taken. Cerise stared straight ahead. Tearing up in front of the whole family wouldn't do. Sixteen days since the Hand took her mom and dad, and just about eighty years to the day since the feud between the family and the Sheeriles had started. A hell of a day.

A bolt sliced past her shoulder and thudded into the bark of a tree ahead. A squirrel writhed, pierced by the shaft.

William rode up to the tree and sliced with his knife, cutting the small furry body in two. A swirling mass of tentacles spilled out and fell into the dirt with a wet plop. She'd seen these tentacles before, inside the bat guided by the Hand's necromancer.

"A deader?" Cerise asked.

William nodded. "You don't have to worry about the Hand today."

"Why not?" Erian asked from the back.

William glanced at him. "If Spider had his people helping the Sheeriles, he wouldn't need a scout to keep an eye on things. He must have cut the Sheeriles off, but he still wants a report from the fight."

That meant Lagar and Arig were on their own. Just the two brothers and whatever hired muscle they brought with them. Cerise raised her eyes to the sky. "Thank you."

"I can kill the necromancer," William said.

"How many people do you need?"

He grinned, flashing white teeth, his face feral. "None."

"I'll see you at the house, then. Happy hunting."

William hopped off his horse and vanished into the brush.

She turned her horse. "The Sheeriles are alone. Let's go pry them out of that damn house."

A ragged chorus answered her. Worry stabbed her, and she crushed it before it had a chance to show on her face.

WILLIAM pulled himself up onto the pine branch at the edge of the clearing and surveyed the scene. The soles of his boots were slick with the Scout Master's blood, and he took an extra second to climb.

The old house sat on a very gentle incline. The Sheeriles must've gotten ahold of a lawnmower, because the grass around the house was freshly mowed. A sixty-yard stretch of rocky ground, dotted with stumps of severed weeds, separated the house from the trees. The Mars lay at the perimeter in a ragged line. They were looking at the house.

He looked, too. It was a two-story dilapidated-looking place, the kind he saw often in the Broken. Everything was peeling, sagging, or rotting, except for the iron grates on the windows. Those looked brand new. The gaps between the bars bristled with rifles. The place was a damn fortress. If it was him, he'd set it on fire and pick the enemy off as they jumped out.

At the tree line Richard saw him and touched Cerise's shoulder. She turned to look in his direction. William raised the Scout Master's head by the hair and dangled it for her. The Hand's necromancer had died with an ugly grimace on his face. Maybe bringing the head wasn't the best idea, but then how would she know he killed the man?

Cerise gave him a thumbs-up. *Ha!*

He set the head in the bend of the branch and glanced back at the Mars. At the far end, Lark sat in a tree, hidden from the house by the bark. She waved at him. He waved back.

A woman rose from a crouch at the tree line, clutching a familiar bronze-colored ball in her hand. A stinker grenade, the Weird military's favorite nonlethal weapon of crowd control. Throw one of those into an enclosed space and watch people trample each other trying to get out. That must've cost Cerise an arm and a leg. How were they going to get it past the bars? He glanced at the house. Ah, there. A rectangular window, a foot long, six inches wide, too small to bother barring.

The woman took a deep breath. A flash of pale green flared from her in a short burst. A defensive flasher. Not very strong either. Chances were, she couldn't keep it up for long.

She ran into the open, her magic flaring like a glowing wall around her. Bullets whistled and bounced off, deflected by the green flash. She didn't have a lot of juice, just enough to bounce off a bullet.

The woman sprinted, in a straight line, shuddering under the hail of bullets. Good plan. *Go,* William cheered her on. *Go, go!*

Thirty yards to the house. Twenty-five, twenty-two . . .

The ground under her left foot gave. Metal teeth flashed. The woman screamed, her foot caught in a huge metal trap. Her flash faltered and vanished.

The first bullet took her in the chest as she was falling. It tore a chunk of flesh from her back in a crimson spray. The second, third, and fourth punched her stomach. The bronze ball rolled from her fingers and fell into the green grass.

A small body burst from the brush and dashed across the clearing, dark hair flying. *Lark.*

At the tree line Cerise screamed.

The kid zigged and zagged like a scared rabbit. Bullets tore the turf on both sides of her. A bolt screeched through the air and sprouted from her chest. It caught the girl in mid-leap, and for a moment Lark flew, weightless, eyes opened wide, mouth opened in a horrified O, face chalk pale, just like the child in a meadow full of dandelions years ago . . .

The wild screamed and raked at him from the inside with its claws. He dropped off the branch and dashed to her. The grass and rocks blurred. He rushed through the world, governed only by the speed of his own heartbeat as only a wolf could run. Bullets grazed him like searing furious bees, shredding his shadow, biting through his tracks. He scooped Lark off the ground and kept running, faster and faster, too fast, to the safety of the trees.

Erian charged past him to the house. Faces jerked into his view, barring his way. William leaped over them, bouncing off the nearest trunk deep into the woods, over the fallen tree, past the bushes to the stand of cypresses, half-sunken in the water.

He realized they were far enough and landed on a dry spot. His heart hammered in his chest. His ears felt full of blood.

Lark stared at him with terrified eyes like a mouse before a cat. He jerked her up. The bolt had punched just above her clavicle, not in her chest. A flesh wound. Only a flesh wound.

"Why?" William snarled, his voice barely human. She said nothing and he shook her once. "Why?"

"I had to help. Nobody will miss a monster," she whispered.

"Never again," he growled in her face. "You hear me? Never again."

She nodded, shaking.

He whipped around. People were coming through the brush. He lowered Lark to the ground. The knife was already in his hand. He smelled their breath, he heard their pulse. Their fear flooded him, filling him with a predatory glee. He bit the air. They backed away from him.

"William!" Cerise's voice cut through his rage. "William!"

She pushed through them and splashed through the water. Her scent sent his senses into overdrive. Cerise grabbed at him, her eyes luminescent. Her lips grazed his and he tasted her for half a second. "Thank you!" she breathed and then she was gone, swiping Lark off the ground and carrying her away, and William had to shake himself, because the excitement strained his body, begging to split it open and let the wild out.

People backed away and followed her, until only one remained. William stared at the familiar face. Wild hair, earring, dark eyes . . . It took him a second. Kaldar.

"Hey, there," the man said.

William growled.

"Easy now. Easy. Put the crazy away. The fight is that way." Kaldar pointed back, over his own shoulder. "That's where the bad guys are."

"I know." William stalked past him.

"Talking is good." Kaldar followed him. "Coherent complete sentences are even better. You're very fast, blueblood."

William pushed through the brush. The fury boiled through him. He needed blood. He needed to rip into warm flesh.

At the house Erian, pressed flat against the wall between two windows, ripped a bolt free of his shoulder with a grimace. The Mars kept up the covering fire, their bolts and bullets clattered against the bars guarding the windows above him, mere feet away from Erian's head. Cerise's cousin crouched and crept to the right, his back glued to the wall. He reached the small window, shattered the glass with his fist, and tossed the stinker inside.

A wave of guttural howls echoed through the tree line.

The wind brought a whiff of an acidic stench, putrid and oily and sour, like decomposing vomit. Bile rose in William's throat. He spat to the side. Too much. Too much excitement, too much adrenaline. He felt the familiar ice slide down his skin, raising every hair on his body. The first precursor of the rending, the battle frenzy that struck his kind when the pressure became too much.

William ground his teeth and tried to hold it back. He would need it later. He would need it for Spider. *Not now, fuck it. Not now.*

"Bet you a dollar I'll kill more than Richard," Kaldar yelled, his fingers clenching a wide-bladed sword.

"That's a losing bet," Richard said.

Inside William, the wild's jaws had opened a crack. He caught a glimpse of its fangs, shining and white like the surface of a glacier. He was losing. The rending was coming.

Erian jerked a short, curved knife from the sheath on his belt. A moment stretched into an eternity. Another . . .

The wild opened its mouth. Bottomless blackness gaped in its maw, guarded by icy fangs. He stared straight into it.

The wild bit at him. The fangs pierced his mind. The wild swallowed. Darkness engulfed him.

The world slowed to a crawl. William walked into the field.

Behind him Kaldar screamed. William paid him no mind.

Another kick rocked the bars and the whole grate came loose and clattered to the ground. A dark-haired woman leaped out of the window. She took two steps and crashed down as a bolt sprouted from her throat.

The Sheerile mercenaries fled from the house, spilling from the window and doors, charging across the clearing. William snarled and lunged at them.

A man hurled himself at him, knife raised. Too slow. William swayed away from the glittering metal arc of the striking blade, sliced the man's armpit, jerked him to the side, cut his throat, and kept moving. A woman lunged from the left. William disemboweled her with a precise slash, stepped over her body, and kept moving. He killed again and again, knowing that nothing short of shedding his skin and biting into living flesh would satisfy him. He had to settle for what he had. Steel rang around him, punctured by isolated shots. He glided through the air thick with metallic blood stench on soft wolf paws, removing obstacles in his path.

The world dissolved into blackness and blood.


**CERISE** saw William sprint across the field. Her mind took a second to comprehend it, and by the time she understood what was happening, he'd swung his knife, quicker than the eye could see. Arterial spray wet the ground, bright, vivid red. The Sheeriles' man fell to his knees, but William had already gone on to his next victim.

He killed the woman in an instant, didn't even pause, and when he turned to strike at the next man in his path, she saw his eyes, hot like two chunks of molten amber.

"Stay back!" she barked. "Stay away from him."

He cut and sliced, raging across the field like a demon, killing with brutal, precise savagery. As if a mad tiger had got loose amid a herd of helpless prey. Fast, tireless, deadly.

A shot rang out. William jerked. Her heart skipped a beat.

William swiped a knife from a fallen opponent, whipped about, and hurled it. The blade sliced through the narrow space between the bars on the second-floor window. A woman sagged against the bars and tumbled down, a knife in her throat.

William grinned, baring his teeth, and kept killing.

Chill bumps marked her arms.

Around her, people stood up to get a better look. Nobody said a word. The family just stood and watched in horrified silence.

So that was what he kept chained inside.

"He's insane," Richard said next to her.

"I know," she told him. "He held it in all this time. He's unbelievable, isn't he?"

Richard stared at her for a long moment and raised his eyes to the sky. "What are all of you doing up there? You've lost your minds."


**"WILLIAM?"**

The girl. Her voice, floating into his mind. Her scent swirling about him, filtering through the scents of hot blood

Cerise. Calling him.

William clawed through the blood-soaked fog.

Her hand touched him. He grabbed her and pulled her to him. His vision snapped into crystal clarity, and he saw her and his hands, gripping her shoulders. His fingers were covered with blood.

Cerise smiled at him. "Hey."

"Hey."

Her fingers stroked his cheek. "Are you back with us?"

"I never left."

He noticed her family now. They had surrounded him in a ragged circle, clutching crossbows and rifles. The field was strewn with corpses. He'd run out of people to kill.

The pressure inside him had eased. He needed more, more blood, more enemies to drain the heated strain in his muscles, but Cerise needed him and what he had done would have to be enough for now.

"I'm going to fight Lagar now," she told him. "Will you watch?"

He let her go and nodded.

Cerise walked to the porch. The sun glinted from the sword in her hand.

William sat in the grass.

Richard sat on one side of him, Kaldar landed on the other.

"Murid has her rifle trained on your head. If you interfere, she'll splatter your brains right on these nice weeds over here," Kaldar said. "Just thought you should know."

"It's good to know," William said. His body cooled slowly. Fatigue mugged him. They were fools. It was her fight. If he interfered, she would never forgive him.

If Cerise faltered, he would end up watching her die. The thought made the wild inside him howl, but one didn't stand between a wolf and her prey.

"How often can you do *that*?" Richard indicated the corpses with a sweep of his hand.

"Not often."

"It's over, Lagar," Cerise called, "Come out. Let's finish this."

A quiet descended on the clearing.

The screen door banged. A man stepped out into the sunshine. He wore a blue robe that reached to his knees. The left sleeve hung in tatters. Lagar shrugged off the other sleeve, letting the robe hang at his waist. He swung his sword. Cords of muscle rolled on his bare chest and arms.

What did she see in him? He was tall, well-built. Handsome enough. Pale hair, blue eyes. They were enemies, but he got Cerise to dance with him. Was he charming? Did he know the right things to say?

They paced from side to side, stretching, keeping their distance. Lagar flexed. Veins bulged on his arms. "How come we never got together, Cerise?"

She looked small compared to him. That made for a smaller target, and she was fast, but Lagar was stronger. He'd muscle her and she didn't have the weight to counter. "I don't know, Lagar. Killing my relatives and kidnapping my parents might have something to do with it."

Lagar stopped. Cerise stopped also.

His flash burst from Lagar's eyes in a torrent of brilliant white. It ran down his hand onto his sword.

Shit.

"Too bad it turned out this way," Lagar said.

Cerise's magic slid along her sword. "We both knew it would," she replied.

Lagar charged, fast like a changeling. Cerise parried, her movements flowing as if her joints were liquid. The two blades crashed against each other, sparking with magic. They danced across the clearing, flashing and thrusting. Steel rang, magic shone.

Cerise pulled back and so did Lagar. For a long breath they stood still, poised like two cats before a fight, and then Lagar moved, stalking Cerise across the grass, his sword pointing straight up. Cerise followed, her blade loose in her fingers, stepping on her toes.

Lagar ran. She matched him. He leapt and struck from above in an overhead blow, banking on his superior strength. They clashed in a blinding burst of magic and broke apart, facing each other.

The scent of blood lashed William's nostrils.

A long cut sliced through Cerise's shirt, swelling with red across her shoulder over her breast. A narrow smile bent Lagar's lips.

If Lagar won, William would kill him.

The Sheerile took a step forward and fell, as if his legs were cut out from under him. Slowly Cerise slumped next to him in the grass. Lagar gasped, sucking in the air in small shallow bites.

A dark stain, deep red, almost black, spread through Lagar's robe. Liver blood, tainted with the stench of bile.

"Gods, it hurts," Lagar whispered.

Cerise picked up his hand and held it. *She touched him.* William choked back a snarl.

Lagar's gut distended, growing like an inflating water balloon. A cut to the aorta or an iliac vessel. Lagar's stomach was filling with his own blood.

"We . . . would've been good . . ." Lagar coughed out blood.

Cerise rubbed his hand. "In another time in another life maybe. You hated my father more than you could ever love me."

"Lucky for you," Lagar said softly. A convulsion rocked him and he clenched her hand.

"You should've left," she told him. "You always wanted to."

"False diamonds," Lagar whispered. "Like swamp lights."

Another convulsion shook him. He screamed. His eyes rolled back in his skull. Blood poured from his mouth.

His pulse stopped.

Cerise untangled her hand from his. Her face turned flat and cold. "String him up."

"You're bleeding," Richard said. "And grandmother isn't here to help you."

"She's right," Ignata walked up to them. "Tomorrow will be too late. String him up, Richard."

He shook his head and walked off.

"What's going on?" William glanced at Kaldar.

Kaldar grimaced and spat into the grass. "Magic. Old swamp magic."

# TWENTY-TWO

CERISE sat in the grass. The cut on her breast had stopped bleeding. Strangely, it didn't hurt, not as much as she thought it would have. Her blood always clotted quickly, and she usually got away with a bandage where other people needed stitches.

A few yards away Erian dragged a corpse by its feet onto the growing pile of the dead. He should've nursed his wounds, instead of pulling corpses around. Erian turned toward her, flipping the corpse. Excitement lit his eyes, his teeth bared in a rigid grin. He looked deranged, lost in a maniacal glee.

Blood poured from the corpse's mouth. Erian laughed, his voice bubbling up from his throat.

The delight on his face disturbed her to her core. This wasn't Erian. Erian was calm and quiet. He didn't laugh at death. Didn't revel in it.

The feud was over, Cerise told herself. He'd waited for his revenge for so long it might have driven him a bit unhinged. The Sheeriles were done, and once they cleared the field, Erian would return to his normal self. But she would remember that rigor mortis smile forever.

She sighed and looked at the body he was dragging. The cadaver's pale head bounced on the ground, and more blood escaped from its mouth. The face seemed familiar . . . Arig. She almost didn't recognize him without that leer. Death wiped all expression off his face, and now he seemed just another boy, cut down too early.

Cerise wished she felt something, something other than

regret. The Sheerile brothers were dead. The feud was over. She should've been celebrating, but instead she felt empty, scraped clean of all emotion. Only regret remained. So many people dead. Such a waste. A waste of people, a waste of life.

If a rock fell from the sky and hit her head, killing her, she wouldn't care. She was spent anyway.

William dropped on the grass next to her. "It was a good fight."

"Yes. You slaughtered thirty people single-handedly."

"I meant you and Lagar."

Cerise sighed. "If I was my father, the family would follow me anywhere, but I'm not. I had to prove that I was good enough. The next time I may have to lead them against the Hand, and I need them to follow."

In the center of the clearing the men had strung up Lagar's body. He hung upright, off a wooden pole, and people piled peat and mud around the base. Three buckets full of mud already waited next to the body. Richard and Kaldar brought a large plastic bin over and set it by the buckets.

William looked at the body. "Why?"

"We're going to invite a swamp spirit into his body. There are many spirits in the swamp. They used to be Gods, the Old Gods of the Old Tribes who fled into the swamp centuries ago. But the tribes are long gone, and now their Gods are just spirits. There is Gospo Adir, he's the spirit of life and death. There is Vodar Adir, he's the spirit of water. I'll be calling Raste Adir, the spirit of plants."

"To what end?"

She sighed. "We don't know where the Hand took my parents or why. We need to find out where they are and what they want. Plants have a lot of vitality. Enough to revive a dead body. The things I'm looking for are locked in Lagar's brain. He was a careful man. He would have to know what Spider planned to do with my parents, or he would've never made a deal with the Hand.

Raste Adir will meld with the body and find that knowledge for me."

"Fusion." William spat the word as if it were rotten.

"Not exactly. Fusion melds a living human with the plant tissue, smothering the person's will. Lagar is dead. There is no will left. We just need the information stored in his mind. Don't look at me like that, William. I'm trying to save my family."

The disgust slid off his face. "Is it dangerous?"

"Yes. The old magic is starving. If I'm not careful, it will devour me."

He opened his mouth.

"I have to go now." Cerise pushed off the ground and strode to Lagar's body, where Ignata and Catherine waited. *Look on, Lord Bill. You showed me your bad side. This is mine.*

Ignata dumped a bucket of mud over herself. Catherine joined her, holding the bucket, awkward and uneasy. Cerise picked up the third one and emptied it over her head. The cool mud slid over her hair, smelling faintly of rot and water.

"I wish Grandmother was here," Catherine murmured.

"She can't," Ignata said.

"I know, I know. I just . . . I wish it was over."

"Me, too," Cerise murmured.

Catherine stopped. "Why, do you think something will go wrong?"

Cerise almost cursed. "No," she lied. "Nothing will go wrong. I'm just tired, bloody, and covered in mud. I'd like to get home and sleep, Cath."

"I think we all would," Ignata said.

Catherine sighed and poured the mud over herself.

"Let's just get this over with."

Cerise popped the lid off the plastic bin. Three bags filled with ash sat inside. She passed two of them to Ignata and Catherine, and kept the third. Fear cringed deep inside her.

*Just get this over with. Just get it done.*

Cerise pulled the bag apart and began pouring ash in an even line, drawing a circle around Lagar's body.

It would've been so much easier if Grandma were here, but she wasn't.

GRANDMOTHER Az took Emily's face into her hands and held her gently, like she used to do when she was a tiny babe. A mere slip of a girl, Emily brimmed with magic. Az sighed. Of all her children, Michelle had the most magic. Little wonder Michelle's only daughter would be the same.

Before them the ward stones shielding the Sheeriles' territory dotted the swamp forest. That's where Kaitlin hid, thinking herself safe and secure in her manor, behind her old wards. She thought them impenetrable. *Well, not for long, you demented crone. Not for long.* It would end today.

Mikita and Petunia watched them.

"Are you sure, chado?"

Emily nodded.

"Such a good girl you are." Az smiled, noticing the tiny tremors troubling the girl's hands. Scared child. Scared, scared. "Very well."

"What do I do?"

"Just stand here next to me. Gaston, are you ready?"

Urow's youngest son nodded his head—butchered his hair that wolf, yes, he did—and adjusted the backpack strapped to his back.

"Remember, the Fisherman's track. That's your way back. The wards keep things out, but they won't keep you in. Don't stay there. Don't wait for it to happen, or you might not get out."

He nodded again.

"Off we go, then." Grandma rested her hand on Emily's shoulder, feeling the hard knot of the muscle. "It's all right," she whispered. "Trust your grandmother, child."

The girl relaxed under her fingers. Grandmother Az stood straighter and gathered her power. It came to her like a cloud of angry bees, pouring from the leaves and the ground in a flood centered on her. This was the old magic. Mire magic. It had once built an empire the likes of which the world had never seen before. All was gone now, but the magic remained.

Emily gasped. Hungry, Az pulled the power from her, more and more. Emily shuddered and went down to her knees. Her head drooped, her dark hair fanning her face, her magic streaming into Az's fingers. In that magic, the magic from a living human body, that was where the real power lay.

Az could see it now, the storm of magic draping her like a dark mantle, billowing in the wind of the phantom currents. The witch's cloak, they called it.

Az felt Emily's heartbeat flutter in her, weaker and weaker. Enough. She could've taken more. Some part of her longed for it, longed for the power, but she shut that part of her soul off, slammed the door in its wailing hungry face. She let her go, although it took all of her will to do it, and her grandbaby fell facedown into the soft earth.

The witch's cloak coalesced, shaped by her will. *Here's to you, Kaitlin. May you rot in hell with your spawn.*

Az punched the air, throwing all of her weight into the strike. The magic burst along her arm, a dreadful needle aimed at the heart of the Sheerile land, where their manor lay. The stones shook in the earth and two of them went black.

A shadowy path opened in the wards, only four feet across and straight as a bolt.

"Now, Gaston! Go!"

Urow's youngest dashed along the path and within two breaths vanished from their view.

"There he goes," Az murmured. "So fast. Like the wind."

Her legs crumbled under her, but Mikita's hands caught her before she fell. The ward stones grew paler and paler, slowly returning to their normal gray color. The protective spells were flaring to life, reclaiming the path she had made.

"Getting too old for this," Az murmured before sleep claimed her.

CERISE emptied the last of the ash, took a small embroidered satchel from the bin, and stepped into the circle, aware of her two cousins joining her. Catherine's face was bloodless even under the mud. Ignata bit her lip.

They stood at the pole. Cerise took a small step forward. No turning back now. She had to do this and she had to do it right. The old magic was unruly and always hungry. Asking it for help was like playing with fire. Give a hair, and it would swallow you whole. Fear skittered down her spine. Cerise pushed it away.

*Mom, Dad, hold on. I'm coming.*

Ignata began to chant, gathering magic to her. A moment later Catherine's low voice joined in.

Cerise tugged the silk strings of the satchel, dipped her hand inside, and brought out a handful of seeds. She had only done this twice before, both times with Grandma Az leading, and it terrified her so bad, she had nightmares for weeks afterward. Raste Adir drove people wild. If you slipped up, your body was no longer yours. It did things on its own, and all you could do was watch in panic. Raste Adir made you forget who you were, and if you weren't careful, you would forget yourself forever.

Her fingers shook.

Cerise passed the satchel to Ignata, who closed it and took it out of the circle and came back, still chanting.

Cerise knelt before the mound of mud and peat under the pole, where Lagar's blood dripped down, and gently dropped the seeds onto the mud.

Magic shot through her in an electrifying pulse and spread, tingling, through her body, spilling from inside out. Beside her Ignata swayed. Catherine murmured the chant like the soft whisper of the wind through the leaves.

Grandmother Az's words streamed through her mind. *Don't give in. Don't forget who you are.*

The magic swirled within her and rushed out, like the tide, sucked into the mound.

The seeds moved. Their outer shells cracked. Tiny green roots thrust through, pale and fragile.

The magic poured out of Cerise in a heady rush, feeding the plants.

The roots thickened, raising the seeds, burrowing deep into the bloody mud, turning brown. Green sprigs spiraled up, twisting about the pole, biting into Lagar's body with green shoots, climbing higher and higher.

Sweat broke out on Cerise's forehead, mixing with the mud.

Leaves burst on the shoots, bright, vivid, their tiny veins red like Lagar's blood. Lagar's corpse disappeared beneath the blanket of green.

A deep ache gnawed at her insides. The mound demanded more magic. More. *More.*

Buds sprung from the greenery and split open. Flowers unfurled, yellow and white and pale purple, sending dizzying perfume into the air. It swirled around Cerise, sweet like honey. A giddy happiness flooded her. So beautiful . . . Her body swayed, dancing. She tried to stop herself, but her limbs escaped her control.

Catherine crashed to her knees and laughed softly.

*Mom . . . Dad . . . Focus. Focus, damn it.* Cerise bent over the mound and spat onto the leaves. "Wake."

The green mass shivered. A muted roar rolled through the clearing as if a dozen ervaurgs declared their territory all at once. Magic shot through the leaves, ancient, powerful, and hungry. So hungry.

Lagar's face thrust through the rustling leaves, framed in the cascade of flowers, his skin dusted with golden pollen.

Raste Adir had answered the call.

Lagar's eyes glowed with verdant wild green. Thin shoots snaked from his body, hidden beneath the moss and leaves, reaching out to her, ready to drain her dry, filling her mind with promises. Cerise saw herself caught in the branches, her body a dry husk, one with the green; saw the shoots surge further, saw kneeling Catherine become a spire of green; saw Ignata lifted off her feet by a vine, her face serene and lost among the blossoms . . .

Cerise jerked back, raising her defenses. *No. You get back!*

The old magic hovered just beyond reach. Its pull was so strong.

On the ground Catherine sobbed, happy tears spilling from her eyes. The vines reached for her.

Cerise stepped in front of them and gathered her magic. It rose behind her in a dark cloud, splaying forth. The shoots shrank back, shivering.

*That's right. Get back, stay in your place.*

Cerise squared her shoulders. She was a swamp witch like her grandmother and her grandmother's mother and her grandmother's grandmother before her. She had skill and she had power, and the old magic wouldn't wrestle her mind from her.

"Where is my mother?"

Lagar's mouth opened. A cloud of pollen erupted from his throat, swirling in a glittering cascade like golden dust.

"Answer me."

Ignata made a small mewing noise behind her.

A shimmer ran through the pollen. An image rose within the cloud: a vast field of water with a lonely gray rock rising out of it like the back of some beast, and beyond it, a hint of a large house . . . Bluestone Rock. Only a day away!

The branches reached for her. She snapped her witch's cloak and they fell back.

"Where is my father?"

The pollen shifted. No image troubled the cloud— Lagar didn't know.

"What does Spider want from our family?"

The branches swirled, winding tighter and tighter. Lagar's eyes flared with dark green like two swamp fire stars. Something burned deep in that glow, something terrible and powerful, clawing its way to the surface.

"Obey!" Cerise snapped.

The pollen glittered once again, shifting into a tattered notebook . . . It looked like one of Grandfather's journals.

Lagar's body split like an opening flower. Dark blue tentacles sprouted from it, streaming to her through the image in the pollen.

She pushed her magic before her like a shield. The tentacles smashed into it with a ghostly howl. The pressure nearly pushed her off her feet.

"Run!"

Behind her Ignata grabbed Catherine and pulled her up to her feet. Cerise backed away. Her nose bled. Her head grew dizzy.

"Clear!" someone called. She stumbled out of the circle. The tentacles flailed behind her, reached the ash, and shrunk, shriveling.

"Burn it!" Richard stepped into the circle and hurled gasoline onto the leaves from a bucket. Someone flicked a match. The greenery went up in flames.

A howl of pain burst from Lagar. He screamed like a living thing being burned alive.

Catherine sobbed, rocking back and forth.

Cerise curled into a ball and tried to block out Lagar's cries. Now they knew. Now they knew where to look.


KAITLIN opened the lid of a mother-of-pearl box. Her fingers brushed the treasures within. A lock of Lagar's blond hair, cut when he was a child. The tip from the first arrow Peva had shot. One of Arig's twigs . . . She remembered when Peva had told him that his fingers were too weak for a good draw, and for a while wherever Arig went, he had a twig in his hands and would be snapping little pieces off of it.

She pursed her lips. Where did she go wrong? How could she have raised weak sons that had failed her?

She looked up at the mirror that hung on the wall and touched the wrinkled skin around her eyes. Old . . . She had grown old. She had given all of herself to her children. That's what a mother was supposed to do. And they failed her.

Kaitlin glared at her reflection. Her skin may be sagging. Her hair may be graying. But her will was iron. It was in her eyes, just like her father used to say. "You have iron in your eyes, Kaitlin. You're strong. Life will hurt you, but you'll survive, my daughter. The iron doesn't give in."

She squared her shoulders. There were magics she could work. Dark things, vicious, forbidden things she could let loose on the Rat pack. And all of the old crone's magic couldn't save them then. Oh, the Guard would come, and the militia would gather and whine about the outlawed magic. Let them come. She would hold them off.

Perhaps she could even start anew. Time had robbed her of her fertility, but there were plenty of children in the Mire. She could pay some woman for a good strong child, and Kaitlin would have another son. And this time, she would make no mistakes.

She turned to the couch where she had left her shawl and frowned when it wasn't there. For a moment she searched and then saw it hanging over the porch railing, where she had stood this morning seeing Arig off.

Strange.

She felt around for a trace of foreign magic and found none. The shield of wards stretching from her house remained intact. Besides, none would dare to enter her domain. Nobody would be that stupid.

Kaitlin strode onto the porch, tiny sparks of power breaking over her skin. She passed her hand over the shawl.

Nothing. Not spelled in any way, the pattern as intricate as ever. She must've forgotten it here on the porch.

Kaitlin lifted the shawl, wrapped it around her shoulders, and stood for a moment, breathing in the Mire smells. The afternoon was winding down. Soon the night would fall. The dark time. The Rats would be in their Rathole, celebrating, bloated with wine and success. She had a few things to show them.

A faint prickling in her hand made her glance at her fingers. Thin gray residue sheathed her fingertips. She stared at it, puzzled, rubbed her fingers with her thumb, and gasped as the skin and muscle peeled off.

Shocked, she whirled, searching for traces of offensive spells, chanting to raise her defenses. Power surged and formed a reassuring, solid wall of magic to guard her from the world. She could chant herself out of it. Again and again she whispered, but the skin on her fingers refused to heal.

The shawl. She tore it from her body and screamed as the skin on her neck came off with it. Numbness crept into her fingers and seeped into her arms.

This couldn't be. She was iron! She was strong.

Her legs failed, and Kaitlin crumpled onto the porch. Numbness clutched at her chest. Her heart skipped a beat . . . The numbness burst into pain. It surged through her body, ripping into her insides with savage teeth.

She tried to call out to the workers in the stable, but pain had locked her throat in a fiery collar and her voice refused to obey.

I'm dying . . .

She wouldn't let the Rats have the land. Not her land, not her house, not the wreck of a body that once had been her husband. With an enormous effort of will, Kaitlin poured the remnants of her life into one last magic.


**GASTON** dashed along the twisted Fisherman's track. He had tossed the sack and iron tongs he had used to han-

dle the shawl into some bushes to reduce the weight, but it
didn't make much difference. His legs were beginning to
tire. Gaston leaped over a fallen tree. The weeds flanking
the overgrown path slapped his shoulders as he ran, dust-
ing his skin with yellow spring pollen.

Behind him a roar rose, a dull muted sound like the
voice of a distant waterfall. He glanced over his shoulder
and saw weeds snap upright in the distance as if pulled
straight by an invisible hand. Pines groaned in protest.

He ran. He ran like he had never run before in his
life, squeezing every drop of speed from his muscles
until he thought they would tear from his bones. The
roar grew louder. Tiny rocks pelted him. The air in his
lungs turned to fire.

Gaston saw a glimpse of the river ahead and launched
himself toward it.

Not going to make it.

He hit the water and dove deep into the gloom. A tiny
ervaurg shot past him, spooked by his presence.

Above him the sky turned yellow.

# TWENTY-THREE

**CERISE** stretched her legs and drank more juice. Her whole body ached like she'd been beaten with a sack of rocks.

"How are we doing?" Ignata asked from the other end of the room.

"We're fine." Cerise glanced at her. The skin on Ignata's face seemed stretched too tight. Dark bags clutched at her eyes. Catherine had hid in her room the moment they entered the house. Cerise sighed. If she had any sense, she would've hidden also. She tried, but the anxiety made her stir-crazy, and once she took a shower, she came down to the library, where Ignata ambushed her with ickberry juice to "replace electrolytes," whatever that meant.

"What a day," Ignata murmured.

Erian shouldered his way into the room and sank into a soft chair, his eyes closed, his arm in a sling. "What a week."

Ignata turned to him. "Why are you still awake? Didn't I give you some valerian half an hour ago?"

He opened his pale eyes and looked at her. "I didn't drink it."

"Why not?"

"Because your valerian has enough sleeping tincture in it to put an elephant to sleep."

Ignata covered her face with her hands. "You know, if you had to hire a doctor, I bet you'd listen to her."

"No, we wouldn't," Cerise murmured.

"Where is the blueblood?" Erian asked.

"With Kaldar."

"I noticed something." Erian turned in his chair. "He's got a memory like a gator trap. There are over fifty of us, and he hasn't confused a single name yet."

Cerise scooted deeper into the chair. That was all she needed, a family discussion about Lord Bill.

"I like him," Ignata said. "He saved Lark." A smile stretched her lips. "And Cerise likes him, too."

"Don't start," Cerise murmured.

"It's about time, too. It's been, what, two years since Tobias ran off?"

"Three," Erian said.

Kaldar walked into the room, followed by William. Their stares connected and Cerise's heart skipped a beat.

Kaldar dropped into a chair, stretching long legs. "What are we talking about?"

"We're trying to decide when you're going to marry Cerise off," Erian said.

Kaldar leaned back, a little light playing in his eyes. "Well . . ."

Cerise set her glass down with a clink. "Enough. Have you figured out which house my mother is in?"

Kaldar grimaced. "Not yet. In case you forgot, Blue-rock is in the middle of a pretty big lake. It takes time to find the right house. We'll know tomorrow. I've got guys on it."

"What guys?"

Kaldar waved his hand. "If I tell you who I sent to spy on the house, you'll bust my balls about how dangerous it is and how I shouldn't put children in peril. It's being handled, that's all you get."

"Now, wait a minute—"

Something thumped against the window.

Cerise grasped her knife. Kaldar was on his feet and moving to the window along the wall, dagger in hand.

Another thump. His back to the wall, Kaldar leaned to glance outside, sighed, and slid the glass panel up.

A small animal scrambled onto the windowsill. Fuzzy

with mouse fur, it sat on its haunches, looking at them with enormous pale green eyes.

*Oh no.*

The beast waddled to the edge of the windowsill. Its bat wings fluttered once, twice, it took the plunge and glided to the table. Tiny claws slid on the polished surface, and the creature flopped on its butt, skidded, and crawled back to sit before her, whiskers moving on the shrewlike nose.

No escape now. "Emel, you almost gave me a seizure."

"Sorry about that," Emel's voice came not from the beast but from about three inches above its head. "I don't have full control of this little fellow yet. I just made him a couple of weeks ago, but I was sure that under the present circumstances anything larger than him would get shot down."

The beast scratched its side with a tiny black foot.

"I'm so sorry about Anya," Emel said.

"Me, too." A pang of guilt stabbed her. Anya had volunteered to run the stinker to the house. If it wasn't for Lagar's gator traps, she would still be alive.

The bat shivered. "Someone summoned Raste Adir to the clearing in front of Sene. Was it you or Grandmother Azan?"

"Me. Grandmother is sleeping."

The beast sneezed and curled into a tiny ball. "Very well done," said Emel's disembodied voice. "You held it a touch too long, but other than that, very well done."

His praise filled her with absurd pride. At least she had done something right. "Thank you."

Richard slipped through the door, followed by Murid and Aunt Pete, her missing left eye hidden by a black leather patch.

The beast fell asleep, its tiny ribcage rising and falling with smooth regularity.

"Did you know that most of the Sheerile estate has been blighted?" Emel continued. "The house is crumbling into dust, and the entire place is raining yellow pine needles. Grandmother didn't have anything to do with that, did she?"

Smart bastard. "Emel, you know perfectly well that blight magic takes a life. All of us care too much about Grandmother to let her throw herself away like that. She's just sleeping. We lost a lot of people today, and it took a toll. Kaitlin was probably so mad that she lost the feud, she sacrificed herself to blight the place."

"I thought as much. Of course, you do remember that aiding a casting of the blight is punishable by death, according to Mire law."

And he would be heartbroken if the Mire militia dragged her off. Unless he got the money first, of course. "Yes, I remember."

A sound of a throat being cleared issued from above the creature. "There is the matter of the eel," Emel said. "I wasn't confident my message would get through to you."

"What are you implying?" Kaldar stopped cleaning his fingernails with the tip of his dagger.

"Nothing offensive. Simply put, all of you had a very difficult day, and I'm sure the eel was the last thing on your mind. However, the problem remains unsolved. The law clearly says that if you purposefully destroy property belonging to another, you must pay restitution. As you know, since we are related by blood, the eel would not have attacked you unprovoked. So, either you provoked it or you did nothing to avoid it. I understand that another person was involved in the altercation, but the fact remains: you are allowed passage through Sect-held property, but he was not. The eel was simply doing its duty. Since you were present at the scene and can't claim ignorance of our traditions, the Sect holds you responsible for not taking care of—"

"How much?" Cerise asked.

"Five thousand."

She reeled back. Kaldar's jaw hung down. Erian's eyes snapped open. Ignata nearly dropped her glass.

Cerise leaned forward. "Five thousand dollars? That's outrageous!"

"It was a fifty-year-old animal."

"Which attacked me in the middle of the swamp in an unmarked stream!"

"There was a marker there. We're just not sure what happened to it."

"This is unfair!"

Emel sighed. "Cerise, you and I both know that you are perfectly capable of avoiding mud eels, especially one of this size. It was hard not to notice the thing—it was fourteen feet long. However, your points are valid and you're my dear cousin, that's why it's only five thousand and not seven as it would've been for anyone else."

"We can't do five thousand," she said flatly.

"I'll go as low as four thousand eight hundred, Cerise. I'm sorry but anything less would be an insult to the Sect. And even so, the missing two hundred will have to come from my own funds."

Gods, where would she get the money? They had to pay the Sect. It was too powerful. Making an enemy of it would mean that their livestock would start dropping dead. First the cows and rolpies, then dogs, then relatives.

"If you do not have the lump sum, we can set up a payment schedule," Emel suggested. "Of course, there would be interest involved . . ."

"Three payments," she said. "No interest."

"Within three months, the first good-faith payment due by the end of this week."

"You're forcing me to choose between clothes for the winter and being forever in debt to the Sect. I don't appreciate that."

"I'm sorry, Cerise. I truly am."

The creature awoke. "I very much care about all of you," Emel said. "The Sect does not wish me involved in this affair with the Hand. But I'll try to help the best I can. I *will* find a way."

The beast took to the air and vanished into the darkness outside.

Kaldar slammed the window closed.

"Where are we going to get the money?" Ignata murmured.

"My grandmother's jewelry," Cerise said. She thought of the elegant emeralds set in the pale white gold, thin like silk. Her link to her mother, the last link to the life that could've been. It felt like ripping a chunk of herself out, but the money had to come from somewhere and that was the last reserve they had. "We'll sell the emeralds."

Ignata gaped. "They are heirloom pieces. She meant them for your wedding. You can't sell them."

Oh, she could. She could. She just had to have a good long cry before she did it, so she didn't break into tears during the sale. "Watch me."

"Cerise!"

"They are just rocks. Rocks and metal. You can't eat them, they won't make you warm. We have to pay the debt and the kids need new clothes. We need new ammunition and food."

"Why can't he pay?" Erian nodded toward William. "He killed it."

"He has no money," Cerise said. "And even if he did, I wouldn't take it."

William opened his mouth, but she stood up. "That's it, the debate is over. I'll see y'all later."

She headed outside onto the verandah before she broke to pieces.


OUTSIDE the cold night air wrapped around Cerise. She took a deep breath and started down around the balcony, to the door leading to her favorite hiding spot.

A dark shape dropped onto the balcony in front of her. Wild eyes glared at her. William.

How in the world did he get ahead of her? She crossed her arms on her chest.

He straightened.

"You're in my way," she told him.

"Don't sell them. I'll give you the money."

"I don't want your money."

"Is this because you're still pissed off about Lagar?"

She threw her hands up. "You stupid man. Don't you get it? Lagar was trapped like me. We were both born into this, we couldn't leave, and we knew we would eventually kill each other. What we wanted made no difference. At least he could've run away, but I'm stuck here because of the family. I didn't love him, William. There was nothing there except regret."

"So take the damn money."

"No!"

"Why?"

"Because I don't want to be obligated to you."

He growled.

Quick steps approached. They both turned.

Aunt Pete came running from around the corner. "Cerise?"

Dear Gods, couldn't they leave her alone for just a moment? Cerise heaved a sigh. "Yes?"

"Kaldar's boys came back. They found the house where the Hand is holed up and took pictures." Aunt Pete wheezed. "Hold on, let me catch my breath." She thrust the photographs out.

Cerise took the pictures and held them up to the weak light filtering outside through the window. Big house with a glass hothouse on the side. Kaldar's guys got really close. She would have to speak to him about that—no need to take chances.

Aunt Pete pulled the pictures from her hand and slapped one on top of the stack. "Never mind all that. This one, look at this one!"

The photograph showed the close up of the hothouse, taken through a clear glass pane. A two-foot tall stump of a tree jutted sadly through dirt. The tree's stem was blue

and translucent, as if made of glass. Borrower's Tree, one
of the Weird's magical plants.

Cerise glanced up.

Aunt Pete huffed. "You know what this tree is used for.
Think, Cerise."

Cerise frowned. In small quantities, Borrower's tree
was harvested to produce catalysts that bound human and
plant. William had said the Hand was full of freaks; some
of them probably had grafted plant parts and needed the
catalysts. It did look like a fairly sizable tree, and it was
cut down to a nub, so they must've needed a hell of a lot
of catalyst.

The only reason to have that much catalyst would be
to actually transform someone through the use of magic.
But who would Spider transform? All his guys were already as transformed as they were going to get. It had to
be the captives. But it wouldn't make sense to graft anything on them; no, he had to be doing very specific things
to achieve mental control over them, in which case it
would be . . .

The pictures fluttered from her hand. Cerise rocked
back. "He's fusing my mother!"

The world went white in a moment of rage and panic.
Her head turned hot, her fingers ice-cold. She froze, like
a child trapped in a moment of getting caught. Memories
streamed past her: mother, with her blue eyes and halo
of soft hair, standing by the stove, a spoon in hand, saying something, so tall . . . Going outside to the porch
hand in hand; fixing her hair; reading together in a big
chair, her head nestled against her mother's shoulder;
her mother's smell, her voice, her . . .

Oh, my Gods. All gone. All gone forever. Mother was
gone. Mother, who could fix anything, couldn't fix this.
Fusion was irreversible. She was gone, *gone*.

*No. No, no, no.*

A crushing heaviness swelled in Cerise's chest and
tried to drag her down to the floor. She clenched against

the pain, her throat caught in a tight ring, and forced herself to walk away, half-blind from the tears. "I have to go now. So nobody will see."

Hands swept her off her feet. William carried her off, away from Aunt Pete, away from the noises from the kitchen, to the door, and up the stairs, and then into her little room. Her face was wet and she stuck it into his shoulder. He gripped her, his warm arms cradling her, and sank to the floor.

"They're fusing my mother." Her voice came out strangled. "They're turning her into a monster and she would know. She would know what they were doing. The whole time."

"Easy," he murmured. "Easy. I have you."

Mother's beautiful smile. Her warm hands, her eyes full of laughter. Her "I have the silliest children." Her "sweetheart, I love you." "You look beautiful, darling." All gone forever. There would be no good-bye and no rescue. All the deaths, all the scrambling, it was all for nothing. Mother wasn't coming back to her and Lark.

Cerise buried her face in William's neck and wept soundlessly, pain leaking out through her tears.

CERISE opened her eyes. She was warm and comfortable, resting against something. She stirred, raised her head, and saw two hazel eyes looking at her.

William.

She must've fallen asleep, all tangled up in him. They sat on the floor, where he first landed. He hadn't moved.

"How long have you sat here?" she asked.

"About two hours."

"You should've put me down."

She wiggled a little, but he kept his hands where they were. "I don't mind. I like holding you."

Cerise leaned back against him and put her head on his shoulder. He stiffened and then hugged her tighter to him.

"Do I look like a mess?" she asked.

"Yes."

That was William for you. No lies.

The soft light of the lamp fell gently, illuminating her hiding room. It looked so pitiful now. Pictures of dead people on the walls. Threadbare chairs. This had been her spot since she was a child and now she saw it, as if for the first time. It would've made her sad, but there was no sad left in her. She'd cried it all out.

"I'll have to explain it to Lark." Her heart cringed at the thought. "And I don't even know if my father is dead or alive."

Her voice trembled. William hugged her tighter.

"You've seen Lark's tree?" he asked quietly.

She nodded. "The monster tree."

"What happened to her?"

Cerise closed her eyes and swallowed. "Slavers. I don't even know where they came from. We never could figure it out. Someone had to have let them in across the border. Celeste, my second cousin, and Lark, she was called Sophie back then, were taking wine down to Sicktree by river. Lark wanted to buy Mom a birthday present . . ."

She choked a little on the words.

"So Celeste took Sophie on a boat to trade a case of wine for some trinket. They shot Celeste in the head. Dropped her with one bullet. She fell overboard and Lark went after her. The slavers hit her with an oar when she came up for air, knocked her right out. They took her down into the Mire to their camp and put her in a hole in the ground. The hole would flood in the evening, and she had to sleep sitting up, up to her knees in water, so she wouldn't drown. We turned everything upside down looking for her. We searched with dogs everywhere."

His arm braced her, pulling her closer.

"She says the second day one of the men got into the hole with her. Probably wanted to molest her. He might have done it, at least partway. Lark can flash a little. She isn't quite there yet with aiming, but it's a strong white flash. She flashed him through the eyes."

"Fried the brain," William said.

"Yeah. The slavers left the body where it was and stopped feeding her. It took us eight days to find her, and then only because of Grandma. She had gone off into the swamp a week before—she does that every year—and when she came out, she called Raste Adir the way I did today. Used one of the slaver corpses we had put into the freezer. I should've done it, but back then I didn't know how."

Cerise swallowed. "When we found the camp, it was full of holes and children. Some were dead—the slavers didn't take good care of their merchandise."

"Did you kill them?" William's voice was a ragged snarl.

"Oh, yes. Left nobody alive. I would've tortured every single one of those motherfuckers if there was time. When we pulled Lark out of that hole, she was weak but alive. She could stand by herself. Seven days without food, she should've been weaker."

Cerise closed her eyes. Telling him was like ripping a scab off a wound.

"You think she ate the body?" he asked.

"I don't know. I didn't ask. I'm just glad she's alive. She came back odd, William. At first it was the hair and the clothes, and then it was running away to the woods and not talking. And then there was the monster tree. Mother was the only one she trusted. Now only I'm left."

"There is a real monster in the woods," he said. "It went after Lark and I fought it."

She raised her head. "What do you mean a monster? Was it one of the Hand's freaks?"

He shook his head. "I don't think so."

"What did it look like?"

William grimaced. "Big. Long tail. Looked like a giant lizard sprinkled with hair here and there. I cut it and it healed right in front of me."

Damn it.

He looked at her. "I don't know what it is, but your Grandmother does. She was singing it a lullaby in Gaulish."

Grandmother Azan? "And you kept it to yourself?"

He raised his free hand. "I wasn't sure if this was a pet, friend of the family, some distant relation, maybe another cousin . . . let me know when I'm getting warmer."

Cerise pulled herself free of his arms. "It's not a family pet or a relative! I don't know what the hell it is. I've never heard of anything like that."

"Ask your grandmother."

"She'll be asleep. She did some hard magic today, and it will take her a few days to recover."

Cerise slumped forward. His hand ran down her back, kneading the tired muscles, the warmth of his fingers soothing her through her shirt. He stroked her like she was a cat. "So will you be pissed off if I kill it?"

"If it comes after us, I'll cut it to pieces myself," she told him.

His hand strayed lower and he took it away. He was back in control. The fierce creature she'd seen that morning hid again.

Cerise leaned back against him. His arm wound around her waist, pulling her closer. He was strong and warm, and sitting in his arms filled the sore empty spot inside her with quiet content.

"When I was twenty, I met a man," she told him. "Tobias."

"Do you have his picture on the wall, too?" he asked, and she sensed traces of a growl in his voice.

"Top left corner."

He turned. His face grew grim. "Handsome," he said.

"Oh, yes. He was very pretty. Like a movie star from the Broken. I was so in love. I would've done anything for him. We were all set to marry. He was almost part of the family. Dad even let him handle some of our business."

"And?"

A familiar cramp gripped her heart. She smiled. "I

found a discrepancy in the books. Some money had gone missing from the sale of the cows. Tobias took it."

"Did you kill him?" William asked.

"What? No. I cornered him and he tried to deny it, but I guess I must've been too scary, because in the end he told me all about his master plan. He was going to get as much money as he could and take off for the Broken. He tried to lie and tell me he did it for us and that he was going to convince me to come with him, but I could tell he was lying. It was always about the money. It was never about me."

"What did you do?" William asked. She couldn't tell by his voice what he thought about the whole thing.

She grinned. "Well, he wanted to go to the Broken. Kaldar and me, we put him in a sack and took him down through the boundary. Kaldar stole a car, and we drove him down to New Orleans, to the big city, and left him, sack and all, on the courthouse steps. The Broken is a funny place. They really don't like it when you show up there with no ID." She tilted her face up. "Would it bother you if I'd killed him?"

He looked at her. She must've thawed a little, Cerise decided, because she had to force herself not to lift up and kiss him.

"No," William said. "But I know it would bother you."

She snuggled closer to him. "Your turn."

"What?"

"Your turn to tell me a story about yourself."

William looked away. "Why?"

"Because I told you mine and asked you nicely."

William growled under his breath. Amber rolled over his eyes and vanished. How in the world hadn't she put two and two together before?

"There was a girl," he said. "I met her in the Edge. I liked her. I did everything right. I said all the smooth things, but it didn't work. I don't know why, but it just didn't. I guess, she didn't need another fixer-upper in her life. She had two brothers to take care of, so she went off with my best friend. It was good for her. He's steady, and he always knows the right thing to do and does it."

She winced. "You're not a fixer-upper."

He bared his teeth. "Don't kid yourself. You saw me this morning."

Cerise took a deep breath. "Do you like me the way you liked that girl?"

"No."

It felt like a slap in the face. He was in love with some other girl. And the idiot didn't even want him. How could she not want him? He ran into an open field to save a kid everybody shunned.

Cerise bit her lip. She wouldn't be a consolation prize; she had some damn pride left.

But before she cut him loose, she had to be 100 percent clear where they stood. If it cost her a tiny bit of pride, that was fine. Nobody but the two of them would ever know.

"How is it different?"

He rolled his head back, sable hair falling down on his shoulders. "With Rose I knew what to say. I could take a step back and talk to her. I remembered all the crap from the magazines. It was easy."

"And with me, it's hard?" Why? Because she was a swamp girl? And how did the magazines fit into it?

William looked away from her. "I don't like it when you're away. If I don't see you, I can't settle down. If I see you talking with another man, I want to claw his throat out. And none of the things you're supposed to say fit."

Oh, this had to be good. "What sort of things?"

He sighed. "The lines. Like 'You're my everything,' or 'Did it hurt when you fell from heaven?' "

She lost it and laughed. She sounded hysterical and broken, but she couldn't stop.

He sighed again. "Why are you laughing?"

It was that or crying.

"Cerise?"

"Are you going to ask me if my daddy was a thief, because he stole the stars and put them in my eyes?"

He pushed away from her. "Forget it."

The laughter finally died. "It's called the rending, isn't it?" she asked. "The thing you did this morning? Your kind does it when you become overwhelmed—"

He lunged at her. A blink and he pinned her to the floor, his big body bracing hers, his eyes on fire.

Excitement zapped through her. She felt her muscles tighten in all the right places.

Now or never.

Cerise bit her lower lip. "Well, this is quite a predicament, Lord Bill."

William snarled. She stared straight into his eyes, at the savage thing he hid inside. "Wolf," she whispered. "I think you are a wolf."

"When did you know?" His voice was a ragged growl, as if she was talking to a beast.

"For a while now. Yesterday when you found me here, I was reading a book about changelings, because I knew."

Cerise caught her breath. Her heart was beating too fast, as if she were running for her life. Anxiety washed over her in a cold wave. The world, which had been so stable a month ago, had fallen apart around her and she couldn't even hold on to the pieces. What if she was wrong? What if it was just wishful thinking? If she misread the need she saw in his eyes, and he turned her down and walked away from her now . . . She would handle it— she knew she would, because she had no choice—but thinking about it, imagining it happen, clenched her throat shut. She struggled to make the words come out.

"You have to be very careful now, Lord Bill. You're in terrible danger."

He stared at her, obviously not understanding. She searched his face but found no answer. Gods, it felt like torture.

Cerise forced her lips into a smile. "Nice changeling
boys like you shouldn't play with swamp girls."

"What?"

She raised her head to his ear. She felt as if she were
standing on the edge of a cliff. One step and she would
plunge or soar. "You'll get bewitched."

His eyes widened, the molten amber in them churning with violent intensity.

She kissed him. Her lips pressed against his, asking,
demanding. *Kiss me back, William. Kiss me back!*

He opened his mouth, and she slid the tip of her
tongue inside, licking his. He tasted just like she imagined he would: delicious and wild, and she kissed him
harder.

He jerked her to him. His mouth locked on hers, taking over the kiss. He kissed her as if he was making love
to her already, as if he had only one chance to seduce her
and this was it. She gripped his rigid body, sliding her
hands around his muscular neck, running her fingers
through his hair, feeling the smooth, silky strands slide
under her fingertips.

He pulled her up. The muscles bulged on his back as
he lifted her higher off the floor and kissed her again,
thrusting his tongue into the heat of her mouth. She was
out of breath and she didn't care.

His rough, hot hands stroked her, touching everywhere,
under her clothes, caressing her neck, her back, her butt,
until she wanted to arch her spine like an eager cat. His
mouth found a sensitive spot on her neck, and a light electric shock burst from her neck all the way down to her
toes. She gasped, and he kissed her again in the same spot,
nipping the skin.

"Oh, Gods."

His eyes shone with want and predatory satisfaction.
"The name's William. It's a common mistake."

She slid her hands over his chest, feeling the hard muscle under the skin. "Jackass."

He laughed that raspy wolfish laugh that made her crazy. His hand slid between her legs, stroking her thigh in just the right way, and she unbuttoned her shirt with feverish speed, eager for the feel of his body on hers. He jerked his own shirt off, grabbed her, and kissed her again with a deep guttural growl, thrusting his tongue into her mouth, the taste of him turning her light-headed.

"Don't leave me," she whispered.

"Never," he told her.

The last cold shreds of fear melted away inside her and only happiness and need remained.

His hand cupped her butt, and he moved her closer, the hard bulge of his erection digging right between her legs through the fabric of their jeans. Cerise grabbed onto his big shoulders and slid lower, grinding against him.

His hand slid up her back and suddenly her bra was off. William looked at her with his crazy amber eyes. "You drive me mad."

Yes! He had no idea how long she had waited for him to say it. "Don't blame me. You're already mad," she breathed and kissed his perfect jaw, tasting the light scrape of stubble. He smelled so good, clean and strong and male. "Mad, mad wolf."

"Look who's talking."

His hand slid over her nipple, sending a shocking burst of pleasure through her, so unexpected, she almost jerked back. He dipped his dark head and licked her breast, sucking on her nipples, first soft, then harder, lifting his head just enough to let the cold air touch them and sliding the sensitive buds into his mouth, again and again, until she was ready to scream.

And then her belt was undone and her jeans were halfway down her butt.

"She's probably up there," Kaldar's voice said from below. "I'll go and check."

"Ceri?" Lark's voice called.

They had to stop. Damn it all to hell. "William!"

He kept going. Oh no, no, she couldn't let her little

sister barge in on her while her jeans were around her knees. Especially not now, not today, not before she had explained that their mother was dying.

"William!" Cerise barked.

William's fingers slid under the band of her panties, teasing their way down.

"Stop!"

Someone's steps approached the door.

She punched him in the head.

William startled, as if shaken awake, and rolled off her. She jerked her jeans back in place.

The door swung open.

William rolled to his feet and dashed across the room, to the balcony and over the rail. She sprinted left and landed in her chair, tugging her bra in place and buttoning her shirt.

Kaldar came up the stairs. "Cerise?"

She yawned. "Yes?"

"Here you are." He dropped into the other chair. Behind him William pulled himself back up with one arm and landed on the balcony's rail.

"Aunt Pete panicked everybody. She thought you might have done something rash."

William stood on the rail. The damn thing was two inches wide. He padded along it like it was solid ground and made some shooing motions at Kaldar's back.

She tried to ignore him. "I never do anything rash."

William mouthed, *"Bullshit."*

"She saw you leave with the blueblood."

Cerise raised her eyebrows. "I had myself a nice long cry and then I fell asleep in the chair. Did you expect to find me on the floor, making out with him half-naked?"

William nodded several times, a big grin painted on his face.

"I wouldn't put it past you," Kaldar said. "Or him. Who knows what the hell he might do?"

William made a cutting motion across his throat.

"He might kill you if you're not careful," she told him.

"Who, Will? We're the best of friends."

William rolled his eyes.

"Thick as thieves, I'm sure," she mumbled.

"If you do decide to make out with him, try to get caught," Kaldar said. "Easier to rope him into marriage that way."

"I'll keep that in mind."

Kaldar looked like he'd bitten into something sour. "The fusing, do you want to talk about it?"

And just like that all sexy thoughts fled from her head. "Not right now."

"You will have to talk about it with the family tomorrow," he warned.

"I know. I'll speak to Lark before we go to bed." Cerise got up. Kaldar did, too. William dropped straight down off the rail, and she almost gasped. "Let me grab my hair tie. I left it outside. I'll be right down."

She walked on the balcony, aware of Kaldar's gaze on her back. William hung off the edge, his feet pressed against the wall. He didn't look like he was straining.

Yes, she was definitely over her head. But when William held her, she felt happy and safe. Everything was falling to pieces, and she wanted to be with him so badly, even if only for a couple of minutes of bliss.

"Tonight," she mouthed. "My room."

He grinned a happy feral grin. Cerise turned and went with Kaldar downstairs.

# TWENTY-FOUR

CERISE awoke. Her bedroom lay dark. It took her a second to place the even, whispery sound next to her, and then she recognized it—Lark, breathing.

The explanations didn't go well. She'd tried her best, but the only thing Lark heard was that Mother wasn't coming back. Ever. The poor kid broke and cried. She cried and cried with feverish desperation. At first Cerise tried to calm her, and then something snapped inside her, and she cried, too. You'd think she had no tears left, but no, she bawled just like Lark. They huddled on the bed and sobbed from the pain and unfairness of it. Finally Cerise made herself stop and held Lark, murmuring soothing things to her and stroking her hair, until her sister curled into a ball and fell asleep, whimpering like a sick kitten.

Cerise looked at the ceiling. No noises disturbed the silence. She heard nothing, she saw nothing, but something had to have woken her up.

She sat up slowly and turned to the tall window opening onto the verandah. A pair of glowing eyes stared through the glass.

William.

He had no shirt on. The moonlight slid over his back and shoulders, tracing the outline of sculpted biceps, sliding over the shield of muscle on his side to the narrow waist. His hair fell on his shoulders in a dark mane. He stood with easy predatory grace, beautiful and terrifying, and he stared at her with the same impossible longing she'd seen in him in the lake house. The intensity of it took her breath away. She wasn't sure if she should swoon, scream, or just wake up.

He moved and tapped the window with his knuckle.

Not dreaming. He'd showed up and he wanted in.

Cerise shook her head. *No.* She needed him so badly, it almost hurt, but Lark needed her more.

He raised his arms. *Why?*

She leaned over and very gently pulled the blanket down, revealing Lark's tousled hair.

His face fell. He rocked forward and bumped his head on the glass.

"Aaaah!" Lark jerked up. "Ceri! Ceri!"

Cerise thrust herself between her sister and the window. "What is it?"

"A monster, a monster at the window!"

Cerise grabbed Lark into a hug and turned, keeping Lark's face away from the glass. William ripped off his pants. A convulsion gripped his body, jerking him, breaking his arms, twisting his shoulders. Cerise gulped. "There's nothing there."

"There is a monster! I saw it."

William's muscles flowed like melted wax. He crashed to all fours. Dense black fur sheathed him. He shook, and a huge black wolf sat at the window, his eyes glowing like two wild moons.

She did not just see that. Surely, she didn't.

Every hair on the back of Cerise's neck stood up. She swallowed. "Look, baby, it's not a monster, it's just a dog. See?"

Lark pulled from her and glanced at the window. "Where did it come from?"

"It's William's dog." The damn wolf was the size of a pony.

William pawed at the glass gently and licked it.

"William doesn't have a dog."

"Sure he does. His dog stays in the woods so he doesn't bother our dogs. He's very nice. See?" Cerise rose

and opened the window. William trotted in, an enormous black shadow, and put his head on the sheets next
to Lark. She reached over and petted his sable fur. "He's
nice."

"Come on." Cerise adjusted the pillows. "Try to get
back to sleep."

She slid under the covers next to Lark. William hopped
on the bed by their legs and lay still. "Behave," she told
him.

He yawned, showing her white teeth the size of her
pinkies, and closed his mouth with a click.

"Ceri?"

"Mmmm . . . ?"

"You won't let them keep Mom that way, right?"

"No, I won't."

"You have to kill her."

"I will, Sophie. I will."

"Soon, right? I don't want her to hurt."

"Very soon. Go to sleep now. It will hurt less in the
morning."

Cerise closed her eyes, felt William shift to make room
for her toes, and relaxed. Tomorrow would be a hellish
day, but for now, with the giant wolf guarding her feet,
she felt strangely safe.

WHEN Cerise awoke, William was nowhere to be seen.
He'd stayed through most of the night—she had awak-
ened earlier, just before sunrise, and he had still been
there, a big shaggy beast sprawled on her bed. Now he
was gone.

It was crazy, she reflected, as she got dressed. She knew
he would eventually turn into an animal. After all, that was
what changelings did. But witnessing it was like staring
Raste Adir in the face. This was magic so old, so primitive, that it didn't fit into any of the neat equations her
grandfather had taught her. It roared, furious and primal,
like an avalanche or a storm.

The journal she had seen in Lagar's mind bothered her. It looked just like one of her grandfather's journals in which he used to write out his planting schedule and research. The journal had to be the key, the last piece in this big tangled puzzle.

She found Richard in the front yard, supervising as Andre sharpened his machete.

"I need to go to Sene," she told him. "Will you come with me?"

He didn't ask why. He just had two horses brought and they rode out.

Half an hour later Cerise stood on the rotten porch of Sene Manor. She used to be so happy in this house, back when the garden was cultivated, the path to the creek swept, and the walls were a bright cheery yellow. *Yellow like the sun,* her grandfather had said after he'd finished painting. Grandmother had shrugged her delicate shoulders. *Congratulations, Vernard. You turned the house into a giant baby chicken.*

She could still hear the muted echoes of their voices, but they were gone. Long gone, stolen by the plague. She never even saw the bodies, only the two closed coffins. By the time the bodies were found, they'd been decomposing for a few days. Father said they were in bad shape and not fit to be displayed. She had to say her good-byes to the wooden lids.

All that remained of her grandparents was the empty shell of their house, abandoned and forgotten. And the garden, once overgrown, was now barren, since Lagar had mowed it down to nothing.

A bright spot of red drew her eye. She squinted at it. Moss. Burial shroud, they called it. Short and stubby, it grew deep in the Mire, feeding on carrion. It would sprout over the corpse of a fallen animal, so dense that after a couple of days all you could see was a blanket of red and a bump underneath. Odd that it would be in the garden.

Richard nodded at a small patch of redwort growing by the porch. "Lagar's thugs missed a spot."

"I hate that plant." Cerise sighed.

"Yes, I remember. The earache tea." Richard nodded. "Grandfather used to make us drink it every morning. It worked. I don't recall ever getting an earache."

"I remember gagging on it. I think I'd take the earache over the tea."

"Oh, I don't know." Richard's narrow lips bent in a smile. "It wasn't that bad."

"It was awful." Cerise hugged herself.

Richard nodded at the door. "The longer you put it off, the harder it will be to go in."

He was right. Cerise took a deep breath and crossed the bloodstained porch to the door, hanging crooked on its hinges. No time to waste. She stepped inside.

The house greeted her with the gloom and musty, damp smell of mildew. A sitting room lay to her right. She passed it. A brick red rug once covered the hallway, but now it lay torn and filthy, little more than an old rag. Floorboards, warped by moisture, glared through the rents.

The house felt cold. Her steps made the floor creak and quiver. Behind her Richard paused, leaning to examine the sitting room.

"No vermin," he said. "No droppings, no gnaw marks. Perhaps, the plague's still here."

"Or maybe it's just a dead house." Its people had died, and the house had withered away, unwilling or unable to support life. "The sooner we get out of here, the better."

A pale door loomed before her. The library. Her memory thrust an image before her: a sunny room, a plain table, walls lined with shelves crammed with books, and Grandfather complaining that sunlight would bleach the ink off the pages . . .

Cerise pushed the door with her fingertips. It swung open on creaky hinges. The oak table lay in shambles.

Pieces of shelves, torn from the walls, lay in a pile of splinters here and there. The books had spilled on the floor in a calico cascade, some closed, some open, like a pile of dead butterflies. The library wasn't just ransacked; it was smashed, as if someone of extraordinary strength had vented his rage on it.

Behind her, Richard made a small noise that sounded like one of William's growls. Destroying Grandfather's library was like ripping open his grave and spitting on his body. It felt like a desecration.

Cerise crouched by the pile of books and touched one of the leather-bound covers. Slick slime stained her fingers. She picked up the edge of the book and pulled. A page ripped, and the book came away from the floor, leaving some paper stuck to the boards. A long gray and yellow stain of mold crawled across the text to the cover, binding the pages together.

"This is an old mess," Richard murmured.

"Yes. Spider didn't do this."

Dread stirred inside her. Anybody could've ransacked the library—the house stood empty for years. Still, something didn't quite fit. A burglar looking for things to steal wouldn't have torn the books apart.

Cerise circled the book pile. She hopped over the ruin of the table to get a better view of the walls, slid on a slimy patch, and almost fell on her butt. Deep gouges marked the old walls. Long, ragged, parallel strokes. Claw marks. She spread her fingers, matching the wounds in the wall, but her hand wasn't big enough. What the hell?

"Come, look at this."

Richard leaped over the book with his usual elegant grace and touched the marks. "A very large animal. Heavy—look at the depth of the scars. I'd say upward of six hundred pounds. An animal would have no reason to enter the house. The place has no food, and it sits in the middle of the clearing. And if this was an animal, we would see other evidence: feces, fur, more claw marks. It looks like this creature broke into the library, demolished it, and left."

"As if it broke in to wreck the books on purpose."

Richard nodded.

"William said he saw a monster in the forest. It looked like a large lizard."

Richard frowned. "What was he doing in the forest?"

"Lark was showing him something. The monster attacked Lark and William fought it off. Apparently Grandmother Azan helped."

"You like the blueblood," Richard said carefully.

"Very much."

"Does he like you?"

"Yes, he does."

"How much do the two of you like each other?"

She couldn't hide a smile. "Enough."

Richard tapped the side of his nose with one long finger.

"Please," she invited with a wave of her hand.

"We know nothing about him. As a blueblood, he may have certain duties and obligations back in his world. Maybe he's on leave from the military. What if he has a wife? Children? Could he stay with you if he wanted to?"

"He's no longer in the military and he has no one."

"How do you know?"

"He told me."

"He could've lied," Richard said gently.

"He's a changeling, Richard. He has a hard time with lying."

Richard drew back. He opened his mouth, obviously struggling. "A changeling," he finally managed.

She nodded.

"What . . ."

"A wolf."

Richard cleared his throat. "Well."

She waited for him.

"It could be worse," he said finally. "Efrenia married

an arsonist. Jake's wife is a kleptomaniac. I suppose, a psychopathic spree killer isn't that odd of a choice, considering. We'll just have to work around it. Gods know, we've had practice. He's certainly good in a fight."

She smiled. "Thank you."

"Of course," Richard said. "We're family. If you love him and he loves you, we'll do whatever we can to let you be happy."

Cerise turned to the corner, where a small bookcase used to contain the planting journals. The book case lay overturned. She picked it up and wrestled it upright. Nothing, except a puddle of soggy pulp that may have been a book at some point, but now served as a shelter for a family of muck bugs. The journals were gone.

They left the library and headed to the kitchen. Both windows stood wide open, the freshly installed metal grates catching the light of the morning sun. Dead leaves rustled on the floor. Shards of broken pottery crunched under Cerise's foot. A shattered plate. And a knife. She picked it up. A thin paring knife that was missing its tip. A dark brown stain marked the blade. She scratched at it and the dark brown crumbled, tiny flecks floating to the floor.

"Blood," Richard said. "The entire blade is stained. This knife went into someone."

"Grandma could've been cooking something."

He shook his head. "Anything she cooked would've been drained of blood. This knife went into a living body."

Cerise looked at the knife. Three inches, maybe four. "It's too small to hurt anyone. I could kill someone with it, but Grandma? She would faint first. Besides, they died of plague."

"Supposedly." Richard strode to the sink.

"What do you mean, supposedly?"

"We never saw the bodies. Look, dishes."

The sink held a small stack of dirty dishes. To the right two dusty glasses sat in a tray upside down. Grandfather set the glasses right side up to dry. He thought they ventilated better. Her grandparents used to bicker about it.

Cerise came to stand by the sink. "So Grandmother was washing the dishes, when something attacked her. She grabbed the first knife she could find, turned . . ." Cerise turned with the paring knife. "The knife broke."

"She must've grabbed a plate, probably several, and threw them at her attacker."

Cerise put the knife on the counter. "And then?"

Richard touched her elbow, steering her from the sink, and pointed to the cabinet. Stains marked the doors, dark patches on dark wood. A thick crust had formed on the cabinet doorknob. Several long silver hairs were stuck to it.

"Whatever it was knocked her down." Richard spread the leaves off the floor, revealing a long dark smudge. "And dragged her off."

They chased the trail of blood through the kitchen, down the hallway, and to the bedroom. Blood spattered the walls. Dried to nearly black, it spanned the boards to the right and left of the headboard as if someone had bathed in blood and then danced around.

"The bed," Richard murmured.

He grasped one side of the torn mattress, she grasped the other. Cerise heaved. The mattress gave, rising off the floor. A large fuzzy blotch of mold marred the underside. It didn't look good. Cerise leaned closer and rubbed at the mold with her sleeve. Dark brown. Blood. Nobody could bleed that much and survive.

There was no plague, no fever, no sickness. Her grandparents were murdered.

She looked at Richard. His face was controlled fury.

"The family lied to us," she said.

"Yes, they did."

THE kitchen buzzed with angry voices. Forty-six adults, stressed to the limit, trying to outscream each other.

The insult to the family was monumental. Gustave kidnapped, Genevieve fused, the house of cherished grandparents robbed.

Cerise let them rage. They had to vent enough to be reasoned with. She wished she had William with her, but he had to stay outside the room. This was a Mar affair.

"They came onto our land," Mikita's voice boomed. "Our land! They took our people. We're Mars. Nobody does that to us and lives. We fuck them up and we fuck them up good."

"We hit them with everything we have," Kaldar yelled out.

"Y'all are out of your minds." One of the older women, Joanna, pushed from the wall. She was Aunt Pete's cousin. "We have kids to think about. That's the Hand we're talking about here."

Kaldar turned to her. "You have three daughters. How the hell am I going to marry them off? We don't have money and we don't have prospects. Right now, the only reason people want to marry into our family is because they know if something happens, we'll back them up. What do you want me to do when your eldest comes to me crying, because she's in love, but the man won't have her and we can't even pay for her wedding? Love fades, fear stays."

"If he really loves her, the name won't matter," Joanna yelled. "Love's what does it."

"Really? Speaking from experience, are you? Where the hell is your Bobby, and why isn't he taking care of his kids?"

"You leave my kids out of it!"

"We must fight," Murid's voice cut through the noise with raspy precision. "We have no choice."

"Aunt Murid." Cerise made an effort to say it just right, sweet but with an edge to it. "You've lied to us."

Instantly the room was silent.

"You, and Aunt Pete, and my parents. You've lied to all

of us. We went down to Sene this morning. My grandparents didn't die of the plague."

Aunt Pete glanced at Murid.

"We found the blood," Richard said. "Too much blood. And claw marks on the walls."

Murid raised her head. "There was no fever. Your grandfather lost his mind and murdered your grandmother in the bedroom."

A wave of cold rolled over Cerise. It couldn't be. "Why?"

"We don't know," Aunt Pete said. "He had become withdrawn over that spring and summer. He rarely visited the main house. Your mother thought he was depressed. When your father and she came down to visit your grandparents, they found your grandmother's body. He'd ripped her apart like a straw doll. All of you loved him very much. We spared you the pain of knowing what he did."

"There were two coffins at the burial." Cerise leveled her gaze at Aunt Murid.

"Your father must've killed Vernard," Murid said. "That's the most logical explanation. I never saw the bodies, and Gustave would not talk about what happened in Sene, except to say that we could never have an open-casket burial. I don't know if it was self-defense or revenge. I only know that he came back with two coffins, with their lids nailed shut."

The memory of the wall with the claw marks rose before her. She just couldn't shake it off. The claws. The monster in the woods. Her grandparents. Somehow it all had to fit.

Cerise searched the room for Erian. "Erian?"

"Yes?" He pushed to the front.

"Once this meeting is over, I want you to take two boys and dig up Grandfather's grave."

A collective gasp rushed through the room.

Cerise stared them down. *Just try and stop me.* "I want

to know how he died." She looked from face to face. "The secrets stop now. Tonight we go to fight the Hand, and I will have to kill my mother. I'd like to have everything out in the open beforehand."

"I don't think you should go," Erian said, his face calm. "I don't think any of us should go. The Hand is too strong. Attacking them is risky."

She stared at him. "Erian, you're the first to run into every fight!"

He nodded, his expression oddly rational. "All the more reason to listen to me now. The Sheeriles are dead. The feud is dead. Our enemy is gone and this war is over. You would put all of us in danger and for what? Your mother is gone, and we don't even know if Gustave is alive."

The betrayal stung. Of all people, she had expected it from Richard, not Erian. Richard was cautious, while Erian hadn't met a fight he didn't want to win. "What the hell is wrong with you? You have been my brother since you were ten. My parents raised you. Erian!"

He crossed his arms on his chest. "Ceri, we must do what is best for the family. Attacking the Hand is plain stupid. You're hurting and it's making you crazy. Think about it. If they weren't your parents, you would agree with me."

She was losing the argument; she could see it in their faces. Cerise clenched her teeth and forced her voice to sound steady. If it was a fight he wanted, she would give it to him. "So you think we should tuck our tail in and hide in the Rathole."

"Yes." Erian's eyes were crystal clear. "They're freaks, Cerise. We aren't strong enough."

"I have a better idea. Why don't the lot of us go down to Sicktree, take our pants off in front of the courthouse, and bend over? That will announce to the entire Mire exactly where we stand." She leaned forward. "Act like you're a Mar, Erian. Or did I miss something, and did the Sheeriles cut off your balls in that fight?"

A grimace clamped his face. "Watch yourself!"

"Think very carefully before you threaten me. I'm stronger and better than you."

Erian leaned forward.

"Stop."

Cerise turned. Clara was looking at her. She sat between her husband and her oldest son, the stump of her leg making a short bulge under her dress. She'd aged, and when their stares crossed, Cerise thought her brown eyes looked gray, as if dusted with ash.

"Clara?"

The entire room focused on Clara's face. Urow bared his teeth, reacting to the pressure. Clara put a hand on his arm.

"Yesterday I sent Mart back to our house," Clara said. "The Hand burned it. There is nothing left. As long as the freaks live, we'll never be safe. Not us, not our children, not even in our own homes. They won't rest until they wipe us out. We will give you our sons, so you can kill the Hand's freaks. Kill them all. To the last one."


WILLIAM leaned against the balcony rail. They'd asked him to wait outside. He didn't see any need to push the issue—they were loud enough that he caught most of what was said.

They battered Cerise. They screamed and argued and carried on. He wanted to walk in there and snarl them silent.

She didn't budge. They voted and gave in. The Mars would attack the Hand at dawn.

A part of him was happy—she won. She got the fight she wanted. The rest of him was pissed off—she got the fight she wanted, and now she would run right into that fight. She was his mate, and he could end up watching her die.

She was his mate.

The wild in him scratched and howled, demanding her, demanding to taste her, to touch her, to take her away somewhere safe, where there would be only him and her. He stared at the Mire pines. It was not a sure thing. She hadn't promised him anything. Her mood might have changed, and he might have missed his chance.

And tomorrow they would be in a fight for their lives.

Cerise was coming up the stairs. He listened to the sound of her steps, light and fluid. She came to stand next to him, looking at the woods.

"I've heard," William told her to save her the trouble.

"How good is your hearing?"

"Good enough."

"It would mean a lot to me if you would brief my family on the kind of enemies they could expect."

She made no move to touch him. He was right. She had changed her mind. "Sure."

"Tonight will be very busy for me," she said. "The afternoon will be very busy, too."

Fine. He got the message. She didn't want him to bother her.

"There is an old storehouse on the edge of our lands, past the wards. We use it to dry out herbs. Because it's past the ward line, the family rarely goes there. In about a minute I'll walk down these steps and head to that storehouse. If someone were to wait about ten minutes, so nobody would get suspicious, he could meet me there."

It took him a minute. She was *inviting* him. "Where's the barn?"

Her eyes sparked with a wicked gleam. "I'm not going to tell you."

What the hell?

Cerise arched her dark eyebrows. "It's too bad that you don't have any dogs, Lord Bill. If you had one, you could track my scent and chase me down, like a hunter. Through the woods. Imagine that."

She turned and headed down the stairs.

Bloody hell. He loved that woman.

Ten minutes later, two hundred yards separated William from the main house. Far enough. He shrugged off his shirt. His boots and pants followed. For a moment William stood, savoring the feel of cold air on his skin, and then he let the wild out.

His body buckled and twisted. His spine bent. Fur sheathed his legs.

William inhaled deep, letting the breath of the forest permeate him. Excitement flooded him, turning him stronger, faster, sharper. The sounds of the swamps amplified in his ears. The colors turned vivid, and he knew his eyes had gained their own glow, the pale yellow fire fed by magic.

William tossed back his head and sang a long lingering note, a hymn to the thrill of the hunt, the pulse of prey between his teeth, and the taste of hot blood, spilled after a long chase. The little furry things shrank back into their hiding places, between the roots and into the hollows, sensing a predator in their midst.

Cerise's scent tasted sweet. William laughed in the quiet wolf way and broke into a run, falling into a long-gaited, smooth rhythm. He had an appointment to keep with a beautiful girl who had agreed to meet a changeling in the deep woods.


A wolf howled. Vur stirred on the branch. It had been nearly a week since Spider sent him and Embelys to spy on the Mar land. He was sick of the outdoors and doubly sick of spending his time in a tree.

Movement. His round yellow eyes fixed on a small figure running at full speed out of the woods. She dashed across the clear ground and ran into a rickety old barn.

Vur reached over and pulled the tangle of dried moss and shredded cloth that served as Embelys's robe. She uncurled, the swirls on her arms and face fluctuating, as she unconsciously mimicked the cypress bark that had grown damp overnight.

Her body bent to an unnatural angle, until her head was level with his. "It's her."

Vur nodded. A single spotted feather fluttered from his shoulder. Spring was in full swing and he was molting again.

They watched the barn door swing closed.

"Should we take her now?" Vur asked.

"It's foolish of her to leave the house alone," Embelys said. "She's meeting someone."

Embelys's hand snapped, and she dragged a squirming bug into her mouth, crunching him with obvious pleasure. "Besides, she's skilled. And unlike Lavern, I find being sliced with a flash painful."

"Lavern is dead." Vur shrugged, sending two more feathers floating to the tangled roots of the cypress.

"My point exactly." She pulled back, settling on the branch, her legs hugging the trunk, and rested her head against the bark.

"So we wait?"

"We wait."

A giant black wolf sprinted to the barn from under the trees.

Embelys hissed.

The wolf leaped. His body twisted, his bone and muscle wrung like a length of dark fabric. Fur shed, melting into the air as it fell. Arms stretched, legs elongated, rocked by convulsions, and a nude man rose from the dirt. He shook himself, and for a moment Vur saw his face and his eyes, hazel, still glowing.

*William the Wolf.*

The man slipped into the barn.

Vur sat petrified, afraid to move.

William the Wolf. William the murderer. The changeling beast who hunted the Hand's agents. The only man who stood against Spider and lived.

Slowly the fear melted. The Wolf was only one man. Just a man.

"We have to warn Spider," Embelys whispered. "He must know."

"You go. I'll stay."

"Are you mad?"

"I can glide. He can't. I'll watch over him. Go."

"Suit yourself."

She twisted, disengaging from the trunk, and slithered down, speeding along the forest floor.

Vur gathered himself, calculating. William was just a man, a man who was meeting a girl, for sex. He would be satiated and sloppy afterward, and the poison on Vur's claws was very potent. If he timed it just right . . . The head of William the Wolf would assure he was set for life.


WILLIAM glanced through a small window. The storehouse was freshly swept. Bundles of herbs hung drying from the rafters, spicing the air with bitter fragrance. He caught a glimpse of Cerise's dark hair as she headed up the ladder to the second story.

He backed up, took a running start, and leapt, scrambling up the wall to the roof. The small attic window was open. Inside Cerise unfolded a quilt over a pile of hay. He dove through the window and rolled to his feet.

Cerise froze with a quilt in her hands. Her pale shirt hugged her breasts. Her long dark hair spilled over it in a glossy wave. Her dark eyes, framed by a fringe of long eyelashes, widened. "You're naked!"

*So pretty. Must have the woman.*

He pulled the wild back. No. Not yet. He had one shot at this.

William circled her, stalking, tasting her scent, watching her watching him. "Do you like what you see?"

She tilted her head, spilling her long hair over one breast. Her gaze traveled slowly from his face down to his toes. She took a deep breath. "Yes."

William stopped and crossed his arms on his chest. "We need to talk."

Cerise hesitated for a second and sat on the hay. "Okay."

He leaned against the wall. "I was born in Adrianglia. I was born as a pup. It's a sign of a strong changeling."

She winced.

He had to keep going. "My mother gave me up to the Adrianglian government the next day. I was sent to the special orphanage for children like me. For the first two weeks of my life, I was blind and helpless, and they didn't think I would survive. I did, and when I turned three years old, I was transferred to Hawk's Academy."

She sat there, quilt draped over her knees, big eyes looking at him. He half expected her to run away screaming.

"From the time I was three until I turned sixteen, I lived in the same room. It was a bare cell with a metal bunk bed welded to the floor and bars on the windows. I shared it with another kid. I was allowed three changes of clothes, a comb, a toothbrush, and a towel. We had no toys, and reading aside from schoolwork was forbidden. My life consisted of exercise, martial training, and study. That was it."

He stopped and looked at her to make sure she understood, afraid he would see pity. He saw none. He couldn't read her, couldn't tell what she was thinking. She just sat very still and looked at him.

"You don't have to stand over there," Cerise said, her voice soothing. "You can come sit here by me."

William shook his head. If he sat by her, it would be all over. "I used to dream that my parents would show up and break me out of that place. When I twelve, I broke into the office, found my file, and realized where I stood. Nobody wanted me. Nobody was coming to save me. I was on my own. So I did the best I could. When I failed, I was whipped and punished by isolation. When

I succeeded, they let me outside for a few minutes of freedom.

"When I was thirteen, I killed my first opponent. When I turned sixteen, I graduated from Hawk's and the signature on my graduation papers served as enrollment into the Red Legion. I was not given a choice about joining, but if I had been, I would have chosen the military anyway. I am a killer."

He was tired of talking, but he had to get all of it out. The memories pressed on him like a crushing weight he couldn't drop.

"I told you I was court-martialed. I have nothing, Cerise. No land, no money, no status, no honor. I'm not normal. Being a changeling is not a disease. I will never get better. I will always be fucked-up and my children will likely be puppies. You need to tell me if you really want this. You and me. I must know. No games, no hints, no flirting. Because if you are doing this so I will fight for your family tomorrow, don't worry. I will anyway. If you don't really want me, I'll fight and then I'll leave, and you won't hear from me again."

William stopped. He'd fought in hundreds of skirmishes, he had done things that no sane man would, but he never remembered feeling that hollow at the end of it.

Cerise opened her mouth.

If she told him to leave, he would have to leave. He said he would and he had to do it.

"I love you," she told him.

The words hung in the air between them.

She said yes. She loved him.

The chain he put on himself shattered. He lunged and caught her in a hug, brushing her hair off her neck, and kissed her, sweeping her off the floor. Her hands caressed his face.

"You should've said no," he snarled. "Now it's too late."

"I don't care, you stupid man," she breathed. "I love you and I want you to love me back."

She was his. His woman, his mate. He kissed her, eager for her taste, and she kissed him back, quickly, feverishly, like she couldn't get enough.

*Mine.*

He buried his face in her neck, smelling her silky hair, licking her smooth skin. She tasted like honeyed wine, sweet and intoxicating under his tongue, and she made him drunk.

"I want you to stay with me," she told him. "I want you to stay with me forever."

Some part of him refused to believe it. He would never be this lucky. Fate didn't reward him; it kicked him and knocked him down, grinding him under its heel. A terrible fear gripped him that somehow she would vanish, dissolve into thin air or die in his arms, and then he would be back in his house, awake, alone, and broken, because she was only a wishful dream.

"Will you, William? Will you stay with me?"

He gripped her to him, to keep her from disappearing. "Yes."

She stroked his back, her slender fingers tracing the contours of his muscles, soothing, inviting him. She kissed his mouth, her soft lips pressing against his. Her pink tongue darted out, and she licked him, stroking him, again and again. He kissed her hard, trying to shut down the annoying warnings in his head, and dropped them down onto the hay. She squirmed under him, warm, flexible, and pliant.

Excitement flooded him. He pulled her shirt off and kissed her breast, sucking on her pink nipple, stroking her soft stomach and down, lower, to the sweet spot between her legs. She purred. He would kill to hear her make that sound again.

She was his mate. It finally sank in. She said yes, she was his, she wanted him to stay, and if she vanished, he would spent the rest of his life looking for her and he would find her again.

She wrapped her hand around his shaft and slid it up and down, spiking the need in him into an overwhelming hunger. She was wet for him, he could smell it, and the scent was driving him out of his skin.

"I love you," he told her.

"I love you, too," she whispered, her velvet eyes bottomless and black.

He thrust into her and she screamed.

"ON the hay," Cerise murmured. "We did it on the itchy, smelly hay. I can't believe it. Why did I even bring a quilt?"

He leaned over, grabbed the quilt, and pulled it over them, clenching her to him. "There."

She pulled a blade of dried grass out of her hair. "This time in the hay. The last time we almost did it on a dirty floor. You've made me into some sort of hillbilly slut. "

*Yeah, that's right.*

"Next time, we have to do it in bed," she said.

"With wine and roses?" he asked.

"Maybe. I'll settle for clean sheets." She snuggled closer to him. William closed his eyes. He couldn't remember ever being this happy.

"You will stay with me, right?" she asked.

"Yes."

"Even though it would mean Kaldar would be your in-law?"

"I could just kill him . . ."

"No, you can't. He's my favorite cousin."

He read a real concern in her eyes and couldn't resist. "He's unmarried. No kids. Nobody to miss him."

Her eyes widened. "William, you can't kill my cousin."

He laughed under his breath and she smacked him.

William gathered her closer. "I'm a wolf. You can't chain me. But now you're mine, my mate, my woman.

Your family are my people now. Nothing they could do
would drive me away. There are things I have to do,
back in the Weird. I may have to leave for a time, but I
will always be back."

She caressed his face. "Things that have to do with
Spider?"

He told her about the dead children and the blood on
the dandelions and the note.

Cerise looked back at him, horrified. "Why? Why
would he do that? They were just children. They weren't
a threat to him."

At the time he hadn't known why either, but now he
had the benefit of the Mirror's intelligence. "Spider's real
name and title is Sebastian Olivier Lafayette, Chevalier,
Comte de Belidor. Very old Gaulish blueblood family.
The bloodline started going weak around his great-
grandmother's time. They're bleeders. Their blood doesn't
clot as it should, and with each generation it was getting
worse. Spider's father was bedridden for most of his life,
and the family was desperate for a cure.

"Spider's father found a woman from a blueblood
family with a dirty secret—they had a changeling a couple of generations back. We're a very healthy lot. Spider's grandfather, Alain de Belidor, violently objected.
Didn't want his precious blood polluted. But Spider's
father married his bride anyway. The changeling blood
fixed all their problems right up—Spider was born healthy
as a horse.

"About that time Alain developed dementia. Since his
son had one foot in the grave most of the time, Alain
ruled the family. He terrorized Spider's mother and the
boy. Somehow he became convinced that Spider was a
changeling."

"How does that work?" Cerise asked.

"If the changeling is strong, like me, he has a ninety
percent chance to pass the magic to the next generation."
He kissed her. "If our kid is born human, the chances of
his kids going furry drop off. Twenty percent in the first

generation and basically nothing in the second. Spider has the changeling blood, but he isn't a changeling. His grandfather couldn't wrap his mind around it. He stalked him, convinced that Spider was hiding an animal inside. Once when Spider was seven, Alain dumped boiling water on him to 'draw the beast out.' When Spider turned eighteen, he got his grandfather declared incompetent and took control over the estate. Nobody knows what exactly happened to Alain, but nobody has seen him for years."

She grimaced. "That's just horrible all around."

William shrugged. "It's a hard world out there. Spider hates my kind, because we're the cause of his misery. I have to kill him. It's more than revenge at this point—he's a threat to any changeling. Hell, he's a threat to the entire damn country. He understands it. He doesn't take it personally."

Cerise frowned next to him. "How do you know?"

"We talked about it before we got into it the last time. It's just the reality of life for him," William explained. "He's a cold bastard. He understands my reasons, and in my place he would do the same thing. He doesn't see himself as evil. In his own eyes he's doing exactly what I used to do—serving his country the best he can. He isn't crazy, Cerise. He's very rational. That makes him more dangerous. What the hell is in that journal? Why does he want it so much?"

Cerise grimaced and rubbed her face. "I've been trying to puzzle it out and I have no idea. The journal is the key to the whole thing. I wish Sene had burned in a fire. I wish my parents would've razed it down to the ground—"

William put his hand over her lips.

"What is it?" she whispered.

"The birds stopped singing."


VUR shifted from foot to foot. How long did it take to fuck? Was the wolf freak romancing her in there with wine and poetry? Vur focused on the flutter of oak branches by the barn and launched himself into the sky. His skin wings snapped open, and Vur flew, gliding on the currents to perch on the oak.

WILLIAM slid to the side, rising silently. Cerise rolled to her feet, thrust her hand into the hay, and pulled her sword out.

William bared his teeth. *That's my girl.*

She moved to the wall. "Oh, baby! Yes! Yes! Give it to me! Yes!"

The roof creaked under the weight of someone's body. William padded along the floor, tracking the creaking.

"Harder, baby! Harder!"

The roof burst. A feathered body fell through the hole, talons spread for the kill. William lunged at the attacker's back, locking his forearm on the slick throat. The creature choked, gurgling. Cerise thrust, impossibly fast, and stepped back.

The creature fell to his knees. William scanned his memory for Hand agents with feathers. Vur. "The claws are poisonous."

Cerise's face gained a harsh edge. She looked like a wolf threatened in her own den. "Let him go, please."

William released the lock. Vur crashed to the floor, gasping. Blood spread through his feathers.

"Hurts, doesn't it?" Cerise took a step closer.

"Yesss," the Hand's agent gurgled.

"It will take you a long time to die, and it will hurt more and more as you slip away. The Hand took my father. Tell me where he is and I will end it now."

Vur's blue eyes blinked.

"Take your time," William told him.

He circled the body and sat in the hay. Cerise sat next to him. Moments dripped by, slow like cold molasses. Vur's moans turned into sharp cries. They waited.

A minute leaked away.

Another.

"Kasis!" he cried out. "He's in Kasis."

Cerise rose, her face grim. Flash sparked, sword sliced, and Vur's trembling body finally became still.

# TWENTY-FIVE

JOHN watched the door swing as Spider emerged from the bowels of the laboratory into the sunlight-flooded hallway. The lean man blinked against the light and raised his hand to shield his eyes. A thick leather binder lay in the crook of his right arm. It commanded John's attention, and he couldn't keep from staring at it.

"The smell is truly abominable," Spider said.

"Sorry. It can't be helped."

Spider nodded. "Walk with me a bit."

They strode side by side along the hallway, the binder swaying gently with Spider's smooth pace.

John watched the floor before his feet. The binder was full of translated notes, the thoughts of a genius mind. The things he could do, armed with that binder. The very idea of what it might be hiding made John light-headed. He braided the fingers of his hands together to keep from reaching for it. He could almost feel the slick leather against the pads of his fingers.

Working for Spider was difficult. He was reasonable, but only when circumstances permitted; understanding of difficulties, yet completely unaffected by them. And he expected impossible things in an impossible timeframe.

John had done the impossible. A fusion, and a relatively stable one at that, in less than a month. He had done well, and Spider appeared content. Yet the fruit of his labors, the prize, lay locked in the binder in the crook of Spider's arm, and John knew better than to trust Spider's seeming felicity.

"We've identified three possible sites," Spider was saying. "It will take us a day or so to examine them and perhaps another day to extract the unit. I'll be gone, oh, for about a week."

Gone. The word rang like a chime in John's head. He will be *gone*.

"Why three sites, m'lord?"

"The journal notes aren't clear as to the landmarks. A local might be able to pinpoint the exact location, but I decided against compromising the document by the presence of an outsider. I'll be taking almost everybody. We have a lot of ground to cover."

A dim light broke through the foggy melancholy in John's head. He was being told this on purpose.

"I'm leaving two slayers and a guardian to protect the house. It's a formality at this point anyway. There is nothing valuable here save for you and Posad, of course, and besides, the traps will do most of the protecting on their own."

"Once the unit is located and the extraction is complete, I'll send a retrieval team for you. I'm sure you'd rather rest here than slog through the mud with the rest of us. I hope your forced isolation won't be a problem?"

John smiled. "No, m'lord. I'm badly in need of sleep."

"Ahhh." Spider nodded, gray eyes neutral under the blond eyebrows. "I'll leave you to the comfort of the sheets and down, then."

They exited onto the second-floor balcony. The wind brought dampness from the flooded plain below. John shivered. "Ghastly place."

"Mildly put." Spider ran his left hand along the balcony's carved rail and smiled, showing even, sharp teeth. The smile shot a bolt of alarm through John's neck all the way to his fingertips. He yawned, trying to mask his discomfort.

"John, you're exhausted." Spider patted his shoulder. "To bed with you."

"By your leave, m'lord."

"Go, go." Spider waved at him. "That yawn of yours is infectious."

John bowed and strode to his quarters. Spider had the translation, but he had left the journal back in the fusion room. He expected him to make a play for it. A man less ambitious and more cowardly would walk away. He should walk away. But the journal called to him. The knowledge it contained . . . A secret to life, perhaps even to everlasting life. Armed with it, he could seek asylum in any realm. He would enjoy the accolades of a genius, protected and admired for the rest of his life, given an opportunity to take his work in the direction he desired, instead of being steered by a thug. For Spider was a thug, an intelligent, urbane, royally licensed one, but still a thug. The difference between him and a common street boss was the degree of devastation he could unleash.

John entered his room and locked the door. He had to wait until Spider left tomorrow and then he would have to be careful. Very careful.

THE scent laced William's nostrils just as he approached the house, the sharp musk of a wolf having freshly marked his territory. He tensed.

A large older man stood before the door within a swarm of giddy dogs. Large, wide at the shoulder, he wore jeans and a leather vest. His hair was long and gray, and it fell over his back.

"Easy," Cerise murmured next to him. "Easy. It's just Uncle Hugh."

The man turned and looked at him. A pale glow rolled over his eyes. A wolf.

A low rumble rolled in his throat. "He's—"

Cerise slipped her arm into the crook of his elbow. "Like you. I only found out a few days ago. He's a very kind man, Will."

Hugh watched them approach. His face showed nothing. William halted a few feet away. When two changelings met outside of the Red Legion, it never worked out well. He didn't want a confrontation now. Not after he had finally mated.

"Uncle Hugh!" Cerise walked over and hugged him.

"Ceri." He hugged her awkwardly and let go. "I came to help."

"Thank you!"

"Who is this?"

"This is my William."

Hugh looked at her, then at William. "*Your* William?"

She nodded. "With all of his fur, claws, and teeth."

Hugh startled as if shocked with a live wire. Cerise petted his forearm. His gaze shifted to William. "Adrianglian?"

William nodded.

"They turn you into killers there."

"We were born killers."

Hugh's eyes turned pale yellow. "If you mistreat her, I'll rip your throat out."

William let a touch of growl slip into his voice. "Old man, I'll drop you where you stand."

"That's nice," Cerise said. "Why don't all of us go inside and have some tea and pie?"

Hugh didn't move.

"Hugh," Murid called from the porch.

He glanced at her.

"Leave the boy alone," she said.

Hugh shrugged his shoulders and petted Cerise's hand. "If he ever—"

"He won't hurt me." Cerise put her other hand on William's forearm. "He loves me, Uncle. Come on."

William growled a bit and let her lead him to the stairs.

The door banged, releasing Kaldar onto the porch.

William sighed and heard Hugh do the exact same thing. They scowled at each other over Cerise's head.

Kaldar rolled his eyes. "Oh, that's just lovely. We've turned the house inside out looking for you, and here you are. Did you have fun, lovebirds?"

"None of your business," Cerise told him.

"To the library with you. We're holding the war council there."

William let himself be ushered into the crowded library, where he was asked to sit in a chair in front of the table containing half a dozen dusty bottles of green wine. The library was full of Mars. No children were present, only the older adolescents and adults. The war party for tomorrow.

Erian passed around cups made of some hollowed-out plant. "Swamp gourd," he said. "Tradition."

"You didn't do this before fighting with the Sheeriles." William took his cup.

"That was different," Erian said.

"The Sheeriles were Edgers, like us," Mikita boomed to the left.

"The Hand and its agents are invaders," Murid added.

Richard looked at Cerise. She pulled out her sword and handed it to him. "I think you should do it."

Richard took the sword. A hush fell on the room.

He held the blade out above the bottles. His face took on an expression of intense concentration.

A second passed. Another.

That was why Cerise was in charge, William decided. In battle, Richard would be dead by now.

Magic flashed from Richard, an intense electric blue. It danced along his blade. He struck and beheaded the six bottles with one strike.

A ragged cheer rolled through the library.

Richard passed the sword back to Cerise. Bottles were grabbed. Ignata splashed some wine into William's cup.

"Today we drink the fifty-year-old wine," Cerise announced, holding her cup up. "To living the next day well."

They drank. William gulped from his cup. The wine rolled down his throat, fire and joy blended into one. For the first time since leaving the Legion, he felt a part of something bigger than himself.

"We were hoping that Lord William would tell us what we're facing," Richard said.

"We want to know about the Hand." Ignata poured more wine into his cup.

William took another sip. All right. He could do that. "As long as we're clear: Spider is mine."

Heads nodded in agreement.

"Spider's standard unit usually consists of twenty-four agents in an advanced state of magic alteration."

"Why twenty-four?" Kaldar asked.

"It's an easy number to divide: two groups of twelve, three groups of eight, four groups of six, and so on. We killed three."

"I thought you only killed two," Kaldar said.

"Three," Cerise told him. "Are you going to let the man talk or will you interrupt some more?"

William tapped his memory. "Spider's close circle, his elite. Karmash Aule. Origin: unknown. Height: seven feet, two inches. Approximate weight: three hundred and sixty pounds. White hair, red eyes. Enhancements: reinforced spine, transplanted glands, resulting in above-average reaction time and increased strength. Position: second in command. Prefers blunt weapons. Likely to rely on and overestimate his own strength. Easily enraged. Moderate pain tolerance. Possible weakness or target areas: joints, glandular implant in the left side directly under the ribcage.

"Velsun. Origin: unknown. Height: five feet, six inches. Approximate weight: one hundred and forty pounds. Bloodred skin, braided blue hair, blue eyes. Enhancements: glandular apothecary, resulting in superior reaction time, extreme speed, enhanced hand-to-eye coordination. Position: slayer. Prefers bladed weapons. Unstable. Once she begins to kill, she will not stop until the catalysts from her apothecary are exhausted. While engaged, unable to distinguish between civilians and military personnel. Possible weaknesses: none."

They were staring at him as if he'd grown a second head.

"You don't do revenge halfway, do you, William?" Murid said.

"No. Ruh. Origin: Northern Province. Height: six feet, two inches. Approximate weight: one hundred and sixty-five pounds . . ."

Richard grabbed a piece of paper and a pen and started taking notes.


POSAD'S dark eyes didn't catch the light of the setting sun. They sat on his face like twin pools of carbon, solid black and sparkless. Spider stared into them until Posad blinked. "Do you understand me?"

"Yes. I finish packing and destroy the garden. Then I wait for the home team to clear the base and leave with them. I've done this before."

"You do not go upstairs."

Several bees landed on Posad's deformed shoulder and pushed past the scale of dried skin sheltering the hive opening. "I do not go upstairs."

Spider nodded and walked away, to where Veisan waited with his saddled horse. The muzzle of her mare glistened with ointment, and Spider grimaced at the strong stench of mint emanating from it. No horse would bear Veisan unless her scent was masked.

He mounted, casting one last look at the mansion. Somewhere within it his prized alteration specialist was taking the first steps on the path to his death.

"A waste," he murmured. It couldn't be helped. The hunger in John's eyes was too strong and the information within the journal too volatile to allow the pair to come into contact. He would miss John, miss his expertise. Yet no expense could be spared for the sake of the realm.

\*    \*    \*

FROM the shadowed depths of his bedroom, John watched
Spider ride away. He forced himself to read for another
hour and set out for the fusion room. He started slowly,
on quiet feet, pretending nonchalance, but the mansion
lay empty around him, and spurred by anticipation, he
walked faster and faster until in the end he was running.

In his haste, he almost burst into the room, but caught
himself at the last moment and halted, with his hand on
the door.

A fused being had no will of its own. It was both sus-
ceptible to instruction and unable to refuse an order.
But the fused being retained traces of its personality. It
couldn't disobey directly, but it could take advantage of a
poorly phrased command. This was especially true if the
human subject had been strong-willed, and Genevieve
Mar had one of the most powerful spirits he had encountered.

John caught his breath and swung the door open. The
ugliness of fusion had ceased to affect him long ago, and
as he stepped into the room, he watched only the creature's weapons: the three long, flexible appendages, studded with thorns. The plant equivalent of a whip. The whips
operated on hydraulic power, flexing when their vascular
bundles flooded with fluid. The supply of liquid was
finite, and the whips were capable of a single devastating
strike. That reserve spent, they would have to rebuild
before striking again. From experience, he knew the time
between strikes ranged from fifteen minutes to half an
hour. Fifteen minutes. A smart man could accomplish a lot
in fifteen minutes.

The journal lay on the desk behind the fusion. Spider's bait.

John stared at the fusion. First things first. He had to
exhaust its hydraulic reservoir. He cracked his knuckles.
"Obey. Use your whip to pick up the journal and gently
place it on the floor at my feet."

* * *

**WILLIAM** stared at a black hair left on the handle of the door leading to his room. The old wine packed a hell of a punch. His head swam. He pulled the hair off and stepped inside.

Gaston jumped off the chair.

"Do me a favor." William tried to sit on the bed. At the last possible moment, the treacherous piece of furniture made a panicked attempt to jerk out from under him. He landed on the covers, pinning the bed in place with his weight. That was some wine. "Don't leave your hair on the door handles. Or across bag handles. Or wrapped around letters."

"I wanted you to know that I was in the room."

William pulled one boot off. "For one, you opened the window, and there was a draft under the door. For another, the door handle was still warm. And then—"

The other boot landed next to its twin.

"And then?" Gaston asked.

"I heard you. And smelled you." William leveled his gaze on the kid. "You are supposed to be asleep, because of your grandmother's magic. Why are you up?"

Gaston locked his teeth. "I want to come with you tomorrow."

"No."

"Why?"

"You're a kid. Tomorrow is a fight to the death. It won't be pretty like in the books and movies. It will be hell. People will hurt and die, and you won't be one of them."

"I'm strong! I'm fast, I can climb, I can hit really hard, and I'm good with a knife . . ."

William shook his head.

"He cut off my mother's leg!"

William hopped off the bed. "I'm drunk. I'm wasted on that damn wine and I'm seeing double. So come on. Give it your best shot."

Gaston hesitated.

William rocked a little on the balls of his feet, trying to keep his balance. "Pussy."

The kid's face went red. He bounced off the wall, leaping, hands outstretched. William grabbed his arm, channeling his momentum, and jerked him out of the air, flipping him. Gaston crashed to the floor and slid into the wall. William tilted his head, looking him over.

The kid shook himself and rolled to his feet. Not a quitter.

"What's the matter? Can't you knock me off my feet? I can barely stand."

Gaston bared his teeth and lunged from a crouch. The kid was fast, William reflected, as he slammed his elbow on the back of Gaston's neck. The boy sprawled on the floor. William kicked him in the kidneys. Gaston gasped.

"What's the lesson?" William asked.

"You're better," Gaston ground out and swiped at William's ankle.

William kicked him again. Gaston curled into a ball, trying to draw some air into his lungs.

"Take your time. Try not to get knocked down. If you're down, keep your stomach flexed, so a kick to the gut doesn't take you out."

The kid inhaled finally.

"What's the lesson?"

Gaston coughed. "Not good enough."

"Not good enough yet. Yet being the important part." William grabbed the kid by the arm and pulled him up. "Going to fight Spider tomorrow is very noble. People like us don't give a flying fuck about noble. We fight to win. We fight dirty and we use everything we've got, because the job is not to throw your life away. The job is to take the other fucker out. And a bastard like Spider takes skill to kill. Being strong and fast doesn't make you good. It just means you have potential."

Gaston wiped his nose.

"If you live long enough, I'll teach you to be like me.

Or you can run in there roaring tomorrow, like your father does, and let Spider turn you into a piece of bleeding meat."

"What if he takes you out tomorrow?"

William sighed. "If he does, go to Sicktree. Find a
guy called Zeke Wallace. He runs a leather shop there.
Tell him what happened and tell him that you need to
speak to Declan Camarine in Adrianglia. Zeke will get
you to Declan, and he will take it from there. In a few
years you can hunt Spider down and kill him in my
memory. Or you can die tomorrow. Your choice."

William opened the door. Gaston walked out and
glanced over his shoulder. "I'll beat you one day."

"Maybe."

William shut the door and fell on the bed. It was good
that he never got hangovers, or he would be a sorry man
in the morning.

He closed his eyes and heard the door swing open.
Cerise slipped into his room and slid into the bed next
to him.

"Am I dreaming?" he asked her.

"No."

"Oh, good."

# TWENTY-SIX

GRAY predawn light snagged on the damp cypress needles. William leaned forward, gripping the cypress branch with his fingers to keep from falling. Above him Kaldar shifted in the tangle of maiden's hair moss.

When he'd volunteered to scout ahead of the Mars, he didn't think Cerise would saddle him with her cousin. Kaldar's body moved quietly enough. His mouth was another matter.

William squinted. From his perch in the cypress he could see the hothouse and a chunk of back wall about four hundred yards away. A short dark figure moved within the hothouse. As they watched, the hunchback swung a short shovel. Glass rang. Shards flew to the ground.

"What is he doing?" Kaldar murmured.

"He's breaking down the garden."

William swung off the branch, leaped down to the lower one, and swung himself down, dropping to the ground.

"Where are you going?" Kaldar hissed.

"Inside. Spider and most of his people are gone. There are only a few agents guarding the place."

"We're supposed to wait for Cerise."

William activated his crossbow and headed to the house. Behind him Kaldar swore under his breath and hopped onto the soft ground. William padded through the cypress grove to the edge of the clearing and halted. The ground smelled odd.

Kaldar caught up. "Trapped?"

"Yes."

Kaldar picked up a rock and tossed it into the clearing. It landed between two wards. A green stem shot out of the ground, and a hail of needle-thin thorns peppered the soil, striking sparks off the rock.

"You got any money on you?"

"No."

Kaldar grimaced. "What do you have?"

William made a mental inventory of some twenty-odd items he'd pulled out of the Mirror's bag of tricks and hid in his clothes this morning. Not much he could part with. "A knife," he said.

"Fine. I'll bet my knife against your knife that I can walk through there unharmed."

William glanced at the eighty-yard clearing separating them from the house. It would be suicide. "No."

Kaldar rolled his eyes. "It's not the same without a bet."

Cerise would skin him alive if he got her cousin blown up. It would be very entertaining. Therapeutic even. But it would make her cry. "No."

"William, I need a bet; otherwise, it won't work. You have nothing to lose. Just bet me the damn knife."

William took out his backup knife and thrust it into the ground at his feet. "Knock yourself out."

Kaldar dropped his own blade to the ground and picked up the knife. His fingers ran along the blade, caressing the metal. He closed his eyes and walked into the field.

His foot hovered over a spot; he turned, his eyes still closed, and veered left, then right. The toe of his right boot almost touched a patch of suspicious ground, then Kaldar swayed and spun away. He kept moving forward, lurching like he was drunk, jumped with liquid grace, froze, poised on the ball of his left foot, and conquered the last ten feet at a straight run.

He spun around, hands raised, self-indulgent smile stretching his lips. "Ah?"

A shadow flickered behind him. William leapt to his feet and fired twice. The first shot caught the agent's eye,

punching him off his feet. The second bolt went wide as
a smooth, spotted tangle of a body clutched Kaldar about
his shoulders and pulled him up to the second-floor window.

Embelys, William's memory told him. The serpent. No
time to waste.

William tossed a handful of the Mirror's bombs into
the clearing. The tiny spheres detonated with an ear-
shattering boom. Geysers of dirt and plant roots blossomed, hurling debris into the air. Guided by his instinct,
William dashed forward as the dirt rained on his shoulders, pulling his favorite knife as he ran.

He sensed the enemy ahead and thrust through the
dirt with his knife. The agent whipped around, her hair a
whirlwind of tiny braids above her muscled shoulders. A
tide of red from the severed femoral vein drenched her
leg. She gasped and went down. He didn't wait for her
death.

Shapes broke free of the brush behind the clearing savaged by his bombs. He caught a glimpse of Cerise out of
the corner of his eye but kept moving.

The house loomed before him. William jumped, caught
the edge of the balcony, and pulled himself up, to where
Kaldar's body had broken the wooden rail. A shattered
window lay on the balcony's floorboards in a spray of glittering glass. He leaped over the razor-sharp dew, dived
into the room, rolling as he hit the floor, and came to his
feet, the blade poised for a strike.

The faint sounds of a choked struggle tagged his hearing. They came from the room to his left. His kick broke
the wall. He lunged inside. An agent spun at him from the
right. William ducked the kick, thrust into the man's armpit, cut the throat of the second attacker and paused as the
bodies fell.

A gasp came from the right. "William!"

Embelys's massive bulk fastened Kaldar to the wall.
Her coil thrust through the paneling and twisted about

his waist and shoulders, pinning his right arm to his side. His left arm lay on top of Embelys's chest, where her body bent before catching a thick iron rod affixed to the ceiling. The pattern on her coils was pallid and dull. Her head hung limply to the side. A long streak of blood stretched to the floor from her neck, where William's knife protruded from her flesh.

"Thanks for the knife." Kaldar's face went red with effort. "Help me get the whore off of me."

A tremor echoed through the house. It reverberated through William's skull, shaking his teeth as if they were loose in his jaw.

"I could use some help," Kaldar's voice rasped.

Another tremor pulsed, like the toll of a colossal bell, and William staggered from the pressure.

"What the hell is wrong with you?"

Inside William, the wild raised its ears. Someone was calling him. He turned toward the door. The call resonated through his skull, directly in his mind, bypassing his ears. If this was magic, he'd never met it before.

"Be still and don't make noise."

"Don't go! Help me, damn it!" Kaldar punched Embelys's corpse with his free fist. "Sonovabitch!"

A cry full of pain and longing echoed through William's head. He ran through the door and to the hallway, heading toward the source of the screaming. The intensity of the mental wail was enough to make his heart skip a beat.

A door came into his view at the end of the hallway, a dark rectangle shivering with tiny magic aftershocks. The source of the call lay behind it. William broke into a run.

The Hand's magic danced on the door's surface, breaking into smoke-thin coils of pale green. He kicked the door. It flew open.

A sweet scent filled his nostrils, heady and liquid-thick, like the odor of old buckwheat honey. Something stirred within the room, outside his field of vision. William bared his teeth, stepped inside, and closed the door behind him.

An enormous flower bloomed in the corner of the room. Its roots, thin and studded with chunky tuber-like vesicles, spread across the floor and walls in a reddish net, leaving only the windows bare. The roots swirled together into a thick squat stem, from which protruded three wide leaves. Red liquid pumped through the veins of the leaves, adding a pink tint to the sections of green.

Three massive petals, gray and spotted with flecks of green, rose above the leaves. They were closed, hiding the center of the flower like hands folded in prayer.

A jerky quickening ran through the network of roots. William stepped back.

The roots crawled, unwinding from the far corner, revealing a desk and three long, flexible tentacles stretching from the flower to a four-feet-tall cocoon.

With a rubbery menacing strength, the tentacles peeled the cocoon from the wall and brought it across the room, uncurling as they moved. The last coils slid, straightened, and a body fell at William's feet with a wet thud. The tentacles froze in the air, as solid and unmoving as a cypress stem.

*Fuck me.*

Hydraulic movement. He'd learned about this during his time in the Adrianglian Legion. The tentacles couldn't move until the plant replenished its supply of liquid.

William knelt by the body. The corpse lay on its back. A man. Probably. The exposed flesh of its face and neck was unnaturally smooth and swollen, its color the deep swollen purple of a fresh bruise. The cadaver's mouth gaped open. The puffy eyelids lay half-closed over the milky orbs of the eyes.

A tiny tendril of the root snaked its way onto the corpse's cheek. The sharp tip of the root, enclosed in a rough, almost bark-like cone, probed the dead flesh, and thrust through it. The skin tore like wet paper. A thick torrent of viscous bloody fluid spilled forth and streamed across the dead cheek to the floor. The nauseating stench of rotting meat erupted from the body. William leaped back.

Other roots reached for the corpse, the vesicles pulsing like tiny hearts. The plant was drinking the corpse's fluids, consuming them like water.

The petals quivered. The spots of green that flecked them crawled, moving away from the petal's edges to blend into a single green stain at the base of the flower. The roots kept pumping. Deep red liquid spread through the veins in the petals, turning their gray to red.

William raised his blade. If it tried to drain him next, it was in for a hell of a surprise.

The flower's veins contracted, pulling the petals apart with agonizing slowness. Something moved with the flower.

With a whisper, the petals snapped open, bright red and stiff like the tail feathers of a posturing peacock. A burst of yellow pollen erupted into the air, floating in the draft like powdered yellow snow. The honeyed odor flooded the chamber.

William coughed. His eyes teared, and he wiped the moisture with his hand.

A body lay within the flower. Nude and bald, frail to the point of emaciation, it rested on its back within the lower bell-shaped petal. Its legs vanished into the flower's core. The bluish tint of the corpse's bloodless flesh offered a stark contrast to the petal's garish crimson.

Another unlucky bastard being eaten.

By now the flower's whips would have regained the liquid. If he were to strike, he would have to get past them first.

The body opened its eyes. They looked at him in silent plea and for a second he thought he was looking at Cerise.

William caught his breath.

The roots crawled aside, opening a narrow path to the flower.

He took it.

The body's hands opened, revealing a sunken chest and thin bags of skin where breasts used to be. The blue eyes tracked his movements. If she was younger, if her face had a bit of fat and her skin was smoother. If she had blond hair . . .

"Genevieve," he whispered and coughed, expelling a mouthful of pollen from his throat.

She stretched her hand to him. He took her icy fingers. The same reddish liquid that had flooded the veins of the petals and leaves was making its way through her torso, bulging the vessels under her nearly transparent skin.

She opened her mouth. A wave of magic smashed against him. William went down to his knees, gasping for breath. A vision of Cerise flickered before him. Her sword was carving Embelys's flaccid body, cutting Kaldar out. She was in the house. He blinked and the image of Cerise vanished.

Genevieve's mouth contorted, struggled to form a word. William's eyes burned from the pollen that swirled in the air about them in a snowfall of tiny powdered stars. It filled his mouth and his nose, it burned his throat. "Before . . ." Genevieve whispered. "My daughter . . ."

Her whip swung toward the desk and rolled back, twisted about his shoulder with a gentleness equivalent to a caress. A leather journal fell at his feet.

"No choice . . . made me . . ."

"She knows," he told her. "Cerise knows."

"Tell Sophie . . . So sorry . . ."

"I will."

She squeezed his hand. "Kill me . . . Please . . . So Ceri . . . doesn't have to . . ."

The knife felt heavy in his hands, as if filled with lead. He raised it.

She smiled. Her fragile sharp-boned face, her sunken

cheeks, her eyes drowning in pain, all of it lit, united and transformed by that weak smile, made radiant and time-less. William knew he would remember it to his death.

He swung. The blade sliced cleanly through her flesh. Her head dropped to the floor and rolled, releasing a torrent of blood from the stump of her neck. It splashed onto the floorboards, and the roots stretched toward it. The vesicles pumped, sucking up the liquid in a canni-balistic cycle even as blood continued to flow from the wound.

William picked up the journal off the floor.

Her head lay on its side. She was still smiling and her blue eyes focused on him. "Thank you," bloodless lips mouthed.

The pollen had clogged his lungs, sapping his strength. William pushed to his feet and staggered to the door, half-blind, stumbling, exhausted, and weak. His hand found the handle, and he lay on it with his weight. It fell away before him, and he crashed into the hallway. The cool smoothness of the wooden floor slapped his cheek.

The door.

William dragged himself upright, shut it, and sagged against it. His lungs burned. The last whiffs of pollen swirled around him.

William concentrated on the rising and falling of his chest. His hands flipped the journal open on their own. Long streaks of cursive lined the pages, too out of focus. He wiped the last tears from his eyes and brought the jour-nal so close the pages nearly touched his nose.

R1DP6WR12DC18HF1CW6BY12WW18BS3VL9S R1DP6WG12E 5aba 1abaa

Gibberish. No, not gibberish, code.

A rapid staccato of footsteps echoed through the hall-way. He dropped his hand to his side, letting the journal hang along his leg.

Cerise rounded the corner, Richard behind her. She raced toward him.

"Are you hurt?"

William shook his head and tried to tell her he was okay, but words wouldn't come out. He dropped the journal into her hands. Understanding slowly crept into her face. She turned corpse white and tried to push past him. "Let me in."

"No," he rasped. His voice finally worked.

"I have to see her!"

"No. She didn't want you to. It's over."

Richard caught her shoulders. "He's right. It's done."

"Let me see my mother!"

She jerked from him, but Richard held on. "It's over. It's all over and she's resting now. Don't taint your memories. Remember her as she was. Come on. Let's get William into the fresh air."

Cerise said nothing. Her shoulders slumped. She gulped and slid her shoulder under his right arm, while Richard pulled him up. Cerise's arm wound her way around William's waist. He thought of telling her he wasn't that weak, but instead leaned on her and let himself be led out of the house into the sunlight.

THEY had set the house on fire. It burned like a funeral pyre, belching thick acrid smoke into the air. The flames consumed the old boards with a loud snapping, snaked their way up the walls, melted the glass of the hothouse, and Posad's plants hissed and wailed as the fire sank its teeth into their green flesh. Nobody arrived to stop the blaze, and even if they had, the fire had spread too far and too fast.

Cerise refused to leave. William sat next to her. He felt her pain, sharp and brutal. There was nothing he could do, except sit next to her. She didn't cry. She didn't rave. She just sat there, radiating grief and fury.

Soon the whole structure stood engulfed, no more than a mere skeleton of stone and timber wearing a mantle of heat. She sat on the edge of the clearing, reading the journal in the light of the raging blaze, until the roof crashed with the thunderous popping of ancient support beams, spraying glowing sparks everywhere, spooking the horses, and forcing the two of them to retreat from the heat.

# TWENTY-SEVEN

**WILLIAM** reclined, sinking deeper into the comfortable softness of the Mars' library chair. Spider was gone. Gone somewhere in the Mire. Everything rode on that damn journal. It would tell him where Spider went and what he wanted from Cerise. Except the fucking thing was in code.

Cerise took a spot by the window with the journal, a pen, and some paper.

The library was crowded. The Mars kept coming in and out, radiating anxiety. William clenched his teeth. All of their tension made him jumpy. In the corner Kaldar brooded over a glass of wine. He, Richard, and Erian sat by the door, like three watch dogs.

William kept running the pattern in his head. He'd memorized a page and a half of code. It was a code, he was sure of it. It had a pattern. For one, the numbers ran in sequence.

R1DP6WR12DC18HF1CW6BY12WW18BS3VL9S R1DP6WG12E

The numbers repeated themselves, but rarely with the same letters—R1, P6, R12, C18, and then F1, W6, Y12 . . . Or was it 1D, 6W? They differed by 6. Except for the first interval from 1 to 6, which differed by 5 . . . But then there was the second sequence—3, 9, 15, 19. Sometimes the numbers would run the entire sequence, and sometimes they ended and a different series started over.

He had hammered his brain against the pattern, ever

since he saw it. Codes weren't his thing, but he knew the basic premise: figure out the combination of letters and numbers occurring most often and try sticking the most often used letter of the alphabet in its place. But he was a hunter, not a code breaker.

Erian swung his legs off the chair and paced, measuring the library's length with long strides. His voice was quiet. "It's been three hours. She's not going to break it."

"She'll break it," Richard said. "It was Vernard's life's work, and she was his favorite grandchild."

"Yeah." A bitter edge in Erian's voice set off an alarm in William's head.

"What is your problem?" Kaldar kept his voice low. "Did she spit in your breakfast?"

Erian pivoted on his foot. "It's over. Why don't the two of you get it? The feud is done, we've won, we're fucking done."

"It's not over until we have Gustave and Spider's head," Richard told him.

Erian swung his hand, his face slapped with disgust. "The whole damn family went mad."

Richard rose smoothly, crossed the library, and pulled a large leather volume off the shelf.

"What is it?" Kaldar asked.

"Grandfather was exiled under Article 8.3 of the Dukedom of Louisiana's Criminal Code. I just realized that I never thought to check what Article 8.3 was."

Richard unlocked the leather flap securing the book, flipped the cover open, and riffled through the yellow pages. He frowned. "Found it."

Richard raised the book, showing them the page. The red-lettered heading read "Malpractice and Corruption of Vows." A long list of subsections crawled down from it.

"Subsection 3," Richard read. "Page 242."

The pages rustled as he turned them. "Malpractice. Unlawful Human Experimentation. Gross Disregard for the Integrity of the Human Body. Intent to Create an Aberration."

"How is that different from what the Hand is doing?" Erian asked.

"The Hand is not supposed to exist," William said. "If captured, the Hand's agent receives no support from Louisiana. They cut him loose because their magic modification is illegal."

"Grandfather was convicted of using magic to tamper with the human body, which broke his Physician's Oath." Mikita walked into the room. "Mother says they had a conversation about it once. He knew they would come after him, but he did whatever it was anyway. He said it was too important to quit."

"What was the nature of the research?" Richard asked.

"He was trying to find a way to teach the human body to regenerate itself. He said that humans had all of the power to heal themselves and take care of any illness. That they just needed to find the right switch inside their bodies."

To break an oath and risk everything, his cushy blue-blood life, his position, a man had to be driven. A man like that, a man with the purpose, wouldn't have let the swamp stop him, William thought. No, he'd keep working on whatever it was. Here. In the swamp.

Looking for a way to teach the body to heal itself.

To regenerate.

His memory forced an image of a monster in the moon-light, its wounds knitting together. Pieces clicked together in his head. A self-healing, indestructible monster. In his life William had seen dozens of different animals, but he'd never met anything like the creature. It wasn't a cat, a wolf, or a bear. It wasn't even related to any of them.

If it wasn't natural, it had to be made. And who would be better to make it than a man like Cerise's grandfather.

If the monster was made, Spider would want to get his hands on it, pull it apart, find out how it came to be.

If Cerise realized that a monster her grandpa made was running around the woods, she'd move heaven and earth to kill it and kill Spider. That's the way her mind worked: she took care of her responsibilities, and she paid her debts. Spider had twenty agents with him. They had . . . the Mars, and at least seven or eight of Cerise's relatives were out of commission. Twenty lethal, trained, magically enhanced freaks against maybe thirty-five regular people. Nothing regular about the Mars, but even if the lot of them pulled every magic talent they had out of their asses, it would be a slaughter. Cerise would be in the front line, and she would die.

His mate would die.

William's hands curled. The skin between his knuckles itched, wanting to release the claws.

They would all die: Richard, Erian, Ignata, Makita, even the idiot Kaldar. None of them would make it. He couldn't stop them from fighting, and worse, he needed them desperately, because he couldn't take on twenty agents alone.

He felt trapped, like a dog on a chain.

He could be wrong. There was no link between the monster and Vernard. Not yet.

"Done," Cerise said.

They looked at her. Her eyes were haunted and wide, as if she'd seen something that wasn't fit to be seen.

"It's a simple substitution cipher," she said, her voice flat. "It's very difficult to break unless you have the key."

"What's the key?" Kaldar asked.

"A Gaulish lullaby. He used to sing it to me when I was little." She pushed from the table. "I think we better call a family meeting."


TWENTY minutes later the Mar family assembled in the library, and Cerise read the journal in a flat voice in air thick with human breath.

"'The art of medicine, as ancient as the human body itself. It began with the first primitive, who, plagued by

ache, stuck a handful of grass in his mouth, chewed, and
found his pain lessened. For ages, we followed in that
primitive's footsteps, holding fast to the notion that the
introduction of a foreign agent into the body was the
only path to cure. We invented medicines, ointments, po-
tions, splints, casts, slings, and endless devices to facili-
tate healing, yet we have never focused on the healing
process itself. For what is healing, if not the body's self-
correction of imperfection? What is the role of medicine
if not to push the organism onto the path of regeneration?

"'On this day, I, Vernard Dûbois, a man and a healer,
state that a human body possesses all of the means to
heal itself, to cure every malady and every defect without intrusion of a surgeon or a physician. I make this
claim, believing that one day I and those like me will
become obsolete. It is in the name of that glorious day, I
now embark on the path of research and experimentation. It is a path strewn with rocks of self-doubt, mistakes, and persecution. Let it be known that I forgive those
who would condemn me, for I comprehend the reasons
that drive them to act. Misguided though they may be,
they hold the interests of humanity close at heart, and I
bear them no ill will.

"'Of the Gods, I ask forgiveness for my past trans-
gressions. Of my wife and my daughter, I beg forgiveness for my future ones. I pray that one day you may
understand the reasons for which I must continue.'"

She kept going, reading pages of formulas and equations. Some heads nodded—Aunt Pete, Mikita, Ignata.
Most people looked the same way he did: blank. As best
he could gather, Vernard had found some kind of micro-
scopic algae that spurred regeneration. The algae emitted
magic that changed the body, accelerating the healing.
Vernard got it to work on mice, but failed when he tried
it on anything larger. Once inside the body, the magic
algae died, and he couldn't get enough of it into his test
subjects to make a difference. He'd tried feeding it to

them, he'd tried injections and blood transfusions, but none of it was fast enough.

Cerise stopped. "There is a page here with one word: EXILE. The next entry reads: 'We've reached the swamps. In the grove behind our new dwelling I found a peculiar moss, red and similar to fur in appearance. It spread across the grove's floor, forming an irregular mound in the middle. Upon examination of the mound I found a rabbit's corpse underneath, partially digested. The moss has an enormous eno concentration. The young man who fancies Gen—I think his name is Gustave—informed me that locals call it the burial shroud and avoid it with superstitious fear.' "

Cerise paused, swallowing with effort, and kept reading.

William zoned out, listening to the words but not understanding. There was something about the moss and the gastric juices of some sort of cavity and combining the moss with the previous plant he'd screwed around with. Finally he raised his hand, feeling like he was ten years old, sitting behind the school desk. "Can you explain it to me?"

Cerise paused.

"There is a plant that looks like moss," Petunia said, scratching at her eye patch. "We call it burial shroud. It's not really a plant, more like an odd cross between plant and animal. It's native only to the Mire and it needs magic to survive. Burial shroud feeds on corpses. Its spores settle on the carcass, and then its shoots pierce the dead animal's skin. It then siphons the liquids from the corpse through its shoots, takes what it needs, and dumps the rest back into the body."

"Like a filter?" William frowned.

"Just like that," Petunia nodded. "These shoots are very, very tiny, but there are so many of them, they can filter all the liquids from a carcass several times within one day. With me so far?"

He nodded.

"Vernard needed a fast way to introduce his miracle algae into the body, fast and in large numbers. He stumbled onto burial shroud and tinkered with it until he managed to get his algae inside the moss and used magic to get it all to play nice. So, he ended up with burial shroud full of regeneration algae. Makes sense?"

William nodded again.

"Then he built himself a casket and lined it with burial shroud. Let's say you put a person into the casket. The burial shroud will attack and start pulling liquids out of this person. It will take some proteins and other things, and dump the rest back into the body. But!" Petunia raised her finger. "As it returns liquids to the body, it will add the miracle algae to it."

"It would hurt," William said.

"Oh, yes. It would hurt like hell, but if you're dying or getting old, you wouldn't care." Petunia grimaced. "Keep going, Ceri. I'm guessing your grandfather experimented with putting creatures into the casket."

Petunia proved right. Vernard had designed five test subjects: a cat, a pig, a calf, someone he called D, and E. Before he could stick them into his coffin, he made them drink some sort of herbal concoction he called the remedy. Cerise's face jerked as she read the ingredients.

"'One-quarter teaspoon crushed redwort leaves, one tube of fisherman's club in full bloom, one-quarter teaspoon minced burial shroud, one cup water. Let steep for twenty hours.

"'Today I've taken the cat, subject A, and slit its side to cause massive bleeding. I've placed it into the Box and shut the lid. I will check on it tomorrow. Tonight I must go fishing. I promised Cerise, and one must always keep a promise given to a child . . .

"'The cat is alive. The gash has healed completely, and a new pink tissue marks the location of the wound I had inflicted. I've beheaded the cat, and upon dissection, found its heart still beating. The pulse continued for nearly six minutes and stopped, I suspect, because the body ran out of blood.'"

The cat wasn't the only victim. William growled in his head. He could see where this was heading. Once Grandpa started putting things into the damn Box, he would crawl into it himself eventually. First, the cat, then the pig, then the calf . . .

"'The calf lives. The bones of its broken leg have healed. It stands renewed in the back corral, together with the piglet. It is time for a true test. Tonight I enter the Box.'"

Ignata buried her head in her hands. "Oh no. No, Vernard, no."

"'Words fail me. At first I felt the agony of each sting puncturing my skin. My world shrank to a red daze and I floated in it, buoyant in my pain, twisted, battered, mangled by it, and yet somehow supported and made whole. The pain tore the very fabric of me, unraveled it strand by strand, and wove it back together anew. As it consumed me, I found deliverance in its red mist. I found strength and vigor. The universe had opened like a flower to my mind, and I saw its secret patterns and hidden truths. I stand before the Box now. My mind is clear, but the insight has left me. The secrets gained have slipped away, beyond the veil of consciousness. I can feel them, yet they pass through the fingers of my mind like smoke coils. I must return to the Box . . .

"'It's easier to breathe. The budding arthritis in my hands troubles me no longer . . .

"'I ran three miles in the morning to test myself, and discovering myself free of fatigue, I ran three more . . .

"'The visions of the red daze haunt me. I must enter the Box again . . .

"'I shall speak nothing of what I glimpsed beyond the red curtain. I must understand it before I commit it to the page . . .

"'The scar on my shin is gone. I've had it since I was a child . . .

"'And then I picked her up into my arms and danced across the house, danced and danced. She laughed, throwing her head back . . . Gods, I haven't seen her laugh like that since we were twenty . . .'"

Cerise's voice kept on, flat and steady, reading Vernard's thoughts as he slid deeper and deeper into delirium. The Box was addictive, and the addiction came with a price. It unhinged Vernard's mind.

"'I'm becoming violent. My moods, my rage are growing difficult to control. I screamed at Genevieve this morning when she brought us drinks. She had spilled my mug of tea. I didn't mean to lash out, yet my body did it seemingly on its own, while I watched it act from the depths of my consciousness. It is as if I'm steering a boat with a broken rudder . . .

"'The remedy failed me. The toxin proved too potent . . .

"'Too late. It's too late for me.

"'Too late . . . Impatient. Too impatient. Too many visits to the red daze. Had I just waited another month, letting the remedy affect me, had I limited myself to three trips and no more . . . Had I, had I . . .

"'Had I been a husband, had I been a father,

"'I shall die alone, abandoned by my lover,

"'Lay me down gently, I'll go no farther,

"'Lay me down gently . . .

"'I found the pig dead in its pen. Its torn body was a mess of blood and bruises. I suspect the calf. I don't like the way he looks at me.'"

Cerise closed her eyes for a long moment and kept going.

"'Today, when I dumped the feed into the calf's trough, it tried to ram me. I saw it coming, yellow eyes burning with a radiant hunger. It galloped to me, hooves striking a thudding battle hymn from the ground. It meant to kill me. I didn't move. I couldn't. I didn't wish to. It reached me, and my body took over. I spun out of the way. My hands closed about its neck and tore into the flesh. Blood

washed over my fingers. Its scent . . . oh, its scent, intoxicating and sickening. It took hold of me and rode me, and
I could not escape its grasp.

"'I buried the calf. The rational part of me is horrified by the sight of the body, by its odor, by the taste of
raw flesh on my tongue. But its voice is growing weak.
The logical center of my being is fading. It leaves a rav-
ening dog in its wake. And I have not the power to contain its rage. But she did fine. She did just fine. Only
once and no more. My gift. My curse. My poor sweet E,
carry it in you. I wanted so much for you and have given
you so little. I'm just a selfish old man, tired and stupid,
sitting on the shards of my tower. I fought against the
forces of nature and was found wanting. I should've let
it die, but couldn't. I would beg for forgiveness, but I
know you'll have none to give. I love you. Gods, how
hopelessly inadequate this simple proclamation feels.

"'The red daze is coming. It will claim me soon.

"'I've hid it. Hid it where the fisherman waits.'"

Cerise stopped. "This is the last coherent entry. On the
next two pages he has written 'poor Vernard' over and
over, and then it dissolves into scribbles."

She slumped in the chair, exhausted.

William's mind raced. That's what Spider wanted. The
Box.

If the Hand's freaks got cooked in the Box, they would
come out more psychotic than they were before. They
would regenerate their wounds in seconds, and they would
kill and kill and kill, never stopping.

Louisiana wanted a weapon against Adrianglia. This
was it.

Vernard never died. The thought dashed through his
mind, illuminating the fractured pieces of the puzzle. Of
course, Vernard never died. Not after that many trips to
the Box. It would make him nearly indestructible.

"This is the day the secrets get told," Grandmother Az
said.

William looked up. She stood in the middle of the

room, wizened and ancient as ever, and deep sadness pooled in her small dark eyes.

"You're awake," Ignata said and rose to offer her chair. Grandmother Az ignored it. She stared at him, and William felt a pull of magic.

"Tell them, child," she said. "Tell them who you've seen in the woods."

"Vernard never died," William said. "I've seen him. I fought him in the Mire."

"The monster? No." Cerise shook her head. "No, it can't be."

"He prowls the night," Grandmother Az said. "He stayed away from the house for many years, but he's come back. He knows something is wrong. He is a monster now, but some memories still linger. The thing he did, the unnatural thing, it changed him too much. The magic was too strong."

Silence fell, tense and charged, like the air before the storm.

"Who is E?" Ignata said. "A was the cat, B was the pig, C was the calf. D was Vernard himself."

Kaldar rose. "The Box. It speeds up the healing, yes?"

He crossed the room. A dagger flashed in his fingers. He took Cerise by the hand and glanced at her. She nodded. Kaldar cut at her forearm. Blood swelled. He wiped the crimson liquid off with his sleeve and raised her arm high. A thin line of red marked the wound but no more blood came.

"Sweet little E," he said. "I've wondered about that for years. She never got a cold. All of us would be down with flu or some other crud, but she would be up and chipper."

Cerise studied her arm as if it were a foreign object. "I don't remember it. The Box. I don't remember it at all."

"He probably sedated you," Ignata said.

"It would have to be a bloody strong sedation," Murid said, "to dull that kind of pain."

Ignata frowned. "Do you remember the remedy?"

Her mother grimaced. "Oh, please. It's the redwort tea. During the last few weeks, he practically drowned her in it every chance he got. That's probably the only reason she is sane now. That's what the remedy does—it keeps you from going mad."

Richard's clear voice filled the room. "The question is what we are going to do with the journal now."

WILLIAM tensed. His every instinct screamed in alarm.

Faces turned to Richard.

"We have the journal. It is too late for Genevieve, but not too late for Gustave. Cerise told me that he's being held in Kasis."

Richard leaned forward. "The place is a fortress and the Earl of Kasis has a lot of guards at his disposal. Not only that, but the place itself sits on the border between Adrianglia and Louisiana in the Weird. It touches the Edge, but that's about it. If we attack it, we'll have people from both countries on our trail. But we must get Gustave back. We must at least try."

"Blackmail," Kaldar said. "We trade Gustave for the journal. Spider will do anything to keep us from turning it over to the Adrianglians."

And it all went to shit. William bared his teeth.

"Spider is too dangerous," Erian said.

"Screw Spider. That journal is monstrous!" Petunia's voice cut him off. "It's the product of an abnormal mind. Brilliant but abnormal. We must destroy it."

Kaldar gaped at her. "As long as we have the journal, we can get Gustave back."

She glared back. "William! How big was the creature you saw?"

They all looked at him. The hair on the back of his neck rose under pressure. "Large. At least six hundred pounds."

Shock slapped the Mars' faces. Even Cerise paused, frozen in an instant.

Aunt Pete whirled to face Grandmother Az. "That's about right, isn't it?"

Grandmother nodded.

Pete's stare pinned Kaldar like a dagger. "So, ask yourself, nephew, do you really want to hand that monster-making blueprint to the world in exchange for one life?"

"It's not our problem," Erian said. "Why are all of you ignoring me? It's not our problem!"

Mikita shook his head. "It is our problem. We are the Mars. It was made by our in-law on the land that's now in our family. We are responsible."

Aunt Pete stomped her foot. "There is a bigger responsibility here. Human responsibility. Vernard knew enough to hide this thing—mad as he was, he locked it away and hid it from humanity. It's not right to let this knowledge out!"

Kaldar threw his arms out. "Who the hell cares if the Weird's nobles kill each other? What did they ever do for us?"

"What he says does have some merit." Richard drummed his fingers on the desk.

Aunt Pete studied him as if he were an insect. "Who are you people?"

William looked at the Mars and knew Aunt Pete would lose. They wanted Gustave back. They were family and family looked out for their own first. He looked at Cerise's face, lit from within by hope. He remembered her head against his chest, how it felt to hold her, the smell of her hair, the hot, sweet taste of her mouth . . .

"We can arrange an exchange someplace public . . ." Kaldar said.

William rose from his chair. "No."

Cerise's eyes found him.

Kaldar frowned. "You said something, blueblood?"

William ignored him. "Adrianglia and Louisiana are grinding against each other. They can't afford to let the other side have any advantage. Once Spider learns that you've got the journal, he will try to wipe you out. Once Adrianglia learns that you have it, they will do the same."

He found Cerise's gaze. "Listen to me. Everyone in this room will die. Everyone. They will kill you, they will murder your kids, they will burn your house, they will shoot your dogs. They will obliterate you. It would be as if you never existed."

"You seem very sure of that." Richard's quiet voice echoed through the silent room.

William almost snarled. *Because they will order me to do it.*

"Adrianglia doesn't know about the journal," Erian said.

"They will very shortly. Burn it. Burn the fucking journal and never speak of it again."

Cerise was looking at him. There was something in her eyes, suspicion, hurt, anger, he couldn't tell. Whatever it was, it reached deep down into his chest and jerked at his heart.

If he told her the whole truth now, if he told her about the Mirror, he would lose her. But if he could make her understand, she would live.

"How will Adrianglia know about the journal, William?" she asked, her voice very soft.

The wild howled and screamed inside him. *No! Shut up. Shut the hell up. Don't lose the woman!*

"Last night I used a drone bug to send the complete report to Zeke Wallace," William told her.

The room shrank to the two of them. He was ice calm. There was no going back.

"You're not a bounty hunter," she said.

"No."

"Is Adrianglia paying you to kill Spider?" she asked.

"No. They don't mind if I kill him, but I'm not here for him. I'm here for the Box and the journal. That's what the Mirror wants, and they will order me to slaughter the lot of you to get it."

"You lied to me."

"I meant the rest of it," he snarled. "Wolves mate for life and you're my mate."

"Wolf?" Erian jumped off his chair. "William Wolf? The one the freaks are so scared of? And you brought William Wolf into the family? Are you out of your mind? He's a fucking changeling."

William bared his teeth.

Erian caught himself but it was too late. Cerise was staring at him, half-risen from her chair, her face bloodless.

"Erian," she said.

Erian stumbled backward, looking lost.

"It was you." Cerise's voice brimmed with pain. "You sold my father and mother to the Hand."

"My own brother." Richard's face contorted and for a moment he couldn't speak. The desk creaked under the pressure of his white-knuckled hands. "Why?"

"Because somebody had to," Erian snarled. His hands shook. "Because neither you nor that fucking waste of space that's our other brother would do anything. I saw our father die. I remember everything: the shot, the blood, the look in his eyes, everything! You know what Gustave told me at the funeral? He told me, 'You will get your revenge.' I waited for revenge. Years I waited, but he didn't give a fuck about it, oh no, he was happy squatting in this house, our father's house, letting his spoiled brat daughter run the place. He would've grown fat and happy, while our father rotted in the ground. Every year I came to him, and every year he told me, 'It's not time, Erian. We can't afford a feud right now.' It would never be time, so yes, I fucking did it. I gave the Sheeriles an edge. I gift-wrapped Gustave for them, because if he stayed here, the feud would never end. Now the Sheeriles are dead. Our father is watching from above and he's happy, Richard. You hear me? He is happy!"

Richard's face turned white. "I must kill you," he said very calmly. "Somebody give me a sword."

Cerise rose. "Uncle Hugh and Mikita, take Erian out.

Lock him in the north building. Make sure he can't hurt himself."

Erian bared his teeth. Hugh hit him on the back of the head. Erian's eyes rolled back in their orbits, and he sagged down in Mikita's arms. They carried him from the room.

Cerise turned to William.

"If you bargain for the journal, you will die," he said. "If you go to fight Spider, you will die, too. Don't. Don't do it."

"I don't have a choice," she said. "I can't live knowing that I had a chance to keep thousands of people from dying and I did nothing."


CERISE clenched her teeth. Her heart pounded in her chest. Her mouth tasted bitter. Erian. Of all people, it had to be Erian.

Her legs had turned to wet cotton. Her chest constricted. She wanted to bend over and cradle the hot knot of pain in the pit of her stomach, but the entire family was here, watching her, waiting to see what she would say, and she held it in.

William stood alone, in the middle of the room, his face pale. She looked into his eyes and saw it all: pain, grief, fury, fear, and resignation. He thought she would leave him. Why not, everybody else in his life did.

"You're a Mirror spy?" she asked softly.

"Yes." His voice was low and ragged.

She sighed. "I wish you had mentioned it earlier."

It took a second to penetrate. Amber rolled over his eyes. Shock slapped his face. It lasted only a moment, but the relief in his eyes was so obvious, it filled her with anger. Anger at the monsters who had damaged him, anger at Erian, anger at the Hand . . . Her hands shook, and she clenched them together.

"I love you," she told him. "When I asked you to stay with me, I meant it."

"He's a changeling," someone said from the back.

Cerise turned in the direction of the voice. Nobody owned up. "I've managed the family's money for the last three years. I know all of your dirty secrets. Think very carefully before you start throwing rocks at the man I love, because I will throw them back and I won't miss."

Silence answered her.

"Okay, then," she said. "Glad we got that settled. Why don't you talk between yourselves." She turned and marched out on the balcony and walked away, around the corner, out of their sight.

Outside the heat of the swamp enveloped her and she exhaled. Tears wet her eyes and ran down her cheeks. She tried to wipe them off, but they just kept coming and coming, and she couldn't stop.

William came around the corner and grabbed her.

She stuck her face into his chest and squeezed her eyes shut, trying to stop the tears.

He clenched her to him.

"I can't believe you didn't tell me," she whispered. "I asked you point-blank back in the swamp, and you didn't tell me."

"You would never have let me come with you," he said.

"We're trapped," she whispered. "I just want to be happy, William. I want to be with you and I don't want anybody to die, and I can't have that."

He gripped her shoulders, pushing her away so he could look in her face. His eyes were driven. "Burn the journal, Cerise. Listen to me, damn you!"

"Too late," she told him. "You know it's too late. The Hand will come for us, if not now, then in a week or a month. You said it yourself: they can't afford to let any of us live. And even if they did, if they use the Box, it won't just mean war. It will mean the end of the world in the Weird, because they will make these creatures and then they won't be able to control them."

"Let me handle it," he told her.

"Twenty agents against you alone? Are you out of your mind?" She wiped her tears with the back of her sleeve. "If I offered to go up against twenty agents, you would pitch a fit. We have no choice."

He hugged her, his hands stroking her hair. They stood together for a long time. Eventually, she stirred. "I have to go back. It won't be okay, will it?"

William swallowed. "No."

"That's what I thought," she said. She turned around and went back to the library.

Inside familiar faces waited for her. Aunt Pete, Aunt Murid, Ignata, Kaldar. Grandmother Az sitting in a corner, letting her run the family into the ground. Cerise sat at the table and braided the fingers of her hands together. Gods, she wished for guidance. But the person in the sky, the one she always asked for advice, was apparently running around in the woods, killing things at random.

Her grandfather had murdered her grandmother. If she thought about it too long, it made her want to rip her hair out.

Richard was off, too, gone to blow off steam.

*Who am I kidding?* she wondered. Richard would never be all right. None of them would ever be all right.

"It has to be the Drowned Dog Puddle," she said. They went to gather berries there every year to make the wine. It was a big family affair: children gathered the berries, women cleaned them, men talked . . . "What else could it be?"

Murid said, "Nothing else. Vernard didn't know anything else."

The question had to be asked and so she asked it. "What do we do now?"

"What do you want us to do?" Murid's clear eyes found her, propped her up like a crutch. "You are in charge. You lead and we follow."

Nobody disputed her words. Cerise had expected them to. "We must destroy the Box."

"Or die trying," Kaldar said.

Aunt Pete shook her head. "We all benefited from

Vernard's knowledge. We studied his books, we learned from him, we made wine together. He was family."

Cerise looked to Kaldar. "Kaldar?"

"They're right," he said. "I hate it, but we must fight. It's a Mar affair. Our land and our war, and it won't be done until we've chased the freaks from our swamp." He hesitated and scowled, deep lines breaking at the corners of his mouth. "I'm glad we have the blueblood. I don't care if he is a changeling. He fights like a demon."

They blocked her on every turn. Cerise turned to Grandmother and knelt by her. An old word slipped out, the one she used when she was a child.

"Meemaw . . ."

Grandmother Az heaved a small sigh and touched Cerise's hair. "Sometimes there are things that are best to be done and things that are right to be done. We all know which is which."

Murid slid her chair back. "That settles it."

Cerise watched them go and a sick feeling of guilt sucked at her stomach. Nausea started low within her belly and crept its way up. She was tired of the last dinners before the big battle. Tired of counting the faces and trying to guess how many more she would lose.

A hard, heavy clump of pain settled in her chest. She rubbed at it.

Her grandmother's fingers ran through her hair. "Poor child," Grandmother Az whispered. "Poor, poor child . . ."


WILLIAM strode down the hill, carrying the Mirror's bag. Gaston chased him.

"So that's it?"

"That's it. We get our shit together and go fight the Hand."

Gaston mulled it over. "Will we win?"

"Nope."

"Where are we going now?"

"We're going to make sure that this insane family doesn't get wiped out, if we win."

Gaston frowned.

"Insurance," William told him.

"Wait!" Lark's voice rang behind them.

William turned. Lark dashed down the slope, skinny legs flashing. She braked in front of them and thrust a teddy bear into William's hands.

"For you. So you don't die."

She whipped around and ran back up the hill.

William looked at the teddy. It was old. The fabric had thinned down to threads in spots, and he could see the stuffing through the weave. It was the same one she had up in her tree.

He pulled his bag open and very carefully put the teddy bear in. "Come on."

They walked down, away from the house, deeper into the swamp.

"'Where the fisherman waits,'" William quoted. "What does that mean to you?"

"It could be a lot of places. There is a whole bunch of Fisherman's this and Fisherman's that in the swamp."

"Vernard wouldn't know many places. This place has to be close. Some place your family would go often."

Gaston frowned. "It might be the Drowned Dog Puddle. It's a bad place. The thoas used to come there to die."

"Tell me about it."

"It's a pond. There is a hill on the west side of it, and it kind of hugs the pond. The water is pitch-black because of all the peat. Nobody knows how deep it is. You can't swim in it and nothing lives there except snakes. The hill and the pond open to some swampy ground, cypress, mud, little streams, and then the river eventually. The family goes there to pick the berries for the wine each year. They grow all around that hill."

"What about the fisherman?"

"There is an old tree growing by the pond, leaning over it. People call it the Black Fisherman."

"Sounds about right." William looked around. Tall pines surrounded them. He couldn't see the house. Far enough. He dug in his bag, taking care not to damage the bear. "How's your handwriting?"

"Um. Okay, I guess."

William got out a small notebook and a pen and handed them to Gaston. "Sit down."

Gaston sat on the log. "Why do I need those?"

"Because Vernard's journal is very long, and my handwriting is shit. I need to write it down because I don't understand any of it, which means my brain will forget it soon."

The kid blinked at him. "What?"

"Write," William told him. "The art of medicine, as ancient as the human body itself. It began with the first primitive, who plagued by ache, stuck a handful of grass in his mouth, chewed, and found his pain lessened . . ."

# TWENTY-EIGHT

**WILLIAM** crouched on the deck of the barge. Before him the shore loomed, black and green in the weak dawn light. Cerise stood next to him, her scent twisting and turning around him. Behind them the Mars waited.

"Are you sure?" Cerise asked.

"Yes. We go our separate ways here. If I take out Spider, the Hand will break." But to get to Spider, he'd have to have a distraction and the Mars were it.

"Don't die," she whispered.

"I won't."

He pulled her to him and kissed her, her taste so sharp and vivid, it almost hurt. So this was it. He'd known it was too good to be true. He had her and now he would lose her.

The barge swung close to the shore. He leaped, clearing the twenty-foot stretch of water, and took off into the woods.

Twenty minutes later William went to ground on the crest of the hill behind the Drowned Dog Puddle. The sun had risen, but the day was gray and dark, the sky overcast. In the weak light the swirls of green, gray, and brown on his face blended with the dense brush cover of the berry bushes. He'd molded himself into the hill so deep, he tasted mud on his lips. He was all but invisible to Spider's agents busy below.

The hill cradled the pond in a ragged crescent, dropping down in a sheer cliff, made soggy and slick with recent rain. Bushes and pines sheathed the hill, but noth-

ing grew down by the pond, save for a lonely cypress. It
rose above the water, a gnarled and grizzled veteran of
countless storms. The cypress cast no reflection. The water of the pond beneath it was pitch-black.

The entire place emanated an odd menacing calm.
The sloshing of the Hand's agents did little to disturb it,
no more than a grave digger would've disturbed the se-
renity of a graveyard.

William shifted slightly to keep the circulation flowing in his arms. He hid above the pond's northern shore,
far enough to be out of the agents' plain sight, but close
enough to miss little. The Mirror's bag provided him
with a distance lens, which he wore over his left eye like
an eye patch. The lens brought the agents so close, he
could count the pimples on their faces.

Three feet beyond him the ground ended abruptly,
and the hill plunged twenty-six feet straight into the
pitch-black water of the pond. Spider didn't pay the hill
a lot of attention, posting only two guards. They had
gone to ground, too, the closest only fifteen yards from
where William lay. Neither would be a problem when
the time came. In Spider's place William would've done
the same— any attack coming from the east, over the hill,
would've ended in the peat, and his instincts screamed at
him to stay the hell away from that black water.

Most of Spider's agents were concentrated around the
pond. William focused on the shock of white hair. Karmash.
The massive agent barked an order to a swarthy thick
woman. She tossed her hair back and went to a chain
lying in the mud. The muscles on her nude back bulged.
Something shifted beneath her skin, like a coiled spring,
and she picked up the chain roll and carried it without
apparent strain to where other agents untangled ropes by
cypress roots.

They were rigging a block and tackle, which they'd
hang from the cypress to pull the Box free. Clever, Spider.

An agent exploded from the mud, all sinew and tentacle, dripping sludge, and flung a wriggling snake clear of

the shore. It spun in the air away from the main body of
agents. A woman lashed out from behind a stack of lumber. Her arm flashed and two halves of the snake fell
twitching into the mud. And there was Veisan . . .

Spider came into the lens's view, leaning on the stack
of wood. The hair on the back of William's neck rose. If
he'd been covered in fur, his hackles would have been
up and his mouth growling. Spider slouched. The lens
picked up dark bags under his eyes. The bastard was tired.
Tired was good.

A hissing dispute broke out between Karmash and
the tentacled monstrosity William's memory identified
as Seth. Seth's tentacles flailed through the tears in his
black robe. Karmash was making short cutting motions
with his shovel-sized hands. Spider pushed free of the
wood stack. Noticing that he was being paid attention
to, Seth stepped back. Karmash was a touch slower to
catch on, but a breath later he, too, found some pressing business that made him walk away. Spider resumed
his slouching.

One of the agents would have to dive into the peat to
attach the chain. William smiled. That should be interesting to watch.

Once the Box came up, all hell would break lose.

He'd done the best he could, William decided. He'd
explained the plan to Gaston and sent him to hide the
copy of the journal and wait. If he didn't make it through,
the boy would take the journal to Zeke. He had done his
job and gotten the Mirror what it wanted. The Mars would
be safe from them.

Now he had to kill Spider. Piece of cake.

A lean sinuous woman stepped to the edge of the
pond. Her robe whispered to her feet, leaving her nude.
The head of every male agent turned. If it weren't for
the scales, she would be perfect.

The woman arched her back and then stretched, pushing her arms back. The gills on her neck snapped open in

a frilly pink collar, bright against her pale green scales. She picked up the rope, slipped it around her waist, and with serpentine grace slid into the peat.

KALDAR maneuvered the barge around the bend and glanced at his uncle. "Almost there."

Hugh stood up. Around him the dog pack rose, sitting on their haunches, staring at the big man with fanatical devotion. You'd never know the barge was full of dogs, Kaldar thought. With eighteen one-hundred-pound dogs on board, not a single bark or a growl. Like they were possessed or something.

Hugh stripped off his shirt, exposing a lean torso. He pulled off his boots, then his pants, and carefully folded his clothes. "So how did they pick you to help me? Lost a bet or something?"

"I don't lose bets. I volunteered. I never got to see you do your thing. Be a shame to miss it."

Cough whined softly.

"Soon," Hugh told him. "Soon."

A strand of cypresses came into view. Kaldar tugged on the reins, sending the pair of rolpies to the shore. "We're here."

"Okay." Hugh took a deep breath and squared his shoulders. "Okay."

His body twisted as if ripped from the inside out. Bones thrust and muscle followed. Acid squirted into Kaldar's mouth. Hugh crashed to the bottom of the barge, convulsing. The dogs whined in unison.

Hugh shook and rolled up to all fours. Dense gray fur slid over him and a giant wolf looked back at Kaldar with green eyes. Kaldar swallowed. The thing towered a foot over the dogs, and Cough was a hundred and twenty pounds.

The barge bumped into the muddy shore. The wolf leaped into the mud. The dogs streamed after him in a brindled flood. Kaldar tied the reins to the tree, grabbed his shotgun, and followed.


THE reptilian woman broke the surface of the puddle for the eighth time. William watched her drag the end of the line out of the peat. She didn't look so good anymore. The woman handed the rope to Karmash and collapsed on the shore. The mud gave under her weight and she sank into the muck. A thick layer of peat sheathed her face and chest. Her chest heaved.

Karmash tossed the rope to another agent, who clung to the branch of the cypress with clawed legs and a prehensile tail. The agent caught the rope and wove it into the block and tackle. They had used the ropes to wrap the Box like a package. William had seen it done before. The rope would squeeze the Box when they dragged it free of the mud. In their place, he'd find some way to break the suction first, lifting the Box from the mud.

Karmash had the same idea. He crossed the shore to the reptilian swimmer and dropped a large iron bar next to her. She shook her head. He prodded her with his foot as if she were a lazy dog. She shook her head again and rolled into a ball as Karmash's foot thudded into her ribs.

Spider broke his leisurely posture and walked over to them. He knelt by the woman and spoke to her. The crosshairs of William's lens centered on his eyes, focused ... Earnest Spider, soft-spoken, persuasive.

The woman nodded finally and took the iron bar into her trembling fingers. Karmash barked orders.

The dense clouds that smothered the sky chose this moment to rupture. Gray, cold rain spilled onto the Mire, pooling on the mud, wetting faces and plastering hair to heads. Spider raised his face to the heavens and swore.

\* \* \*

THE muddy hole in which Cerise lay slowly filled with water. Beside her Richard made a tiny movement, flicking a twig that had fallen on his face.

The agents didn't expect anyone to come from the south. To an outsider's eyes the labyrinth of sludge, water, and trees probably seemed impassable. Somewhere out there William lay in wait, ready to pounce.

Thirty yards away the Hand's agents grasped the rope and strained in a muscle-bulging, tendon-ripping heave. A huge white-haired agent—Karmash, William had called him—in the front roared, "Again!" in Gaulish. They heaved again.

It wasn't fair. It wasn't fair that they took her parents, that Lark was a monster, that Erian betrayed them. It wasn't fair that she had to lead her family into the slaughter. It wasn't fair that she loved William and now he could die.

Cerise squeezed her eyes shut for a second. *Get a damn grip.*

Where was Hugh with his dogs? Cerise's gaze strayed to the left. There, sandwiched between Richard and Mikita, Erian lay. Even under the swirls of forest paint, his face was bloodless.

For twelve years he was her brother. They ate at the same table. They went to sleep under the same roof. And then he almost killed Urow, he caused Clara to lose her leg, he let the Hand capture her parents . . . And for what? So he could see Lagar Sheerile die? It just hurt, deep inside, like someone sawed on her chest with a rusty saw.

She went to see him this morning. He stared at her like she was a stranger. She told him the family wanted his head and he had a choice. They could take him out back and shoot him like a rabid dog. Or he could fight the Hand and die with his sword in his hand. He chose the sword. She had known he would.

The surface of the pond boiled. A solid mass emerged, a dark rectangle, spilling clumps of bottom slime into the pond. The thick scent of rotting algae spread through the clearing. They had to move now. Cerise wished the dogs were here. But something had delayed Hugh and they had no choice.

Cerise raised her arm. Behind her a ragged line of Mars broke free from the mud. She chanced a single glance at the grim painted faces. Family . . .

The agents still pulled the ropes, unaware of their presence. Cerise rose on one knee, preparing the first insane charge . . .

Loud sucking noises came from the left, as if someone was trudging his way through the mud and carrying half the Mire worth of it on his boots.

*Shlop. Shlop. Shlop.*

Cerise dropped back into her hole.

Karmash raised his hand and turned in the direction of the sound.

A tall gangly figure in a crimson robe strode down the hill.

Emel. Dear Gods, why?

Emel stopped, gathered the edge of his crimson vestments, already mud-soaked, and shlopped his way past the bewildered agents to face the mud where the Mars hid. "Cerise," he called. "I really must talk to you."

The agents stared at him.

*I'm going to kill him.* Cerise clenched her teeth. *A dead man. He is a dead man.*

"The payment still hasn't been made," Emel said, fiddling with the hem of his wet robe. "Usually at this point I start killing the relatives of the guilty party, but since you are my relatives, the matter is a bit more complicated."

Next to her, Richard turned on his back, his hands behind his head. His face assumed a serene expression as he slowly sank into the mud. Apparently it was just too much for him.

Emel tucked his hem in the crook of his elbow and put the fingers of his two hands together. "Now then, I believe we've made an agreement for one thousand seven hun-

dred and twenty-five U.S. dollars due yesterday. I really
would like to resolve this matter here and now, before you
may charge to your probable death. Not that I wish you to
perish, by any means, but should you expire, our agreement would become void, and I would hate to go through
negotiations again. I do hate to be crude, but I would like
the money now. Please."

Did he think she brought it with her? The Hand wouldn't
let him walk away. He was going to get himself killed.
What in the world was he doing, making himself a target?

Karmash was looking past Emel, straight at her. She realized he had seen them.

The Hand would have to go through Emel to get to
them.

*Oh no.*

The Sect didn't want him involved, but if he was attacked, they would expect him to defend himself. Emel
was trying to pick a fight.

"Kill them!" Karmash howled. "Kill the corpse buggerer
and his family!"

The agents dashed for the necromancer, leaving their
leader struggling to secure the rope. The monstrous muscles on his arms bulged, he gritted his teeth, and began
circling the cypress, winding the rope around the bloated
stem. Beyond him, Cerise glimpsed a lean blond man
shout commands to the group guarding the southwestern
path.

Emel turned. "Corpse buggerer?" He dropped the hem
of his robe. "Nobody insults the acolyte of Gospo Adir."

His face trembled. His hands reached out, rigid fingers
raking the air like talons. Power accreted around him,
compacting into a dense cocoon. The black surface of the
pond gasped as a ball of foul-smelling gas erupted from
its middle.

Cerise dashed to him. Behind her the Mars charged at
the Hand.

Emel grunted like an animal. His hands clawed the air.

Shapes burst from the peat, huge hulking forms of skeleton and rotting flesh. Too big, too broad for human corpses. Thoas, the dead of the moon people.

The first of the Hand's agents reached Emel. Cerise lunged, flashing across her blade, and stepped back, as the top half of the agent's body slid from the torso and crashed into the mud.

"Thank you." Emel brought his hands together and exhaled sharply. The dead thoas ripped into the agents.

"Thank you for helping."

"Of course. We're family. You go. I'm well protected now."

She sprinted into the thick of the battle.

The thoas tore into the agents with all the wrath Emel could muster. Three of them hung on the white-haired giant. He tried to push them off, but they clung to him, taloned hands ripping, rotting teeth biting. He slammed his back against the cypress and knocked one of the corpses loose.

A grunt of pain made Cerise whirl. She turned just in time to see Mikita go down. A furry creature leaped onto his prone body with a triumphant shout. Before she knew it, Cerise was running, running desperately fast across the slick sludge. She was ten yards away when the furry beast bared needle teeth and ripped out Mikita's throat.


THE pack halted before the mouth of the path, breaking against the hillside like a brown deluge. Kaldar tried to stop and slid, waving his arms to keep his balance. His hand grasped a sapling, and he caught himself, avoiding a collision with the dogs.

A single form detached from the pack and sailed over their backs in a mighty leap. It landed next to Kaldar. Nightmarish eyes glared at him from a wolf's face.

Something was wrong.

Kaldar pushed to the front. The hill on one side, deep swamp on the other. They had to pass through a narrow

stretch of ground about twenty feet wide. The ground
looked freshly raked. Traps, Kaldar realized. Many, many
traps.

"A bet. I need a bet or I can't make it work."

The pack growled. A brindled dog moved before him
and dropped a dead swamp rat at his feet. Cold sweat
broke on his forehead.

"Fresh kill. Good bet." Kaldar swallowed. He picked
up the rat. The tiny body was still warm to the touch.
Closing his eyes, Kaldar moved into the path.

He felt the magic coalesce above him. That was his
talent, his own personal power. It had pulled him out of
many scrapes before, and he counted on it now to lead
him through the field of traps.

The shivering current hovered above him and plunged
through the top of his head, through his spine, through the
rat corpse in his arms, into his feet and the ground beneath
him. The surge nipped at his entrails with sharp hot fingers. It guided him to where it wanted him to go and he
obeyed.


WILLIAM saw Karmash go down beneath a roiling mass
of thoas corpses. The agent had managed to secure the
lines before they dragged him down, and the Box hung
suspended above the water from the branches of the cypress.

Good time to jump in.

William leapt to his feet and ran along the crest of the
hill. The first agent never saw him coming. He slashed
the man's throat, spun about, and sliced the other agent
to pieces.

Below him the fight raged. The Hand's agents had recovered from the initial assault and struck back. He saw
Seth's pink tentacles close about a body and release it a
second later, limp and twisted, like a cloth doll chewed
by a dog.

William turned and ran to the cypress. If he sank the

Box now, they wouldn't get it out a second time. He had to get down to the cypress and cut above the block and tackle, or the lines would snap and take him with them.

Ten yards to the cypress.

Eight.

Spider burst from the thick of the fighting.

William sprinted.

Spider jumped unnaturally high and scuttled up the cypress, landing on the hill in front of the tree.

William halted, his knife out. "Spider."

Spider grinned and pulled a curved knife from his sheath. "William."

William bared his teeth.

"Is this really where you want to die, William? In this awful place?"

"No, but it's good enough for your grave."

"Are you working for the Mirror now? It's nice. We must be winning if the Adrianglians are desperate enough to hire your kind."

William bared his teeth. "They hired the best."

Spider smiled. "I see. So tell me, is it business or pleasure? Are you doing it for the girl or for your country?"

"Both. Are we going to finish this or do you want to chitchat some more?"

Spider bowed with an elaborate flourish.

William snarled and charged.

# TWENTY-NINE

**THE** magic jerked, nearly sending Kaldar to his feet. Something was wrong. Kaldar opened his eyes. He was almost to the end of the path. Through the gap in the hill he saw the battleground and clumps of fighters tearing at each other in a chaotic frenzy. To the left and above Aunt Murid stood on the slope, her hands a blur as she spanned her crossbow and fired, sending bolt after bolt into the fray. Above her something shivered on the edge of the greenery. A long pink tentacle snaked out from the brush, rippling with reddish eno fire.

"Murid! Look out! Murid!" Kaldar ran. Something popped under his foot with a dry click. He kept running, too late realizing that he had stepped on a mine, and it had failed to detonate.

The tentacle slivered forward, dragging a thick tangle of appendages free of the bushes. They squirmed like a nest of grotesque snakes. A human torso rode in the midst of it all, topped by a bald head glaring at the world with solid black eyes.

"Murid!"

She kept firing.

Kaldar jerked his shotgun and fired. The shot bit into the creature.

The abomination hovered on the edge of the cliff and plunged down. Murid vanished beneath the squirming mass.

Kaldar screamed.

His legs carried him to the creature, and he hacked into

the writhing mass with his knife and kept screaming and screaming as blood and tissue flew in a salty spray from his blade. Tentacles raked his back but he kept slicing, oblivious to the pain. He carved his way to the torso and plunged his blade into the human stomach. Tentacles flailed, and the monster's human mouth hissed. Kaldar jerked his knife free and stabbed again and again and again . . .

CERISE kicked a body off her blade. All around her the fight raged: reanimated corpses jerky on their feet, huge dogs, the Hand's freaks, furry, scaled, armored, clawed, fanged, feathered, and the family, all clawing at each other in an insane race to kill. Blood spilled into the sludge, and lives were torn from the still-warm bodies.

She'd killed and killed and killed, slashing again and again. Now she was tired, and the fight wasn't anywhere near over.

In front of her a scaled clay paused in his killing spree and raised his arm with a shout. She followed his gesture and saw William on the hill.

Her heart skipped a beat.

He clashed with a lean blond man—Spider, she realized. They moved so fast, it took her breath away.

She had to get to that hill.

Cerise dashed forward, slicing at the scaled clay in passing. Her flash-blade severed his thigh, cleaving through the bone. He crashed down. She didn't pause. Someone else would finish him.

A red-skinned woman broke from a mound of torn thoas corpses and ran toward the cliff and the two men fighting on it. Veisan, Cerise's memory supplied. Spider's assassin.

Cerise sprinted across the muddy ground. Veisan squeezed out a burst of speed, but Cerise was closer to the cliff. She reached the pond and spun about it.

Veisan saw her. Her hands balanced two wide curved

blades, thin and sharpened to razor precision. They would slice a limb in a single strike. A grimace raked Veisan's face. Her mouth gaped, her eyes turned wide.

She was afraid for Spider.

Cerise rubbed the ground with her foot to gauge the slickness.

Veisan looked at her.

"No," Cerise told her.

Veisan flipped her blades and charged.


SOMETHING steel-hard clamped onto Kaldar's leg and pulled. He fell forward into the bloody mass. The force dragged him away from the body. He clawed at the slick ground, but the thing that held his leg was too strong. It pulled him free. Kaldar squirmed onto his back and found dog jaws on his leg. Erian loomed in the rain.

"They're dead," Erian said. His voice was dull. Pain contorted his face. "They're both dead."

He turned and hurled himself at the nearest freak. Kaldar sat up. A tangled mass of flesh lay on the hillside. The rain diluted the blood spilling from the severed tentacles, and it spread in a pale red across the sludge. Kaldar rushed to his feet and dove at the gory mess, hurling the severed pieces of flesh out of the way. He dug in through the corpse until a human arm emerged. He grabbed it and pulled, slid on the mud, fell clumsily, scrambled to his feet, and pulled again. The twisted mound of flesh shifted and Murid's shoulder and then her head came free. He grabbed her by the shoulders and dragged her out.

Murid stared at the sky. The raindrops fell into her eyes and bounced off her bloodless cheeks.

Kaldar shook her. He clasped her shoulders and shook, sending her black braid flapping, willing her to live. "Don't. Don't!"

She lay limp in his arms.

He shook her one more time and then set her gently

down on the ground. His knife lay in the mud a few inches away. It was still sharp and there were still freaks to kill.


**VEISAN** cried out, spinning wildly, her blades a glittering whirlwind of metal. *Strike, strike, strike, strike.*

Cerise swayed from the first, dodged the second. The third caught her on the shoulder, slicing through the sleeve and skin. She parried the fourth with her sword. Veisan kept striking, leaving no openings, backing her to the pond.

Cerise sank into the rhythm. Time slowed to a ponderous crawl. She saw Veisan with crystal clarity: the white knuckles of her fingers straining as she gripped her knives, the panicked expression on her face, the cords of veins bulging in her neck, as she advanced, her dreadlocks flying.

*Slash.*

*Slash.*

*Slash.*

Cerise moved with the blow, sweeping past Veisan. The line of magic slid along her blade, pulling the last of her reserves from her body. Cerise struck.

Blood spatter flew. The red-skinned woman kept moving, her body not realizing that she was already dead. Veisan whirled to deliver another blow and halted. Blood gushed from a hairline cut on her neck.

Her mouth opened.

Veisan dropped her swords. Her hands went to her neck, trying to stem the gush of life from her neck. She grabbed at her neck. Her head slid off her shoulders and fell into the mud.

For a long second the body stood frozen and then it, too, toppled over like a log.

Cerise turned to the cliff.

\* \* \*

**WILLIAM** parried a barrage of blows and ducked. Spider's knife swept above his head and severed a sapling to his right. The wood slowed Spider's speed by a fraction. William lunged through Spider's defenses and slashed at Spider's midsection. The blade grazed Spider's chest, and he smashed his elbow into William's back. Pain burst in his spine.

William lunged to the side and rolled clear. Spider's breath was coming in ragged gasps. He sucked air into his lungs and charged again. William parried, counterattacked in a flash. His blade sliced Spider's thigh, as hot metal whisked along his left arm. He withdrew again.

He was getting tired.

William gritted his teeth. He had to stay calm now. Spider was too good, and if he let his fury take over, Spider would kill him.

Spider bled from a dozen minor wounds. So did he. Neither of them could keep this up for long.

If he lost, Cerise would be the next one to die. Spider would never pass on the chance to kill her.

He had to end it now. Whatever it took.


**WILLIAM** faltered. Cerise gasped, her heart caught in her throat. Spider lunged, but William recovered within the same breath, hammered a vicious kick into Spider's midsection, and leapt away. They ripped and clawed at each other, kicked, elbowed, sliced. She'd never seen anything like it.

William lunged. He was slowing down. He had to be tired. Spider parried with quick short strokes and hammered his knee into William's leg. William jumped and the kick missed.

They were both bleeding. William's eyes shone. Spider bared his teeth. He seemed barely human.

William thrust, trying to sink his blade into Spider's stomach. The Hand's agent parried, knocking William's blade to the right, in the direction of William's swing. Without a pause, William slashed back in a vicious riposte, the tip of his sword drawing a bloody line across Spider's chest.

*Too wide!* Cerise almost screamed. *Too wide, William.*

Spider swayed and lunged into the gap in William's defense. His blade dived for William's left armpit and William stepped into it.

The curved knife sliced like a metal claw.

Cerise choked on her scream.

William's arm clamped down Spider's blade. Spider jerked at it in disbelief, but the curve of the blade held it in place. The knife was wedged in William's armpit.

William clasped Spider's elbow with his left hand and stepped close. His right arm embraced Spider, as if they were two long-lost friends, whispering a secret into each other's ear. William clasped Spider to him. His knife flashed and William sliced deep across Spider's spine.

Cerise knew they were too far for the sound to carry over, but she could've sworn she heard the sickening crunch of metal severing the bone.

Spider's mouth gaped in shock. Blood poured from his back in a red stream.

He won. William won.

"Damn, that was a fine move!" Richard screamed by her side.

The Hand's agent jerked back, pushing at William with both hands. William's bloody fingers slid off Spider's shoulder. He raised his knife to cut the man's throat, but Spider toppled backward, blond hair spilling, his face a pale mask, and plunged into the black water of the pond. His body vanished in the peat.

William watched it sink. His eyes found Cerise. He smiled, staggered back, and fell.

*No!*

She scrambled up the slope. The slick mud gave under her fingers in handfuls, and then Richard grabbed her and hoisted her up. She caught a root and pulled herself on the slick grass.

William slumped against a tree. Spider's knife lay on his lap. Blood slicked the edge. William looked at her, his hazel eyes soft. His whole side had turned bright red.

Cerise dashed to him. He opened his mouth, trying to say something. Blood gurgled from his lips and spilled on his chin. She sobbed and clutched him to her. More blood poured, wetting her fingers. His pulse fluttered weaker and weaker beneath the fingers she pressed to his neck.

"No," she begged. "No, no, no . . ."

"It's okay," he told her. "Love you."

"Don't die!"

"Sorry. Live. You . . . live."

She kissed his face, his bloody lips, his dirt-smeared cheek. William brushed at her hair with fatigued fingers. His body shuddered. His eyes rolled back in his head.

"You can't leave me like this!"

His heartbeat shivered one last time and vanished like a snuffed-out candle.

The world screeched to a halt, and Cerise skidded through it, lost and alone. A terrible pain tore through her and squeezed her heart in a steel fist. There wasn't enough air to fill her lungs.

*I love you. Don't leave me. Please, please don't leave me.*

Richard's soft voice came from behind her. "He's gone, Cerise."

*No. Not yet.* She struggled to pick him up. Hands took her by her shoulders. "He's dead, Cerise," Ignata whispered. "Let him be."

"No!"

Cerise pushed to her feet, dragging the body up. Richard grasped her shoulders. "Cerise, let go . . ."

"No! Let me!"

"Where are you taking him?"

Frantic, she wrenched herself free. She wasn't thinking at all, her head full of fragmented thoughts and pain, and it took a lot of effort to spit out two words. "The Box."

"That's insane." Ignata blocked her way.

"The Box will heal him. Get out of my way!"

"Even if it does revive him, he will come out mad. He has no protection like you do. He didn't have the remedy!"

"I'll go in there with him."

"Why?"

"The burial shroud in the Box, it will take my fluids and mix them with his. Whatever the remedy did, it's still in me."

Ignata jerked her hands up. "What if you both die? Or he comes out crazy? Richard, help me."

For a long moment Richard froze, caught between them. Then he bent down and picked up William's legs. "She deserves it. Because she deserves to have this one thing go right."

Cerise gripped William's shoulder and together they wrestled the body down the hill. "Help me! Please help me."

Ignata bit her lip and spun to the family gathered below. "Pull the Box ashore!"


WHEN William awoke, the world was red and it hurt. It hurt so much; he panicked and thrashed, trying to break free of the red mist. And then a woman's arms closed around him. He couldn't hear and he couldn't see, but when he brushed her face, he knew it was Cerise and she was crying. He pulled her closer, trying to tell her that it would be okay and they would get out of here, but pain drowned him and he went under.


THE scent of blood permeated the battleground. As Ruh walked along the hill to the black pond, he read the savagery of the fight in the churned mud. Crimson pooling in footsteps, dog tracks, the corpses of murdered clays blended into a vivid, cohesive picture, a map he read and navigated. Here Karmash fell, dragged down by corpses. They lay lifeless now, little more than heaps of bone and rotten tissue. The white-haired brute survived. Somehow he always persevered. Ruh wrinkled his nose at the stench emanating from the decomposing flesh. The peat had preserved the corpses of the thoas, and now, exposed to open air, they rotted at an accelerated rate.

He stepped over Veisan's corpse. Her footprints told her story: violent struggle, lightning-fast attacks, and then a single devastating blow. All that violence rolled into a small package, constantly straining at its fragile wrapper, ready to burst free. She was at peace now.

The enemy had come and gone. The ropes hung abandoned on the cypress. They had taken Spider's treasure with them. No matter. He would find them. None escaped Ruh.

Ruh reached the shore and crouched in the mud, careful not to step on the small spike spheres of magic bombs scattered in the sludge. They weren't his, nor did they belong to anyone from Spider's crew. Tentacles whispered from his shoulder in a rush of ichor. The magic licked the bombs. They tasted foreign. They tasted like the Mirror.

He stared at the mud marks. Interesting. Someone had stripped a body here. The clothes lay in a soggy pile. The bombs must've fallen from the pockets as the clothes were pulled off the corpse. The enemy wasn't above looting the dead. Even the Mirror's dead.

He scooted closer to the black pond and dipped his tentacles into the water. The cilia within them trembled, eager to taste the scents and flavors, but he kept them hidden. They were too fragile for this task.

He sank the tentacles and felt them snake their way through slick water, combing the pond.

Something brushed against them. He held still. A hand gripped them, and through the sensitive tissue, Ruh perceived a familiar taste. Familiar yet odd, as if something wasn't quite right with the magic the person generated. The hand released him.

Ruh withdrew and retrieved a length of rope, still attached to the tree limb. He dropped the end of the rope into the pond and fed it to the black water.

The weight clamped onto the line and Ruh strained to pull it up. His hands slid a little, finding little purchase on the peat-slicked line, but despite his weak grip, the rope slowly coiled at his feet. Finally a head broke the surface, grotesque with its skin and hair blackened. A mouth gaped wide and gulped the air.

Ruh grasped Spider's hand, wrenched him ashore, and crouched as the cell leader rested. The peat-sheathed water had little air in it. A few minutes longer and Spider would've suffocated. Or perhaps drowned was the more appropriate word. Ruh puzzled over it.

"I've made arrangements for the pickup as you've instructed me," he said. "Four operatives will meet us at a creek a mile and a half to the southwest. Through that path." He pointed to the narrow trail that sliced through the hill.

"I can't feel my legs." Spider's voice sounded even.

So that explained the odd taste.

Ruh nodded. "Then I will carry you, m'lord."

"The Box?"

"They've taken it. But I will track it down."

"I know you will . . ." Spider nodded and paused. His eyes focused on something beyond Ruh. "In the bushes," he said softly.

A tentacle slivered from Ruh's shoulder and tasted the air. The scent lanced the cilia on his arm. Animal fur. The stench of urine, unlike any he had encountered. The moist odor of breath, laced with scents of rotting meat. And magic. Strange, contorted, abnormal magic, pulsing with fury.

"It's not an animal," he whispered. His hand found the heavy knife and loosed it from his belt.

He spun around just as the huge shape launched from the top of the hill. It sailed into the open in an impossibly long leap, its tail lashing like a whip. The spiked curve of the spine flexed. Sickle talons rent the air, aiming for Ruh's chest. Too stunned to dodge, he slashed at the horrid jaws, gaping open on the abominable face. The knife sliced deep into the flesh and met bone.

The beast snapped. Triangular teeth bit Ruh's arm. He felt nothing, no tug, no jerk, but suddenly his arm vanished. Blood spurted in a hot fountain from the stump of his elbow. The beast gulped.

An explosion of pain in his shoulder nearly shocked him into unconsciousness. The monster gulped again and turned toward him, paw over paw, blood stretching in long strands from between the yellowed fangs.

Ruh ran. On his third step, a heavy weight smashed into him, crushing him, pinning him down. The world went dark, and Ruh saw the inside of the beast's mouth before the jaws severed his head from his shoulders. Foul stench filled his nostrils. The sticky tongue smothered his face, snuffing out awareness.


SPIDER plunged his hands into the ground and pulled. The hot wedge of pain that sat in the small of his back flared into a blinding daze. He stretched, chancing a glance at the beast. It tore into Ruh's back and flung a piece of bloody meat into the air.

Desperately, Spider stretched. His fingers closed about a spiked sphere. The Mirror's bombs. Probably from William. The irony . . .

The beast growled. The hair on Spider's arms rose. He stifled the instinctual reaction and pushed himself forward, through the pain, to another tiny sphere.

The beast stepped over Ruh's savaged corpse and started toward him.

Pull, flash of pain, bitter taste in the mouth. Three. Now he had three. If three didn't do it . . .

A huge paw sank into the muck next to him. Talons bit into his side and flipped him on his back. He kept the bombs clutched in his fist. The tiny bumps on the surface of the spheres sank in under the pressure of his fingers. The bombs would explode a second after he let them go.

The beast lowered his head. Drool dripped on Spider's chest. He looked at the grotesque face. Red eyes stared back at him, deliberate, smart. They caught him. Mesmerized him. He sank deep into their depths, stunned by their ferocity and intellect and pain. One chance. He had one chance, or it would end right here.

The massive jaws opened wide, wider, cavernous.

"Hello, Vernard," he whispered.

A low groan broke free of the beast's mouth. It stretched into an ululating cry and suddenly shifted into a long coherent word.

"Genevieve . . ."

"I fused her," Spider said. "Took her from your family."

The thing that used to be Vernard Dubois snarled in rage.

"I'll take Cerise, too," Spider promised. "I will kill you, and then I'll find her and take her, too."

The jaws unhinged and plunged down to bite. Spider tossed the bombs into the black throat and shoved himself to the side.

Vernard's head exploded. A wet mist of blood and brains showered Spider's stomach. Thick slabs of meat pelted him. The stump of the body toppled and crashed forward. Spider threw his hands out to shield himself, but the weight was too great, and it plunged on top of him. A wide gap glared where the beast's neck used to be, and as it fell, blood gushed from it in a hot sticky flood, drenching Spider's face.

With sick dread, Spider waited for the body of the beast to glue itself together.

A moment passed.

Another.

Spider strained, gripping the ground. The corpse pinned

him down, and in the wide gash he saw the black, moist sack of the heart still pumping. He reached into the ruined body, ripped out the bulging organ, and bit into its flesh. The blood burned his mouth. He tore the still living flesh with his teeth and forced it down.

If there was any truth in Vernard's journal, the beast's heart would restore him. He choked down another bite and let it go before nausea made him lose it.

Spider clenched his muscles, thrusting himself into agony. His torso slid from under the beast. He dragged his hand across his mouth, wiping away the blood, unable to believe he lived. He breathed in deeply and savored the damp Mire air he so used to hate. It tasted sweet.

Spider rolled to his stomach. A mud field stretched before him, seemingly endless. An eternity away the southwestern path gaped. A mile and a half.

Spider clutched at the ground with dirty fingers and pulled himself six inches forward. Pain lashed him. He caught his breath and pulled again.

# THIRTY

WILLIAM opened his eyes. Wooden boards ran above his head. He blinked. Pain swept through him in a torrent, ripping out a groan. Things swam out of focus.

A door banged. A dim shape thrust into the room. William struck at it, but his arm fell limp.

"It's me, it's me," Gaston's voice said. A hand restrained him.

William snarled.

"Come on now, friend," Zeke's voice said. "You're safe, it's all good. All good. Gaston, slide him back into bed, before he chokes himself. There we go."

"Where is she?"

"Safe," Gaston said. "She's safe."

Alive. Cerise was alive.

A cup bumped against his lips.

"Drink," Zeke said. "You'll feel all better after you drink."

The liquid spilled into his mouth. It tasted vile, bitter, and metallic. William tried to spit it out but somehow it worked its way down his throat into his stomach. Warmth spread through him, dulling the pain.

Slowly his vision returned to normal, and he stared at Gaston kneeling by the bed, his face two inches away.

There was something on his neck. William reached over. His fingers grazed leather.

"Hang on." Zeke reached over and unhooked something, lifting a large dog collar free. "Sorry about that. You went wolf on us a couple of times. Had to keep you put."

William shook his head. His voice came out hoarse. "Where is Cerise?"

"She had to go home," Gaston said.

"Where am I?" He tried to rise, but they clamped him down.

"Settle down," Zeke told him. "I will explain everything to you, but you've got to lie still or we'll tie your ass to the bed. You got me?"

Fine. William lay back down.

"They brought you to me four days ago. They had you in some sort of casket, and you were barely breathing. Apparently you were hurt bad, and whatever the casket did kept you alive, but you weren't getting any better. Cerise said that we had to get you to the Weird because the Mire didn't have enough magic, and if we left you where you were, you'd die."

They put him in the Box. He'd died. He remembered dying and the mist and then nothing.

"We didn't have a lot of time," Zeke said. "You were hanging by a thread. The Hand's freaks were still after the Mars, and we had to move fast. There is only one way out of the Mire into the Weird and that's through Louisiana. We had to grease the Border Guard's hand. It took everything I had and all the money the Mars had. Wiped us out clean, but we got you and the kid out, because she didn't trust me alone. I better get reimbursed for this. We're in Louisiana now, in the country, in one of the Mirror's safe houses."

Zeke reached to the table and lifted a square of lined paper. "Here. She wrote you a note."

William clenched the paper in his hand, focusing on it with all of his will. The tiny scribbles solidified into words.

*I love you so much. I'm so sorry, I can't go with you. There are only fifteen adults left, and most of them are hurt. The Hand's freaks ran after you killed Spider, but they keep coming back. We've been attacked twice, and we don't have enough money to get everyone over the border. I have to stay behind to protect the kids and Lark.*

*Live, William. Get better, get strong again, and find me if you can. Even if I never see you again, I regret nothing. I only wish we had more time.*

He read it again. And again. It didn't say anything different.

He would find her again. But before he did that, he had to make her safe from everyone. Her and her whole damn family. Until he saved the lot of them, they would never let her go.

The kid raised a cup and held it up to his mouth. "You need more of this tea."

"No." Every word was an effort. "The Box?"

"He broke it," Zeke said in disgust. "Shattered the thing to pieces. When I woke up, it was burning."

"Cerise told me to." Gaston bumped the cup against William's lips. "She said for you to drink this. It's good for you. It will make you better."

"No."

Gaston's face radiated grim determination. "You don't have to like it. You have to drink it. Don't make me hold your nose closed."

William cursed and drank. There was only one man who could help him now. He had to get stronger so he could travel, and if it meant he had to chug the vomit-inducing tea, he would do it.

By evening, he managed to keep down some broth. The next day he sat up, two days later he walked, and two days after that, he and Gaston crossed the border between Louisiana and Adrianglia, heading north.

"WOW." Gaston gaped at the two-story mansion, situated on a perfectly manicured lawn. "Wow. Is that all one house?"

William grumbled. Gaston had never set foot out of the swamp. The entire way through the Weird, the kid would stare at things in amazement, get embarrassed, and then try to be a smart-ass about it. It was getting old.

"Who lives here?"

"Earl Declan Camarine, Marshal of the Southern Provinces."

"Are we going to get arrested?"

"No."

"Are you sure?"

William growled at him.

A window on the second floor burst in an explosion of glittering shards. A body hurled through it and a boy dropped into a half crouch onto the balcony rail, his crazy auburn hair blazing with red streaks like a shock of dark flame. Wild yellow eyes stared at William from a narrow face. The kid looked at least a foot taller than he remembered.

"Jack!" Rose's voice called.

Jack's eyes flared with feral fire. He hissed and leaped off the balcony, changing in mid-jump, shredding his clothes. A spotted adolescent lynx landed into the green grass and took off at a dead run, heading toward the trees.

Wouldn't be able to pull it off in the Edge, William reflected. In the Edge, changing shapes took a few seconds, but in the Weird with magic full force, you could go furry with no pain on the fly. Jack spilled out of his clothes quickly. No pause, no awkwardness. The kid had practice going from dressed to furry. "Jack!" Rose ran out onto the balcony. She wore a peach-colored gown and her hair was up. "Jack, wait! Damn it."

She saw them below. Her eyes widened.

"I'm here to see Declan," William told her.

Two minutes later he sat in Declan's study. He'd left Gaston with Rose, who took him to the kitchen. The kid ate like a horse.

Declan looked at him from behind the desk. He hadn't changed a bit: same hard eyes, same blond hair. Except he was growing it out again. He grew it long every few years to use as a power resource in case he had to sacrifice a part of himself to magic. Where William was leaner and taller, Declan looked like he could punch through walls. Judging by the look in his eyes, he wouldn't mind bashing his fist against a few bricks.

Declan surveyed him. "Doing well?"

"Yeah."

"Looking kind of thin there. My mother's always looking for a new diet. Maybe you can share some tips?"

William bared his teeth. "Yeah. Shouldn't you be all fat by now? Is that some flab on your sides?"

"Fuck you."

They looked at each other.

"Two fucking years." Declan spread his hands. "Two fucking years you're gone without a word. So. What can the Office of Marshal do for you?"

William unclenched his teeth. It killed him to say it. "I need help."

Declan nodded. "Tell me about it."

Half an hour later William finished. It would've taken less time, but two minutes into the story he'd mentioned Nancy Virai, and Declan had turned pale and taken a big square bottle of Southern bourbon out of the cabinet. The bottle was half-empty now.

"So let me get it straight." Declan leaned forward. "You've got the journal."

"Not on me."

Declan rolled his eyes. "Give me some credit. You do have it, though?"

"Yes."

"Chances are, the girl's father is still in Kasis. Once what's left of Spider's flunkies report back to their home office, the Hand will come after her, and they will want to use him as leverage. You want to save her, but she left you. And if you don't give the journal to the Mirror, they will skin you alive. You want to get the girl and what's left of her family out of the Mire, but you can't do it through the border with the Broken, because they have too much magic. Have I got it right?"

"Yeah, pretty much."

Declan nodded his blond head and gulped more bourbon. "I'll need a favor in return."

Figured. "What is it?"

"Jack. He's a good kid, but . . . he needs guidance. He needs understanding and I can't give it to him because I have no idea what goes on in his head."

William nodded. "Fine. I'll help with Jack. I would've anyway."

"I know, but you hate to owe anyone. This way we're even."

Declan pulled a copper sphere from the corner of his desk and tapped it. The sphere cracked in the middle. The two halves slid apart, revealing a pale crystal. A spark of light flared within the crystalline depths and streamed in a ray of light to form a map six inches above the sphere.

*"Louisiana. Border. Mire."* Declan pronounced the words with crisp exactness. The map centered on the green blob of the Mire where it touched the border of the Louisiana.

*"Kasis,"* Declan said.

The map remained where it was.

"Blasted thing. *Kasis Castle.*"

The map slid to the Adrianglian border. A small dot of white glow flared on the boundary and grew into a gray castle. Declan scowled at it. "I've had a run-in with Antoine de Kasis before. The de Kasis family has treaties in place with both the Gauls and us that keep them out of our border squabbles. They were put in place a century ago due to some classified service the family provided to both Louisiana and Adrianglia. I never could find out what exactly they did. The treaties forbid any sort of military action on their land. The price of this sweet deal is complete neutrality from the Kasis family: they can't aid either Louisiana or Adrianglia."

William nodded. "I wondered why the Mirror didn't just walk me into the Mire through Kasis. Now I know."

"There is another reason. Antoine de Kasis is dirty. He's a Louisiana sympathizer, and he's very useful to them. His lands are the only way into the Mire without the bother of dealing with the Louisiana border guard. The Mirror has to suspect he's dirty, because if I know, they definitely know. However, they lack proof of his involvement. If they're holding the girl's father there, it's likely he's guarded by the Hand's agents, which would implicate Antoine. The Mirror won't like invading Kasis for two reasons. First, they know Antoine is dirty and they observe him in order to gather intelligence on the Hand's movements. If they take him out, there goes their chance to spy on the Hand. Second, if the Hand isn't there for some reason and if the Mirror's agents don't find any clear-cut proof of Antoine's involvement with the Gauls, invading Kasis would cause an international incident of huge proportions."

William nodded again. "I have it figured out. I will use the journal as leverage."

"That's a really dangerous game to play," Declan said. "If you get burned, William, there is nothing any of us can do."

"Thanks, Dad."

"My job is to warn. Here is the interesting thing. According to the treaties, if de Kasis is found to have violated his agreements, the realm that proves his wrongdoing gets to confiscate his lands. There isn't much land there, but whatever there is will become the property of Adrianglia. You need to buy that land from the government. They wouldn't sell it to you normally, so you have to make that part of your deal with the Mirror. It will give you access to the Mire, and you can smuggle your girl and her family out."

William exhaled. "So all I need is to get the money to buy the place. Borrow it, steal it . . ."

Declan stared at him.

"What?"

Declan braided the fingers of his hands. "*Borrow* it?"

William shrugged.

"When Casshorn died, his possessions passed to you. You're his adopted son and his only heir. You own two castles, half of the Darkwood, a forty-mile stretch of Darron River, for the use of which you charge the shipping companies a sizable toll, and the land on which the city of Blueshire sits. They pay you rent. Why the devil would you need to borrow the money, you dumb bastard? You're richer than I am."

William's brain screeched to a halt.

Declan got up. "While you had your two-year-long pity party and hid out in a shitty trailer, playing with your toys and drinking beer, I had to take care of your financials. And if you think I don't have my own shit to deal with, you're sadly mistaken." He pulled several large ledgers from the shelf and dropped them in a stack on the table. "There you go. All yours now, Lord William Sandine. Have a go at it. Don't spend it all in one place and hire somebody good with money to manage it for you."

WILLIAM sat alone in the silence of Declan's library. It had been twenty-four hours since he made the call to Erwin through Declan's scryer unit. He'd outlined the details of the deal. Erwin said nothing. He simply bowed and severed the connection.

Declan insisted on both him and the kid staying in the manor, reasoning that if the Mirror didn't like the deal, they would be more reluctant to rain hellfire and meteorites upon the house of the Marshal. He even deployed his most effective weapon, in case things went really sour—two hours after the scrying took place, the carriage of the Duchess of the Southern Provinces pulled up to the front gates. William had met the Duchess before. He would rather go up barehanded against a rabid bear.

The ache inside his chest gnawed on him. It started when he woke up and found out Cerise had left him. Over the next few days it grew stronger and stronger. She had left him. The rational part of him reassured him that she had done it to save him. But the rational part of him grew weaker and weaker. She had left him. Like so many people before. Even if everything went his way, even if he managed to pull it off, she could still walk away from him. And there wouldn't be a damn thing he could do about it.

He got up and stepped onto the balcony. The sun was slowly setting. They would serve dinner soon—he could smell it from the kitchen.

Voices came from below. William leaned over and looked down. Three kids, George's blond head, Jack's auburn mane, and Gaston's closely cropped hair. He'd barely seen the kids since he arrived. By the time he and Declan had hammered out and delivered the terms of the deal, he was dead on his feet and he passed out for about twelve hours.

"So what are you?" Jack asked, aggression vibrating in his voice.

This ought to be interesting.

"Are you like William's kid or something?" Jack asked.

"Leave it alone," George said, his voice calm.

Gaston leaned back a bit. "Who's asking?"

This wouldn't go well

"What do you mean, who's asking? I'm asking. Are you that stupid? What are you, some kind of inbred hick?"

"Here we go," George muttered.

Gaston shrugged. "I tell you what, run along. I have no time for spoiled rich babies."

"Yeah?"

"Yeah."

Jack lunged forward. He was fast, but not faster than George, who stepped out of the way half a second before Jack struck. Gaston threw his hand up, and Jack ran face-first into his fist.

That had to hurt. William winced. Gaston had fists like

hammers. He wasn't quite sure what to do with them yet, but Jack wasn't hard to stop. He all but threw himself.

Jack spun from the impact. A low feline growl tore from his mouth.

Okay, that was about enough of that. William hopped over the balcony and landed between them. The jump almost took him off his legs. He was still too weak, but the kids didn't know it.

William looked the boys over. In two years George had grown taller and filled out. He'd never be bulky, but he was no longer thin and sickly. His pale hair was cut in the same manner as Declan's when Declan kept it short. His clothes were meticulously clean.

Jack wore a ripped-up shirt. His nose was bleeding. His eyes shone every time he turned his head. The kid was strung up too high.

"What the hell are you doing?" William asked.

Jack wiped the blood from his nose. "Nothing."

"Why the hell would you run at him? He outweighs you by sixty pounds."

Jack looked away.

"He's also taller than you by eight inches. First order of business—make him shorter."

William dropped down and swiped with his leg, knocking Jack's feet out from under him. The kid was fast, but he wasn't paying attention. His legs went one way, his head went the other. He fell into the grass and bounced back up, hissing like a pissed-off cat.

"Your turn," William said. "Go for it."

Jack lunged at Gaston's legs. Gaston tensed and jumped, catching the lower branch of an oak.

Jack rolled up. "What the hell?"

"Did you expect him to stand still for you?"

Gaston grinned.

"Go on," William said. "Try to get to higher ground."

Jack scrambled up the tree, trying to get a drop on the older kid. They squared off in the branches, kicking and talking shit.

William and George watched them.

"How have you been, George?"

"Good, thank you. I'm really glad you are back," George said. "Will you stay?"

"I don't know."

George sighed and for a moment he looked just like the weak, pale kid William had met two years ago. "I wish you would stay," the boy said. "It would be better for everyone. Especially Jack."


THE dining room was huge, William reflected. His whole house would fit into it. It was also mostly empty. The Duchess had pulled Rose away to her rooms for some sort of female reason, and it was only Declan, him, and the kids sitting at the enormous table.

George sliced his food with surgical precision, as if he'd spent the entire two years in the Weird taking etiquette lessons. He was meticulously clean. Both Gaston and Jack were filthy, smeared with dirt and covered with scratches. Jack had stuffed some wadded paper up his nose—Gaston had tapped him again—while his ward sported a shiner where Jack managed to kick him.

"What happened?" Declan asked.

Jack bared his teeth at him. "We fell."

"Together?" Declan said.

Gaston looked at his plate.

"Tell him," William said.

"He made a comment about hicks. Then I made a comment about spoiled babies. Then he ran into my fist and we had words."

Declan looked at Jack. "Why the hell would you run at him? Should've gone for the legs."

Jack opened his mouth.

Nancy Virai walked through the door.

Declan choked on his steak.

Erwin followed Nancy, wearing the familiar apologetic smile.

William started to get up.

"Don't rise on my account."

Declan rose anyway and bowed. "Lady V. What a pleasure. Please sit down."

Erwin stepped out from behind Nancy and held out a chair. She sat, and he positioned himself behind her chair.

Nancy's sharp eyes fastened on William. "If you are wrong, the assault of Kasis will cause a diplomatic mess."

"I'm not wrong," William said.

"Ten years. That's my price for this foolishness."

William blinked. "Ten years?"

Nancy rested one long leg over the other. "If I do this for you, the Mirror will have the use of your services for ten years. And of course, you will turn the journal over to us."

"Don't do it," Declan cut in.

Nancy turned to him. Her raptor eyes stared at him for a second. "The Mirror appreciates Earl Camarine's zeal in offering advice to his friend. However, from where I am sitting, it seems that Lord Sandine is, in fact, wearing his big-boy pants, as they say in the Broken. He's capable of making that decision on his own. Yes or no, William?"

"Gustave lives and I get to take the Mars out of the Mire. They will receive Adrianglian citizenship."

Nancy tilted her head. "Does the girl mean that much to you?"

He bared his teeth at her. "Take it or leave it, Nancy."

"No," Declan repeated.

Nancy smiled. George drew back. Jack hissed.

"You have your deal. Earl Camarine, the wards of the House of Camarine, and the ward of the House of Sandine, will bear witnesses to this agreement on their honor."

Declan dragged his hand across his face.

"I understand the Duchess is in residence," Nancy said.

"Yes," Declan nodded. "She would be sorely disappointed if you left without speaking to her."

Nancy smiled again. "I wouldn't dream of it."

*  *  *

**WILLIAM** left for Kasis the next morning, Gaston with
him. Declan decided to come at the last minute. It felt
off, William reflected. Almost as if they were back in
the Legion.

Before they left, Jack came by his room. He looked
younger somehow, timid and dejected. "Are you coming
back?"

William nodded. "Eventually."

"Okay, then." Jack opened his mouth to say something and closed it.

"How's it going?" William asked.

Jack looked at his feet. "I don't want to go to Hawk's."

Fury flashed through William. "Are they talking about
sending you there?"

Jack shook his head. "No. Just . . . I can't do anything
right. It's always Jack, Jack, Jack. Jack ruined that and
Jack broke this. I'm trying, but it's not working."

"You won't have to go to Hawk's," William said. "If
it comes to that, I'll take you with me."

Jack froze. "Promise."

"I promise."

"Don't take too long to come back."

"I won't." William reached over to the table, to a basket of snacks someone left in his room, plucked out a
square of chocolate wrapped in foil, and handed it to
Jack.

"A smart kid once told me it helps," he said. "Wait for
me and don't do anything stupid."


**FIVE** days later William stood on the balcony of Kasis
Castle and looked over the vast field of cypresses dripping silvery moss. Just two miles south, the boundary
offered passage to the Mire.

The attack on Kasis had taken less than an hour. Four
of the Hand's agents were killed in the Keep, and Erwin's

people found enough damaging papers to keep them happy for months. Nobody in their right mind could claim that de Kasis was neutral.

Antoine de Kasis died resisting apprehension. He didn't resist very much, William reflected. He'd been pissed off and hurting, and de Kasis died under his knife before offering any real resistance.

Two hours later William traded the deed to Kasis for the copy of the journal. The journal was missing a couple of crucial pages, but his memory wasn't *that* perfect and most of the research was there and Nancy was pleased. If she suspected he held anything back, she didn't let it show.

While William exchanged the journal for the deed, Erwin briefed Gustave and escorted him back home, with a detachment of the Mirror's agents to keep the Mars safe during their evacuation. It was better this way, William reflected. He wasn't sure what the man would think of him.

Three days had passed now with no word from Cerise. She was only a day away in the Mire. He'd done everything he could. She couldn't be with him because of the threat to her family. He had taken care of it. William grimaced. He'd thought about going back to the Rathole, but decided against it. He knew the way she thought. If he showed up, after saving her father and her family, she would have to be with him whether she liked it or not. So he sat here, alone, and waited. Waited for her to decide if she wanted him or if she didn't.


SHE came to him in his dreams. Her face was smudged, but he knew it was her, because he could smell her scent and hear her voice, soothing, calling his name. When he awoke, the wild inside him snarled and howled, abandoned, hurting, and so alone he wondered if he would go mad. So every morning he came to the damn balcony and stared at the Mire. It wasn't up to him anymore. All he could do was wait.

CERISE raised her face from her arms. Outside night had fallen on the Mire. Familiar quick steps ran up the stairs leading to her hideout.

"Can I come in?" her father asked from the stairway.

She nodded.

He came and sat in a chair across from her. He was thinner than she remembered. Older. He'd been home for almost two weeks now, and she still woke up convinced that he was missing.

"The packing is almost done," he said. "We're leaving the Mire the day after tomorrow."

She looked away. She'd packed nothing.

"Do you need help with your things?" he asked.

"I'm not going."

Gustave frowned, wrinkles gathering on his forehead. "So you plan to abandon all of us? Grandma, your cousins, me. Sophie."

Cerise glanced at the soft chair, where Lark curled up, asleep.

She didn't have an answer, so she just looked away.

"Tell me about it," he said.

She shook her head. "No."

"Do you think I wouldn't understand?" he asked softly. "They took your mother away from me. Ripped her out of my hands. That was the last time I saw her, terrified, dragged away. I know what it feels like, Ceri. I do."

She swallowed. "He didn't come for me. I love him. I thought he loved me, but he didn't come for me."

"Maybe you should go to him," he said gently. "He might be waiting."

She shook her head. "I talked to the Mirror's people. He lied to me again, Papa. He told me he had nothing, but apparently he's rich. He's related to the Marshal of the

Southern Provinces. It's a big deal, from what they say. He told me he was a bounty hunter, that he was normal, that he had nothing, and I believed him. Why is it I always believe him? Am I stupid?"

"Men lie for many reasons," Gustave said. "Perhaps he wanted to make sure that you love him for who he is, not for his money."

"He told me he loved me, too. How do I know it's not another lie?"

Gustave sighed. "The man came to get me out of Kasis. He didn't owe that to us, Ceri. He came for me because I'm your father."

She shook her head. "He knows where the house is. It would take him a day to get down here. If he wanted to, he would be here already. He's changed his mind, Papa. He decided he doesn't want me, and I'm not going to beg. I won't be showing up on his doorstep in all of my Mire glory, asking him to come and lift me from the mud. I have some damn pride left."

Gustave sighed. "I want you to start packing tomorrow."

She didn't answer. What was the point of talking anyway?

He sighed again and left. Cerise waited until he closed the door and then cried quietly, curled up in her chair.


ANOTHER gray day. The view from the balcony looked much the same.

William shook his head. She wasn't coming. He had to clench his teeth and move on.

Steps echoed behind him. One of Declan's deputy marshals, on loan until William could get his own people sorted out. He had no idea how to do that.

"M'lord, Gustave Mar is here."

*Great.* "Show him in, please."

A few moments later Gustave joined him on the balcony. Lean, dark. Like Cerise. Same eyes, same posture.

Gustave bowed.

"Don't," William told him. "Here." He pulled a chair from the small picnic table and sat in the other chair himself. "What can I do for you?"

"I came to thank you for saving my family. And for helping Genevieve and sparing my daughter that burden. I don't know what is proper to say, but I want you to know, I'm grateful. If you need me, I'll be there. All of us will be there."

William nodded, uncomfortable. "Thank you."

They looked at each other. Silence stretched.

"A drink?" William asked.

Gustave exhaled. "Yes."

William went inside and brought out a bottle of wine and two glasses. He filled the glasses. Gustave sampled his. "Good wine."

"Not as strong as the one at your house."

"Ahh, yes. I will miss that. We may have to make excursions into the Mire to gather the berries."

"Better bring a small army," William said.

Gustave grimaced. They drained their glasses and William refilled them.

"How's the moving going?" William said to say something.

"Good," Gustave said. "A bit slow. There are only fifteen able-bodied adults left, and half of them are injured. Cerise is doing the best she can. We should be about done. The end of this week will be our last dinner at the house. We would be honored if you joined us. We're easy to find from here—just follow the river. I know it would mean a lot to my daughter."

"She doesn't want to see me," William said.

Gustave rubbed his face. "You're right. She doesn't want to see you. That's why, ever since I've returned, my daughter is snarling at everyone and everything. She's not sleeping. She is not eating. And let's not forget the crying. She never was a crier. Even as a child."

"What are you saying?"

Gustave rose. "I'm saying that my daughter thinks you've abandoned her. She thinks that you don't want her anymore, that it's all over, and it's breaking her heart. She is too proud to come and beg, and I have gathered that you are too proud to come and get her. The Hand and the feud ripped away my wife, William. She was my life . . . my everything. They almost destroyed my family. I hate to stand by and watch this cursed mess crush my daughter as well. Think on it. Please."

He left.

Ten minutes later William left for the Mire.


THE Rathole was as he remembered, William decided, flicking his furry ears. He lay downwind of the house by the roots of a large pine. He'd gone to ground here for about an hour. The Mirror's people guarding the house spotted him but let him be.

Cerise was inside.

He kept trying to catch her scent, but it just wasn't there.

If he went in and she told him to leave . . . He wasn't sure he would. He didn't know what the hell he wanted. All his plans ended with "Get to the house." Now he was at the house, and he wasn't sure what to do about it.

The screen door opened. Lark ran down the steps. She wore jeans. Her shirt was clean and her hair was brushed out. She carried a stack of clothes in her hands.

She turned and headed straight for him.

William sank deep into shadows under the pine trying to look smaller.

She stopped a few feet away. "I can see you, you know. You're as big as a horse."

William whined at her. *Go away, kid.*

Lark put the clothes on the ground. "She's in the inner yard. Dad said you can go around over there through the door in the side, so you don't have to go through the whole place."

She turned and left. William sighed and pulled the wild deep inside him. Pain racked his bones and then he was human again. He slid his clothes on and went to the side door, through the hallway, and into the inner yard.

The flowers still bloomed in the small garden along the wall. The weapon rack was out, and past it, Cerise practiced just as she had on that morning four weeks ago. All that was missing were Kaldar and Gaston chatting on the sidelines and Grandmother Az perched on the stone bench.

Cerise's blade sliced through the air with refined grace. So beautiful . . . So, so beautiful. So fast and deadly and . . .

She saw him. Her cuts gained a new vicious edge.

He had to be smart about this, but he didn't know what to say. He would do anything if she still wanted him.

"Hello, Lord Sandine," she said. "Thank you for saving my father. We owe you a debt."

William strode to the weapon rack and chose a seneschal blade. It was the biggest, longest, heaviest sword on the rack. It would take him ages to swing it.

Cerise battled the air with lithe quickness, still preternaturally fast in her strikes.

William cleared his throat. She turned and looked at him.

"A deal," he said. "We fight. If you win, I'll walk out of here and never bother you again. If I win, you'll come away with me. You'll be my mate and you will live with me always."

He almost cursed. *Smooth, right.*

Her sword pointed at him. Cerise looked at his weapon. "You'll lose. I'll slice you to ribbons."

William swung his bulky sword, warming up his wrist. "That's fine."

"You are a stupid, stupid wolf."

"Less talk, more fighting."

They clashed in a clang of steel.

Cerise dropped her blade and threw her arms around his neck.

# EPILOGUE

CERISE sipped her tea. The morning was gray and a little damp. The night left some dew on the wicker chairs sitting on the balcony and it was making her jeans wet, but she didn't care. She liked sitting like this, early in the morning.

The woods here came almost right to the house. These were real woods, thick oaks and maples and pines. From her perch she could see clear across the lawn to where the trees started. Somewhere out there William prowled. He liked to take off early in the morning and hunt. The house grated on him a little. He would've preferred a much smaller place and so would she, but this was the only house among Casshorn's holdings that was close enough to Declan's manor. It would be all right. They would make it into a home eventually. Or just build a smaller place. She did kind of like the huge stone balcony. And the pool was nice. Gaston loved it to pieces. But a smaller place would be better.

Cerise sipped her tea. So nice and quiet. Yesterday the four kids—Lark, Gaston, George, and Jack—had gotten ahold of some Rollerblades, specially made for them by someone in Declan's family. They had themselves a race down the long marble hallway, and then somehow it turned into a brawl, the way it usually did.

The kids were at Declan and Rose's today. Cerise first met Declan and Rose about two months ago. Lark and the boys hit it off right away, and Declan and William were friends, but she wasn't that wild about meeting Rose. For one thing, William had liked her at some point.

He was hers now. Her wolf. Cerise smiled. Still, when she first saw Rose, it didn't help either. Rose was taller than her by about four inches. Her hair was honey brown and perfectly styled, her gown looked expensive, and she was pretty. Too pretty.

Cerise had worn jeans, a white blouse, and she'd left her hair down because William liked it that way.

The kids went one way, the men went the other, and Cerise had to sit with Rose on the terrace.

"So you're from the Mire in the Edge?" Rose said after a while.

"Yes."

"That's why the jeans?"

"Well, I tried a gown," Cerise said. "I looked very nice in it. I wore it long enough to take a picture, and then I took it off. It looks very pretty hanging in a closet."

Rose looked at her. "Will you excuse me?"

"Sure."

About five minutes later Rose came out wearing a pair of threadbare jeans and a T-shirt and carrying two bottles of beer. "I've been saving them. They're from the Broken."

She popped the tops and passed one over to Cerise. They clinked beer necks and drank.

The boys and Lark disappeared into the trees.

"My youngest brother killed a lynx yesterday," Rose said. "Apparently it came into his territory and left some spray marks. He skinned it, smeared himself in its blood, and put its pelt on his shoulders like a cape. And that's how he came dressed for breakfast."

Cerise drank some beer. "My sister kills small animals and hangs their corpses on a tree, because she thinks she is a monster and she's convinced we'll eventually banish her from the house. They're her rations. Just in case."

Rose blinked. "I see. I think we're going to get along just fine, don't you?"

"I think so, yes."

And somehow they did. Now they had a babysitting arrangement: one weekend Rose had the kids and one weekend she did. She didn't mind. Jack was a small feral William. He was trouble, but he was a good kid. He worshipped William, and Lark and he were like two peas in a pod. She couldn't quite figure out George yet. He was very quiet and polite, but once in a while his eyes would light up and he'd say something really funny. It was almost like there were two Georges: the well-mannered version and the hidden wry one who lived to make trouble.

But today they were gone, off to Rose and Declan's. Which meant that this morning she and William would be alone in the house.

A black wolf burst from the forest and charged the house. Cerise smiled.

The wolf changed in mid-leap, turning into a very naked William. She craned her neck a little to get a better look. Mmmm . . . He vanished below the balcony. A moment later William swung himself over the balcony rail and flopped in the chair next to her, still stark naked and slightly sweaty.

She looked at him through half-closed eyes. "You're lucky the kids aren't here."

He leaned over, his eyes wild. "But the kids are gone. We can have a nice lazy breakfast and then we can nap."

"We just got up."

"You just got up. I've been up for hours." He leaned over and kissed her lips. She tasted him, smelled the light musk of his sweat. His tongue explored her mouth, and when they broke apart for a breath, she had to remind herself that taking her clothes off on the balcony wasn't a good idea.

"You're right, we should take a nap," she told him.

He grinned at her.

A sharp forlorn cry rolled above them. She looked up and saw a small blue speck rapidly growing bigger.

"What's that?"

William swore. "That would be an Air Force wyvern. A small one."

The speck grew into a huge scaled creature, a cross between a dinosaur and a dragon, sheathed in blue and white feathers. Enormous wings churned the air and the wyvern touched down in the middle of the lawn. A small cabin perched on the back of the wyvern.

Cerise took a towel off the table and thrust it at William. He looked at her like she was crazy.

"Cover yourself."

"Why?"

"Because most men don't stand there with their stuff hanging out for all to see."

William wrapped the cloth around his hips.

The wyvern lay down. The cabin door opened and a man jumped out.

William growled.

"Who is that?"

"That's Erwin."

Erwin came up to the house and waved at them. "Lord Sandine. The Mirror requires your services."

They wanted him to go spy. He would be off in danger on his own. Her throat constricted. No. They hadn't had nearly enough time together.

"I'll go get dressed," William growled.

"Both of you, m'lord."

"I get to go?" Cerise jumped to her feet.

"Yes, my lady. That is, unless you refuse. Lord Sandine is bound by our agreement, but you are—"

"Save it," she told him. "I'll be right there. Let me just get my sword."

Read on for an exciting excerpt from
the next Kate Daniels novel

# MAGIC SLAYS

by Ilona Andrews

Coming June 2011
from Ace Books!

I sat in my new office, between my enchanted saber and a stack of bills, and contemplated my sanity. Right now it was very much in question.

The amount of money I didn't have was shocking.

The world's pulse skipped a beat. The twisted tubes of feylanterns in the walls of my office faded to black. The ward that guarded the building vanished. Something buzzed in the wall, and the electric floor lamp on the left blinked and snapped to life, illuminating my desk with a warm yellow glow. I reached over and turned it off. The electric bill was killing me.

Magic had drained from the world, and technology had once again gained the upper hand. People called it the post-Shift resonance. Magic came and went as it pleased, flooding the world like a tsunami, dragging bizarre monsters into our reality, stalling engines, jamming guns, eating tall buildings, and vanishing again without warning. Nobody knew when it would assault us or how long each wave would last. Eventually magic would win this war, but for now technology was putting up one hell of a fight, and we were stuck in the middle, struggling to rebuild a half-ruined world according to new rules.

Lots of people found ways to make money off the magic chaos. First, there was the Mercenary Guild. Mercs cleared magic hazmat for the right price and asked no questions. I had been a member of the Guild for more years than I cared to admit, and although I was still a merc and carried a Guild card with my name, Kate Daniels,

printed on it in pretty letters, I hadn't worked full-time
for the Guild in over a year.

Then, there was the Order of Merciful Aid. The Order
offered to help everyone, rich and poor, criminal and
law-abiding citizen—as long as they were human. Once
you entered into a contract with the knights, you gave
them broad, sweeping authority over your life to dig as
deeply as they needed to resolve the problem. The Order
was feared and respected, and I had worked for it as well.
I never made a full-fledged knight. One had to graduate
from the Academy to do that, and I had dropped out. The
best I managed to become was an agent, a half-assed
knight, with all of the responsibility but only a fraction
of the authority. Still I had a good run there and got to
help some people along the way. But the Order had its
own agenda: the survival of the human race at any cost.
It turned out that our definitions of human didn't match.
I quit.

Two months after my fall from the Order's grace, I
started my own business, Cutting Edge Investigations,
bankrolled by the shapeshifter Pack. The shapeshifters
had advanced me a very large loan in return for a slice of
my currently nonexistent profits. I took out an ad in a
newspaper, I put the word out on the street, the office
had been open for a month, and so far nobody had hired
me to do anything.

I'd thought I had built a decent reputation in Atlanta.
Apparently, not decent enough to drum up any business.
If things kept going this way, I would be forced to run up
and down the street screaming, "We kill things for money."
Maybe someone would take pity and throw some change
at me.

The phone rang. I stared at it. You never know. It could
be a trick.

The phone rang again. I picked it up. "Cutting Edge."

"Kate," a dry voice vibrated with urgency.

Long time no kill. "Hello, Ghastek." And what would
Atlanta's premier Master of the Dead want with me?

The Masters of the Dead piloted vampires. When a victim of *Immortuus* pathogen died, his mind and ego died with him, leaving only a shell of the body: superstrong, superfast, lethal, and ruled by bloodlust. The Masters of the Dead grabbed hold of that empty mind and drove the vampire like a remote-controlled car. They dictated the vampire's every twitch; they saw through its eyes, heard through its ears, and spoke through its mouth. In the hands of an exceptional navigator, a vampire was the stuff of human nightmares.

Riding vampire minds was a well-paying business. Ghastek, like 90 percent of navigators, worked for the People, a cringe-worthy hybrid of a cult, business corporation, and research facility. I hated the People with a passion, and I hated Roland, the man who led them, even more.

Unfortunately, beggars couldn't be choosers. "What can I do for you?"

"A loose vampire is heading your way."

Crap. Only the will of the navigator kept a vampire in check. Without that restraint, an insatiable hunger drove the bloodsuckers to slaughter. A loose vampire would massacre anything it came across. It could kill a dozen people in half a minute. The city would be a bloodbath.

"What do you need?"

"I'm less than twelve miles behind her. I need you to delay her, until I come into range."

"From which direction?"

"Northwest. And Kate, try not to damage her. She's expensive . . ."

I dropped the phone and dashed outside, bursting into almost painfully cold air. People filled the street—laborers, shoppers, random passersby hurrying home. Food to be slaughtered. I sucked in a lungful of cold and screamed. "Vampire! Loose vampire! Run!"

For a fraction of a second nothing happened, and then people scattered like fish before a shark. In a breath I was alone.

A thick chain lay coiled on the side of the building. I used it to block my parking lot at night so weirdos wouldn't park there. Perfect.

I ran inside and swiped the keys off the hook on the wall.

Two seconds to the parking lot.

A second to unlock the padlock securing the chain.

Too slow. I ran, dragging the chain behind me, and dropped it before an old tree.

Three seconds to loop the chain around the trunk and work the other end into a slip knot.

I needed blood to bait the vamp. Lots and lots of blood.

A team of oxen turned the corner. I ran at them, pulling a throwing knife . The driver, an older Latino man, stared at me. His hand reached for a rifle lying on the seat next to him.

"Get off! Loose vampire!"

He scrambled out of the cart. I sliced a long shallow gash down the ox's flank. It bellowed. Blood dripped on the ground. I ran my hand along the cut. It came off wet with hot crimson, and I waved it, flinging red drops into the wind.

The ox moaned. I grabbed the chain loop.

An emaciated shape leapt off the rooftop. Ropes of muscle knotted its frame under skin so tight that every ligament and vein stood out beneath it. The vampire landed on the pavement on all fours, skidded, its long sickle claws scraping the asphalt with a screech, and whirled. Ruby eyes glared at me from a horrible face. Massive jaws gaped open, showing sharp fangs, bone white against the black mouth.

The vampire charged.

It all but flew above the ground with preternatural speed, straight at the ox, pulled by the intoxicating scent of blood.

I thrust myself into its path, my heartbeat impossibly slow in my ears.

The vamp's eyes fixed on my bloody hand. I'd have only one shot at this.

The vampire leaped, covering the few feet between us. It flew, limbs out, claws raised for the kill.

I thrust the chain loop up and over its head.

Its body hit me. The impact knocked me off my feet. I crashed to the ground and rolled upright. The vamp lunged at me. The chain snapped taut on its throat, jerking it off the pavement. The bloodsucker fell and sprang up again, twisting and jerking on the end of the chain like a feral cat caught in a dog catcher's leash.

The ox bellowed in pain. I breathed, short and shallow.

The vampire flipped and lunged in the ox's direction. The tree shook and groaned. Blood spurted from under the chain on its neck. Either it would snap the tree or the chain would slice its throat.

The bloodsucker threw itself at the ox again and fell to the ground, its leap aborted by the chain. It picked itself up and sat. Intelligence flooded into its burning red eyes. The huge jaws unhinged and Ghastek's voice came forth.

"A chain?"

"You're welcome," I growled, fighting the urge to bend over in relief. Ghastek must've gotten close enough to grab the bloodsucker's mind. "I had to cut an ox to get the vamp fixed on me. The bill is all yours."

"Of course."

You bet your ass, of course. An ox cost about a grand. A vampire, especially one as old as this one, went for about thirty times that. And Ghastek didn't even have to buy a new ox, he just had to pick up the vet bill.

The vampire squatted in the snow. "How did you manage to get a chain on her?"

I sagged against the ox cart. "I have mad skills." My face was hot, my hands were cold. My mouth tasted bitter. The adrenaline rush was wearing off.

"What the hell happened?" I asked.

"One of Rowena's journeymen fainted," Ghastek said.

"It happens. Needless to say, she's now barred from navigation."

The journeymen, Masters of the Dead in training, were perfectly aware that if their control over the undead slipped, the vampire would turn the city into a slaughterhouse. They had nerves like fighter pilots pre-Shift. They didn't faint. There was more to it, but Ghastek's tone made it clear that getting any more information out of him would take a team of lawyers and a medieval torture device.

Just as well. The less I interacted with the People, the better. "Did it kill anybody?"

"There were no casualties."

My pulse finally slowed down.

To my right, a humvee swung into the parking lot at a breakneck speed. Armored like a tank, it carried an M240B, a medium machine gun, mounted on the roof. The gunner was pale as a sheet.

"Cavalry," I said.

The vampire grimaced, mimicking Ghastek's expression. "Of course. The jocks got all dressed up to kill a vampire, and now they won't get to shoot the big gun. Kate, would you mind stepping closer? Otherwise they might shoot her anyway."

You've got to be kidding me. I moved to body shield the vampire. "You owe me."

"Indeed." The bloodsucker rose next to me, waving its front limbs. "There is no need for concern. The matter is under control."

A black SUV turned the corner into the parking lot from the left. The two vehicles came to a screeching stop in front of me and the vampire. The humvee disgorged four cops in blue Paranormal Activity Division armor. The taller of the four leveled a shotgun at the vamp and snarled. "What the hell do you think you're doing? You've could've killed half of the city!"

The SUV's door opened and Ghastek stepped out. Thin and somber, he wore a perfectly pressed gray suit with a barely visible pinstripe. Three members of the People emerged from the SUV behind him, a man and two women, a thin brunette and a red-haired woman that looked barely old enough to wear a suit. All three were meticulously groomed and would've looked at home in a high-pressure boardroom.

"There is no need to exaggerate." Ghastek strode to the vampire. "No lives were lost."

"No thanks to you." The taller cop showed no signs of lowering the shotgun.

"She is completely safe now," Ghastek said. "Allow me to demonstrate." The vampire rose from its haunches and curtsied.

The PAD collectively turned purple with rage.

I backpedaled toward my office, before they decided to remember I was there and dragged me into this mess.

"See? I have complete control of the unde . . ." Ghastek's eyes rolled back into his head. His mouth went slack. For a long second he remained upright, his body completely still, then his legs gave. He swayed once and crashed into the dirty snow.

The vampire's eyes flared with bright murderous red. It opened its mouth, revealing twin sickles of ivory fangs.

The PAD opened fire.

The guns roared.

The first bullet sliced into the vampire's chest, punched through dry muscle, and bit Ghastek's journeyman in the shoulder. He spun from the impact, and the steady stream of rounds from the M240B punctured the vampire and cut across the journeyman's spine, nearly severing him in two. Blood sprayed.

The women hit the ground.

The bullets chipped the pavement. Half a foot to the right, and Ghastek's head would've exploded like a watermelon under a sledgehammer. I dived under the gunfire, grabbed Ghastek's legs, and pulled him out of the line of fire, backing up to my office.

The women crawled toward me through the snow.

The vamp twisted around, shuddering under the barrage of bullets, leaped on to the fallen man, and tore into his back, flinging blood and flesh into the air.

I dragged Ghastek's body over the doorstep and dropped him. Behind me, a woman screamed. I ran back, jumping over the dark-haired woman as she pulled herself through the doorway of my office. In the street, the redheaded girl hugged the ground, clenching her thigh, her eyes huge as saucers. Blood stained the snow a painfully bright scarlet. Shot in the leg.

I had to get her out of here before the vamp keyed in on her or the PAD shot her.

I dropped on the pavement, crawled to her, grabbed her arm, and pulled with everything I had. She screamed, but slid a foot toward me across the pockmarked asphalt flooded with melting snow. I backed up and pulled again. Another scream, another foot to the door.

Breathe, pull, scream, slide.

Breathe, pull, scream, slide.

Door.

I pushed her inside my office building, slammed the door shut, and barred it. It was a good door, metal, reinforced, with a four-inch bar. It would hold.

A wide red stain spread on the floor from the wounded woman's leg. I knelt down and sliced the pant leg. Blood spurted out of bullet-shredded muscle. The leg was ripped wide open. Bone shards glared at me, bathed in wet redness. Femoral artery cut, great saphenous vein cut, everything cut. Femur shattered.

Shit.

We would need a tourniquet.

"You! Put pressure here!"

The dark-haired girl stared at me with shocked glassy eyes. No intelligent life there. Every second counted.

I grabbed the redhead's hand and put it over her femoral artery. "Hold or you'll bleed out."

She moaned but pressed down.

I ran to the store room to get the medical supplies.

Tourniquets were last-resort devices. Mine was a C-A-T,

military issue, but no matter how good it was, if you kept
one on too long, you risked major nerve damage, loss of a
limb, and death. And once it went on, it stayed on. Taking
it off outside an emergency room would get you killed in
a hurry.

I needed paramedics, but calling them would do nothing. Standard operating procedure when faced with a loose
vampire was to seal off the area. The ambulance wouldn't
come unless the cops gave the paramedics the all-clear. It
was just me, the tourniquet, and the girl who would likely
bleed her life out.

I knelt by the woman and pulled the C-A-T out of the
bag.

"No!" The girl tried to push away from me. "No, I'll
lose my leg."

"You're bleeding to death."

"No, it's not that bad! It doesn't hurt!"

I gripped her shoulders and propped her up. She saw
the shredded mess of her thigh. "Oh God."

"What's your name?"

She sobbed.

"Your name?"

"Emily."

"Emily, your leg is almost amputated. If I put the tourniquet on it now, it will stop the bleeding and you might
survive. If I don't put it on, you'll bleed to death in minutes."

She clutched at me, crying into my shoulder. "I'll be
a cripple."

"You'll be alive. And with magic, your chances of keeping your leg are pretty good. You know medmages heal all
of sorts of wounds. But we've got to keep you alive until
the magic wave hits. Yes?"

She just cried, big tears rolling down her face.

"Yes, Emily?"

"Yes."

"Good."

I slipped the band under her leg, threaded it through

the buckle, pulled it tight, and wound the windlass until the bleeding stopped.

Four minutes later the gunfire finally died. Ghastek was still out. His pulse was steady, his breathing even. Emily lay still, whimpering in pain, her leg cinched by the wide tourniquet cuff. Her friend hugged herself, rocking back and forth and mumbling over and over, "They shot at us, they shot at us."

Peachy.

That was the problem with the People: most of them saw action only through a vampire's eyes while they sat in a safe, well-armored room within the Casino, sipping coffee and indulging in an occasional sugary snack. Getting shot at while riding a vampire's mind and dodging the actual bullets were two different animals.

A loud bang resonated through the door. A male voice barked, "Atlanta Paranormal Squad. Open the door."

The dark-haired girl froze. Her voice fell to a horrified whisper. "Don't open it."

"Don't worry. I got it under control." Sort of.

I slid a narrow panel aside, revealing a two-inch-by-four-inch peephole. A shadow shifted to my left—the officer pressed against the wall so I couldn't shoot him through the opening. I did the same on the other end of the door.

"Did you get the vamp?"

"We got it. Open the door."

"Why?"

There was a small pause. "Open. The. Door."

"No." They were hot from killing the vampire and still trigger happy. There was no telling what they would do if I opened the door.

"What do you mean no?"

He seemed genuinely puzzled.

"Why do you need me to open the door?"

"So we can apprehend the sonovabitch who dropped a vampire in the middle of the city."

Great. "You just killed one member of the People in

the cross fire, wounded another, and you want me to let you have the rest of the witnesses. I don't know you well enough to do that."

The PAD generally stuck to the straight and narrow, but there were certain things one didn't do: you didn't turn over a cop killer to his partner, and you didn't surrender a necromancer to the First Response Unit. They were all volunteer and sanity was an optional requirement. If I gave Ghastek and his people to them, there was a good chance they would never make it to the hospital. The official term was "died of their injuries en route."

The male voice huffed. "How about this: open the door or we'll break it down."

"You need a warrant for that."

"I don't need a warrant if I think you're in immediate danger. Say, Charlie, do you think she is in danger?"

"Oh, I think she's in a lot of danger," Charlie said.

"And would it be our duty as law enforcement officers to rescue her from said danger?"

"It would be a crime not to."

One person dead, one painting the floor with her blood. I guess it was time for jokes.

"You heard Charlie. Open the door or we'll open it for you."

I leaned a touch farther from the peephole. If they tried to break in, I could probably take them, but I could also kiss any sort of future cooperation from the PAD goodbye. "Look up above the door. You see a metal paw welded into the wood?"

"And?"

"This business is the property of the Pack. If you're going to break the door down, you need to be prepared to appear before a judge and explain why you invaded these premises without a warrant, arrested guests of the Pack, and caused damage to Pack property."

A long silence followed. The Pack's lawyers were nothing to sneeze at, as I was learning, and they were tenacious as hell.

"What exactly are you saying?" the cop growled.

"First, you kill a civilian in the cross fire, then you break into the Pack's property without a warrant. That's a lot for one day."

"It was a justifiable kill," the cop said. "I'm not going to debate it with you."

"Look, I worked with you guys before. Call Detective Michael Gray. He's got a file on me. If you get him down here or if you bring me a warrant, I'll open the door. No fuss, no damage, everybody is happy, nobody gets hauled to court. We're going to need an ambulance pretty soon, too. I've got one of the girls in a tourniquet, and if we don't hurry this along, she'll bleed to death."

"Tell you what, open the door, let us take the wounded girl out, and we'll call Gray."

Like I was born yesterday. "The moment I open the door, you'll rush me. I'll wait until the paramedics get here."

"Fine. I'll make the call, but you're playing with her life. She dies—it's on you, and I'll personally book you."

I slid the metal guard shut and went back to the women.

The dark-haired woman stared at me with haunted eyes. "You're going to let them have us?"

"If it's a choice between your friend's life and your freedom, yes. For now, we'll wait."

Emily looked at me. "Am I going to die?"

"Not if I can help it."

# ABOUT THE AUTHOR

**Ilona Andrews** is the pseudonym for a husband-and-wife writing team. Ilona is a native-born Russian, and Andrew is a former communications sergeant in the U.S. Army. Contrary to popular belief, Andrew was never an intelligence officer with a license to kill, and Ilona was never the mysterious Russian spy who seduced him. They met in college, in English Composition 101, where Ilona got a better grade. (Andrew is still sore about that.) Together, Andrew and Ilona are the coauthors of the *New York Times* bestselling Kate Daniels urban-fantasy series and the romantic urban-fantasy novels of the Edge. They currently reside in Portland, Oregon, with their two children and numerous pets. For sample chapters, news, and more, visit www.ilona-andrews.com.

DON'T MISS THE NEW SERIES FROM
*NEW YORK TIMES* BESTSELLING AUTHOR

# ILONA ANDREWS

# ON THE
# EDGE

Rose Drayton lives on the Edge, between two worlds: on one side lies the Broken, a place where people shop at Wal-Mart and magic is nothing more than a fairy tale; on the other is the Weird, a realm where blueblood aristocrats rule and the strength of your magic can change your destiny. Only Edgers like Rose can easily travel between the worlds—but they never truly belong in either.

penguin.com

M634T0110

Don't miss the new Kate Daniels novel from
*New York Times* bestselling author

# ILONA ANDREWS

# MAGIC
# BLEEDS

———◆———

Kate Daniels cleans up the paranormal problems no
one else wants to deal with—especially if they involve
Atlanta's shapeshifting community.

And now there's a new player in town—a foe who
may be too much for even Kate and Curran, the Beast
Lord, to handle. Because this time Kate will be taking
on family.

M707T0510

# Penguin Group (USA) Online

*What will you be reading tomorrow?*

Patricia Cornwell, Nora Roberts, Catherine Coulter,
Ken Follett, John Sandford, Clive Cussler,
Tom Clancy, Laurell K. Hamilton, Charlaine Harris,
J. R. Ward, W.E.B. Griffin, William Gibson,
Robin Cook, Brian Jacques, Stephen King,
Dean Koontz, Eric Jerome Dickey, Terry McMillan,
Sue Monk Kidd, Amy Tan, Jayne Ann Krentz,
Daniel Silva, Kate Jacobs...

You'll find them all at
**penguin.com**

*Read excerpts and newsletters,
find tour schedules and reading group guides,
and enter contests.*

Subscribe to Penguin Group (USA) newsletters
and get an exclusive inside look
at exciting new titles and the authors you love
long before everyone else does.

## PENGUIN GROUP (USA)
penguin.com